Praise for Uzma Aslam Khan's *The Geometry of God*

"[F]uses the romantic, the spiritual and the political… the characters, the poetry and the philosophical questions she raises are rendered with a power and beauty that make this novel linger in the mind and heart."

—*Kirkus*, starred review

"Elegant, sensuous and fiercely intelligent, *The Geometry of God* takes an argument that is in danger of becoming stale—that of fundamentalism vs. free thinking among Muslims—and animates it in a wonderfully inventive story that pits science against politics and the freedom of women against the insecurities of men."

—Kamila Shamsie

"Uzma Aslam Khan, a fearless young Pakistani novelist, writes about what lies beneath the surface—ancient fossils embedded in desert hillsides, truths hidden inside the language of everyday life… Khan's urgent defense of free thought and action—often galvanized by strong-minded, sensuous women—courses through every page of this gorgeously complex book; but what really draws the reader in is the way Mehwish taste-tests the words she hears, as if they were pieces of fruit, and probes the meaning of human connection in a culture of intolerance, but also of stubborn hope."

—Cathleen Medwick, *O magazine*

"*The Geometry of God* is a novel that you don't just read; you listen to it. It can be irreverent, perverse. It can speak with a whole, fluid beauty. It can be curious, wondrous, noncompliant, like the English in Mehwish's head… Mehwish is the zauq of the book, the sensory pulse of the novel, who pulls you into a world of her own making. Expect a simultaneous rush that has funniness, absurdity, shock, tenderness… [and] great sex."

—*First City*, India

"Such wonderful and persuasive writing. No one writes like her about the body, about the senses, about the physical world. Uzma Aslam Khan is the writer whose new novel I look forward to the most."

—Nadeem Aslam

"Uzma Aslam Khan has boldly tapped uncharted themes in her latest book, *The Geometry of God*. She carves a sublime story of new and old with contemporary panache, in which people are real and their fears are prevalent and believable. Khan weaves a complex story whose narrative has a casual energy to it: each voice telling his or her story. Khan is not afraid to say anything."

—*Dawn*, Pakistan

"Throughout this complex narrative, Khan writes with unfailing intelligence and linguistic magic. For Westerners, she unlocks doors and windows onto Pakistan and its Islamic culture."

—Claire Hopley, *The Washington Times*

"[V]ivid and rich. The reader is rewarded with new viewpoints, a welcome change from the sensationalized and often macabre portrayals of Pakistani people and the country they fight so hard to preserve."

—*Story Circle Book Reviews*

"Uzma Aslam Khan's novel is an eloquent rebuttal to its own character's claim about modern Islam's single-mindedness. Skipping across eras and registers of culture—and showing devotion to pleasures as diverse as Elvis Presley and the Mu'tazilites, Aflatoon (the Arabic name for Plato) and evolutionary biology—it is both an example of and an argument for the essential hybridity of every society."

—*Ploughshares*

"Uzma Aslam Khan comes from a younger generation of Pakistani authors born and raised in the disrupted decades of the 1980s and 90s whose fiction looks back to those earlier times... As in her previous work, Aslam Khan deploys several narrators, both male and female... but it is the abstract perspectives offered by Mehwish, a character who sees the world with her inner eye, tastes its truths and tells them 'slant', that are the most original and captivating... we become attuned to her quietly anarchic voice... complex... inventive... "

—*Times Literary Supplement*

Thinner than Skin

Uzma Aslam Khan

FOURTH ESTATE • *New Delhi*

First published in the United States in 2012 by Clockroot Books
An imprint of Interlink Publishing Group, Inc

First published in India in 2012 by Fourth Estate
An imprint of HarperCollins *Publishers* India

Building 10, Tower A, 4th Floor, DLF Cyber City, Phase II,
Gurugram Haryana – 122002, India
www.harpercollins.co.in

ISBN: 978-93-5029-413-0

2 4 6 8 10 9 7 5 3 1

Grateful acknowledgment is made to *Granta* and to the *Massachusetts Review*,
where excerpts of this novel have appeared, titled respectively
"Ice, Mating" and "The News at His Back"

Book design by Pam Fontes-May

Printed and bound at
MicroPrints India, New Delhi

It is far harder to kill a phantom than a reality.
—Virginia Woolf, *The Death of the Moth and Other Essays*

There are one or two murderers in any crowd.
    They do not suspect their destinies yet.
—Charles Simic, "Memories of the Future"

She had felt this way once before and it might have been the wind then too.

There had been the scent of the horse right before he ran. The steam rising from the manure he had left in a thick pile on the glacier. The wind carrying the dissipating heat to her nostrils just as the horse's nostrils flared in panic. Then he was racing forward, straight into a fence of barbed wire masked in a thicket of pine. The mother of his foal lifted her neck. The goats too. They sensed it, even the stupid sheep sensed it, the fat Australian ones the government tricked them into buying. Every living creature had felt the horse impale himself just before his cry rang through the valley like a series of barbed wires.

That was years ago. Now the wind carried a similar foreboding, not in the shape of a scent but of a wingbeat, and the lake froze in anticipation. Maryam waited, and nearby her daughter Kiran waited too. So did the mare and the filly, the three buffaloes, the four goats, and all the stupid sheep. What would it be this time? Whose cry was about to cut through the valley?

She walked along the shores of the lake, feeling the weight of her past, the one she left behind each year when her family moved up from the plains to the highlands. She absently stroked her daughter's unbraided hair, her brow crinkled as the skin of a newborn lamb.

The trouble with memory: it awakened her mother. When alive, her mother would say that horses are the wings to this world, owls to the next. She had stories for the mountains that enclosed them too, stories in the shape of names. The Karakoram was the black door. The Pamirs the white door. The Himalayas the abyss. At times she saw no point in distinguishing between them, and all the mountains became, simply, the wall. On such days, her mother herself became a wall, pushing Maryam into corners and cracks. "Walk along walls, not toward them," she would snap. "One footloop at a time." Other times, she would counsel Maryam to look for individual peaks—such as the two lovers, Malika Parbat and Nanga Parbat, the Queen and the Nude—that might appear as windows in a door, or as footholds in a void. And Maryam always looked.

Tonight, the peaks were draped in a deep blue sheet of mist. No windows. No footloops. She had lived with them her entire life and knew that the taller mountain, Nanga Parbat, could not be seen from here so much as felt, and that only on very particular days, when he was drawing closer to Malika Parbat. She understood that the mountains were not as fixed as many believed. She knew too that when undressed, the taller mountain had as many angles as a buffalo hip. He moved in much the same way. A slow slip into a socket, a turn of the tail, a shadow sloping deep into a crotch. In the sunlight his summit was cast in gold, and this was what she looked for each spring, during the trek to the highland pasture, the herd lowing before her, each buffalo hip mimicking the movement in the sky. She looked for it, even if she found it only in her imagination.

It was the snowmelt of the two peaks that created the lake where she now paused. The melt had been too strong this year, obsessive even. As if last year's vices had not been smoked out completely. They had followed them all the way up from the plains, these vices, hitching a ride on the backs of their horses and even the bells of their goats; if you did not get rid of such things they had a way of getting rid of you.

She gazed into the lake that lay between the mountains, till, gradually, her eye adjusted to the picture surfacing from the water's depths. It was a picture of a man, his back to her. Though Maryam could not see him she could see the peak on which he lay trapped. She knew every color and curve of this valley; the peak he lay on she did not recognize. What was he doing here, at the foot of the two mountains, at the bottom of the lovers' lake?

Maryam looked away from the image. Her fingers fussed over Kiran's chaotic hair with increasing fervor and the girl complained. Her eyes darted back to the water. Nothing, except that thick sheet of mist in the sky, reflected in the lake. The picture of a man trapped on an unfamiliar mountain was gone. Her fingers tried to relax.

Her daughter was squirming but she tried to keep her, whistling softly through her teeth. She was answered with the chime of a bell. She liked the animals. *When you call, they come.* It was the buffalo Noor, gazing casually over her shoulder from the shore, a stalk of grass between her lips that she twirled like a cigarette. There were no barbed wires here. No one tearing down the trees. And no forest inspectors telling the nomads to stretch their limbs barely as far as the length of a blanket, only to deprive them of a blanket altogether. She yanked Kiran's hair. No! All that had been left behind, down in the plains! Up here, they were free to graze. The highlands belonged to those who had been coming here for so many summers only they knew how the Queen and the Nude behaved when no one was watching.

The wind slackened. The air began to ring with bells as faint yet bright as stars. There was no nervous scent, no echoing cry. No owl's wingbeat gliding to the next world. Kiran skipped away from Maryam, and Maryam, drawing the night around her shoulders like a shawl, began to chase after her, forgetting entirely that only moments earlier, she had been wondering who would find him, the man glimpsed for just that second in the water, the man who walked into a wall.

ONE

Say an Owl

It was a barn owl outside my window that night in Kaghan. She—all beautiful things are feminine to me, I make no apologies—perched on the bough of an almond tree at the edge of the river and the moon was high. As I opened the door of my cabin, she swung her neck and looked full into my face. There is no creature more direct than an owl. A rose has thorns, a cat has claws, but an owl the ferocity of her gaze. Unable to pull free from the ruffle of white feathers billowing around her ice-black stare, I delayed ducking back inside for my camera.

It was in my jacket in the closet on the far side of the room. Moving quickly, I remembered the night in San Francisco when Farhana and I had been returning home from a late dinner. The car's headlights had shone on something large and white on the road. We'd stopped. Farhana fell to her knees, and began caressing the ring of down delineating the eerie, heart-shaped face. Its eyes were open—ah, dead beauty loses her sex!—and a cloud of feathers fluttered around a gaze with a softness that made me shiver. I stroked a limp wing with the pattern of cream and toffee swirls, wishing I had my camera, even if this upset Farhana. As my fingers moved to the still breast, she said an owl was a symbol of many wonders, evil and wise, and "ours" was wise. I wondered if this would be a good time to propose. And while I'm at it, I thought, I might also suggest a honeymoon (somewhere in a forest, she loved lushness, the propinquity of green), though not immediately after the wedding; I still wasn't earning enough. In which case, should I wait? When Farhana started to cry, saying she wanted me to look as peaceful as the owl when I died, I decided to wait. I remembered hoping that I wouldn't die in an accident late at night, tossed on the roadside till some inquisitive passersby stopped to admire my breathless form, only to leave me and drive away.

The living owl was an obliging model. I shot two dozen photographs while she glared, swiveled, and glared again. There was the heart-shaped face and the wings with the delicate markings. There, the heart beneath my fingertip. I could feel it beat this time, caught in a small silver button yielding to my touch. I could squeeze the drumming of an enraged predator's pulse.

When I returned inside the cabin to review my handiwork, all the images were white. Nothing else. Only a sallow blur. Stupefied, I rechecked the settings, the battery, the light. All as should be. By the time I resolved to try a second time, my visitor had vanished.

Leaving my cabin again, I finally did what I'd stepped out to do. I set out on my nightly walk. I didn't interpret the owl as evil or wise. To me she only meant that I should have listened to my father and not become a man who "spends his life hiding behind a lens."

On the other hand, he'd wanted me to be an engineer. If I couldn't take a few simple shots of a creature who *wanted* herself seen, imagine what else I might have failed at. Who'd feel safe walking across (or even under) a bridge of my design? Such were my thoughts as I headed for the river, inhaling a mid-summer chill deep into my lungs.

Breathing was like sucking a hookah filled with flakes of glass. Strangely, the sensation was pleasant. No doubt it had to do with the elevation—*five mountain peaks over 8,000 meters, fifty over 7,000* was a common boast—but that would only impress a man impressed by facts. Surely, it had more to do with the purity of the place, which was why it was here, more than anywhere else, that I came closest to feeling I'd rather be here than anywhere else. Rare for me, a man who likes to move. Fitting, then, that I was running beside a river in a valley shadowed and graced by nomads. Even if this hadn't been the plan.

It was our first night here, on the ancient Silk Route, a route which had never been *the* route at all, not for us, nor for a single man, horse, or fly. There were as many routes through these mountains as veins in a rock, and, true to the spirits of the routes, our own track had changed since our arrival in the country. We were never meant to stop in Kaghan Valley. Which was why, earlier in the day, Farhana and I had argued. We'd barely spoken since and she was sleeping in the cabin while I photographed the owl. Or tried to. It occurred to me as I jogged along the river breathing phantom glass and feeling energized in a way that only happened to me late at night, that had I succeeded in capturing the owl on my screen, I could have shown the images to Farhana in the morning after waking her with a kiss and we might have made up.

Then again, perhaps not. She frequently complained that I was a photographer by day, a happy man by night. Like my father, she saw my passion as a disguise rather than an art, as if the two are dissimilar. She dismissed my camera as a veil that I only removed when the sun set. She was right about the timing. I always leave my camera behind on my nightly walks. She was also right that leaving it behind made me look at the world differently. Sometimes I liked the world more, sometimes less. Since meeting her, I'd begun to think of my two states as "with" and "without." Without, Farhana weighed more prominently on my mind. But while photographing the owl, I hadn't thought of Farhana even once.

I met her soon after moving to the Bay Area from Tucson, two years ago. I'd left my job with a design and construction company and couldn't return home a failure. It would have been hard to explain that, having turned out better at shooting engineering projects than erecting them, I'd become a photographer.

It was landscapes I excelled at, or wanted to. I left Tucson and spent the next few weeks making my way up the West Coast, occasionally veering back into the desert after hitching a ride. I still have them in my portfolio, those who stopped for me, and the shadows of the many who didn't: pick-up trucks, scuffed boots, silver belts glistening in the sun. There was old man prickly-pear cactus all around and of course the Joshua trees, as the wind blew in from the northwest and purple clouds draped us. For all the tales of murder and kidnapping in these parts, I never chose poorly. I was more often mistaken for Latino than A-rab, even by Latinos, including the one so amused by his mistake he followed me deeper into the desert. Anywhere else, I'd mistake him for Punjabi.

"So, you *Mooz*lim or what?" he asked.

"Or what?" I took his photograph as his shoulders shook and I eventually saw that he was laughing. There is something about large men with quiet laughs. Laughs that boil up slowly from within. A single raindrop splashed his nose. Only his belt, his teeth, and a patch of the distant San Bernardino mountains reflected the sun. After the second raindrop he was still laughing. I thanked him for the ride, walked into the desert, and did what I feared I could spend the rest of my life doing. I really looked at cactus. I really looked at triumph. Blossoming in shocking gimcrack hues of scarlet and gold in a world that watched with arms crossed, if it watched at all. It reminded me of the festive dresses worn by gypsies in Pakistan's desert borderlands and mountain valleys. The drier the land, the thirstier the spirit.

When I finally arrived in San Francisco, for no reason other than that it was San Francisco, I had a stack of photographs of the Sonora Desert, the Petrified Forest, and Canyon de Chelly. I mailed off the best and waited for someone to bite, while renting an apartment with two other men. I had two interviews. The first went something like this:

"Why are you, Nadir Sheikh"—he said Nader Shake—"wasting time taking photographs of American landscapes when you have material at your own doorstep?"

"Excuse me?"

"This is a stock-photo agency. We sell photographs to magazines and sometimes directly to customers and sometimes for a lot of money. We might be interested in you, but not in your landscapes."

"In what then?"

"Americans already know their trees."

"Do they know their cactus?"

"Next time you go home, take some photographs." When it was obvious I still didn't get it, he dumbed it down. "Show us the dirt. The misery. Don't waste your time trying to be a nature photographer. Use your advantage."

Back at the apartment, my housemate Matthew felt sorry for me. He said a former boyfriend knew a nice little Pakistani girl. I ate his nachos while he talked on the phone.

I walked along the River Kunhar, thinking of Farhana. My way was lit by the moon and the rush of the current and the silhouettes of the trees and the hut down the way where we'd eaten trout earlier and it thrilled me to know that the others were asleep so I unlaced my boots and peeled off my clothes and stood buck-naked.

I heard a story once. A long time ago, on the banks of the river before it bends to meet the Jhelum, the Mughal queen Noor Jehan paused on her way to Kashmir. She was suffering from an eye infection and decided to dip her hands in the river to wash her face. The water was so cool and pure her eyes were cured. Ever since, the river has been called *nain sukh*, that which soothes the eye. I knew

I was further upriver than the bend where the queen had once stopped, and I knew glacial water was not the cleansing stuff of myth. Yet something compelled me to kneel at the Kunhar's edge and rinse my eyes, and even to drink her noxious fumes.

Which is what I was doing when I saw her again. The owl, soaring across the opal moon breaking in the water. Flapping twice before circling back toward me, she came to rest on a giant walnut tree. There, looking directly down at me, she spoke. "*Shreet!*" It was the voice, more than her flight from my camera, or her return now, when I was without, that made me feel signaled. No, singled. Singled out.

I was being sighted.

I arranged to meet her the afternoon of my second interview. This time I included in my portfolio a series of photographs taken on a previous return to Pakistan. It was a series of my mother's marble tabletop, which she'd inherited from her mother, and which dated back to the 1800s. The swirling cream-and-rust pattern changed as I played with the light, sometimes slick as a sheet of silk, sometimes pillowing like a bowl of ice cream. A few frames were, if I say so myself, as sensuous as Linde Waidhofer's stones.

The second interview did not go very differently from the first.

"Your photographs lack authenticity."

"Authenticity?"

"Where are the beggars and bazaars or anything that resembles your culture?"

"The marble is a real part of my family history. It's old, from 1800—"

He waved his hand. "It seems to me that when a war's going on, a table is trivial." I wished for the courage—or desire—to ask what images of what war he was looking for.

He stood up. "I'm a busy man. Could've ignored you. Didn't, know why? There's something there." He leaned forward expectantly, so I thanked him for thinking there was something there.

I left the office and walked down the corridor to the stairs, passing the photographs that hung on the walls, photographs I loved with an ardor that stung. I'd recognized them all on my way in, of course. There were prints by Linde Waidhofer to taunt me, including one from her *Stone & Silence* series. A Waidhofer can be a nature photographer of the Wild West but a Sheikh must be a war photographer of the Wild East! He must wow the world not with the assurance of grace. He must wow the world with the assurance of horror.

I wound my way slowly through prints from Ansel Adams' *Yosemite* series—it was the wrong moment to view *Bridalveil Fall*, the sheer force of the torrent almost making me weep, and I found myself wishing, childishly, *if only the drop weren't so steep*—before halting, finally, at *Golden Gate Bridge from Baker Beach*.

The coincidence hadn't hit me on my way into the interview but it hit me now, as my eye swooped down from the whiteness of the clouds to admit the whiteness of the surf breaking on the shore. I was meeting Farhana on Baker Beach in one hour. It had been her idea, and she'd been specific about where on the beach I'd find her. I stared at the photograph, surprised at the fluttering in my breast. It astonished me that I was hoping to find her on the exact same length of shore depicted in the frame. Worse, I believed that once there, perhaps without her knowing it, I'd look up and see the bridge from exactly the same perspective as I was seeing it now.

Did I want the picture to be a sign? Possibly. It happens this way when you have just been tossed down a roaring cataract. You grope for a raft, anywhere. You even tell yourself that you have found it.

Before the owl swooped across the moon's reflection in the River Kunhar, I'd been thinking about that word, *Kunhar*, how *kun* sounded like *kus* which sounded like a cross between *cunt* and *kiss*. Do we desire and despise in the same sounds in all tongues? I'd held the bitter taste of glacier melt in my mouth as the silver disc eased deep into the river's skin. I'd dipped my head to taste her again, and, gathering filigree into the fold of my tongue, gazed down the Kunhar's length. She cut through the valley for one hundred and sixty kilometers. I'd been thinking of a long labia.

"*Shreet!*"

The thought scattered like moonseed.

"*Shreet!*"

The second time, the sour glacier water inside me froze and my fingers grew so stiff that when I reached for my clothes, I simply poked at them, as though with sticks. I crouched to my knees for warmth, bewitched by those gleaming black eyes in the pretty heart-shaped face. Instead of the owl, I saw the face of a girl. She had morphed into human at an hour no human should see. She had spoken at an hour no human should speak. How many minutes or hours passed before she shot up into the sky and flew in the direction of the lake we would head for tomorrow?

I eventually returned to my cabin, still naked, and slid into bed beside Farhana. She shifted. I was never more grateful for the heat she radiated under our sheets. I curled into her back and she turned, presenting me with the same gift as on our first night of love: she slipped her finger in my navel. Mocking my "proper Convent-boy English," she whispered, "I'm going to *have a listen*." She put her ear to the hollow, exhaling her sweet hot breath over my cold skin till it thawed.

"What do you hear?" Her hair was spread in a fan across the pit of my stomach.

"*Shh!*"

As her lips enclosed me, I thought, *Bliss! I will not have to make up with her in the morning, she is making up with me!* And I heard it again. The rush of wings, the moon diving in the Kunhar. *Shreet!* An ascending—higher, higher, through a smooth, silvery sky—a falling—deeper, deeper, down a silky, slippery skein.

I walked briskly to Baker Beach in joyous agitation. Descending from the parking lot, I pulled off my shoes, expecting to see a girl of Farhana's description—"look for a long braid, the longest on the beach, black, of course"—waiting at the edge of the sea, as per her instructions, her back to me (showing off the braid), with Golden Gate Bridge looming to her right. Instead, I wound up in a volleyball game, with all the players entirely in the nude.

Was she among them? Damn, how was I to know?

There *was* a player with a dark braid, though she had two, neither as long as I'd been led to believe. Leaping for the ball, she made a full-frontal turn, and my God, how astonishingly she was built! I gawked at the hair between her legs, wondering if this were a cruel joke. (Granted, not entirely cruel.) Matthew must have arranged it, getting "Farhana" to lure me here. He was probably watching, laughing till he hurt. *Nice little Pakistani girl.* Funny, Matthew, *funny*. I stared at the volleyball player one last time—no, that couldn't be Farhana, please let it not be Farhana! Please let it *be* Farhana!—and turned to my right to scan the bathers on the shore.

Almost all naked, mostly men. Obscenely overdressed, I jogged in mild panic toward a cluster of rocks on the far side of a thick cypress grove. Along the way, I tried to hunt discreetly for a long braid slithering down a shapely back, but many figures lay *on* their backs, some on their hair. I could see the rocks now. She wasn't there. Two naked men were, one walking out to the water, hand on hip. Long cock, wide grin. I waded into the sea, my back safely to him, but the water was too cold for my taste. After a few minutes, I trundled closer to the boulders, trying to look-not-look.

She was sitting there, smiling. Her braid was pulled to the side, draping her left shoulder, and she waved it at me like a flag.

"We must have just missed each other!"

"I thought you told me to wait on the beach?"

"I'm sorry. It got late."

I was on the verge of asking how she got all the way here without my noticing when I saw how her eyes sparkled. It wasn't

Matthew who'd been watching me but Farhana. I clambered up without another word, crossing a series of tide pools and a snug sandy enclosure between the boulders that sprawled in a V. I crouched down beside her and looked to her right: there loomed Golden Gate Bridge.

"Did you think you'd recognize me better with clothes on?" she giggled.

"Your clothes *are* on."

"Are you disappointed?"

"I'm relieved."

"How disappointing."

So I learned this immediately about my Farhana. She was one of those people who liked to receive a reaction, and she didn't like to wait very long for it. That day she must have been pleased enough with what I gave, because we met almost every day afterward. And what did I give? Embarrassment. Curiosity. I know she caught me wondering how much she was going to reveal, and she knew that I knew that beneath her T-shirt, she wore no bra. For weeks, that was all I'd see. *Nice little Pakistani girl.*

"Why do you keep looking up at the bridge?" she asked, about an hour into our rendezvous on the rocks.

I said nothing about the photograph. I never did. But as the sun set, I took several shots of the bridge. In the foreground, there was no surf and no sand, only a line of jagged rocks—without Farhana. She wouldn't let me photograph her that day.

When we finally stood up to leave, I realized how tall she was. And how boyish.

She knew. "I would have gone topless if I had breasts." Again, she required a reaction.

I am not an eloquent man and am usually tongue-tied around directness, but directness attracts me. I looked at Farhana and took all of her in, all that she'd spent the afternoon telling me: her work with glaciers, her father in Berkeley, her mother's death, leaving Pakistan as a young child, her life in this city where she grew up. I took that in while absorbing her height, her leanness, the paleness of her skin, and the way her braid now wrapped around her in a diagonal curve that extended from left shoulder to right hip. I realized I was maybe three-quarters besotted, perhaps halfway in love. I said she looked more like a calla lily than any woman I'd ever met.

"Not just any calla lily," I added. "Jeffrey Conley's calla lily. Have you seen it?"

She bowed her head, suddenly self-conscious. Turning her back to me, she took off her T-shirt. "I'll see you tomorrow then."

"When?"

"Same time."

How hard it was to pull away!

Scrambling off the rocks, I glanced up a final time before turning toward my apartment. She'd twisted to one side so her long, deep spine was now perfectly aligned with the braid and both encircled her like an embrace.

The next day, I began courting Farhana. At first empty-handed, and wherever she chose, but by the second month, at her home, and with a gift. I courted her with calla lilies. Nothing delighted me more than descending the hill into the Mission District where she lived, a potted plant in my arms. I knew the flower shops with the widest varieties, from white to mauve to yellow, some with funnels as long and slender as her wrists, slanting in the same way her braid embraced her spine that first time we met, and still embraced her each night as she torqued her body to undress. I longed to photograph that spine but she wouldn't let me. So instead, with my naked eye, I watched her fingers undo the knots of her braid. I'd learned not to interfere with this lengthy ritual, during which her strokes grew increasingly harsh and her face wore a million different permutations of annoyance. The comb always came away with a wad of black wool that she tossed in the dustbin before climbing into bed, beaming. I loved seeing that smile approach me every night.

This morning in Kaghan, it was I who beamed, as I watched her sleep. I tasted her breath with the roof of my mouth. Pine and glacier steam. I traced the fleshiness of her lips with the tip of my nose. Her mouth was a pale beige tinted with the softest pink, the delicate rim so subtle in its arch. She seldom wore lipstick, for which I was thankful, because her naked mouth blended beautifully with the rest of her. When worried, her tongue would dig the subtle indent at that luscious lower lip, and sometimes the thumb would cooperate, picking at plumpness, drawing blood. I learned this gesture in the days after we first met. I learned it especially on the bus to Kaghan Valley. But this morning, she slept peacefully; the tongue was still and so was the thumb. I tasted her again. More steam than pine. Farhana's morning breath was never her worst feature, though she'd cringe at that, demanding, What's worse?

Our cabin was old. Perhaps its walls were the source of the pinewood scent enveloping our bed. The doorframe was a medley of pale and dark wood. I imagined the hand that must have reached for blond walnut when the dark cedar was gone, reached for red polish when the brown was upturned. Perhaps the man attached to the hand had been unable to walk to wherever the red was kept. Perhaps he'd been older than the cabin was now. Perhaps he didn't belong to this land but had come from a windier, sandier world.

I lay on my back, rolling the word *Kaghan* around my tongue the way last night I'd played with *Kunhar*. Did the word come from Kagan, a woman who'd arrived in this valley long ago? On a previous trip, I'd heard stories, fragments that never extended far enough into history books but lingered in the air. Some said Kagan was descended from the pagan Kafir-Kalash tribe of Chitral Valley, to the west. Others said in secret that she was barely human, and belonged to a world of fairies and spirits. She was accessible only to those who worshipped her, and when she appeared, she wasn't dressed like a Kalash woman at all. She wore mist and rode a horse.

Or had the word *Kaghan* come from K*h*agan, a grander version of Khan? The Turkic rulers who'd spread from Turkey to China on the ancient Silk Road had divided into two, one branch becoming the lion khans, the other, camel khans. Now this valley had neither lions nor camels. But it did have owls. And horses. Were its earliest inhabitants owl khans? Horse khans?

Most of the horses in the valley belonged to the semi-nomadic tribes that spent their summers in the mountain pastures and winters down in the plains. We'd be seeing them later today at the lake. No one knew where the nomads had come from but they were believed to have ridden down from the Caspian steppe thousands of years ago, and perhaps had once been Turkic-speaking. A third rumor held that Kagan had been one of them. And she had been a pari khan—ruler of fairies.

Beside me, Farhana inched a little higher on her pillow, blowing glacier steam in my eyes. Apart from her, nothing stirred. Kaghan mornings in our cabin were windless.

I walked to her side of the bed. On the bedside table lay a map, with Kaghan Valley circled in red at the easternmost corner of the North-West Frontier Province, on the edge of Kashmir. I'd drawn the circle on the bus to the valley, telling Farhana that to see the Frontier, you had to imagine it as the profile of a buffalo's bust, facing west, with the capital Peshawar the nose, Chitral Valley the backward tilting horn, Swat Valley the eye, and Kaghan Valley the ear. The Frontier listened to Kashmir at its back while facing Afghanistan ahead, and it listened with Kaghan.

On the bus, Farhana had refused to listen to me, or to Kaghan. She'd picked at her lip, reminding me that we were never meant to be here at all. Until last night, I didn't think she'd ever forgive me.

I opened the cabin door. I listened to Kaghan. Around me rose rounded hills, scoops of velvet green on a brick-red floor. Like the mossy moistness of rain-kissed tailorbirds. It was for this I'd come, not to upset my beloved. Around us the valley undulated like the River Kunhar that gave it shape, cupping nine lakes in its curves, sprouting thick forests of deodar and pine, towering over 4,000 meters before halting abruptly at the temples of the Himalayas and the Karakoram. The only way through the mountainous block was by snaking along hair-thin passes, as if by witchery. Here the overwhelming sensation was not a closing or crowding. Not exactly. It was more a cautioning—a slope to the side, a wait and see. The buffalo's ear is always cocked.

I knew that in colonial times, the British considered it a pretty sort of wedge, this ear, nicely if incidentally squeezed between the more considerable Kashmir and the more incomprehensible, and feared, hill tribes of the west. And so they mostly left the valley alone. Today, most of the hotels, restaurants, and shops were run, though not owned, by Kashmiris and Sawatis. Even those who couldn't read or own a television were keenly aware of what was going on, and where. They liked to say that the buffalo is as attuned to what lies behind as what lies ahead. Why else did shivers keep running up and down its spine? Why else did it keep sweeping its hide with the smack of its tail?

I'd noticed military convoys yesterday, soon after our arrival. It was unusual in this valley. I'd been too preoccupied to give this much thought. The trucks were as twitchy as buffalo tails, creeping up and down the valley's spine, seeing nothing, fearing the worst. The whole country was teeming with convoys of one kind or another. So what? We were here to enjoy the place, even if we couldn't enjoy the time.

A shadow flickered on the doorframe. There were other areas—the ceiling beams, the paneling by the bed—also randomly spotted with light and dark timber. With the curtain drawn, despite the checkerboard paneling, it was night in the cabin.

That flickering shadow was a lizard, sidling for a mate.

I kissed her, slowly, drinking her, hoping to keep her beside me a little longer, just us.

"I once heard a story," I whispered, stroking her hair. The scent of her shampoo pooled with the musk lingering on my fingers from last night. It wasn't the walls that exuded the scent, it was Farhana. And it wasn't pine, or even musk. It was, curiously, tobacco. She'd never smoked in her life and abhorred the habit. How to tell her that her own most intimate odor was that of a cigar? I slid between her knees.

She smiled into her pillow. "They'll be here any minute."

"Maybe they're already eating."

"You were going to tell me a story."

"It can wait."

"I think I hear them."

"You hear us."

She laughed. "I *can* hear them. I bet they're coming here for breakfast. Who wants to walk to the restaurant?" She pressed her knees, whispering, "Tell me the story."

I ignored this.

"Is it the one about the lake? And the jinn. And the princess. Please?" She arched her back. I threw off the sheets.

"You already know it."

"I work with facts. I forget the fairy tales."

So I told her again.

As soon as we finished, we heard the knock. Farhana's colleague, Wes, and an old friend of mine from Karachi, Irfan. They were staying in the adjoining cabin. We were meant to meet at the restaurant for breakfast before leaving for the lake, but here they were now, as Farhana predicted, because no one felt like trudging a quarter mile for eggs. So we dressed in a hurry, welcomed them inside, and ordered in.

The omelettes were cold by the time the waiter arrived, but still crisp around the edges, the interior plump with finely minced tomatoes and green chilies. Irfan and the waiter talked at length in Kashmiri. Or was it Hindko? I could identify only a few sounds—*akh*, *gari gari*—focusing more on Irfan's expression. The news wasn't good.

Wes and Farhana discussed glaciers. They might as well have spoken Gujri. I chewed my omelette in silence. Red, yellow, and green. The colors made a familiar flag, though I couldn't remember which. Afghanistan's had the red and green, though its eggs weren't yellow but black. And I wasn't even sure what flag it flew these days; after the American invasion, Taliban white had been dyed to something like the flag that had flown under the monarchy. Senegal; Sri Lanka. Yes, they flew these three colors. On the plate before me, I replaced the lion of Sri Lanka with the owl of last night. I decided to tell everyone.

Irfan said the sighting was an ill omen (though I still couldn't help thinking I was the one being sighted). Irfan was the reason our route had changed, which was the reason Farhana and I had argued yesterday, at a shop that sold shawls. My hurt at the way she rejected the one I'd draped around her shoulders, and her anger—"We didn't need to come to Kaghan at all"—was all of it still raw? I looked at her now, afraid of losing the peace of waking up together this morning. Was it already beginning to fade? But she remained cheerful—no lip-picking today!—saying that in some places, owls were believed to be holy spirits of shamans, and when I said, "As holy as ours?" she tossed me a winsome look and Irfan shifted disapprovingly. Perhaps he'd heard us last night. Or this morning.

Wes glowed as if he were the one we'd all stayed up listening to. "Take any pictures?"

"Yes."

"Let's see." He chewed with his mouth open.

"They didn't come out."

"What do you mean they didn't come out?" His smile was an oval of eggy goo.

"Just that."

"With a digital? You're literally in the wrong business."

Farhana laughed. "Don't tease him. That's a touchy topic."

What if I revealed all her touchy topics?

"We should leave." I stood up. "The lake is crowded by noon."

Irfan returned to his cabin for his jacket. Farhana picked hot peppers out of a second omelette for Wes. She called him "Wesley" and he called her "Farrah." She called him "wimpy" and he called her "hella sweet."

As I packed my bag with my camera and lens, I resisted the urge to glance again at Farhana. I suppressed a longing to sweep everyone away—like a buffalo clearing its back with a tail!—so we could start again, just us. But what I could not resist—though I knew it would ignite that prickle resting so close to the skin, I knew I would regret it before I could even begin—was replaying the past week in my head.

The Roads to Kaghan

Before Kaghan there was Karachi, and that is where the plan had changed. Karachi. To my disgust, this time I *had* taken photographs of beggars and children running naked in the street, sucking mango pits and smearing their sooty cheeks with orange stains. "For rich men with retirement homes in Napa Valley," I said to no one in particular, hitting *delete*.

We stayed five days. The talk was mostly of disappearances, young men picked up on the streets of Karachi and Peshawar. Every time a plane flew over us, Irfan said it was one of the unmarked ones, the CIA condemning some dead soul to hell.

Many times in those days I thought of my interview with the man who said I was lucky to come from a place always in the news. If he only knew how rapidly the glamour of chaos recedes the closer you come to it. If he only knew never to slit its belly. It is already slit, and the insides are always raw, and people in Karachi spent a lot of time looking around, trying not to slip in a city damaged not by one but a series of attacks, each more malevolent, more multi-pronged. On any given day, the target would be a mosque and a hotel; on another, a bus and a train. The next, Chinese officials in

Balochistan and Pakistani generals in Punjab. Soon, it was just about everything except the two everyone resented most, the army on the ground and the drones in the air, because you can't kill a drone, it's a drone. And you can't kill an army, it's an army.

I watched my parents age. Sickness, fear. The multi-pronged pincers feeding on the anguish of growing old in a land consumed equally by terror as by trivia. Getting the phone fixed, the toilet fixed, the air conditioner fixed, the cable fixed, the road fixed. A day lost begging for electricity, the alms lost in an hour. Where was the space for higher aspirations, for revolution?

And yet, despite the monotony of dread, something lived. Resilience can flower in the muck of death and despair, particularly when it doesn't even know it. I saw this especially around my sister. Hers was an elasticity I didn't think Farhana expected to see and I wasn't sure she was glad to see it. It made her feel… irrelevant.

I compared them, my sister Sonia and Farhana. I knew Farhana did too. Had she expected to come from a position of—improvement? She was better educated. Wealthier. Sonia taught at a private school that paid 15,000 rupees per month. Farhana made more than two hundred times as much. When they shopped together, Sonia bargained for her as though for herself, and bought her gifts. Farhana never reciprocated. She would have been right in identifying herself in the position of receiver in a culture that took pride in its hospitality. But she didn't really reveal any desire to give. Wes, on the other hand, frequently presented my mother with flowers and fruit, and I'll admit I was surprised, surprised also that we were comparing at all, Farhana and I. Sonia to Farhana, Farhana to Wes. Why?

It didn't stop. We kept matching them up. Sonia hadn't enjoyed much freedom or affection from my father; Farhana received much from hers. And yet. Sonia had a comfortable, casual air about her that came from complete ease in an environment she claimed to envy me for leaving. Farhana was seldom as relaxed, not in San Francisco, certainly not here. Sonia laughed more than Farhana. She flirted with shopkeepers. She had a cabal of "best friends." Her cell phone never stopped ringing. Her benign husband observed everything about her with a benign gaze, no matter how she was dressed. But dress did matter to Farhana.

She'd come equipped with two outfits, both once belonged to her mother, both with kurtas falling halfway down her shins, both in colors unbecoming. She was too pale for parrot green and mouse brown made her look, well, mousy. Besides, the starched cotton flared around her torso. She complained of looking pregnant, which she did, though I said the best lay underneath. She asked why I hadn't told her about the latest fashions. I asked why she hadn't searched the internet. To which she replied, tetchily, "I didn't know your sister was so fashionable." To which I didn't know how to reply.

How much of this contributed to the quarrel we were about to have? I couldn't say. Though by the third day she started deferring to Sonia's taste, and started looking the better for it, Farhana's feeling of insignificance was only to increase.

On that third day, we heard it on the news: *A bomb exploded in a hotel this morning, killing one foreigner and seven Pakistanis.* Wes wondered if instead of heading north for the mountains we should be heading west across the Atlantic.

"You're not the target," I said, and Farhana complained I wasn't being sympathetic.

"Sympathetic? One foreigner dies and seven locals. Where's *his* sympathy?" I didn't say, *Where's yours?* We were again weighing lives against each other, one against seven, relevance against irrelevance. Instead of answering me she called out to Wes, and, while I watched, they both strode into the kitchen, where my mother was to lavish them with yet another ridiculously complicated meal.

The next two days, we spent apart. And unfortunately, the nights. We'd barely slept together in the weeks before leaving San Francisco, but since arriving in this city, where lust was a life-size secret, I wanted her again. Farhana was reserved. Why did I want her if I didn't want to hold her hand? she asked, when I sneaked into her room. The question astonished me because, obviously, the answer was born of it. I wanted her *because* I couldn't hold her hand. Or any other part. A quick fuck is a dead end, she said, forcing me back to my room.

Instead of focusing on events in the house, I focused on events in Waziristan, on the Afghan border, where lust was no secret at all. The local tribes of Waziristan harbored Arabs, Tajiks, Uzbeks, Chechens, and Chinese Uyghur Muslims. Some of them were fleeing the war in Afghanistan, but others were fleeing their own governments. Waziristan's tribal chiefs welcomed everyone except Pakistanis from outside their own tribe. Call it hospitality. Irfan and I decided the entrance to Waziristan should have a statue holding a Kalashnikov and a Quran. *Give me your tired, your poor... the wretched refuse of your teeming shore. Send these to me—unless they're Pakistani!*

"And what about Pakistan's hospitality to the US?" I said.

Irfan thought about it. "*Give me your missiles, your drones... the furtive raptors of your teeming war. Drop these on me—because I'm Pakistani!*"

We were sitting in a café with four other friends. The café had tinted windows and a smell that suggested no one ever came here, except our large and fair-skinned waiter, whom we decided looked just like Tahir Yuldashev, the Uzbek mentor of the Waziristan lord Baitullah Mehsud. Until this summer, there'd been a ceasefire between Mehsud and the Pakistan Army. Since the end of the ceasefire, Yuldashev was again supplying Mehsud with Uzbek bodyguards hardened from decades of fighting the Soviets in Afghanistan. Yuldashev, and Central Asia in general, captured our imagination more than the bombings in our own city. We still didn't know who'd bombed the hotel. We were already resigned to never knowing. Yuldashev, on the other hand, was organized and known. For instance, he'd raised an army to avenge the American bombing of Shahi-Kot Valley in Afghanistan in 2002. That was organized.

Three years later, we still didn't know why America had called the bombing Operation Anaconda.

"Ask him," Irfan pointed to the waiter hovering near the door.

We waved him over. I said, "Why name the siege of Shahi-Kot in Central Asia after a water snake in South America?"

The waiter walked outside for a smoke.

"They think we're an extension of Vietnam," answered Irfan.

"Are there anaconda in Vietnam?"

"What would you rather they had called it?"

"Operation Cobra."

"Too typical."

"Operation Antelope?"

The war had the benefit of giving me something to discuss not only with my friends in place of my failure as a boyfriend, but also with my father, in place of my failure as a son.

One morning, the newspaper carried a cartoon that moved the ice between us by a few millimeters. It was this. A white hand belonging to a white man with a top hat and stars and stripes gives a brown man in tattered clothes money. The brown man, delighted, starts sewing together a doll. In the next panel, the same white hand gives the merry tailor twice as much money. This time, the brown man, fuming, tears apart his invention, dress, beard, et al. For those who didn't get it, the caption read: *Pakistan spends billions of dollars destroying what it spent millions of dollars creating.*

My father chuckled. I chuckled.

Two days later, we were in Islamabad.

On the bus up, Farhana picked at her lip. She said nothing even when the bus broke down and we waited three hours for another one. All foreigners had to register with the military almost every hour, so the bus kept stopping and everyone was forced to wait for her and Wes. No one complained, not even those with six or seven children at their knee. I didn't know if Farhana's aloofness had to do with annoyance at these stops (curiously, Wes was cheerful throughout), embarrassment at keeping the bus waiting, or if it was aimed only at me. Some holdover from Karachi? Or did she imagine I had the power to prevent the stops? Or that I was mocking her for thinking she would be treated as if from here? She was courteous with the passengers; overly courteous, in fact, telling Wes repeatedly how friendly and dignified everyone was, as if he needed to be told. She was even courteous with the military men, who delighted in chatting with her, who would not have delighted in chatting with her had she not been a guest. They were even more delighted to have their picture taken (with my camera! That she despised!) while proudly displaying their guns. Afterward, they offered Wes a free lesson in Automatic Weapons 101 that he gladly accepted. The people on the bus waited, some cheering, others in dignified silence.

It wasn't till we reached Naran that I finally learned what was bothering her. We were at a shop that sold Kashmiri shawls and fleece blankets and I bought her one of each saying we were going to need them. I could tell she liked the shawl. It had a silky lightness and a reversible pattern, black on one side, white on the other, and on both, cherry-colored embroidery of interlaced vines. But she turned away and began looking at a row of walnut-wood salad bowls. When I draped the shawl around her shoulders she said it made her feel cheap the way I thought I could win her back so easily.

"Why do I have to win you back?"

"You really don't know, do you?"

"We buy each other gifts all the time. I don't do it to gain anything. Do you?"

"You didn't hear me."

"Did you?"

"Why is Irfan with us?"

Irfan and Wes were outside the shop. We could hear Wes telling Irfan that he'd always wanted to see India "from the other side." We could hear Irfan's silence. (What would I say to that?) We could hear Wes add, "This doesn't even look like Pakistan."

"Why's Wes with us?" I turned back to Farhana.

She sighed. "We're here on work. You know that."

"I thought we were here because you wanted to return to your country?"

Her neck turned red.

Finally, she said, "I like Irfan and I know you guys are close. But he acts like he's the boss and you say nothing. He keeps deciding where to stop and for how long."

Well, that was true. But so was this: she was changing the subject. I took two breaths and decided to state another truth. "Irfan knows these mountains better than anyone I know."

"We didn't have to come to Kaghan Valley at all," she kept on. "We could have gone straight into the Northern Areas, as planned."

"Wes doesn't seem to mind."

"So you like him now?"

"I don't dislike him."

She laughed. It was not her usual laugh.

"But you'll like this valley," I said at last. "It's a lush alpine forest and you love lush alpine forests! Trust me, when we leave here you're going to miss all the green. You won't get that higher up. And it does have glaciers. And it gives us more time together. You'll love the cabin, you'll see. It's by the river and we'll have time for the lakes. You'll love the lakes."

"Please stop."

As she left the shop the shawl fell to the floor. Dusting it lovingly, the shopkeeper handed it back to me.

So I left out the most important detail about Karachi.

It was in Karachi that Irfan suggested going to Kaghan first. We were at one of those grand yet rundown old restaurants with long tables meant to seat entire tribes. (The smallest table was for six—who'd eat out with fewer than that?) There were twenty-two of us. Irfan, Farhana, and I sat at one corner. Wes—who, with his lumberjack build and bleach-blond hair with the green stripe had been attracting a lot of attention from the moment he stepped off the plane—was wedged somewhere between my sister's husband and his mother, who could not stop touching him. She fed him all her seekh kebabs, then her barbecue fish, then everyone else's.

Farhana spoke with Irfan. I wasn't really paying attention. I thought he was helping her with her Urdu, and I registered, vaguely, that their talk was drifting to the rise in winter snowfall in the Western Himalayas and the Karakoram, and how this was feeding the glaciers, and perhaps it was that word *feeding* which sent my mind whirling. I began thinking how odd it was, the way the best-fed man at the table over there was the one being lavished, when three-quarters of the Pakistani population lived under $2 a day. 40 percent had no access to drinking water. 50 percent no sanitation. I could smell the open gutter out on the street. Where was our hospitality when it came to this? It wasn't that I was upset with my brother-in-law's mother, or with Wes, and I'm not sure I was even upset. It was simply a profound sense of—whitewash.

Farhana began describing to Irfan the redwood forests of California. I looked at her. She'd not been attracting as much attention as Wes. With her pale complexion, dark thicket of hair, and dark eyes hooded by bushy brows routinely pruned, her German-Pakistani ancestry had resulted in a quite Iranian look, and there were plenty of people in the country with her coloring. She stood out less for her features and more for her accent, and her height, and, of course, her walk, her stomp, swinging both arms with rigor, feet to the side, as if cross-country skiing.

"They like the valley bottoms," she was saying. "And the floods, though not too often, and they like the fog belt. They like the non-stop drip of dampness. Nadir could never be a redwood." She turned to me.

I smiled. She leaned very slightly, as if to kiss me, and I pulled back very slightly, reminding her where we were. She got up to use the bathroom.

Irfan absently chewed on the burnt edge of a naan and suggested that Farhana would enjoy the forests of Kaghan Valley. "It's very lush, she'd like that. And not so out of the way. We have time. There are glaciers there too."

Then I thought about it. Yes, she *would* love the valley. It was damp, shadowy, fecund. It was Farhana!

So we decided. And we forgot to tell her till it was time to change buses in Abbottabad. We didn't take the one to Gilgit in the Northern Areas but the one to the town of Naran in Kaghan Valley, in the Frontier Province. It was just to be a three-day detour before heading north to the landscape of vertical wildernesses I'd described to her once. She sat with Wes on the bus and he must have told her and it must have pained her that he'd been told while she had not—I do remember Irfan explaining it to Wes, but where had she been? The bathroom? Shopping with my sister? I couldn't remember!—and it was uncharacteristic of her, the way she said nothing till that time in the shop, when she tossed off the shawl.

But then the night before we trekked up to the lake I believed she'd forgiven me, and I believed the same in the morning. I believed it even when I heard her complain to Wes about the detour, as she fed him those cold, tri-colored eggs, moments before we left the cabin. I believed it even on the walk up the glacier, when she turned her back to me, and I had to—how swiftly she and Wes moved on the ice!—I had to hold back—with what ferocity I wanted her just then!—reminding myself that the best reunions are like the best stories, and the best sex, raising questions while delaying answers. Yes. I believed she'd forgiven me, but I did not entirely believe I'd forgiven her. Because though it's true that I left out the most important detail about Karachi and that I then disclosed it, it is also true that I continue to leave out the most important detail.

Kaghan or no Kaghan, what was she doing here at all?

Ice, Mating

Sometimes, after Farhana untangled the knots of her braid and tossed a wad of hair in the dustbin, she'd pull me out of bed, to recline at her five-sided bay window in San Francisco. It pitched so far out into the street, she claimed it was the one that caused the city to pass an ordinance limiting the projection of all bay windows. We'd sit there, nestled in glass in a purple house. Even by the city's standards, the house was spectacular. Slender spiraling columns at the alcove, each with gold rings, like cufflinks on a white and crinkly sleeve. Halfway down the door of unfinished wood ran a tinted oval glass. *Mirror mirror* she'd giggle, the first few times I kissed her there. The bedroom balcony—with little gold-tipped minarets—was where I left her calla lilies, like an offering to the god of extravagance. Art-glass windowpanes under the roof.

At the window, we watched others on the street.

At the window, she asked, "What's the most beautiful thing you ever witnessed? I mean a moment."

At the window, we played opposites. The Mission, where she lived, was once moist, fecund. In contrast, the stark, windswept Richmond, where I lived, was once a desolate bank of sand. We said she sprang from marsh, I from desert. She loved the damp closeness of curves, the rich debris of glaciers and deltas. She loved her gloves and her socks. I, though always cold, hated to cover my extremities. I preferred the raw, violent beauty of the Pacific coast to the secret tides of the protected bays. We said "opposites attract" and we were right. Converging is what divided us.

On her first birthday after we met, the year before we left for Kaghan, in one hand I held a calla lily with a lip pinker than her own, in the other, a bottle of champagne. As I descended the hill to her purple palace, the sun drew the fog from my flesh, and I was salivating as the scent of refried beans followed me all the way to her door. There she met me, dressed in woolens and boots, saying she knew what she wanted instead.

"What?"

"Let me show you."

I shut my eyes, counted to ten, opened them. "So, where is it?"

"Not here, silly. Let's go for a walk. To *your* neighborhood, the one you love to photograph, with all the cliffs and cypresses." She rolled her eyes as though cliffs and cypresses were toys for men. I found her delicious.

It was an especially cold day in May and though I did love the bluffs, I'd been hoping for a more close-fitting day. Call it role reversal. I chilled the champagne and headed for the bay window, to, well, anticipate some tidal advances. The last time we'd made love I'd teased that her needs were growing as strong as the tides rushing up the channels of a salt marsh, and, inshallah, they'd also be twice daily.

Well, it was not to be.

She'd planned the route. First, the ruins of the Sutro Baths, which looked especially green and scummy that day, thick as a Karachi sewer. We watched the pelicans. Dark hunkered shadows, sometimes in gangs of twenty or more, closing in on the fecund orgy at the microbe-gilded pools like evil clouds, like missiles. They launched headlong, scattering the seagulls and the swifts, dropping one after the other in a heavy, gut-wrenching fall. A rain of bombshells. The invasion mesmerized us.

I moved my camera in search of the prison island of Alcatraz, floating somewhere in the bay, but it was shrouded in fog. *Alcatraz.* The archaic Spanish word for pelican, from the Arabic *al-qatras*. It was the rule of silence that drove the inmates insane, reminding them that their exile was complete. I moved my camera back to the baths, and from there, to the austere silhouette of a cormorant. He seemed to be watching the assault of the pelicans with as little interest as God.

"Nadir, talk to me for a minute, without that."

I didn't have to see through the lens to see her point to it. "In a minute."

The pelicans gone, the seagulls multiplied. I watched a pair land on the boulders along the shore. It was the softest landing, the gulls allowing the wind to pull them down gently, lovingly. And the hummingbirds—how did they survive in this wind, and at this height? And the succulents to her side—those red waxy leaves, juicy as capsicum—and the purple flowers with the bright white hearts! Here it was again: the tenacity of the small. What I'd seen in the Sonoran Desert and the valleys of the Himalayas.

"It's over a minute." I put the camera in its case. She cleared her throat. "Nadir, are you as happy here, with me, as you are alone on your nightly walks?"

"I'm much happier."

She looked away. We were balanced on the farthest wall of the ruins. The water here was less slimy; a thin sun shimmered in its depths. As Farhana's orange scarf blew across the pale green peat, I took my camera out again. She sometimes let me photograph her now, though still not often enough, and only when dressed. I got a beautiful profile of her gazing at the baths, perhaps imagining them as the rambling maze of salt water swimming pools they'd once been, thumb at lower lip, the mist rolling across the steps in the background.

"Happier than in the mountains of Pakistan?"

Perhaps I hesitated. "Well, yes."

"So," she tossed her head back, pulled the scarf tight around her neck, "which is more beautiful. The desert, or the mountains?"

"Hard to say." I paused, wanting to play along with this birthday guessing game. "Both. Equally. Differently." How to compare a horizontal wilderness with a perpendicular one? Especially the most impenetrable perpendicular wilderness in the world? What I couldn't even begin to explain was how both energized me by removing me from myself. Like seeing the world from behind a camera. She wouldn't understand. She'd call it hiding. She'd call it cowardly. But it was none of these things. It was disappearing. I could see better this way.

She watched me hesitate. "Okay, which makes you happiest, the desert, the mountains, or these scummy baths with me."

This time I am sure I did not hesitate. "I'm happy anywhere with you."

She laughed. "You don't have to say that. But since you did, why?"

I was still photographing her. From behind the lens, I replied, "Because you don't remind me of my past." And as I stepped onto a lower wall to get more of the ruins behind her, I realized that this was exactly so. She wasn't like any of the women I knew in Karachi. Her energy was—different. It wasn't sultry, wasn't eastern. She was walking away from me now, walking away from my lens, and I noticed that her walk was determined and—how can I put it?—unstudied. As if no aunt had ever told her that women walk with one foot before the other. It wasn't graceful but it was vigorous. There are men on the Pakistan–Afghanistan border who can spot a foreign journalist hiding in a burqa by the way she moves. Farhana would never pass. She could, however, keep up with them on the mountains. Not many women from Karachi could. And yet—of course I didn't tell her this—they had more patience in bed. Farhana didn't like to linger, not over food, shopping, or sex. The only thing I'd ever seen her linger over was her hair, and that was not with pleasure. All the languor was in her spine, the part of her she never let me put behind my lens. Everything else about her had the slightly lunatic energy of Nor Cal, uncomplicated and nervy. I mean, for heaven's sake, she was passionate about *glaciers*. How many Pakistani women know two things about them? It was Farhana who told me that Pakistan has more glaciers than anywhere outside the poles. And I've *seen* them! I've even seen them *fuck*!

She was sobbing. I saw it first through the lens. I saw it too late, after I'd taken the photograph of her wiping her nose with the back of her hand. She said it was the worst thing I could have said.

The seagulls hovered, teetering in the breeze. Before they touched the rock it was beginning to sink in, yet each time I approached a landing, the wind pulled me away again. We loved each other, Farhana and I, for precisely opposite reasons. If I loved her because she did not remind me of my past, Farhana loved me because she believed I was her past. That day I came close to understanding; by the time I fully understood, we were already immersed in separate rituals of silence.

I expected to keep to the coast to Point Lobos, but, veering inland, she began following the signs for Fort Miley. I said nothing. I didn't know what to say. How could I apologize for all that drew me to her? Perhaps I'd been crude in trying to sum it up in the first place. (Or she'd been crude in asking.) That's the line I eventually took, as we clambered uphill. "There's too much about you that makes me happy to say why."

"Too late. You already said it."

Silence, then.

There were picnickers in the grass. Behind them rose a plaque commemorating what had once been gun emplacements, from before World War I. The plaque read,

> Although they never fired on an enemy, coastal batteries here and throughout the Bay Area stood ready—a strong deterrent to attack.

"You had enemies back then, too?" I muttered, before catching myself. "I didn't mean *you* you."

She cut me a furious look. I bounced foolishly on my toes. She climbed further up to where enormous guns had once pointed out to the Pacific, guarding all three approaches to Golden Gate. There was a sublime view of Ocean Beach, but I knew it wasn't for the view that she'd brought me here.

Without looking at me, she said, "Take me back."

I assumed she meant to her warm purple house in the Mission. "Let's go."

"Take me back to the places in Pakistan that you love."

I was stunned. If she'd never been to them, why did she say *back*? And why now? And why ever?

When she said it a third time I understood that she presented her idea as a condition: take me back and I will keep loving you.

For always? I wanted to ask. No matter where?

I looked at her boldly now, and she returned my stare. I was hoping she'd understand that this is what my eyes said.

It was here that a man loved her, a man with whom she could spend an unknowable quantity of time doing just about anything: walking, going to the movies, eating sushi and Guatemalan tamales on the same day, gossiping about a father in Berkeley, a father I'd still not met because, as I was growing tired of hearing, he was unpredictable—I didn't know whom she was protecting more, him or me—but who'd brought her to this country when she was three and stayed. I didn't understand why a thirty-year-old woman—yes, she turned thirty today, it was meant to be a happy day!—with a great job and a great house in a pretty neighborhood in a pretty city didn't feel this was home. All I understood was that she didn't. She was at a time in her life when other women long for a child. Farhana longed for a country.

"You're going home next summer. I'm coming with you. That's what I want you to give me for my birthday. I want this promise."

I didn't want to return. With her, that is. Nor did I want to explain that for me it was a return, but I didn't think it was for her. Nor that, just as she took joy in showing me this corner of the world because I was new to it, I could only take joy in showing her mine if she acknowledged it as new to her. Not if she claimed it as her own. I'd spent the past year lingering over northern California and could freely admit there was much I'd yet to learn. How many months was she prepared to linger over Pakistan? How many years? Would she have the patience to wait and yield till the geography really did begin to construct the person, the way the breakers beneath us constructed the shore? Did she *want* to yield? Of course not. It was a country practically under siege. *We might be interested in you but not in your landscapes.* What images did she want to see and to which land did she want to return?

We'd been happy. I wanted to stay happy. I said, "I'm going for work."

It wasn't a lie. The plan was to spend next summer in the Northern Areas with a friend from school, Irfan, to take pictures. Though loath to admit it to Farhana, this past year I'd sought Irfan's help in paying my share of the rent. Irfan always wired the money without complaining, though of course it was meant to be the other way around. I should be wiring money home, not receiving it. Till I could pay him back, I'd keep working long hours at a brew pub a few blocks from my apartment and take whatever other work I could find, usually as a wedding photographer. I anticipated doing the same even after next summer, no matter how many images I shot of vertical or horizontal wildernesses. Yet her reply stunned me.

"Work? What's the point? You'll never sell any. At least I know glaciers."

I stopped rolling on my toes.

"Perhaps you're going back for the wrong reason," she kept on.

"And being your tour guide is the right reason?"

She bestowed upon me an ice-black stare, the kind I was to receive the following year from a very different creature, in a very different place. Behind Farhana, I could see the guns that once pointed to the minefields outside Golden Gate. How easy it is to envision enemies lurking in the tide. As I looked over her shoulder, imagining what shapes those phantoms had once taken, I couldn't have guessed that within fourteen months, she and I would be posted at our own separate lookouts, not on a headland overlooking the Pacific, but near a glacier overlooking Kashmir.

"What's the most beautiful thing you ever witnessed?" she'd ask, as we lay together by her five-sided bay window, playing opposites. "I mean, a moment."

I always said it was the mating of glaciers. I'd seen the ritual once, with Irfan and his wife Zulekha, on that previous trip to Pakistan's north. I tried to communicate the wonder of it to Farhana, while she stretched on her stomach, swinging her legs.

First, I'd say, the village elders discussed at length which glaciers to mate. The female ice was picked from a village where women were especially beautiful and, because this wasn't enough, talented. Talent meant knowledge of yak milk, butter, fertilizer, and, of course, wool. From caps to sweaters all the way down to socks, the questions were always the same. How delicately was the sheep's wool spun? And what about the kubri embroidery on the caps—was it colorful and fine? Most importantly, did all the women cooperate?

"And the male?" Farhana laughed. "I suppose beauty and cooperation aren't high on that list?"

He was picked from another village, I said. One where men were strong, and, because this wasn't enough, successful. Success meant knowledge of firewood, agriculture, trekking, and herding. There was a fifth, bonus area, and this was yak hair. From this, some men could spin sharma, a type of coarse rug. A glacier in a village with such men had to be male.

She swung her feet, happy in woolen socks. "And where do they consummate their love?"

"In a hole dug into the side of a cliff." I told her it was a ceremony I'd only been allowed to watch after swearing an oath of silence. There was a belief that words disturbed the balance between lovers-in-transit. Perhaps I was breaking the oath by describing it to her in detail there in her purple house, miles away from the sacred soil to which the ceremony belonged.

"The location of the hole had been as carefully selected as the bride and groom," I continued, "by gauging which side of the mountain attracted the right length of shadow for the snow to hold for ten months, 14,000 feet above sea level. Two porters had heaved the ice on their backs the entire way. We were brought in a jeep, after taking that oath."

I remembered Zulekha kissing Irfan's cheek, hurriedly, making sure no one was looking. She had curls down to her shoulders and features as impish as his. They'd been neighbors in Peshawar and had gone to the same college in Karachi. They'd been in love since the age of six.

I remembered the girl I was with at the time, Rida, which means inner peace. The chapstick on her lips had the scent of mint crackling in firewood. Later, I'd feed her purple roses that left blood marks on our lips. (Of course, I left this detail out for Farhana.)

At the marital hole, we all stood, waiting. The porters lowered the ice-bride and ice-groom from off their backs without hurting them. They tossed the male in first. *Whooshoo! Whooshoo!* A loop of air seemed to dance right back up the hole and circle around again, inside my chest. The female was released on top. She fell without a sound.

I thought it a beautiful thing. The most beautiful thing I'd seen. A pilgrimage to love.

We were told it was bad luck for other eyes to watch. Eyes from somewhere else. Karachi eyes. Peshawar eyes. But even then I'd not been able to resist. I'd taken out my camera and aimed. Had it brought us bad luck?

I left this detail out as well.

"What happened next?" She rolled onto her back, said the ice imagery was making her thirsty. I put wet glasses in the freezer for dark beer later. Then I told her the rest. The elders waited politely for the male and female glaciers to finish in their marital bed, after which the porters shielded the hole with a mat of grass, wheat husks, and walnut shells that they'd uncover in the winter, so the snow could collect around the two ice blocks. When the female was fat, freshwater children would spring from her womb and the village would drink them and irrigate their fields with them. After five winters, the couple would begin to creep downhill as one, becoming a natural glacier.

I always concluded by asking, "And you, what's your most beautiful moment?"

She never hesitated. "The way you looked at me, the first time, standing down in the sand on Baker Beach in your trousers while I sat sunning myself on the rocks. You compared me to a calla lily. That was the moment."

The first time she said it, I had to look away. I was the best thing to happen to her? *Me*? I did not deserve my luck. I know I did not, or I would have seen that it was when we played together in her window and I received her unguarded love, these were my most beautiful moments. They were not witnessed. They were lived.

We played differently now.

Jinn, Jeannie

Glaciers in the eastern Himalayas are receding. Some say the Alps will be ice-free by 2100. Greenland's glaciers are melting so fast they could sink southern California and Bangladesh. But in parts of Pakistan, glaciers could be expanding. It was a possibility Wes and Farhana had come to explore.

We finally left our cabin, though not as early as I'd have liked. Wes and Farhana decided to scrape up every last bite of my cold omelette too; perhaps the air was making them hungry. An hour later, as I watched Farhana trek up the glacier to Lake Saiful Maluk with Wes, I feared her love for me was like a Pakistani glacier. It was difficult to say if it was growing or retreating.

What did she love about them? Glaciers, I mean. They weren't shady or concealed, nothing marshy there, except perhaps the slushy, slippery surface. Unlike her, glaciers were slow-moving, sluggish, with bouts of extreme rage. Between stasis and thrust, they rattled and creaked, moaned and bickered, adjusting and readjusting their old, old bones. Like a ghost in the family, and unlike Farhana, they were insistent lingerers. (Granted, she did linger over those damn eggs.) Snails must be born of them. (I once made a photo-collage of a glacier speckled in snails; the snails looked like little glacier turds.) Was that the attraction—the promise of a deep, stubborn rootedness? Rejection of the New World? Here in the land to which she "returned," she found glaciers that weathered global gas emissions and spurned newness. Except this wasn't true, of course. Glacial growth and decline were equal indicators of global warming, as she herself liked to remind me, and if glaciers were growing in the Old World, they were also growing in the New. They were growing in Mount Shasta in northern California, for instance, and Farhana was here to compare the rate of growth in the western Himalayas to that of the southern Cascades.

Apart from returning, of course.

There were others trekking up the glacier with us, as well as a line of jeeps, all heading up to the lake, all leaving brown scud marks across the glittery white expanse. (Snails!) The jeeps slid across the ice, white-knuckled drivers steering wheels that kicked like steeds. To our right was a drop thousands of feet down into the river. I peered over the edge. A school bus lay on its side. I overheard the driver of one jeep tell his passengers that the accident was only two days old. There were no survivors. A whiff of hashish circled us as the jeep continued up.

Leaning over the edge, Irfan said the schoolchildren had probably been listening to their teacher tell the story of how the lake got its name, just as the bus had skidded.

"What a happy thought," I replied.

"She had probably just gotten to the part about the prince falling in love with a fairy princess," he added cheerfully. "Or the part about the jinn."

I looked at him. With his clipped pointy beard and sharp cheekbones, Irfan had an elfin look about him, except that his eyes, hard with sorrow, belonged to this world. He had a way of hunching his shoulders and pursing his lips when reminded of all that caused him pain, which was most things. His wife Zulekha had died soon after their marriage; she'd died in a car hijacking in Karachi, on her way home from a wedding with her brother. The hijackers had shot them both before driving off with her Honda Civic. Irfan was near Kaghan when it happened, working on a water management project for a Norwegian company. It was before the days of the cell phone. He returned to Karachi to find his wife already buried.

In America, a shrink would say Irfan needed closure. In Pakistan, he needed God. But he lost Him when he lost his wife, and his brooding posture enfolded a man nothing like the Irfan I'd gone to school with, the one with whom I'd trekked across these valleys before, to see the mating of glaciers. I thought it was to remember being here with Zulekha that Irfan had changed the plan and decided on this detour to Kaghan. I assumed it wasn't *entirely* because Farhana loved forests.

Now I mumbled, "A lot has changed since we were here last."

He grinned, somewhat devilishly, as if to say, *all for a Honda Civic.*

As I raised my arm to offer something—perhaps a thump of camaraderie to his back—I nearly slipped. I pulled his jacket for balance and we found our footing barely two inches from the edge.

"Not even a fairy princess is worth falling for," he laughed as we turned away from the bus to follow Farhana and Wes back up the glacier.

They were far ahead of us now, two tall figures, both identifiable by the color of their coats—Farhana a red blur, Wes a mustard—the ends of her braid occasionally scattering sunlight across my field of vision like a lens flare. They were probably taking readings as they went; people seemed to be watching them. I walked in the dirt track her shoes left behind as the glacier creaked. There were unimaginable pressures stored in the ice beneath our feet.

This morning, as we lay in bed in our cabin, before Wes and Irfan disturbed us, I'd told Farhana the story about the jinn and the lovers. She lay on her back, knees slowly tracing arcs in the air, casting spells across her damp bush. Before she pulled the covers over her, for those few moments, we were naked together, enjoying the warmth we still held between us. I was glad there were no dishes to wash in our cabin and no access to email, or I could never have kept her there long enough to whisper the tale in her ear.

"There was a jinn who fell in love with a fairy princess. The jinn was the guard of Malika Parbat, the mountain that borders the lake."

"And Malika Parbat means?"

"Queen of the Mountains."

"Go on."

"The fairy princess was called Badar Jamal, and she was a water creature, all silvery and slight, dipping in and out of the lake, stretching pleasingly on Malika Parbat's slopes. The jinn would watch her. Trouble was, a prince began watching too. He was called Saiful Maluk, and he came from across the steppes."

"So the lake is named after him, not her."

"Well, yes."

"Go on."

"To Badar Jamal, the prince was everything a man should be. On a horse, in a turban, and most importantly, from a distant land. The jinn, well, he was a household thing. You can imagine the rest."

She ran her feet up my calves. "The exotic prince whisks her away to a life of adventure."

"Not quite. To put it bluntly, the jinn was a jealous fiend. His scalding fury caused Malika Parbat's snow to melt with such force it breached the banks of the lake and nearly drowned the poor lovers."

"Nearly?"

"Fortunately, they had a cave to run to."

"So, the jinn's wrath melted the snow? The jinn is global warming."

"No, the jinn is an evil spirit that cannot experience love or happiness, but is tormented when others do. The cave is copulation. It's our only hope."

She laughed. "You don't think there are parallels between mother wit and science?"

"I think there are parallels between you and heaven." I blew gently on her skin.

"Did you ever find the cave?" I asked Irfan on the glacier, pulling myself away from the sweet memory of this morning. "I want to show it to Farhana."

"What cave?"

"You know, the one in which Saiful Maluk and the fairy princess take refuge when the jealous jinn gets jealous."

"That cave!" Irfan smiled, casting me a look I couldn't understand. "Yes. I know where it is. But it's far from here. We'll need Farhana's consent." This time I understood the look. The old Irfan would have accepted the love between Farhana and me, vacillating though it may be, without judgment.

I ignored his comment and the look, focusing instead on Malika Parbat looming to the east. The mountain rose just over 5,000 meters, a modest height compared with all the giants to the north. But it was to see her reflection in the lake that lay 3,000 meters above sea level and was named after an alien prince that everyone trooped all the way up.

Irfan pulled his cell phone out of his pocket, frowning. "We've lost contact."

"Good." I'd left my phone behind in Karachi and not missed it once.

"Maybe not so good," Irfan muttered.

I left him to his phone as I increased my speed up the glacier. By now it was packed with tourists and trekkers and I could barely spot Farhana ahead. *Take care of her*, her father had commanded me, before we left. *She is all I have.* The sun soared directly above us; her red coat flickered irregularly over an icy horizon now blindingly white. So blinding that I was almost grateful for the filth left behind by those transgressing against the glacier's beauty, some while slipping to their knees, others while gliding forward, as if on fairy wings.

In the weeks following our fight at the fort, I returned to the coast often, always alone. A small part of me knew it was to cleanse my palette, as if to revive something that had been lost on that wild stretch of land when it included Farhana.

My eye was hungry. I photographed the Monterey pines and the valley Quercus. The agave that bloomed before death. The pups that replaced them. California buckeye, star tulips, and bell-shaped pussy ears with stems as thin as saliva. Diogenes' Lantern, the sweetest of flowers, yellow as the yawning sun.

How did they survive the onslaught of the Pacific wind? Why didn't the stems snap, the buds fall? They flourished at the edge of chaos, in a nursery of knotted cypresses, while I was an intruder, a gray wolf with coarse mane unnuzzled, neck arched plaintively to a remote moon.

I crawled back to her house. *Mirror, mirror*, I bayed at her glass. *Forgive the ugliest of them all!* She wouldn't let me in. Once, through the glass, I saw a small dark man approach the door, and I knew he was going to open it. Before he could, I heard Farhana shout *Baba!* and he turned away. Another time, a tall white man paused at the door, and Farhana was nowhere. We stared at each other through the glass, his image wavering as though he were gazing at me from under water, before swimming away.

I worked longer hours at the brew pub. I gave up trying to push my landscapes, including my mother's marble-top table. *What's the point? You'll never sell any*. Perhaps she was right. The pub allowed me to advertise my skills as a wedding photographer, for which I was developing a reasonable reputation. The irony of it. A Pakistani goes all the way to the land of opportunity only to end up taking photographs of brides. As if there weren't enough brides at home. With the exception of Farhana, women seemed to like me photographing them.

Then one evening, she came into the pub, smiling. It happened as quietly as that. We spent all evening smiling at each other. We smiled through the night, and through the subsequent days. We said very little, and when we did, it was politely coquettish. "How's work?" "Fine. Yours?" When after several more days additional words were spoken, they were about her father. She was finally ready to introduce me to him.

The meeting was arranged for an afternoon in October, eight months before we were to leave for Pakistan, though I didn't know the we part yet. We hadn't dared revisit the birthday promise she'd tried to extract from me in May, though it filled the air around us more oppressively than the fog. As we walked to the BART station, I decided I wasn't looking forward to this visit. I'd been kept in suspense about her *unpredictable* father for so long it was as if now I'd somehow passed a test. (I'd considered wearing a tie.) Perhaps this was part of our patching up, but I couldn't help thinking that she was *allowing* the meeting. Worse, the concession was a way to get a concession from me. Our quarrel grew two legs; it walked beside us all the way to the station, demanding, *Take me back*. It was as if she'd proposed to me. Take me back was to be our marriage. Take me back was to take us forward. (For the millionth time I thought, Dammit, for her, it isn't even *back*!) If I said no, she'd move forward by leaving me.

I stuffed my hands in the torn lining of my windbreaker's pockets, irritation turning to anger. Is this what marriage would be, the appearance of favor for favor, when, in fact, it's two to none? Stacking your chips, keeping score? Living in a damn game of mahjong?

I glanced at her. There was a smile lurking around the corners of her mouth. Not a smile of cunning. A smile of sweetness. I found no justification for my dreary mood. I drew her to me. "I love you." A kiss without chips.

She started to laugh. "You can't kiss me like that in front of him."

"So we should kiss like that now."

"All right then." After a time she broke away. "I should warn you. He can be unpredictable."

"You've warned me many times. I couldn't be more terrified."

"Terrified? But he's *wonderful*."

"Wonderful?"

"Well… You just can't know."

I nodded. "Unpredictable. Wonderful. No kissing."

"Sometimes he talks a lot, sometimes he smiles happily at the dust."

"You make him sound senile."

"Oh, don't be fooled. It only means he's sizing you up. He never remarried, you know—"

"You've told me."

"I'm his only child. He hasn't been great with former boyfriends."

Though I'd heard it before, it was hardly reassuring to hear again.

I tried to distract myself with stories of a mother she'd described for me many times, a mother whose photograph hung above her bed, inside a carved sandalwood frame that still smelled musky, and always reminded me of my grandmother. Her name was Jutta. She came from Bavaria, and she was of Celtic descent. Every summer, Jutta's stern Catholic father would lavish his one indulgence on the family, a trip to Kaltenberg castle, to taste the dark lager that had been brewed there since the days of King Ludwig. Farhana had her grandfather's palette, enjoying beer more than anyone I knew, and she loved to sample the flavors of the brewery where I worked. The more bitter-chocolate, the sweeter she would grow.

Jutta had come to Karachi when her first husband became the director of the Goethe Institute. Farhana's father, a gifted musician, according to her, was the tabla player for a concert at the institute one night. It was the player, not the raag, that mesmerized the German woman. Their affair turned them into castaways even before Farhana was born (too few months after her mother left her first husband). Farhana's maternal grandparents still never answered her letters while her paternal grandfather, recently deceased, never did forgive his son.

We got off the train in Berkeley. Three blocks later, Farhana spotted her father at a window seat of a dark tavern not unlike the one where I worked. I thought I could recognize him from the time I saw him through the glass, approaching the front door. Was it to let me in or to yell at me? Both?

She was saying, "Dada's death has made Baba even more unpredictable. You know the history between them, because of my mother. Still," she swung her arm in mine (not a kiss, but it was something), "though he hasn't been kind to other boyfriends, I just know he's going to like you."

And she was right. And it was mutual. At least at first. Our conversation bore no trace of the *So what does my daughter see in you?* assessment I'd been dreading. In fact, to Farhana's dismay, we didn't talk about her at all. At least at first.

"For heaven's sake," he said, sitting back down after shaking my hand, stretching spindly legs in baggy jeans, "don't call me Mr. Rahim. Call me Niaz." I could imagine him saying the same while easing into a chair with the same languorous grace (that had skipped Farhana) in mid-seventies Karachi, outside one of the tea shops in the Saddar area that teemed with poets and revolutionaries. Thirty years later, he still had the air of a Saddar hippie. In fact, he still had the same jeans. They drooped around his waist, the belt tied ludicrously loose, forcing him to yank them up each time he moved. It made him look both comical and vulnerable. Maybe this was why women left their husbands for him.

Somehow it was perfect that the beer he was drinking was called Moose Drool. And that he had a cup of cappuccino next to it. We ordered coffee.

He looked at me. "So, where have you been hiding all this time?"

I looked at Farhana.

"You know how hard he works," she replied.

"I'm unpredictable," I added. Under the table, Farhana pinched my knee.

He finished his beer, smiling her smile. She asked after his health. Apparently, he had diabetes. He ordered a second beer. They quibbled about his diet. (He also ordered fries.) He didn't look diabetic at all. He had the body of a young and lean rapper, a Lil Wayne lookalike, while his face was that of an exceptionally gaunt Kris Kristofferson. I was startled when I put his two halves together and came up with Jesus Christ. So startled that when he asked me a question, I nodded without hearing it.

When the second beer arrived Farhana pushed it toward me. I glanced at her as if to say, Why aren't you having it? She ignored me.

He chewed the end of a pipe while his cappuccino got cold. "So, what are they?"

"Sorry, what?" I asked, embarrassed.

He frowned. "I asked if there are religious reasons for your father's dislike of your work."

I shot a glance at Farhana. She had an irritating habit of telling the world that my work was a touchy topic. Of course the world wants to touch that.

I cleared my throat. "I never thought of it that way."

"He must have assumed you would. A good son should think about why the Prophet forbade images of himself, and forbade figurative art in general, no?"

I opened my mouth for no apparent reason.

He flashed me a toothy grin. "I was not a good son either." He took a sip of his cappuccino. "Don't they make hot drinks hot anymore?" He pushed the cup aside and reached for my—his—pint. "About which I couldn't be happier. I photographed Farhana's mother many times before she died. Before I knew she was dying." He sucked on the unlit pipe in silence.

I shot another glance at Farhana. It hadn't occurred to me that the photograph above her bed was taken by her father, nor had the irony struck me till now. She cherished the image, yet she wouldn't let me cherish enough of hers.

Farhana moved the beer back toward me. "Let's sit outside so Baba can smoke." I chuckled inwardly. He could die of cancer but not diabetes. Carrying my coffee—which was, as usual, too strong—I left the second pint inside.

We settled around a small table on the sidewalk. There was no milk and I thought it might be rude to go back inside to get it myself. Why did Americans make coffee like mud and tea like rain? When I turned back to Mr. Rahim he was watching me over his pipe, now lit, and over a helix of fries.

He said, "My father never let me take any photos of him, you know. He said that you can reproduce an image, but you cannot reproduce a soul."

"It's so much warmer out here," said Farhana, "than in the city."

"You cannot reproduce a soul," Mr. Rahim repeated. "Every picture tears the body from the soul. He saw paintings and photographs as theft, a way of owning and even destroying someone else."

"Baba," said Farhana, "don't scare Nadir. He's given enough flak for what he does."

This astonished me. It was one thing to steer conversation away from her dead grandfather to protect her father, but another to use me as the pretext! I went back inside for the milk. When I stepped out again, it was her father who tried to defuse the pressure building in my chest. "I think he's less annoyed with me and more with you for thinking him so easily scared."

She smiled at him. "Do you want another cappuccino?"

He tapped his cup. "Your smile is warming this one."

Satisfied, she leaned across the table and kissed him.

He turned to me again. "Where was I? Yes. Maybe it was the time he spent in Malaya during the Second World War. Whatever the reason, my father had a fierce aversion to what he called the fascist eye. He was terrified of its power to replicate an imagination that could not resist it. He bemoaned it, right until his death, the way the Third World is seen by the First World that makes up these terms. What he called *ghoorna.* Their gaze. On us."

I was startled by the intensity of Mr. Rahim's gaze, on *me*.

"Should we go for a walk?" said Farhana.

"He said the public gaze acted no differently from a camera," continued Mr. Rahim. "For him, even the act of seeing became a theft. Even a murder."

"Baba," whispered Farhana. "Don't go into all that now."

He stood up, went inside, came out with a pint half-consumed and resumed talking as if there'd been no interruption. "He had seen the gaze in the way the British looked at women in his village, with both desire and disdain, as if it was beneath them to desire *blacks*, as if this justified deepening the gaze. He saw it again when deployed in Malaya, in the way the Japanese regarded local women. When he returned from the war, he returned to an India on the verge of independence and partition, but because his friends had scorned him for fighting for the British, he felt himself under *their* gaze. He returned both decorated and humiliated. He died a complete hermit."

Farhana asked for the bill.

"But isn't it ironic?" Her father sat on the edge of his seat, shirt collar pulled to one side, clavicle jutting like a bluff. "He grew so paranoid about the public gaze that he enforced strict purdah, both on himself and his wife, obsessed not with seeing but how we are seen, saving his morality—and that of his family's—to the point where there was hardly any *spirit* left to save."

"But you are so spirited!" She curled her fingers around his.

He threw back the pint. "You tell me, was he resisting tyranny or yielding to it?"

I shifted, an intruder in a private conversation between a father and a daughter; no, between a son and a spirit.

Farhana tapped his hand. "Please stop, Baba. You're meeting Nadir for the first time."

He regarded her the way he must have regarded her when she was born, and his eyes grew misty. "But I already know him! Why have you told him nothing about me?"

"But he knows everything!" She played along. "Don't you?" They both looked at me. I looked at the sidewalk.

"Then he knows that you are nothing like me, and everything like your mother. I thank God for that every day!" Now his eyes danced with mischief as he looked from Farhana to me. "At least Farhana is not married."

I choked on my coffee.

She examined the bill.

His eyes stopped dancing. There it was at last: his assessment of me.

He paid the bill and stood up to leave. "You must show me your photographs some time." He pulled up his jeans.

I also stood up. "It was wonderful to meet you." The farewell sounded as stale as his interest in my work.

"Well, I'm glad Farhana is not hiding you from me anymore. The next time we meet, it should be at my house." This, with more gusto. He had deep vertical worry lines between his brows; they seemed to grow deeper as his face brightened.

"I'd like that." I shook his hand more vigorously.

He walked away as abruptly as his moods had changed.

Once assured that he would not turn around again, Farhana flung her arm into mine. "Okay, so he was more unpredictable than ever."

"I like him." It was all I could think to say.

"Who wouldn't?" She smiled.

I could imagine a lot of people not liking him, but decided not to say so. We started walking back to the station. "So, you've told me everything about him, huh?"

"Well, all the juicy parts. My parents were very in love."

At least Farhana is not married.

"What are you thinking?" She looked at me.

"What happened in Malaya?"

She frowned. "I don't know much."

"What do you know?"

"Only what Baba told me once, in a fit of despair, after my mother died. Whenever he's upset, he thinks of his father. Or is it the other way around? Anyway, do you really want to know?"

"Of course." A curl had caught in her mouth. I pulled it free with my fingers.

"It was soon after my grandfather was sent to the peninsula. A group of Indians and Malayans pointed him to a bombsite littered with reams of photographs of local Chinese women, as Japanese soldiers—many still in boots and belts—raped them. Before the war, Dada had already considered life imagery to be prohibited. These photographs haunted him till his death. The entire village had seen them. In fact, there were those who pointed out the photographs to Indian soldiers the way they'd pointed out the girls to Japanese soldiers. They called them, 'Cheeni! Cheeni!' They deliberately left them there, in the open, for all eyes to devour what little was left of the *Cheenis*."

"They could have been left for other reasons."

"Such as?"

"To inform." I shrugged. "Elicit outrage."

She shook her head. "No one had any idea what happened to the girls and no one cared. Baba said it was this episode that led to Dada's becoming a recluse later in life—this, and his unpopularity with his friends for fighting for the British. It was as if Dada felt that he too was trapped in those photos. He believed himself to be in the power of everyone who'd picked one up, whether accidentally or deliberately, indifferently or greedily. Sooner or later, every single person who'd ever entered the village became complicit in the crime. Maybe identifying with the victims was a way of feeling less complicit."

"That is a horrific story," I whispered.

She nodded. We rode the train in silence, arms entwined.

Back in San Francisco, the fog had cleared and the day was surprisingly warm. I was learning that October was spring in the Bay. "Seems we're the only ones not jogging, or walking a dog," I said idly.

She turned to me. "Nadir, I don't dismiss what you do. You only think I do. I just wish, well, that you were equally happy with me as when you're alone, at night, running, without your camera."

"I *am*."

"What's the north of Pakistan like?"

My stomach clenched. *Here it comes.* "It's—isolated. Isolating. Cleansing. I don't know how to explain. People who live there have names for what we don't. But—you find your own."

She did something like a hop before swiveling to face me, walking backward on the pavement as I moved forward, keeping step with me, barely avoiding a streetlamp, her pace growing in speed as she pronounced, "Oh Nadir, I can arrange for us to go!"

"What do you mean?"

"We've applied for funding. We'll get it."

"We?"

"Wesley. You'll meet him. A comparative study of glaciers in northern Pakistan and northern California. Call it a fact-finding mission, to see if I *can* work in my country!"

"You will get it, or—already have?"

She soared into my arms, flinging us side to side, before presenting the route she believed we ought to take. We'd fly from Karachi to Rawalpindi, then, depending on the weather, take either a bus or plane to Gilgit. From Gilgit we'd take a bus to Hunza, from where the two glaciers that would best fit the requirements of her preliminary study were easily accessible. These were Batura Glacier and Ultar Glacier. Did I know of them? Of course. Did I know how dangerous they could be? Of course. Did I need to practice climbing around here, first? I shot her a look. She brought that man called Wesley into the conversation too. They'd apparently worked together on Whitney Glacier on Mount Shasta, where they collected and "dated" ice samples. Did I care how? No, I did not.

Naturally, throughout this monologue, there was no mention of Kaghan Valley.

Later that night, back in my apartment, she let me photograph her naked for once, torquing her spine to artificially recreate the image I first fell in love with.

"Why?" I asked. "Why today?"

She peeled off her sweater, shirt, bra, still delirious with the joy of having skillfully engineered her *return*. And all this time I'd believed she was waiting for me to say yes. There was never any consent involved. We were going.

"Why today?" I insisted.

She giggled. It was as if she were drunk and wanting to have sex with me after refusing when sober. It was her choice, yet I was having to make it.

"Come on, Nadir. Pick up your camera. I know you're dying to."

"Actually, I'm not."

"Sure about that?"

I hesitated. To say yes would mean choosing no. I picked up my camera.

I didn't enjoy it. In those moments, I didn't want Farhana, neither behind my lens nor in the flesh. Even when she wound her braid around her, I couldn't see the calla lily. It was all too conscious, too rehearsed. Hadn't she planned it all—the visit to her father, the walk home, the seemingly innocent question about northern Pakistan, the news, *the news*, and now this? And yet, and yet. As I put her through my lens and captured that twisting torso, her ribs so protruding tonight, a thought flickered in my mind. Was it her pleasure that was dulling mine? I shook the thought away. No, this jeannie was just *fine* out of the bottle (even if she bent so far out of the bottle surely her spine would crack). I snapped another dozen shots. No, that wasn't it. It wasn't even pleasure. More like victory. I could see it in her gaze. It had killed the wonder this moment was always meant to hold. As she adjusted her hips and I kept on snapping, I tried to conjure it up, this wonder, this thing which cannot always be there, which is entirely fleeting and numinous, which, like luck, or talent, or wealth, cannot be equally distributed between those who love, between those who mate. *Snap!* She was raising her chin so high. She was rising from the bed. She was turning off all the lights.

When it was over and she fell asleep, I hurried out into the night, a disturbed man.

Even the act of seeing becomes a theft, even a murder.

I hated the conversation I'd had with her father earlier that day. It wasn't even a conversation. I hated today.

So I was to go back as her escort. When I had just begun earning. She had a great salary. She'd keep building up her resumé, while I became the porter. Photographing her was my payment for her pleasure.

No, no, I had to stop thinking of her this way.

I asked God to help me feel the way I normally felt on my solitary walks. *Empty my mind, make me a happy man.* I increased my pace.

The weather had turned again. It was now colder than on our way to the BART this afternoon. Gusty too, even for the Richmond. So much for spring in October. Why couldn't San Francisco be still? Oh, if only for tonight! In my haste, I'd left my sweater behind and worn only a windbreaker over my shirt. I'd also left my umbrella. Not that it would have helped. When the rain came, the wind scattered it in every direction, opals spinning cartwheels under streetlights. I passed a man and a woman hunched beneath the same coat, and a solitary man talking soothingly into his phone—such composure, at this hour, and in this weather!—but they were the only ones I noticed as I walked down Balboa Street toward the Great Highway, a stretch of coastal road that always reminded me of Clifton Boulevard in Karachi and gave me a kind of peace. From there it wasn't a short hike to the Sutro Baths but I knew that's where I was headed.

It always happened this way when I set out at night. My body knew where it wanted to go, as if it had programmed the route from some earlier time. So I let my legs guide me, aware that to second-guess the purpose in my stride was as fruitless as second-guessing the need to flip onto my right side when I'd crawl into bed later to sleep.

My legs were sure, but my mind remained troubled. I tried to immerse myself in the glittering loops of rain, each drop dazzling, each cluster of multiple drops elastic and yielding. Instead, for no apparent reason, something I once heard Farhana say to my roommate Matthew danced around me instead. It was a silly thing and I'd had no right to eavesdrop. Nonetheless, it stuck.

"... put up with his farts and smelly underwear and the toilet with the urine stains all the way to the floor, and then to accompany him to a public soiree where he is *so* charming, *so* delightful. Do women really not know that underneath all that charm a man is farts and stains? Why do we fall for it, again and again?"

I'd heard Matthew laugh; his toilet was pristine.

First of all, we weren't living together, so I couldn't understand why she was having to put up with my smelly underwear et al. as if we were. Second, was she really talking about *me*? In a way, I hoped so. I didn't know I possessed charm. I would like to, even for a few facetious moments at a public soiree. Third, public soiree? What the hell was that? Ergo, was she talking about *me*? Fourth, I didn't fart as much as Matthew; I washed my underwear more often than she washed hers; I confess to the crusty commode. Ergo, it would have made sense if instead she'd said, "... put up with his finicky taste buds (no food is as good as my mother's), his restless sleep (whenever I returned to bed after a walk, she claimed I woke her up), the toilet with the stains (yes yes), and then to have him accompany me to monologues by my father, who is *so* charming, *so* delightful..."

I felt a blade at my stomach. I was very far from the baths, drenched, and there was this man who must have been born of the opal rain, moving swiftly to wedge a knife under my windbreaker and through my shirt, just left of my navel. I wondered if I was being punished for having petty thoughts. Or punished for taking the photographs. Or just fucking punished.

"What do you want?" I heard a rasp exit my throat.

He was shorter than me and of paler complexion. High cheekbones, very obtrusive chin. Though this section of the road—definitely not the Great Highway, so where the hell was I?—was too dark to be sure, there could have been gray in the chin.

He could have been anyone.

He stared at me for a long time, and his breath was acrid, a mix of stale white wine and an illness, a stomach illness, perhaps, or a mental one. He gave me a lopsided grin and I could hear the sea. It had stopped raining. I was far from my apartment.

"What do you want?" I repeated. His knife poked harder into my flesh; still he did not reply. There was drool on his lips and he seemed to be shaking, with cold, or with laughter. I told myself the dampness at my belly was my soaked shirt. I wasn't walking, or running, I was standing still, still as a dried urine stain. Yet I was drifting, as though bewitched, and the air was a checkerboard of moving points, flashes of color darting by.

His fist suddenly jerked to indicate my windbreaker.

"Jacket?" I asked. The knife was no longer at my belly. There was a sharp pain instead. He threw me a ghoulish grin.

In the wind my jacket inflated like a pneumatic device, as if I were blowing it with a rubber tube in a desperate attempt to escape on a solo flight across the Pacific. It would save me. It would save me, but only if I took it off. I began to undress slowly.

He was wheezing. I could hear words behind the wheeze. "Jack-eet. Jack-eet. Gee-ve-me-your-jack-eet." They were not words but sounds merging into one roll, one hymn. While he repeated this hymn, I freed one arm and then the next, realizing, too late, that my wallet and my keys were in the jacket pocket. He began to hop; I saw Farhana hopping earlier that day. When my jacket was off he began to skip—away. And then he bolted across the street.

This was worse. He hadn't taken a thing. He'd double back, follow me home.

I pressed my stomach and my fingers came away sticky. I was bleeding. I did not put the jacket back on but I did remove my wallet and keys. I held the jacket out to him as I crept away.

I must have walked south from Balboa, not north, because I could see the silhouette of the Dutch windmill when I looked over my shoulder for him; there it loomed, at the corner of Golden Gate Park. It was the first time my legs had misled me. He'd disappeared under the bridge, toward the park. I heard hushed footsteps but saw no chin, no gray sweats, and no soiled, thick-soled joggers without laces on the left foot. I only knew I'd been staring at the shoes when I searched for them on my way home.

I don't remember entering my apartment. I remember smearing my stomach with an antibiotic cream from Matthew's medicine cabinet (above his pristine toilet), bandaging it, taking two Tylenol, and climbing under the blankets with an icepack, naked and shivering. Farhana didn't stir, didn't curl into me.

It was still dark when I woke up again, bleeding. Beside me sat a friend of Farhana's. His name was Wesley.

Eyes Are Heavy

My parents first saw themselves as a married couple in a mirror. It was considered bad luck to gaze directly into each other's eyes. This was an invitation to a jinn. But it was good luck to gaze at each other's reflection. And so, at the wedding, my mother's sister held a mirror across my mother's lap and the newlyweds looked down, and, according to my aunt, smiled. "Your mother made a coy attempt at covering her lips so your father could not see how broadly she smiled, though of course, she was sitting next to him. He could hear the smile. And she could hear his."

The same was true for the slopes of Malika Parbat, Queen of the Mountains. Her lovers were not meant to gaze at her directly. We were meant to gaze at her in the lake.

By the time we crossed the glacier and arrived on the banks of Lake Saiful Maluk, Malika Parbat's reflection was being admired and broken by a stream of exhausted pilgrims and a dozen boats. Irfan warned Wes and Farhana to avoid the boats, declaring, simply, "They sink."

It was Malika Parbat's snowmelt that created the lake that reflected her. Her melt, tossed in with that of the surrounding mountains. If you let your imagination soar, far in the distance to the northwest of the Queen appeared a tiny fragment of what might have been the most photographed and feared peak in the Himalayan chain: Nanga Parbat. Naked Mountain. Or perhaps it was just some mystery mountain that only looked like him, for he was too far away to actually be seen from here. Whoever he was, by all accounts, he rarely showed himself as clearly as on that day. Even those who negotiated the lake's treacherously deep and icy waters in creaky boats to better gaze upon the reflection of the Queen now lifted their chins to gawk across the cerulean sky at that phantom peak, who was her rival, or darling, depending on whom you asked.

Irfan stared in disbelief. "I've never seen him. It isn't possible."

"This *is* fairy lake," I said.

"—Though I've heard it can happen," continued Irfan, still staring, open-mouthed.

Apparently, people believed that on days when the mountain appeared—the one that only looked like Nanga Parbat, but could not have been—the Queen's snow melted even faster, due either to her rage at having her beauty overshadowed, or her excitement at beholding her lover. And on such days his snow also melted faster, due either to his rage at having his beauty uncloaked—whose eyes were worthy enough?—or his triumph at beholding the Queen's ferment. Whatever the reason, the lake that day had a strong tide. We could see it from the way the water rolled onto shore; we could have been by the sea.

"I've never seen it so rough," said Irfan, now even more perplexed.

"Maybe the jinn is here," said Farhana.

"He's jealous of the love I have for my princess," I murmured.

"Then step back!"

"But first, look at yourself." I pulled her closer to the water's edge.

She was flushed from the hike and her cheeks were as crimson as her jacket. Her hair framed her face in a wild halo of black frizz and her smile was especially radiant. I pulled her, and though our socks and shoes would remain wet for the rest of the day, we waded in further so she could see how lovely she was, and so we could see each other's reflection in the mirror.

I didn't know if I was imagining it but at that moment, the water was exceptionally calm. The tide seemed to wait. The lake lay flat as a puddle, and when Farhana craned her neck, the picture that answered back was of a girl as clear and unharried as the water itself, and of a boy beside her, bewitched.

"The jinn isn't here," I whispered. "The mountains are making deep, quiet love."

I would have kissed her then, except it would have offended those around me. It seemed so unjust, the land could express its love but we could not. *Later*, I thought, gazing at her in the lake.

I caught a slight frown fleet across her reflection before she gave me a smile half of pity, half of promise. In the icy depths below, the Queen's twin peaks fanned into triangular wings, enclosing us in a jagged cape of blessings. We stored her consent and pulled ourselves back to shore. Behind me, I heard the tide roll again.

Irfan was greeting the semi-nomadic tribes who made their summer homes on the lake's shores. He spoke in a language I didn't know, but I also heard some Urdu. I could tell that a lot of their communication involved names: names of those who'd moved to these heights for the summer and those who were staying down in the plains. They'd come with their cattle, horses, and sheepdogs. I spotted a few goats near the lake and several more on the hills to the north. Around us, goat bells chimed. There was a young child in a magenta kameez and a green satin shalwar brandishing a stick, while following a small black goat up a hill and there were half a dozen tourists following her, photographing her. She walked confidently, scratching her head, looking back and grinning. Her hair was the light tawny-blonde shade common to people of the valley, and it was so knotted it didn't hang over her neck so much as rise from it, as if in the process of becoming dust. Her cheek was stained with dirt; front teeth were missing. I could hear a wet, rattling cough. Around her neck were heavy necklaces and her wrists were encased in even heavier bracelets. The older women must have been inside the tents.

"She's beautiful," said Farhana.

"She would be, if she were better taken care of."

"You should have told me, I would have brought some supplies."

"Told you what?"

She ignored my question and started following the girl. The small black goat had completely vanished, no doubt finding a tasty bit of scrub between the deodar and pine trees.

Though I knew it was no use, I called out after Farhana, "You know the British called the Gujjars a martial race? You know why?"

"Why?" It was Wes, standing behind me.

To be honest, I'd forgotten him. To be honest, I'd wanted to.

I said, "They're naturally warlike and deceitful when not on your side, naturally brave and loyal when on your side."

"Yeah?"

"Point is, that girl doesn't need Farhana."

He shrugged. "Maybe Farrah needs her."

He put it so plainly. Notwithstanding the irritating nickname. "Sandwich?"

"My thoughts exactly."

I unzipped my backpack and pulled out a plastic bag bulging with chicken sandwiches. They were soggy with butter and I'd lost my appetite for white bread since living in America, but otherwise, I was so hungry that nothing ever tasted better. Despite the company. What did Farhana see in him?

He was on his third sandwich and I on my second when Irfan joined us. In silence, Irfan poured himself a thermos cup of water.

"What did you talk about?" asked Wes.

Irfan pointed to the sky. "The clouds. They say it's going to rain. They think we should walk back now, or stay the night."

"Stay where?"

"I brought a tent."

"Clever," I murmured, and Wes whistled, impressed.

"You should have too," Irfan said in our general direction.

"You should have said so," Wes retorted.

"The weather is changeable." This time he addressed me. "You know that."

I'll admit it, by this time Irfan's glumness was beginning to irk. First the owl was a bad omen, then the school bus had fallen off the glacier while the poor schoolchildren were learning of princesses and jinns, then that comment about needing Farhana's permission before we could look for the cave. Did I mention his repeated need to check his cell phone? He'd been pleasant enough in Karachi—not the way he used to be, before Zulekha's death, but pleasant—so what had happened since? Down in the cabin, he was cordial with the staff; he knew the local khan well, and was friendly with him too. Moments earlier, he'd greeted the nomads with downright warmth. He could have expended some cheer on us. Or at least on me.

"I'm going boating," said Wes, walking away, daring Irfan to tell him otherwise.

"Will we all fit in one tent?" I asked.

"You and Farhana can take it. Wes and I will sleep outside."

"In the rain?"

"I can ask them," he pointed to the nomads.

"Is it easier just to head back?"

"The rain isn't all we were talking about. The rain isn't important."

I waited. Instead of telling me what was important, Irfan again checked his phone for a signal. It was about the twentieth time since the morning.

"Nothing," he snapped it shut.

"What's wrong with you?" I couldn't help myself. "You can't enjoy yourself so nobody should?"

I regretted it at once. His shoulders stooped even lower; his eyes, already mournful (his wife had called them *soulful*), closed shut, as if my words had torn a nerve and his only comfort was in darkness. I thought of that night in San Francisco, near the park, when I'd been stabbed. My attacker had spared me. Perhaps he'd never intended otherwise. Irfan's wife had not been so lucky. It could easily have been the other way.

He opened his eyes. "You do know about the arrest in Peshawar yesterday?"

I shook my head. "How would I? Haven't read a newspaper for days."

Now he cast me a look of disdain, as if to say, *Who has license to shut himself away from the world anymore?* The old Irfan would have understood the desire for that privilege, even if the privilege itself eluded us. The old Irfan would have let this day be filled with princesses and mountain love. But the new Irfan was agitated, and he was my friend. If I couldn't lighten the grief of losing Zulekha, I had to lighten whatever grief I could. Hadn't he been there for me? All that time in San Francisco, when I couldn't pay my rent? Irfan had shared my burden without ever acting burdened.

"Tell me."

"Didn't you hear the waiter this morning? The man is being blamed for the hotel bombing in Karachi. There have been protests. One protester was shot dead."

I paused. "Who was he?" It struck me that I was already referring to the man in past tense.

Irfan did the same. "His accusers say he was disguised as a shepherd, and that he had an accomplice who was last seen—around here."

"Here?" This was a surprise. So far no one handed over to the CIA had come from these valleys. South of here, yes, in Baitullah Mehsud's Waziristan on the Afghan border, but not all the way here, in this high corner of the North-West Frontier Province, at the foot of the Himalayas. These valleys belonged to the farmers down in the plains, and the herders around us. "That's impossible."

"Of course it is. And people here are nervous. They believe the man was innocent—they call both the prisoner and the accomplice 'the man,' they've become one and the same—but they're sure he wasn't from here." He paused. "They also say that down in the plains, there are more military convoys moving in, and plainclothes spies." And now he threw me yet another look of disapproval. "You did notice the convoys?"

I briefly regretted my oblivion to all that had been happening outside our cabin, Farhana's and mine. Yes, I'd noticed the convoys, though barely. Apparently, while I'd been running along the River Kunhar, chased by a crazed owl, another world existed. Amazingly, in this parallel world, another chase was in progress.

"Why?" I asked. "When the police could say he was last seen anywhere, why say here?"

He shrugged. "An accident of geography. To people who don't care, all geographies are the same, and anyway, accidents can happen anywhere."

The young girl in the magenta kameez was walking up the hill, and I could see Farhana beside her, holding her hand. They seemed to be having a kind of conversation; Farhana's broken Urdu would be no less broken than the girl's.

"I'm not sure it's a good idea for them to be here," Irfan nudged his chin at Farhana, and then at Wes, who was getting into a boat. "The tribes are divided about who the man really was. Some say he came down from Kashmir. They say that all the way to Gilgit, people are talking about him, fearing he's hiding somewhere in their midst. Others say he came from Central Asia, and is connected to the fighting in Waziristan. It's hard to know one fight from another."

Both of us were still looking at the lake, at Wes pulling away from the shore.

"Hard times make hard people," Irfan continued. "These herders would normally never turn away a guest, but they won't host someone who'll bring in the ISI, though they fear it may already be too late. Anyone could be a spy. Including a tourist. They want the tourists to leave. It isn't like them."

"We're not tourists."

"No." Irfan smiled, and the smile was kind.

"I'm sorry about what I said—earlier."

He looked away. "If you haven't brought a tent, at least give me a sandwich."

Half an hour later, Farhana was walking toward the lake with the girl. Wes was rowing along the far shore. They were waving to him; I doubt he saw them. I set aside the last two sandwiches for Farhana and was filling the gurgling in my still-empty stomach with water when a boy with brown curls strode toward us, bearing gifts. Pears and apricots. Potatoes and hot maize bread. He carried the aroma of salt on a flame, and a cloth rolled in a knot with black thread. When I plucked the knot from the boy my fingers came away sticky. Honey inside. We embraced, telling him to thank his mother for the gifts, Irfan polishing our gratitude in flecks of Hindko, or Gujri, I couldn't tell which.

I tore the bread and left it on my tongue, letting the heat dissolve slowly. I added an apricot and rejoiced at my menu. Then I poured the topping: a finger of fresh honey. It tasted of flowers unknown to me, flowers vaguely aquatic. Like honey from the bottom of the lake. No one alive had ever touched the bottom, yet here was proof of life in those depths. Next I peeled a roasted potato with my teeth, telling Irfan that part of the thrill of being away from home was mixing dessert with vegetables.

"I always do that," he replied. "No matter where I am."

He held half a pear in one hand, half a potato in the other, and, as the clouds rolled across us and the light grew lavender, the two halves mirrored each other. I scraped my pear over the honey cloth and handed the cloth to Irfan, who drew the remaining drops with his tongue. As boys we'd do the same with imli wrappers. And we were boys again.

I'd been missing this, the ease of being with someone without speaking, without suppressing speech. I'd grown up with it in Karachi, where groups of men will congregate in the smallest spaces—the grass between houses, a doorway, a roundabout—spaces made more generous through companionable silence. It existed between women too, this bond. My sister and her friends could spend hours reclining together on a bed, or a carpet. If secrets were murmured, it happened in a style so intuited it was pre-verbal. I hadn't experienced this very much in the West, where it seemed people had a reason for everything, including intimacy. The only exception I could find was the time I spent with Farhana at her bay window in her purple house. But those moments had been too few in the months before we'd left.

Lying there beside Irfan at the bottom of a hill not far from the nomads' tents, our wet socks and shoes tossed a few feet away, I was now entirely at peace.

"We'll save them the potatoes," Irfan chuckled, setting these aside, gathering fruit peels and seeds into the bag where our sandwiches had been packed.

It was the first time since leaving Karachi that I felt easeful in his company. The way we used to be, when his wife was alive, before she was even his wife. He hadn't mentioned her once, but of course she was with us. Though he hadn't mentioned this either, I knew that on our way north, we'd stop and pay homage to the glacier whose mating we'd witnessed with Zulekha. For her. For closure, even, if this were ever possible. And maybe even for God. Surely there was a ritual of departure to this ritual of return, and he needed me with him to complete the cycle, somehow.

He was also lost in thought. I believed I could guess what he was thinking, apart from Zulekha, of course.

It was soon after we'd witnessed the mating of glaciers that Irfan had begun devoting himself to bringing water to these and neighboring areas. And ever since, one question had never ceased needling him. It was this: *Do they need it?* If for thousands of years people had survived, with varying degrees of success, by building irrigation channels from glacial melt, despite their poverty and isolation, did they need a man from the city bringing them pipes and taps? It was a fine line, the one between helping and hurting. To do nothing could mean becoming a passive witness to a potential calamity. To do something could mean becoming the agent of a worse calamity. In the beginning, Irfan frequently turned to the Quran (remember it was before Zulekha's death), which placed a high premium on niyat. Intent. He told himself his niyat was good.

I could smell the fire from outside the tents of the nomads. There were two women squatting by the flame, perhaps cooking more bread. One of them stood up, and though I was too far to see her face, I noticed how tall she was, how straight her back. She wore a black shirt with brightly colored embroidery—pinks and oranges as fiery as cactus blooms—and her hair was either tucked beneath a pale-hued cap, or pulled tight into a braid. I could hear bangles chime.

We lay there, me looking behind at the tents, Irfan looking ahead at the tourists trekking back down toward the glacier. He decided the wind was changing direction, the clouds would soon disperse. "They'll be fine going down," he pointed to the different groups. "We could leave too, if you still wanted."

"It's so calm here. Let's stay." From the corner of my eye I could see him reach for his phone. "Don't. It's probably still not working anyway."

"All right." He pulled his hand away, then crossed both arms behind his neck and reclined again. "Have Farhana and Wes ever been lovers?"

"No."

"You said that too quickly."

"No."

"I believe you."

In the distance, gray clouds circled the summit of Naked Mountain's lookalike. Was it possible that the clouds arranged themselves just so, creating mirrors upon mirrors, drawing him closer to us from his real position far to the north? They seemed to be teasing him, offering cover, then withholding it. Irfan was right about the clouds dispersing elsewhere, though. They were breaking above the hill where we reclined. A growing niagara of golden light flowed into the bowl of the lake. Fire falling into honey.

What had made him ask? Getting back at me for his own unhappiness—because I'd dared to remind him of it?

And just like that, our easeful time congealed.

"Maybe you *should* check your phone," I said.

He chuckled softly. "I also saved them a pear."

I rolled onto my side, my back to him.

"Up in Hunza, they have a proverb. *Beware the guest one does not feed.*"

What the hell did that mean? I shut my eyes. I wasn't going to let anything spoil what was turning out to be a sublime afternoon.

Queen of the Mountains: Pagan Rituals

Maryam stood up from the fire and glanced at the water's edge. Her fingers drifted to the braid around her face, feeling the tightness of the weave. This morning, her daughter Kiran had again refused to have her hair braided, despite being shown both styles, a single braid around the cusp of the face, like Maryam's, or a cluster of braids down the back, the way Maryam's mother had preferred. Still Kiran insisted on wearing it loose. She had worn her hair loose all summer, ever since they had left the plains down near Balakot, if you could call the mess on her head a way of wearing it.

Pushing her frustration aside, Maryam said a quick prayer for her dead mother, and for every mountain, and for every name her mother bestowed on every mountain. The black door, the white door, the abyss. And the single peaks, like the ones soaring before Maryam now, the ones that could become windows or footholds, allowing you to scale a void. Her mother's two beloved peaks, Malika Parbat and Nanga Parbat. Though some might say it was not possible to see him from here, how well he lived up to his name today! He was a naked white spear towering high above the Queen, breathing down the nape of her neck, the slope of her thighs. Not surprisingly, their snowmelt was thick today. Like her daughter when she tried to comb her hair, the lake could barely hold still.

There was a jinn here too. She could feel it. The Prince Saiful Maluk, the Princess Badar Jamal, Malika Parbat, Nanga Parbat, and the jinn. They were all here today. If she were her mother, she would smoke some juniper leaves and see deeper into the void. But she was not her mother. Visions did not come to her. Misgivings, well, that was another thing. She had felt them all summer long, ever since leaving the plains in a hurry, when she had removed all signs of the lowland shrine in a manner unbecoming to a shaman's daughter. She had even failed to cleanse her lowland home according to the ceremony. She had not blown into its sacred spaces the smoke of juniper leaves. Partly, this was because she could not wait to come up here, to these highland pastures, where her past was left behind. Partly, because her husband discouraged it. "Pagan rituals for a pagan wife," the others said, so he asked her to stop. These were difficult times, he said. The valley was crawling with men who wanted proof of innocence, and pagan rituals were not innocent.

Up here in the mountains she could do as she pleased, and the curses of the sedentary folk were forgotten, if she only let herself forget. There was a line between the highland and the lowland that the troubled times could not see, let alone cross. Only those who came in peace could cross this line. And they would find that up here, everything moved—the mountains, the clouds, the fairies and the jinn, even the caves—but one thing did not move. The thing that did not move here was time.

It gave Maryam a kind of solace, knowing that she could reach time, even sit on it as she might sit on a horse, while all around her, the world was spinning. And for Maryam, solace came in many shapes. For instance, the shape of a cave. Like the one she used as her summer shrine (and much preferred to the one she had covered in haste down in the plains). It was over the hill and downaways and a man had once told her it led all the way to Tashkent. It was a cool womb of rock her mother believed their people once sheltered in, on their way down from the Caspian steppe. They'd come on horseback, though no one could say exactly when—they could not even say roughly when, it was two, maybe three thousand years ago—and they'd come from a faraway place that lay on the shores of a great sea surrounded by land. The sea was deep and it was black. The cave was cool and it was safe.

Two, maybe three thousand years later, her family still piled clothes, matkas, and tents onto the backs of their horses for green velveteen pastures every summer and for cold colorless plains every winter. Always on the move. Like the sea. Like the footholds in the sky, or the void down below. Like Lake Saiful Maluk, especially on this afternoon, as Maryam now watched her son take his time returning to her after carrying the gift to the two men from the city and the two Angrez from even farther away than the steppes of her imagination. Honey, bread, potatoes. The honey, of course, the most valued item they had carried on the horse. Her husband approved. Guests must be made welcome.

One of them, Irfan was his name, was not unknown in these parts. He was as much a friend as a man from the city could be. He spoke their tongue. He knew about the cave. He hid in it for days after his wife had died, wanting to live alone from now on, he said, like a gypsy. Her husband had told him gypsies did not live alone. "We have our families and our animals," he said. "Only saints live in caves, and there has not been a saint around here for some time."

Irfan had answered with a proverb—*a Gujjar will sleep where no man will walk*—which made her husband smile, before he replied, "Many men have walked *and* slept in that cave. I assure you, none became saints." He sat so tidily, this Irfan. Even when trying to inflict penance on himself in the cave, his shoes still looked polished. He had eventually returned home to the city. But now he was back, and Maryam could see he had not recovered. His cheek had sunk; his eye was dim. She was glad they had momentarily lit up when he walked toward their tent earlier this afternoon, to embrace her husband again.

The other—Irfan had pointed him out in the distance, she had not caught the name—had apparently also been here before, but Maryam found no recollection of him. He seemed to her to have no tongue. He followed Irfan's lead while his eye drifted constantly, toward her tent, toward the lake, toward the Angrez woman reaching for Kiran's hand.

The woman walked like a goat. She was too eager. Maryam had seen it before, good-hearted foreigners wanting to be friendly with local folk. They often selected the children, as that woman did now. Perhaps these Angrez needed to feel differently about themselves when they came all the way across the seas and all the way up the glacier to see the lake. She was not unfamiliar with the need. The lake seemed to inspire it. When you looked in the mirror of its surface you wanted to see something you wanted to see. And Maryam had seen the two looking in the lake, the friend of Irfan and the woman, when they first arrived. Though she was too far away to know, she took a guess. They were pleased with whatever else the lake had given.

Maryam also wanted to see something else whenever she peered inside, though she could never say what. Still or ruffled, the water's surface only heightened her desire but never sated it. Perhaps it was because she came—two, maybe three thousand years ago—from a landlocked sea. If a sea has nowhere to go, it must go in circles, like this lake at the foot of Malika Parbat, churning round and round in a bowl, the clouds reflected in dizzying speed, stirring up some limitless need. Yes, it was like that, she thought, watching Kiran chase her goat up a hill while the woman who walked like a goat chased her. In Maryam there was no simple need, such as the need to be charitable with the children of the poor. She had nothing to repent, or correct, really. It was more the need to, to… She frowned, unable to speak the word, or even put her finger on it.

She went back to fingering her braid, back to thinking of the cave, the one that could change shape.

If her grandmothers had once sheltered in it on their way down from the steppe, earlier this year, her children had sheltered in it on their way up from the plains. The cave was low and stained black from a million fires, including her own. But only she knew about that—she, and Ghafoor. The man who first showed her the cave, telling her it led all the way to Tashkent. She shook her head. No, she would not think of him now.

Her husband believed the cave was unsafe. Instead of becoming saints, the men who slept in its bowels became thieves. They saw the telltale sparkle in the seams of the rock and, over time, had scraped it clean. Crude attempts at holding the ceiling up still remained; wooden pillars were jammed haphazardly everywhere across the uneven floor. Her children had played with the pillars, shaking them like salt. She let them. She knew the ceiling would hold. They asked for the story every spring, on their way up to the lake, the story of Prince Saiful Maluk and Princess Badar Jamal. If it rained and they needed to step into the cave for a time, as had happened this year, the story grew even more magical because it grew even more real: *this* was the cave that had cradled the lovers as they fled the terrible jinn who lived by the lake. And when at last her family had continued on their way, a thirsty herd lowing and bleating beside them, shepherded by two gaddi dogs, when they had reached the lake this April, as on every April, the story became even more deliciously terrible: *this* was the jinn's lake. He lived along its shore—*this* shore!

But he had never hurt them, the jinn. Not in all the springs and summers they had camped at Malika Parbat's feet. He had blessed the lake where the fairies came to bathe at full moon. He had blessed these hills where Maryam could roam as freely as the goats and horses. He had blessed the peak of Malika Parbat, who was a pari khan, a ruler of all fairies, and who entrusted him with the task of keeping the fairies in check. He had blessed Maryam's secret shrine too, so that Maryam could pray undisturbed in its womb. He had even blessed her taste buds, so that everything here tasted true, the fruit and the honey.

Then why the misgivings? Perhaps it was the wind, again.

A little honey stuck to her flesh from the food wrapped for the guests. Licking it clean, she watched the clouds drift and Malika Parbat scatter into segments in the lake like the rungs of a ladder. What *else* did she want to see? She could still find no word for it, though the ladder was there, at the bottom of the lake, and if she wanted, she might step right into the void.

TWO

Queen of the Mountains: A Land Outside Land

Her earliest memories were of movement. On horseback, in her father's arms, on her brother's back. She could not say if it was her own crossing she remembered, or that of her mother, grandmother, or some woman whose name she would never know. What she did know was that theirs had always been a fight for mobility. They could only be governed if they stayed. For every way of limiting movement, there was a way to move.

No one knew this better than Ghafoor.

So, she could no longer push thoughts of him away.

Maryam walked to the far side of the lake, which was free of boats. Though the scent lingered, her fingers were licked clean of the honey. The water swayed.

The first time she saw him, she saw through him. He was the tunnel in the mountain, the break in the hill, the hand in the hollow. He was the air that teased the braid circling her face, the cloud that yawned apart in the lake. He was a door to the other world, the world outside the mountains. And he had left her a sign in the cave.

She had seen the sign on their way up from the plains, when her family took shelter from the rain, but she had not dared acknowledge it in their presence. Her husband might say the cave was dangerous, turning would-be saints into thieves, but to her it was many things, and none were dangerous. It was, for instance, a shrine. And a messenger. Because of the cave she knew he was coming. In the months since camping here at the edge of the lake, each time she withdrew to the shrine in secret, she fingered the sign.

Now Maryam's footsteps hastened as she reached the far shore. When she thought no one was looking, she climbed up the hill furthest from the boats and tents, looking over her shoulder one last time for just the briefest moment. Their tent, made of plastic sheeting, was still sagging at one corner. Earlier today, she had told Kiran to fix the stick that propped it, but Kiran was with that Angrez woman, the one who walked like a goat, and her other two children were playing with the children of a neighboring tol. No one noticed Maryam. This was her window.

She walked briskly. Far to the north, hidden behind clouds, hidden from those who could not imagine him, Nanga Parbat kept watch while Malika Parbat admired her reflection in the lake.

He had come to her, at first, like a prophet. Honey on his fingers and a tale to tell. There was a land outside land, outside mountains, even, and it was where she had come from, and where a part of her would return. *Over the Pamirs*. That far.

They lingered outside the cave, that first time, and he walked with her, at her child's pace, this friend of her brother's, this prophet. He held out his hand. "If it crystallizes, it's pure," he said. She sucked his finger clean of the honey. Dark amber crystals conjoined in a hard knot, oozing into a muddy slush around the edges, from his heat. Though young, she was not too young. She looked up, twice, hot and cold sugar in her eyes. He had to tell her to hurry up. He had work to do.

She fed her own children honey in the same way. Kiran, especially, who pulled her finger like a nipple. But that would happen later.

Maryam's mind fled the shores of the lake and even the mouth of the cave to inhabit subsequent days with her brother's friend, the one who could see the world, and through whom she could see it too. The one she had loved as a not-too-young child. Underneath the honey was the taste of his skin, which, though not pleasant, made something inside her turn to slush. It made her hold the crystals on her tongue a little longer so she could melt them with her saliva and hold his taste of young, green garlic a little longer too. The crystals were cold as ice and grazed her teeth. His finger was always cold. The body heat was not his but hers.

He said to always be proud of the legend she was named after. She had been concentrating on the taste on her tongue so intently she had to ask him to repeat it. He pulled his hand away.

"I said, haven't you heard of Maryam Zamani? Others will say you were named after her. Don't believe them. She was named after you." And Maryam giggled, because Maryam Zamani was *famous*, she was a *legend*, while Maryam was only Maryam.

And Maryam who was only Maryam was more interested in stories from beyond the mountains than the stuff of legend. She already knew all the legends of the valley. She knew about the princess and the jinn and the prince who came from far away, perhaps with honey on his garlic-scented skin. She knew about Kagan, after whom the valley was named. Kagan had never appeared to Maryam, but she had, apparently, appeared many times to her mother, who could see her particularly well after smoking juniper leaves and drinking juniper brandy. And then she would show her things. Future things. And help her mother change shape. Even after death. She knew that Kagan, like her own mother, flew in vehicles in the shape of owls. She knew that Kagan had shrines devoted to her all over the valley, and that, at one time, her devotees had left her offerings in temples decorated with ram horns and yak tails. She knew that most of these shrines had now been abandoned, and that Kagan's wrath was far worse than the jagged spear of Naked Mountain. She knew that her wrath was especially reserved for those who broke the line: the clumsy children of devotees, the ones who, when their mothers were dead, performed the cleansing ritual sloppily each spring, before leaving the plains for the mountains. Maryam knew these legends.

So she was not terribly interested in this other legend, the one about Maryam Zamani, which she had also heard before but did not consider worth remembering now. Instead, she asked, "What is it like over there, in the north, where the women wear tall hats and walk alongside men?"

"Over there, they have all heard about you. The girl who moved the rock."

Well, perhaps the legend was worth hearing again. Infused with his pride, she dwelled on it a while, the one about the Gujjar girl whose name was Maryam Zamani, who would go with her friends to Balakot to bring water from a stream. Every day, the girls had to cross a huge stone of uneven, sharp surfaces. Every day they cut themselves, returning home with feet bloodied and knees ragged. It occurred to Maryam Zamani one day that they could simply remove the stone instead. The others asked how. "With courage," she replied. And the stone rolled away.

She did not believe it, of course, the legendary Maryam had nothing to do with her, nor did she believe the legend itself (how could a stone roll away on its own?) but if she pretended to be impressed, Ghafoor, the traveler, the trader, the garlic breather and honey carrier, would tell her what it was like over there.

And he did. He showed her the nugget of white jade he had traded in the higher highlands, from a Chinese merchant who told him that every color of jade changed the one who wore it. White jade made you calm and helped you focus on a task, such as the moving of a stone. He grinned. He was a higher highland Gujjar, unhemmed in by the lowlands where she was stuck, with legends. She worried, briefly, that this business with the jade and the merchant too was unreal, that it too was the stuff of legend. She was perfectly able to concentrate *already*, without the jade, on the taste on her tongue. All she needed was his finger and the honey. He was laughing. "Never let anyone make an old woman of you." He paused. "Even when you marry. My travels will keep me young and I never want to see you old."

When they entered the cave, he teased that her prayers were pagan prayers, what with all the burning of juniper branches and the smoke staining the cave walls and the visions she claimed to have. (A lie Kagan would surely forgive. She could never admit to him that though a shaman's child, she never had any visions.)

"Not to mention all the offerings of food," he looked around.

"Silly," she said with a frown, "the food is for you." And from a crack in the rock she removed a small stash of rice and misri (hoping again for Kagan's forgiveness, for these were indeed offerings to the goddess).

And then he sang for her, the same song that would be sung on her wedding, and when each of her three children were born. First Younis, then Kiran, then Jumanah. It was the poem called Saiful Maluk, about the prince who fell in love with the fairy princess of the lake. And again she saw them as one. Like Ghafoor, the prince had come from over the mountains, though, in the song, the prince was bow-legged and tied his turban all wrong. Moreover, he lost his sword when he saw the princess bathing in the lake. The song made her laugh, it made her blush.

The prince with the turban on backwards
Dropped his sword when the fairy leaned forwards
And when he jumped off his horse
Oh the arc of his legs!
Oh the slope of her breasts!
Oh the jinn with his fire and his flame!

Sometimes he brought his flute, or, if she were lucky, his algoja, the twin flute of the Rajasthan desert that was equally beloved by mountain gypsies. She loved how he made the first flute hum with his nose while trilling a melody on the second with his tongue. (Sometimes, while drawing honey from his fingers, she would imagine the flute; it was her tongue and her nose creating the notes.) She loved also the jangling ornaments that were strung around the length of the wood, the way they bobbed with the beat as he moved his head and shut his eyes so as not to see her dance. If he opened his eyes, she kept swaying, keeping her gaze intent on the beads and the golden thread.

When he got to the part about the prince and princess fleeing the jinn and sheltering in a cave, she could not help but meet his eyes, for they were in the same cave, and it was theirs. The jade around her neck was smooth and hot against her naked flesh, when it ought to have been cold.

Years later, she still wore the jade. She could feel it against her skin, under her black shirt, as she entered the cave and stared at the sign. It had been years since the last one. Why now? Why was he about to return, and from where? There was a churning in her gut. That misgiving again. And yet, there was excitement too. She was never unhappy to see him.

Maryam offered her prayers and scattered rice in the crack in the wall. She asked the goddess to protect her. She asked her mother to protect her. She asked her father too. But even the white jade around her neck did nothing to help her focus. While praying, she could not stop staring at the sign. A single blue feather, from a kingfisher's wing. Might it be a coincidence? Perhaps a kingfisher had nestled here through the winter and left behind this gift.

Maryam hastily ended her prayers—she did everything in a hurry this year!—and walked around the pillars, the ones left behind from an age of rubies. They held up the cave the way sticks are meant to hold up a tent—again her thoughts drifted to the plastic sheeting, sagging and leaky, and to Kiran, whose movements could not be contained—though in truth, the cave did not need them. Like a womb, it was complete in itself. The deeper inside the womb she moved, the narrower it grew, and cooler. The drop in temperature soothed her. She pressed her palms to the walls, hunched her shoulders, let the tightening enclose her. Her fingers traced scratches from a time before. Hunters with turbans, hunters with bare heads. Antelope and buffalo. Owls and horses. Her favorite glyph was that of three horses, one bowing, one dancing, and the third looking back. Hospitality, liberty, and memory. On either side of the trinity hovered an owl, each vaguely ovoid, with eyes wide as wheels. Each time she stood here, fingering the dreams of the dead, she could hear her mother say, *Horses are the wings to this world, owls to the next.*

She could hear wings. Not the rapid wingbeats of birth or the slow wingbeats of death. These were oily, sly. Bats: wings to the in-between. She dropped to her knees on the ground, which was littered with sharp stones—the *legend* Maryam could have willed these away—and crawled deeper into the cave that embraced her till there was nowhere left for her to press. Long ago, Ghafoor would swear, the cave led all the way through the mountains to places she would never see. Kashgar, Bishkek, Tashkent. And she would think, *only if you were a bat.* Now she ran her hands along the walls. Drawings, yes, but no windows, no doors. No trace of a second feather either. Or a nest. Or an eggshell. Or a ruby, for that matter. The blue feather had not been left by a nesting kingfisher; this was a bird that kept to open skies. The blue feather had been left as a sign. He was coming.

She thought of the other sign she had been given just last night. An owl had swooped across the lake. She was leaving her drooping tent to bathe at the water's edge—her husband enjoyed that she performed the ritual each time they had sex no matter where they had it—when she saw the white wings. Circling and circling. Followed by a call. She had not gone back to sleep.

The churning in her stomach quickened. She prayed to her mother again—this time refusing to stare at the blue feather, or the drawings, or the bats—before leaving the cave. Then she hurried back toward the lake and the tents. Naked Mountain was at her back. Queen of the Mountains lay ahead, still preening. And Kiran was still with the woman who walked like a goat.

She thought she could see the white man rowing back to shore. Irfan and his friend were too far away to see, but it seemed to her that the woman was pulling Kiran toward them. She would have to teach Kiran to mingle less with guests. She rehearsed the warning in her head. *Stay near the pastures where your goats graze, or at least within sight of our tent.* After which she would add, *the one I told you to fix.*

Maryam walked faster. It was Ghafoor's wish that she always keep her youth, even once married, and she had. Her pace never slowed. Each spring, on their long trek up to these slopes, she was the one who kept moving when all the others stopped to rest. Ghafoor would also have kept his youth, she was certain. And when her children were grown, so would they. She always prayed for this at the shrine.

Maryam contemplated heading straight for the guests to pull Kiran away and scold her, but she knew it would not do to approach them herself. So she made for her tent, pulled back the flap—black and tattered like bat wings—and hastened inside to tell her husband that tea would have to wait. First, he needed to bring Kiran back.

Cold Feet

I hadn't forgotten Irfan's question.

The clouds continued circling the mountain summit, a scarlet whirlpool in the sky. They caressed him like a memory, so pretty, so mean. And the honey on my fingers so sweet. Beside me, Irfan lay peaceful and still, arms folded behind his neck, perhaps asleep. I, on the other hand, lay fully awake. Too awake.

Wes and Farhana. My fingers probed the scar. There they went, under my jacket, under my shirt. It was a long scar, though the cut had not been deep. But there had been a lot of blood.

They say that after a car accident, it's best not to delay getting behind the wheel again. In the same way, after my encounter with the man who almost desired my jacket, I resolved not to forfeit my nightly walks. Or so I told myself that same night, once back in my apartment. I slept in discomfort, listening to him hiss, *Jack-eet. Jack-eet. Gee-ve-me-your-jack-eet.* I could hear the squelch of footsteps I could not see. But I saw the shoes, soiled and thick-soled. I saw my hand carrying the jacket out to him, a hand removed from my body. And I saw myself getting up from the bed, again, and again, reaching for the jacket, telling myself I had to go back out into the night, because to lose those walks would mean losing normalcy. In truth, I was only walking to the freezer, repeatedly. In my half-wakeful state each walk to the freezer for an ice pack became a step back out the door. I told myself I was on my way to recovery. And when I woke up in the morning, Wes was sitting beside me.

I was back in my apartment in the Richmond, waking up to a look of horror on Farhana's face.

"You're bleeding," she said.

"Huh?" I tried to sit up.

"Nadir, you're *bleeding*."

Granted, there was a sharp pain in my gut. The sheets were aflare with blood. Against them, the exposed parts of my flesh—an arm, a leg—seemed very pale. I remembered falling asleep cheerful in the knowledge that the cut had been a shallow one. Now I heard Farhana through a wave of mist, saying something about needing stitches and medical care and a car. I rolled over and vomited on the floor. I passed out.

She had no car. Neither did I. My housemates were with their lovers.

She called Wes.

Later, it would occur to me to wonder why she didn't call an ambulance. It was 4:00 a.m. and I'd only been sleeping periodically for two hours and woken her up with all my waking and, apparently, whimpering. Why did she bother Wes?

On the way to the hospital, he comforted her. "I doubt the peritoneal cavity is busted." After a moment, he graciously added, "That would literally suck."

I passed out again.

In the operating room, under the lights, I looked closely at the wound. Surprisingly long, the length of a forefinger and a half, but better long than deep. It needed exploring to see if, as Wes supposed, the lining of my abdomen remained unpierced. He was wrong. It had been punctured, but not so far as to penetrate any organs, the doctor announced, rummaging around. Or were those the fingers of anesthesia? I compared the sensation to having a wisdom tooth extracted. It wasn't that different, except nothing was being taken out, while a whole lot was, hopefully, being kept in. I lay there wishing my liver all the best. I also said a prayer for my small bowel.

Next I was wrapped up and sent home.

In the afternoon, Farhana introduced him as Wesley.

He said, "Call me Wes."

"You're not a Wes." She smiled at him, spooning something brothy into my mouth.

He wrapped his arm around her neck, nudging her chin with his fist. The broth dribbled down my chin. "How you feeling, Nad*e*r?"

Nadir, I thought, between leaky spoonfuls.

"Wesley was in med school," Farhana explained. "Gave it up for the environment." What exactly she was explaining I couldn't say. Nor could I understand why he was doing something very peculiar. He was calling her Farrah.

"Farrah, you go rest. I'll take care of him."

She thanked him, kissed me on the nose, and left the room, I presumed, to curl up on the living room couch with *Nature* magazine.

He picked up the bowl of soup.

"Don't you dare."

Chuckling, he put it back down.

I wiped my chin with the back of my hand. I tilted my head. "Why Farrah?"

He shrugged.

"Farrah Fawcett?"

"My mother knew her at UT Austin. Same sorority. Delta Delta Delta."

"So that's why?"

He shrugged.

Did he know, I asked, that Ms. Fawcett's father was Lebanese, that he'd named his angel Farah, which she later changed to Farrah? Or that Farhana meant the same—joy?

He didn't seem to care, or maybe he didn't hear. "They look alike."

"You mean, the same dark hair, dark eyes, tall frame?"

He chuckled.

"The noses are different."

"Despite their different noses, yeah, sure."

I closed my eyes and eventually, he loped away.

I had reason to forget about him the next day.

Farhana woke me with a finger in my navel, just shy of the bandages, thus announcing the beginning of a long spell of bedridden bliss, full with feasting and being doted upon. She tried several of my mother's recipes—the chicken karhai turned out fabulous—and whipped up salads with flowers. It was a time of cardamom, artichokes, and art. She gifted me with photography books I couldn't afford, including a collector's edition of Elizabeth Carmel's *Brilliant Waters*. That was the day my bandages came off. Carmel's waters were the texture of skin, her stones so organic my fingers hovered at my gut, lightly memorizing the cut, reassured in the knowledge that my insides were safe.

"Thanks for cooking," I told her from the bed. "I know it's not your favorite thing to do."

"I'm just very picky who I cook for."

I could have lain there for weeks.

As I recovered, we discussed details of our trip. Karachi, Islamabad, Gilgit, Hunza. She had maps, one of which showed the way to Ultar Glacier, and beyond, to Batura Glacier. With a gaiety that made her glow, she spoke of the work she'd do, called it reading the ice. My eye drifted to a different point on a map. So you read the ice? I mused, not thinking to ask if she'd keep reading it, when it formed between us. We were on a pre-honeymoon, and, unlike the first time she described what she'd do in Pakistan, now I was interested. I learned something about myself in those bedridden days, something I hoped I'd never need to admit. I adored her adoration. I wanted her to feed me, tuck me into bed, swaddle me like a child. I did want to return to my solitary nocturnal habit, it was true, but this hiatus, during which I was entirely in her keep, was delicious. I wanted to be absolutely spoiled by her. So I leafed through her maps, and grew intrigued. "Glaciers might have been growing in north Pakistan for three decades," she said, sensing what a brilliant audience her patient made, "in some of the most isolated places on earth. I want to start an archive of geochemical and isotopic data." I grew to love the language of glaciers. They galloped and groaned, cracked and crept. They were foul-mouthed. They were serene. Twice more my eye fell on the point on a map we were never meant to see as anything other than a point: the shape of a buffalo in profile, with Kaghan Valley his ear, cocked, listening to voices at his back, while facing west. Though I remembered climbing up the buffalo ear with Irfan and his soon-to-be wife (and soon-to-be dead wife), I said none of this to Farhana as we pored over the maps. Ours was to be a different route. Never once during this time did she mention that Wes would be coming with us. *Who* and *where*. The elementals of a shared voyage. I thought I knew who; she thought she knew where.

On the day of a final check at the hospital, we took Matthew's car. The doctor declared the cut had healed "beautifully" and, to celebrate (a little wistfully on my part), we stayed out late, browsing in bookshops, enjoying a dinner of mussels and wine at the Cliff House. Then we got on the Great Highway, the stretch of coastal road that always transported me to Karachi, the one I thought I'd been heading for when I'd met my attacker. About a kilometer from Balboa Street, we saw something white in the middle of the road. A barn owl, the heart-shaped face luminous. She said an owl was a symbol of so many wonders, evil and wise, and ours was wise. I reconsidered her father's hint—*at least she isn't married*—and found it did not scare me as much, at least not till she began to cry, saying she wanted me to look so peaceful when I died.

Back in my apartment, she presented me with a gift. A collection of prints by Robert Frank. The pages had been marked—at first I mistook it for secondhand—with phrases underlined, such as, *he mapped the void between public and private memory* and *he chronicled the racism infusing the collective consciousness of his generation.* I flipped to a series of shots of his wife and child inside a car, taken from outside. There was an expression on his wife's face so complex I couldn't pull myself away. Sometimes I saw resignation, other times, I saw judgment. Sometimes the car was her cage, other times, a comfort, as much as she was cage and comfort to the child. But I barely noticed the child. It was the layers of entrapment in her gaze that arrested me. The quiet confrontation between woman, child, and voyeur.

Farhana skipped a few pages ahead, and began reading aloud. "*He needed to rid himself of the burden of the past to live more immediately in the present.*"

There is nothing wrong with that, I wanted to say.

She was watching me. "What are you most burdened by?"

I had made the mistake once before of answering her when she was in this mood. I said, "I only know what isn't a burden. You, Farhana. You are my joy."

"My needs can be a burden, though," she laughed. "If you deny it your nose will grow."

"I understand your needs."

She pinched my nose, laughing. "I love you. And a long nose suits you."

"Can I photograph you—now? Your legs?"

"So much for stealing the soul!"

"Just your legs."

When she looked up she wore the same look as on that night she undressed for me, only this time, I was ready.

I shot a series of black and white prints as she lay on her side, legs in dark sheets, muscles bright as planets. Hers were steep legs built by steepness. Mountain legs. Calves tapering tidily to the ankles. Stocky yet slanting. Her sartorius cut a ribbony dialogue on her flesh; it was the slope of the calla lily again—I saw it once more in that moment—only now the braid was a muscle snaking along her taut thigh. They were legs that defined themselves as much from the front as the side. We created our own version of another book she'd found this week, as a joke, a square, slender book that made me think of children's hands. *The Male and Female Figure in Motion*. It featured a naked man and woman engaged in various "everyday" activities to show off their anatomies, including walking upstairs with a bucket in each hand, throwing hankies over shoulders, and rolling wheels uphill, activities that were hardly everyday. The shots were wide-angle, the figures so remote they were less in motion than in deep freeze. It *could* have been a children's book; the gingerbread man doing laundry, Goldilocks plumping pillows.

For our version, over our shoulders, instead of hankies, we threw dirty underwear, and walked "uphill" to bed. Unlike the wholesome originals, our shots filled the frame. When Farhana bent, I shot her ass; when I torqued in surprise, she shot my penis. We opened three bottles of wine, drinking two and wasting one. By evening, after making love once and trying again without success, we collapsed, naked and in love.

Two months of bliss. Months that felt like the sunny side of the cut on my skin. Months that did not feel like a hiatus, or a dressing. We had nothing to seek cover from, or to cover up. We were simply returning to the way we'd been. But can we know the interval from the song? And does it matter which it is, if both must end? And when exactly did it end, for us? With her announcement that she was bringing Wes? Or earlier that same day in December, with her father's visit? Or an email from Irfan? On the banks of a lake in Kaghan the coming year, Irfan would say of the Karachi bomber and his accomplice that it was hard to know one fight from another. Equally sticky was knowing when it even became a fight.

I saw Farhana's father several times during those months and, as on that first day in Berkeley, each encounter began with him appearing light-hearted, almost childlike. Somewhere along the way, his temperature always changed, without my understanding why. That day in December, two months after our first meeting (and my attack), he arrived at my door brandishing a box of salted caramels with one hand and pulling his jeans up with the other. We agreed that whoever made the caramels had spent time in Pakistan, where salt and sugar have a natural affinity.

"Of course you put salt in your lemonade, your fruit salad," he said, as Farhana made a face. (I once told her in Pakistan a sexy woman is considered *numkeen*. Salty.) Settling on the sofa beside me, he pointed to my gut. "Completely A-one?" I nodded respectfully. On the table beside him, Farhana arranged a fruit platter—salt shaker prominently displayed—in a failed attempt at coaxing him away from the chocolates.

I helped myself to a caramel. So did he. While chewing, he sighed. "You never can guess where it's coming from, the trouble, but also the relief."

It was anyone's guess; I nodded respectfully.

"Has Farhana told you how I supported myself when I first came to this country?"

"I'm late for work," she said, reaching for her purse. In my ear, she whispered, "Love you." It was the most affection she'd displayed toward me in front of her father.

He shook salt on an orange. It dusted the floor. Farhana left. He returned the orange, picked up a second caramel. Not waiting for me to answer his question, he said, "I didn't even have money for milk in my tea—the tea of course I brought from home. I worked very hard."

He kept on about his struggles. I nodded, wondering unkindly when he'd leave. I wasn't due at the pub for a few hours so had no reason to excuse myself. Nor could I count on my roommates for diversion. Matthew's new boyfriend lived in Maui so he'd all but moved out, while the other one, Cesar, an up-and-coming aerosol artist, kept strange hours, lifting weights in front of the TV all day, then disappearing for weeks. (According to Matthew, Cesar had been on the verge of converting to Islam till he met me.)

"Yes, I had to work hard. But your relief has come. You did not have to wait."

My relief? Did he mean Farhana? Was he suggesting I didn't have to try hard enough to get her? Or hard enough at anything? He waved the caramels under my chin, smiling beatifically. "Finish them. Even with salt they go stale." It wasn't even 9:30 in the morning. I took a second.

"*My* relief I had to work for. But it came in the shape of…"

I missed the part about how he came to purchase milk for his tea.

I was imagining the woman in the photograph over Farhana's bed. Jutta, her mother. She reminded me of Robert Frank's wife. The expression on her face was not entirely the same—Jutta's gaze being more pensive than challenging—but neither could break free of the frame.

He was saying, "Who would have guessed where the trouble began? Where the cancer in her mother first took root? It was already in the brain when we found out." He looked at me in a way that made me feel accused, just as he had the first time we met, though for what I couldn't say. "It always begins before you think it does."

I ate a third caramel.

"Look after her this summer. She's all I have." After a string of truisms justifying why he'd left Pakistan ("society frowned on us, her mother and I") and justifying why he hadn't been back ("hard work eventually pays off"), he began justifying why he knew what was happening there better than most ("it is the mentality").

When he left I checked my email.

There was a message from Irfan, with news from home. It didn't help. More trouble in Waziristan, where the Pakistan Army's hunt for Baitullah Mehsud and his "guests" from Uzbekistan and China was turning increasingly bloody. No one believed the drone attacks were launched by Pakistan, at least not only by Pakistan. Irfan called the drones stupid eyes—"If they're so accurate, how come the war gets bloodier?"—and forwarded links to various articles on their "accuracy." As if I wanted to read them.

I spent the morning in pajamas. In the afternoon, my life receded in the cool, dark walls of a tavern where I existed only in the moment of pouring drinks and collecting bills and wiping counters and listening to others who also felt their lives recede. At night, I fell asleep on the couch in the living room while leafing through photographs by Robert Frank and Elizabeth Carmel and eating salted caramels.

I awoke to Farhana pushing me deeper into the couch with a kiss. And then she told me. Wes was coming with us. He'd been to India and wouldn't mind seeing it from the other side.

"The other side?" I tried to sit up. My mouth was gummy and dry.

"Besides, he did save your life."

"What?" My feet found the floor. "It was a minor stab wound, you know that."

"And what if you hadn't made it to the hospital?"

"And what if we had ambulances?"

"Let's not fight. He's very experienced. We were on Mount Shasta together, drilling the ice, you know, reading it. He's taught me a lot. He could teach you a lot too."

"About what? India?"

She pinched my knee, almost fondly. "I've had a long day, while you've been eating caramels." She waved the half-empty box under my chin, reminding me of her father.

On the table beside us lay the copy of *Brilliant Waters*, open at the photograph of a lake, the surface so rich and still.

Beside me, Irfan lay peaceful and motionless, though his eyes were now open. We said nothing, the evening too dramatic for speech. High above the lake, the mystery mountain was now entirely free of clouds and glistened a silvery amethyst so pure it belonged to another world, a world of princes and princesses, jinns and fairies.

Down below, near where the mortals lay, the lake continued breaking on the shore like a troubled sea, and it was hard to know which to believe: the triumph in the sky or the restiveness in the snowmelt. Goat bells rang like heralds between the two worlds.

To my left, Farhana and the girl had descended the hill. They moved toward us, the goat happily at the girl's feet. I noticed a dog now too, black as the goat. The two animals casually circled each other, like lovers who know their love was there all along.

"She isn't still upset about the detour to this valley," said Irfan. It was a declaration, not a question.

I answered anyway. "I don't think so."

He nodded. "This time tomorrow, we'll be in Gilgit. Two days after that, Ultar Glacier. Then she and Wes can take all the readings they want."

"She nearly didn't come at all, you know."

He twisted his neck to look at me. "I thought it was her idea."

"It was. But a few months before we left, she started getting cold feet."

"Why?"

"It might have been her father. He didn't want her to come."

"Neither did you."

"My reasons were different."

"What were his?"

"What do you think? *It's not safe*. He wouldn't hear otherwise. Telling an immigrant the country he left is not as he imagines is like telling a father the daughter who grew up is not as he imagines."

He laughed. "We'll be passing our glacier."

I smiled. "I know."

She'd text me messages. *Did you hear about the bomb blast?* I'd text back: *Don't panic. Everything will be all right.* She began fixating on Pakistan's "border badlands" and our conversations were increasingly about al-Qaeda hideouts, suicide bombers, bearded fanatics. She decided that Pakistan was a place where women couldn't survive. I asked what she thought 85 million Pakistani women were—unsurviving? Still the nervous texting didn't stop. *Another. That makes more than last year, right?*

One day I sat at my desk, wondering how it happened. After establishing the need for me to accept her "return," she was suddenly establishing the need for me to prevent it. *How did that happen?*

I logged on to the internet. A Yahoo! headline announced the terror threat was red. There was a message from Irfan with an image of a Predator unmanned aerial vehicle armed with Hellfire missiles, described as MALE. Medium-altitude, long-endurance.

I looked closely at the image. The drone was white, lean. It looked a little like a capsule I inserted into my rectum once, as a child, when I had worms. (Come to think of it, I'd seen something similar in Matthew's pristine toilet: hemorrhoid suppositories.) The drone had wings, a tail. The tail was spinning, and I could feel the nerves of my rectum tingle, anticipating the speed with which I was about to get reamed.

It was taking off from a runway in Nevada, from a place called Cactus Springs. I liked the name. I liked how it could be read in many ways. It could be a declaration of the ability of cactus to leap, which some do, if you brush up against them. Or it could have nothing to do with movement. The cactus could be standing still, but in the middle of a well, or a fountain, or several fountains, all gushing copiously. Or it could be long seasons of cactus—entire years made up only of March, April, May.

This was how it worked.

There was a pilot who stayed on the ground. Once the robot plane was in the air, the pilot could set its path as it flew over

Afghanistan and Pakistan, hunting for al-Qaeda fighters. Inside the drone was a camera capturing entire villages, where dark figures slid quickly into labyrinths, their shadows shifting, crisscrossing, into walls, into rooms, into each other. A target became a non-target, a non-target became a target. Before the camera could tell them apart, the world could be saved.

Beneath the photograph was a caption. *If the target is taking cover or lying down the effect is reduced, but if it can be caught standing up or running then the full effective casualty radius of 200 feet will apply.* It ended with a wistful afterthought. *While a drone can drop two 500-pound bombs with each strike, its camera shows us images of daily life in an area most of us never think about.*

To be the one looking up at that.

And to be the one at a Playstation in Cactus Springs, looking down on a land that wasn't even down there, as you were about to destroy it.

A small part of me felt exhilarated at the power of the drone's camera. (A large part of me felt exhilarated at the power of *all* cameras.) That bird's eye view. My life as a pelican. Or an owl.

Irfan's messages were increasingly concerned with where the unmanned planes were taking off from. Cactus Springs in Nevada, or Shamsi Airfield in Pakistan, near the Afghan border? Since the start of Operation Enduring Freedom, Shamsi was being used as a base for US Special Forces—that much was known. Prior to that, Irfan reminded me needlessly, it was used by wealthy Arabs to launch a different predator. Falcons. They were flown in on jets to hunt the endangered Houbara Bustard, a pheasant with aphrodisiac meat, though the real aphrodisiac was watching a falcon spray a Houbara's feathers. (Falconry was forbidden to Pakistanis, yet Pakistan produced more falconry gear than any other country, all for its Arab patrons. Call it hospitality.) Ironically, since the start of the war and use of the airfield by US forces, the bustards could no longer be hunted on the same scale. But people could. Had Shamsi Airfield been gifted to the CIA to launch predator MALE? Irfan threw these questions at me.

As well as this detail: in the sand dunes near Shamsi lay another airbase that could, after a sandstorm, disappear for days. It was in these sands that, soon after the war began, a Pakistani shepherd found unexploded US cluster bombs. He kicked one by accident while herding his sheep. It tore apart his hands and legs and made the news and elicited anger. Since then, if any shepherd lost his limbs, even the story was lost.

I heard the ring in my pocket. A text from Farhana. *Fourteen killed in a mosque. Why a mosque, Nadir?* I texted back, *Um, ask God?* I shut off my phone. I shut off my computer. I went for a walk.

I passed a newsstand. *Kidnappings Traverse Border.* I assumed it meant the Afghanistan–Pakistan border. But as I moved away, the word Mexico jumped out at me, and I thought, Oh—*that* border. Then I thought, Oh—*this* border.

I kept reading. Phoenix, Arizona, was becoming the kidnapping capital of America, and, outside Mexico City, of the world. The torture tactics of Mexico's drug cartels—including ripping off hands and legs—had spread across the border. It concluded, *Are we too obsessed with al-Qaeda to care about our own backyard? For California or Arizona, terrorists linked to the drug trade are a more immediate threat.*

The article excited me. See! We're not the world's biggest danger! Mexicans are worse! Even if I look like both! I carried the paper all the way to Farhana's house, as though for reward.

She said I was being racist. "Stereotyping Mexicans as drug dealers and violent gangsters is not a productive way of thinking. It engenders fear. Makes you think of fellow human beings as 'them.'"

"And fear of Pakistanis?"

"Are you calling me racist?"

"Why would I?"

"Why aren't you answering me? You know I'm sorry this is hard for you."

"I am. You know I'm sorry you're afraid, but we're not going anywhere near the Afghanistan–Pakistan border." (I thought fleetingly, we *are* the border.)

"I'm not. What should we have for dinner?"

"Okay then. Sushi?"

Later, she was in the mood. I wasn't. We tried again in the morning. I was as floppy as ahi.

When she got out of bed, I asked the shadow between us if her "return" was a way to somehow purge her fear of the place she called home. A fear that had only recently been made known to me. A fear that would haunt us right till our departure in July (and, I was to find out, even after we arrived). She wanted a role in it, this home, but didn't know what. It was still only March; the shadow stretched its limbs and bared its teeth and said nothing. On subsequent failed attempts—still no altitude or endurance—the shadow would only keep growing in length, as would its silence.

Did I finally hear the answer in July?

Was saving Kiran by dragging her into the boat the role?

A woman, a child, a voyeur. How quiet the confrontation. How murderous the gaze.

Kiran

"Come with us in the boat," said Farhana, bounding toward me from the shores of Lake Saiful Maluk.

I'd been watching her descend the hill and move toward us for a while. Irfan now sat up, blinking in bewilderment. He'd fallen asleep again.

"You guys!" Farhana rolled her eyes. "Come on, Nadir. Wes says it's safe."

"Safe as a leaking boat can be," said Wes. He'd found the potatoes and the pear.

Irfan rubbed his eyes and looked at Farhana. "You haven't eaten lunch yet."

"No," I added. "We saved you sandwiches."

"I'm not hungry." She was looking away, at the lake, now a bowl of amber light flecked with clouds—or were those whitecaps? "Nadir's done it before, haven't you?" She sounded dubious.

I said I had in the past, and the boats did leak. I watched the brow furrow, the tongue slide into the indent of her lower lip. But she'd made the proposal and I knew she wouldn't retract it. If she didn't want to follow through, she'd want me to prevent it from happening. I'd seen the same conflict play out in the weeks running up to our departure from San Francisco. She was protecting her own fear while desiring to be free of it.

Irfan was still wiping the sleep from his eyes. From behind his fingers, I heard him mutter, "Well, if Wes says it's safe..."

"We could take a long walk instead," I offered. "Look for the cave."

"What cave?" Wes sliced the pear with his penknife, presenting half to Farrah.

She took the half. It was like breakfast all over again. "What cave?" she echoed, a trickle of pear juice on her chin.

"The one where the fairy princess took shelter with her lover, Saiful Maluk. You remember, after the jinn got jealous and tried to drown them."

"Awesome," said Wes.

"It's far," said Irfan.

Farhana turned to me. "No. I want to get in a boat. With you. And the girl."

"The girl?"

She nodded. "She's never been in one."

Irfan laughed. "Of course not! The boats are for tourists."

"That would explain why you've done it," she shot back.

"She may not want to." He glared at her.

"Oh, she *wants* to. No one's ever *asked* what *she* wants."

"Have you?" He stared harder.

"Oh shit!" Wes laughed.

Irfan turned to me, said loudly this time, "If Wes says it's safe."

I was about ready to take the boat—by myself.

While Irfan and Farhana glowered at each other, the child hung back, behind Farhana. To be honest, I'd only been vaguely aware of her standing there till just this moment. Now I saw that she was eyeing the tents along the lake's shore. And then, as suddenly as I spotted her, she skipped away, her bracelets jingling.

"Where are you going?" Farhana called after her.

"She's going home," said Irfan.

Farhana was walking away, toward the tents.

"Where are you going?" I called after her.

"To tell her family I'm taking her with us."

Irfan turned to me. "Teach her something. She'll be putting them in a very awkward position. They won't want their child going off with a group of strangers and they won't want to say no to Farhana, who's a guest. She should accept their hospitality," he pointed to the empty plates, "instead of pressing for more."

"She thinks she's doing the girl a favor." My defense ended up sounding like criticism.

"That's exactly the problem," Irfan agreed.

"It's a ride in a boat." Wes shrugged. "You guys talk as if poor Farrah were trying to abduct her."

Poor Farrah?

"Give her a break," he added, maddeningly.

I followed Farhana.

Farhana followed the girl.

Irfan followed me.

Wes literally inhaled poor Farrah's sandwiches.

It was as Irfan said it would be. The girl, whose name was Kiran, appeared fairly neutral to the outing. Her family was against it. Farhana pleaded with them and eventually, Kiran's father agreed. At least that is how I understood his quiet responses to her fragmented Urdu, and later, while walking us to the lake, how Irfan translated their more rapid conversation. "It's even harder to say no to a female guest," Irfan added, Farhana ignoring him. "It's considered bad manners."

Kiran's father and brother—the same boy who'd brought the food—were standing outside the tent, watching us walk away. I could hear a woman's voice from inside the tent. Later, as I held the boat so Farhana could climb inside, I turned back to see two women watching us as well. One held a young child in her arms, and she was arguing furiously with Kiran's father. I saw her black shirt billow in the breeze; the cuffs of her sleeves were rimmed in fluorescent pink thread and I could hear bangles chime as the arms gesticulated in protest. It might have been the same woman I'd seen by the fire. Kiran's bangles as she arranged herself in the boat—folding her hands in her lap before unfolding them again—were like an echo of the woman's bangles. There was such perfect synchronicity between them that it had to have been a private conversation. I knew, as we pulled away, that the woman was her mother.

I rowed backward at first, looking behind me as the bow pierced the lake's skin, cutting a wide triangle the shape of a fin. Somewhere over my left shoulder must have loomed the actual summit of Naked Mountain, radiant in the evening light, I was sure. I could imagine the clouds circling him like a promise; he was above their promise now. Below us, in the glacial water, Queen of the Mountains' valleys and crests plunged all the way down to a depth that was surely our own nadir.

The boat was shaped like a tub and it was heavy. It wobbled. Apart from the ungainly shape, the rocking made no sense; there was almost no breeze. I rowed out about twenty feet before swiveling the boat around to face in the general direction of Naked Mountain. The tide did not recede. It was the same tide that had confounded us when we first got here; it was the tide of his ardor for the Queen, hers for him, and we were intruders, duly rebuked by being splashed from all sides. The further out I rowed, the larger grew the swells. Kiran and Farhana shared the plank in the stern of the boat, and every time the whitecaps hit her, Kiran shifted in her seat, rocking the boat more. She was light but her disquiet was heavy. She'd been talkative with Farhana when they walked into the hills together, but not now. I asked Farhana if it was me.

"Maybe." She frowned. Switching to Urdu, she asked, "Are you enjoying yourself?"

The girl shook her head.

"At least she's honest," I said.

Farhana wrapped an arm around her. "Is it because you're cold?"

She hesitated, then nodded. Her bangles still chimed; there was still the compulsive folding and unfolding of hands in her lap. But there was no longer a reply.

A pool of water was collecting inside the tub. It was impossible to say how much was coming in from the sides and how much was the leak. The heaviness grew. It was much harder to row that day than it had been the last time I was on the lake. Farhana offered to take over but though her legs were strong, she had no strength in her arms. When I told her this she reminded me that I had none either.

"Still," she conceded, "you do have shoulders." In English, so the girl wouldn't understand, she said that if we were alone we could both take a break.

I played along. "I could show you that vein in my shoulders that makes you wonder if I go running at night, or weightlifting."

She smiled. "This air suits you. You look—" She glanced at the girl. "She doesn't seem happy. Maybe I made a mistake."

"I look what?"

She rubbed Kiran's back. "Should we have brought your goat with us?"

Kiran grinned, showing two gaps in the front row of her teeth.

"I look what?" I repeated.

She met my reflection in the lake. "Like something I'd like to…"

There were no other boats nearby. If we'd been alone.

Beside Farhana rolled the Queen's deepest hollows. She was there, beneath my oar, tempting me to dive, face first. "In Karachi you said a quick fuck is a dead end."

"We've done it quickly since. Never on the water."

I was unutterably aroused. And grateful that I'd worn loose jeans. And mortified. Kiran wrapped her arms around herself, shivering. Couples who have children must have to deal with this all the time. Forced to navigate a third wheel, how do they keep their balance? But she wasn't even our child. And I wanted this moment with Farhana. We'd made love twice already in under twenty-four hours. Hat trick? This was just the thrill, just the *newness*, our long weeks before leaving San Francisco had lacked.

I spoke quickly. "Let's turn back, drop her, then come out again."

"We can't do that. We brought her with us."

We.

Kiran was looking down at the lake now, and her gaze was one of resignation. She was the child of gypsies, her bare feet caked with the soil of mountains. She sat hunkered in the boat as if in a cage. Water was a solid barrier, a mountain pass she could not traverse. There were no pine trees to lead the way, no goat bells to chase. The only markers were down below, in the lake bed, and these would slip through her fingers before she could tap them. Between the big toe and second toe of her right foot protruded a single pine needle, the thickness of her hair, darker than her hair. It had caught in a toe ring. She lifted this foot out of the pool of water rising past her ankles and rested it on Farhana's leg. She wiggled her toes. Bells on her toes.

"Tell Nadir your goat's name," said Farhana.

Kiran looked at me, and I realized she'd been avoiding looking at me till then. She knew I did not want her there. Her large green eyes were the color of sun-quenched grapes. "Kola," she said, daring me to take an interest.

"Like Kala Kola hair tonic or Coca-Cola drink?" I made a poor attempt at raising my voice in a friendly, child-accessible way.

She turned to Farhana as if to register her dismay at the degree to which I was capable of stupid questions.

"And the others, the ones you didn't have to chase?" pressed Farhana.

"Bhuri! Makheri!" She stared ahead, at the shore.

"And what is your favorite color?"

"Billoo." She stared at the sky.

Farhana laughed. I tried to smile. There was an awkward pause.

Well, my moment with Farhana on the water was over.

Or so I thought.

"Last night—" she began, switching to English again.

I waited. When she continued to hesitate, I urged, "Your timing was perfect."

"I know I'm not patient enough for you sometimes."

"You're just right for me."

"Last night, have I ever told you how good you…"

"What?"

"Well, better than salted caramel."

"Jesus, Farhana! You never talk to me like this when we're alone!"

Farhana hugged Kiran, tightly. "I'm sorry! It's not fair we brought her, even though she wanted to come! We should take her back!"

"And then return."

She nodded.

I spun the boat around, too quickly, straight into a wave. It crashed over Kiran's face, dousing her in ice water. She screamed. Then she stood up and the boat pitched and she screamed again. I did not see whether her right foot ever came down or if it was still pressed into Farhana's leg. But I did see her left foot skid in the puddle as she lost her balance, falling backward into the side of the teetering boat. "Sit down!" I heard Farhana shout, clinging to the opposite end of the boat with both hands. It occurred to me only later that Farhana had been thinking more clearly than I. She'd tried to balance the boat. If she'd reached for the girl instead, the boat would surely have capsized. I have no recollection of what I did. None. Not until I heard Kiran hit something—perhaps her hips. And then she was in the lake.

How long before I jumped in after her?

It must be that not even a second passed. Because I had no time to blink or even breathe after I heard the splash and the kick and the shriek that started as a piercing whistle but ended as a dull rattle; I heard it, again and again—how did I hear it, if I wasn't in the water too? Was it coming from me?

Then I heard myself shout—and this time, I knew it was me—"*It's freezing*!" And then time could not move fast enough. A fist curled around my spine and squeezed, a cold wet eel crushing my lungs, my limbs. My shoulders contorted, my muscles screamed, all of me convulsed. I could feel the feeling bleed from me as I became dead weight, plunging vertically to the bottom of the lake. When the pain in my legs returned, it was killing me. *It will kill me*. That damn eel was shooting electric currents deep into my veins.

"Kick!" I yelled, and this time I swallowed the lake.

"Kick!"

Surfacing at last, I spat into the air.

I moved rapidly now. I moved without thinking where I was going, all I knew was that I had to keep moving. When I looked around me, the boat was very far away. I could not see inside it. I did not know if Farhana had jumped or stayed. I could see no one in the water. I began to kick toward the boat.

No one. I shut my eyes and dived.

I opened my eyes and saw a downpour of silt. How did the water appear clear from above? How could it reflect us so sweetly when filthy inside? I surfaced. Blinked. Dived again. Again an avalanche of debris, falling softly all around, and then a fish—large, too large. I surfaced. "Farhana!" I dived again. I could now touch the bottom of the boat. I circled the boat. More fish. White, with yellow eyes. Orbiting me as I orbited them. We'd eaten trout every night since arriving in Kaghan but none had looked like this. Curious without a care. Their cold engagement ignited in me a panic of a familiar kind, unrelated to the likelihood of drowning. That was knowing what might be. The panic now creeping under my skin was the panic of not knowing. It was the panic of walking home in the dark with my jacket held out as a flag of peace to anyone, from anywhere.

I must have circled the boat four times before I heard a keening from above. I pressed my palm to the wood and for a moment, it was as if the boat were weeping. I could comfort her simply by placing my hands here, there. I could wrap myself around her, or, if her girth were too wide, I could receive her embrace of me. And so I did, as yet another form of panic seized me. This was the panic of knowing what might be. Now it was land that frightened me.

I dived again. That was Farhana in the boat. So where was the girl? I kicked my way deeper, deeper still. I had only ever dived into a swimming pool in Karachi, with Irfan and others from our class. We'd throw coins and believe them hard to see, glistening bronze in the blue sting of chlorine. I could barely make it to the bottom of the pool before the pressure in my ears forced me back up. Now I was looking for a girl in a lake so deep no one had ever measured it. I shut my eyes; I would count to ten then dive again.

When I opened my eyes Farhana was peering down at me from the side of the boat. Then her face vanished and instead I saw her legs. Dangling muscular. They were naked now; she'd taken off her shalwar. Or were those Kiran's legs? Limp, skinny. Again a face appeared but it was neither Farhana's nor the girl's and it was saying something I couldn't hear. My ears hummed. My head was screwed in a metal box half its size. I dived again.

I dived with Farhana's father. I heard him say, "Even the act of seeing."

I dived with my father. I heard him say, "Coward, come out."

I dived with Farhana's mother. I heard her say, "We die so young."

I dived with my mother. I heard her say, "God be with you."

I dived with Farhana.

I dived alone.

I dived alone.

Kiran's mother had pale green eyes, like her daughter. But they were smaller, and twice as piercing. Her hair was a shade darker than Kiran's, though not as dark as the pine needle that had caught between those plump, wiggling toes. She wore the hair in a tight braid woven neatly around her face, framing it like the feathers of an owl. She was a very tall woman, almost as tall as her husband, taller than Farhana, and she carried herself high, with a smooth oval chin perpendicular to a regal neck. Her stride was long and sure as she walked toward us on the shore, the black shirt billowing around her the way it had done barely an hour earlier, as she'd watched her daughter being pulled away from her, carried off in a boat with strangers. If Queen of the Mountains could have taken human form, she would have been Kiran's mother.

Her bangles were still.

They'd heard us out there, watched us dive, understood the screams. Irfan and Kiran's brother had come for us in another boat. I could barely remember it. I must have gotten back into our boat somehow, and held Farhana, and said something. It was as if the sight of Kiran's mother joining her husband as he waited for us brought me back to the world, only to remind me that I had wanted to leave it. Still did. I wanted to dive back down to those large white fish and their cold yellow eyes. I wanted them circling me, reminding me of my panic, forbidding my escape. I wanted to live inside that threat. It would free me from the agony of the man and woman awaiting us on shore. *Their* shore.

I imagined her wrapping the honey in the cloth, twisting the knot. She'd baked the bread for us, sacrificed a pear, potatoes.

When we stepped off the boat Farhana began sobbing again. She reached for Kiran's mother but her mother stepped away. Then the woman fell to her knees and screamed into the dirt, and I knew that this must be the first time she had ever crumpled, let alone allowed a witness, and we were the cause. Her shoulders shook in spasms as she lifted fistfuls of sand and tossed them into her hair and slammed her fists, broken nails digging through the bowels of the world, two lines of saliva hanging from her chin. Her husband stood nearby, weeping quietly into the cloth around his neck. His head was bare now. He had thick, beautiful curls.

Wes had pitched Irfan's tent. I was infinitely grateful for this. He stood outside, holding the front flap open. He could not have seen the diaphanous wings approaching us from the direction of Naked Mountain, as if born of the mountain's collar of clouds, soaring high above the tent before circumnavigating the lake. I knew she'd sleep with us tonight, heart-cut face in mine, ice-black stare inches from my throat. I crawled inside, as if into reprieve.

Before Prayers

My dreams were of my mother, of Farhana's mother, of mothers I couldn't identify, with children I never knew. Her face a knot of feathers, her neck as thin as air. I was inside: inside wings, inside caves. I was diving in my grandmother's scent, the scent of Farhana's mother, hanging on the wall above her bed. A bed in a different place, on which I lay, while a hundred different smells moved beside me. Burritos. Enchiladas. Coriander and lime. Smells I once loved, but that now made me wretch. And then my mother was there, in Farhana's bay window in the Mission, and I was sorry I'd barely seen her in those few days in Karachi, before leaving for these mountains. I'd call her on Irfan's cell. I'd tell her I was leaving the valley.

Someone was feeding me stones. Rolling them on my skin, tucking them in my chin, armpit, groin. They were covered in blood and slime. Coriander and lime. The smell the smell. I'd call my mother. If Farhana let me. She kept waking me. She said to stop clawing deeper into the skin of the tent. I was tearing it, and it was cold. If this was so, why did she leave the front flap open? Why did she keep showing me the way out?

Early in the morning, she screamed. Did I not care about the smell? I opened my eyes. I saw why she was upset. Between dreams, I'd spent the night vomiting glacial water. Apparently, I'd swallowed buckets of it, the day before. *The day before.* What day was that? A day that couldn't be! I told her I was sorry about the smell.

I tried to go back to sleep but now I was awake. I wanted badly not to be awake. I felt feverish, and yet my temperature hadn't risen, it had dropped. I learned that Irfan had spent the night warming stones with his hands, his breath, and his armpits before placing them in my armpits and even my groin. I wondered weakly if he, or Wes, had done the same for Farhana, who lay swathed in extra blankets. Where did she get them? I groaned: Kiran's family! Not possible! So too the warm fluids both of us were made to drink! Irfan assured me that mine included herbs to help both my conditions—the vomiting and the hypothermia—as if I had only two.

"Has her body been found?" I asked.

"Of course not," he snapped. He had a deep frown—I could have hidden in the furrow, I would have liked to—and his voice was gruff. He could barely keep from shouting. "Even if you're too weak to walk, push yourself. Movement will keep you warm."

"Let me rest," I groaned again. "Will it be found?"

"Shut up. Get up."

"Will it be found?"

"You know how deep the lake is."

"Actually, I don't."

"That's right."

"But there was a tide. There still is. I can feel it."

Farhana said she could stand it no more and crawled outside with all her blankets. I heard no stones fall.

"What does Bhuri mean?" I asked.

"Why?"

"What does it mean?"

"Brown."

"And Makheri?"

He glared at me. Eventually, he answered, "Naughty."

"They are the names of Kiran's goats."

Irfan was heating them again, long pebbles the shape of pears, and short round ones, so round I wanted to curl myself around them. They went from under his armpits to between his hands, as he juggled and squeezed, as though to soften them, like dough. He was an illusionist entwined in tricks. And in moods. As suddenly as it had begun, the magic act came to a halt, and the softness of his movements was lost. He clenched his fists, pressing furiously to heat those nuggets for me. So angry! So kind! "You're my friend," I choked, and he grunted, securing them roughly against my nuts.

I slept deeply this time. If I had dreams, I don't remember. When I awoke I was lying in a hollow of sound that began in the dark sleeve of some other sleep, from a time before my own. It grew louder, rippling rapidly toward me through that sleeve, till I recognized the echo as a voice, and I knew it was Farhana's. Except, flatter than hers. She wasn't speaking so much as reciting, from a letter inscribed on a treasure, perhaps, dug out from somewhere in the hollow. I imagined her shaking out the dust, shining a flashlight, murmuring words in a language I couldn't understand. Exhausted from trying to decipher her meaning, I went back to sleep.

It happened again. Some time in the middle of the night—or day, the same one? I didn't know—I heard Farhana beside me. I couldn't tell if she knew I was listening. I couldn't tell if she cared. Her voice was unusually melodious this time, yet somehow, still flat. I felt she was speaking to a third person in the tent. Calling to them, giving a testimony of sorts, on whatever she'd unearthed earlier—I briefly pictured her holding an Asokan rock edict—as though speaking into a tape recorder at a police station. Was she dreaming? Sleeptalking? I glanced around me quickly: no one else. Perhaps she herself was the third person. I didn't look at her. I didn't want her to look back with eyes open, or shut. I lay still in our tent.

The longer she spoke, the more my blood chilled again—where was Irfan with his beautiful stones!—surely it was the voice of delirium.

"And I dream of my mother when I am scared..."

Well, I thought, so do *I*. We were having the same dreams!

"You could say she is the closest thing I have to God. It is her image that hovers over me as I try to sleep, her image freed from the frame above my bed. It lifts into the sky like a puffy white cloud, blowing cool air down on me. She would do that. I was young but I remember. She learned it from her time here. You don't just pray *for* someone, you pray *on* them. You blow the prayer into their pores, till it reaches their soul. Breath for breath. That is how you love someone. With your breath. Baba said she never truly became a Muslim, except on nights when she would wish something for me—Dear God, please let my daughter have a mother at my age!—and blow it over me."

I woke up early. This time I was sure it was morning by the way the light filtered through the blue weave of the tent, giving our sleeping bags a thin yellow edge, making the woman next to me identifiable again. My throat was drier than the stones at my side but my temperature was normal. I knew I was the only one awake. I also knew that the lake was resting, even asleep. The tide had turned.

I took my bag. I stepped outside. The nomads rose very early, to pray. They might already be awake, waiting for the sun to break behind Malika Parbat. I looked over my shoulder but she was in darkness. A spray of stars winked in her place and thin wisps of cloud smeared the violet sky. Clouds in the shape of runners and acrobats. Fairies trailing princes. Jinns trailing fairies. Lovers on ice.

I walked to the water's edge knowing what I would find.

I took my time, my bare feet just outside the lake. Even when the water lapped tenderly at my toes, I was quick to step away. I told myself I avoided contact with the bone-chilling lake out of consideration for Irfan. If my temperature dropped again, he'd sooner smash my head with rocks than warm them. And then he'd be a murderer.

The bundle was in a semi-fetal position, on the northeast shore. It must have washed up as I approached; we arrived at the same time. It lay between the two mountains, at their feet. I couldn't reach it without passing the tents, which I did, as silently as I could. Two dogs shook themselves awake, one tiptoeing out toward me. Thankfully, it was tethered, though I needn't have worried. It didn't even bark. The other lay still, one ear slightly cocked. Of more concern was a horse, dark red in color, and with ferocious eyes, who bared its teeth at me and began to neigh. A smaller horse skipped forward and bucked and kicked the sand. It circled me and bucked again. The third time, it nearly kicked my shin. I kept walking. I was getting closer.

My head was as clear as the air, and with clarity comes coldness. Before sitting beside her I noted the beach was wet. I gathered a bouquet of pine needles and small stones and made myself a cushion of these. The sun would light the west shore before it would touch this spot. She'd washed up on the darkest corner of the lake. I wouldn't be able to see her face till after prayers.

And so I sat, beside her, listening to the azaan float in from the hills. I must have been too unconscious to notice any call to prayer until now. Though faint, this morning's call echoed clearly over the lake and across the valley. Within moments, a second and a third call joined in the chorus, each swooping past the other at a different speed, racing through stairwells of air currents, a whole family of owls.

Slowly, Queen of the Mountains' face began to appear in the water.

I detected the first signs of activity from the tents. I heard pots clanging, water flowing. I saw the dogs scratch themselves. I heard goat bells and buffalo bells and a long, drawn-out low, as soulful as a call to prayer. It was answered by a series of lows and soon the valley was ringing with a second azaan. The tent where I'd slept, on the southwest shore, lay completely still. I had no idea where Irfan and Wes had been sleeping.

The sun crept further along the lake. I could still see fairies in the clouds; I could see peaks and hollows. I did not glance at the body again till I was sure I could see it. I stood up, shook my legs, walked along the shore again. Irfan had said that lakes as cold and deep as this seldom gave up their victims. Without a strong current, it could take weeks. So the current that had cursed us was now a blessing.

I walked east, away from the body, farther than expected; my legs have a habit of taking me away. Perhaps it was this that alerted Kiran's mother to my presence here. Or that nasty horse and the foal, both of whom would continue bucking and braying all day.

When I turned back I saw a shadow in the sand crisscrossing my own. Gradually, I saw the woman not the shadow, a child in her arms. I remembered she'd held a child that day too. I hesitated. She'd been watching me. I'd heard no footsteps, no clothes rustle, no bangles chime, nor even a cry, not even from the child. For all I knew, they'd been there all along. Should I pull away, return to my tent? She walked with the same sure stride as she always walked; she wore the same black shirt. The child climbed out of her arms and ran toward the body and the woman barely stopped. Nor did she accelerate. Why had she brought the child? Of what use was it for a toddler to see a dead sister?

The little girl had curls like her brother and father. Her plump legs were squeezed into a yellow pajama torn below one knee. Her frock was dark green and embellished in festive gold embroidery. She cocked her head toward Kiran, now fully in the sun. The dead face was marbled bright pink and gray; the neck was darker. The ice water had washed away the stains from her cheek. The eyes glistened, as though alive. The little girl folded onto her knees, tucking her small feet beneath her. A small brown hand reached for a cold blue neck. The living hand stayed there, at the bathed neck, brown on blue, and the girl did not cry. She gazed at death with a sadness as deep and liquid as the lake, a sadness from which, her dark wide eyes said, she was going to have to learn to surface.

That is what her mother wanted me to see.

Queen of the Mountains: Thinner than Skin

Before she had seen twelve full moons, Kiran saw her first disemboweled goat. It lay in a pasture they had stopped in for just that night, for it was full with the tents of nomads from the west, and unsafe. In the morning, the goat's entrails lay splattered in the green, her juices mixing with those of the wet earth, the flies thick and droopy. It might have been a wolf. It might have been a man. Kiran sat on her haunches, lost in study. The goat's skin was peeled back, like a shawl, and the sun lit the sheen underneath. Perhaps it was this that left her thunderstruck. The sun, with which they prayed and sang, could cause a hurt to turn shiny before your eyes. Or perhaps it was the frailness of the hide. In later years, she would ask Maryam if her skin was as thin as a goat's. And Maryam would tell her the truth. It was thinner. Which meant, of course, that if a goat could be shred that easily, so could a woman.

She would also tell Kiran that, like herself, she would have to grow a second skin to protect the thin one that was eventually left to the sun and the earth, the wind and the flies. This second skin lay beneath the frailer one, not on top. It had to be kept hidden in order to work. But all this she would tell Kiran later. That year,

Kiran's first in the world, she measured the distance between life and death as lying between Kiran's finger and the goat's shiny entrails. Then she pulled Kiran away and shrugged, telling herself that Gujjar children were no strangers to death, and this was only the first of many Kiran would have to know. She was right, of course. If that spring death found Kiran in the skin of a goat, by autumn, before they returned to the plains, it would find her again, this time, in the eyes of a buffalo. During the long winter months in the homestead, death would become resident, taking her cousin's pony, and her grandmother. Wherever they went, it followed them. Death was a wind. He was a gypsy.

By her second year, Kiran had also witnessed the pain of birth and the way a mare will cry if her foal is born still. She was too young to understand the bitterness of age, but not too young to note that bitterness could immobilize two legs *and* four. Soon after the mare Namasha lost her foal, she gave birth to her second and only living filly, but at a price. She lost the steed that sired it. Early one morning, he dropped his dung high up a glacier and descended at a run, straight into a barbed wire fence. Before they could ask him why, he was dead. Maryam pressed the puncture wound with her palm while Kiran watched, dry-eyed and trembling, the blood running down her arms. She touched the wound without applying pressure to it, as though knowing the bleeding would never stop. Afterward, Namasha only took food from Kiran. At Maryam she snarled and she kicked. It took two years before the mare forgave her, and by then Kiran had learned that forgiveness was thinner than skin.

This year, death had again showed himself in the sun. Their first morning on the move, soon after they unloaded their bags off the animals and while the rest of the dera was pitching the tents, Maryam's eldest brother-in-law stretched his arms and simply fell, right there in the middle of his flock, at Kiran's feet. Kiran waited a long time before delivering the news: Baro bai was dead.

It was part of life. The endless roaming, loading, unloading. The bodies that folded, the spirits that fled, when you traveled by caravan, in groups of families bound together by the intimacies of gaiety and grief. The dera of Maryam's brother-in-law was not the most popular in the tol; there had been opposition to the price at which he sold his butter and milk, down in the plains. But once they left the plains, these disagreements became petty. It always happened this way each year, during the migration. The higher up they moved, the more the spirit was cleansed. The children played drums and the women sang. The men told stories and the horses stretched their wings. Even Baro bai's death became occasion for renewal. After burying him by a stream, they spent the rest of their month-long trek sharing stories of his youth. This was a death you lived with. It was not a death that made you stop. Stopping was not an option.

Which was why you had to have the necessary kind of death behind you to carry the other kind. You had to have the years. Otherwise you might halt, and then you really were dead.

The baby did not have years. The mother did not have years. And, from the looks of him, the killer did not have years either.

As she watched him move away, she remembered her mother say that none were more cursed than those destined to watch in silence. There was no deeper hell than a pair of eyes without a voice. And she would say that a broken heart should never grow cold. It was the cruelest of burdens. Not even God would carry it. She had experience with this, having asked Him numerous times to carry hers. He always refused. He was not about to carry any other. And so, her mother said, while you cannot stop a heart from breaking, you can keep the pieces warm. Of course, she never told her how.

Now Maryam found that her heart had not merely broken, or even grown cold. It had simply stopped. It was dead weight that only grew heavier as she moved closer to Kiran lying there in the sand, unmoving, without shedding blood, without a trail of shiny guts, without even a droopy fly. This time, it seemed, death had not wanted to find Kiran at all.

She had pleaded with her husband. How could he let Kiran get in the boat with strangers? Kiran was afraid of water. Did he not see the fear on his own daughter's face?

He replied, coldly, "I am lame, not blind. You know we cannot refuse them. They are guests. Remember where you come from."

Cannot refuse them, even our daughter?

"It is just for a short while, Maryam." And now his voice softened. He was like her father in this way, when he called her by name it was never without tenderness.

"And them?" she ventured. "Where do they come from? Is it a place where a child is pulled from her family for amusement?"

His voice curdled. "You were always fond of drama. Kiran will be fine."

Kiran will be fine.

For the hour Kiran was in the boat, what did her husband do? He sat with the men of their tribe, debating the trouble in the valley. Down where their homestead lay, things had changed. There were military convoys looking for a killer. There were spies. There were accomplices. But there were no eyes, not up here, not for a girl afraid. And there were no ears, not up here, not for the bangles that called. Only Maryam could hear them, while sitting by the open hearth on the shores of the lake, her baby Jumanah beating a tune on the kangri firepot—perhaps she heard them too—in a circle made of copper bowls. They were calling her, but all she could do was listen. Eventually, she could neither see the boat nor hear the bangles. All she could do was nothing. Perhaps in that hour her heart had already begun to stop.

The night the boat returned without Kiran, she slipped out of her husband's tent. There was a blue tent in the distance, neither sagging nor leaky, like her own, and inside lay the girl who walked like a goat and the man who had no tongue. The two killers. Her husband was asleep. She crept under the moon and over the hills, to her cave.

She did the same the next night. She saw their tent. She ran to her cave. She might have cried freely there, but preferred, instead, to scream and curse. She would leave no more offerings to a goddess that gave her misgivings but no signs. At least none she could read. How many times had she fought with her husband to keep their ancient rituals alive, even as others called her a pagan wife? How many risks had she taken by protecting the shrine down in the plains, a shrine that did not lead all the way to Tashkent, nor encase her like a womb, nor hold the dreams of the dead in the drawings on the wall, but that was dark and lifeless and mean? Was this just payment for her devotion? She kicked the rice, and offered it. She spat on the feather—that meant *he* was coming—and kissed it. She cried to her mother—where are your footholds now, your doors?—and praised her.

The second night, her baby daughter Jumanah followed her out of their tent. Maryam carried her to the cave, and showed her the drawings, and cursed her luck.

Before dawn of the third morning, she was winding her way back to the lake, only to find him. The man with no tongue, committing a second murder. He would not even allow her the dignity of being the first to welcome her daughter back. He would not even abstain from the sacrilege of looking at Kiran without love, without history.

It was the baby who found a way to punish him. She placed her small hand on Kiran's cold neck. The child and the child. Neither ready for death. Maryam held his gaze, the killer's, the one who had stolen their youth. He retreated, tail between legs.

Watching him go, she remembered the legendary Maryam Zamani, who willed a stone to retreat. And she thought of the man who once likened her to the legend, the one for whom Maryam was not just Maryam, the one who had come to her, at first, like a prophet. A color filled her eyes. Blue. Kiran's favorite shade. She had tried to braid Kiran's hair with a blue thread once, a cluster of braids raining down her back, all gathered in blue. She had almost succeeded. Blue for the still neck lying on the shore. Blue for the feather from a kingfisher's tail. She was sure Kiran would fly now, with her grandmother, and all the spirits from the plains, and from these mountains, and from the steppe beyond a dark sea, from where they had come, two, maybe three thousand years ago. And as the blue filled her eyes she told herself: *He will fix this. Ghafoor is on his way.*

She kept her gaze on the killer's legs, the way they buckled as he hunkered back toward his tent. She watched for so long the baby began to fidget. But she did not cry. When Maryam finally tore her eyes away, she leaned into Kiran and kissed her brow, and stroked her cheek. She ran her hands over her wet clothes. Kiran's shalwar was torn. From the fall or from a bite? Not a drop of blood, not a droopy fly. The child feared death less than she had feared water. She blew prayers over her cold flesh.

She picked her up. The dead were heavy, after only six years of life. So this was the weight that had permanently lodged itself in her chest. Very well, she would carry it. She adjusted Kiran in her arms till the cold chin of one pressed into the warm curve of the other and broken knees bunched against a heart that had stopped. She breathed in Kiran's ear. "The sun is hot now, I'll take you home."

Beside Maryam, but several feet closer to the ground, Jumanah ran to keep up with her mother. For assistance, she clutched her sister's bloating feet. She had once seen a man on a bicycle do the same. He held on to a racing bus as it carried him far and away. Now her mother was the bus, Kiran's feet the two bicycle handles, and her own plump legs the wheels. She needed a third hand, really, to hold onto her mother the bus, but she could pedal faster. The air rushed around them as she heard her mother chant: *He will fix this he will fix this he will fix this.*

THREE

Naked Mountain: A View from Above

He sat in a café many miles north of the lake, in a town called Gilgit. He was taking his time appraising the two men from Xinjiang Province. He was a tradesman; he knew nothing was free. But the choice he faced now was different. The men did not have fingers and toes, at least not all of them. Studying their hands, he calculated the sum of their words.

They described to him, in minute detail, China's plan to raze the old city of Kashgar. They had brought photographs as evidence of their pain: cobblestone alleys, labyrinthine in design, as interconnected as ancient trade routes. Spectacular mosques, also to be razed. On the walls of one mosque hung a poster forbidding individual pilgrimages to Mecca. The men also had images of abandoned internet cafés, after the freeze by the government last year, ensuring the complete isolation of their fight. The clean-up meted out to protesters involved a different kind of freeze. They were hosed with ice water, several hours at a time, in winter. The lucky few, like the two men beside him, were freed without fingers and toes.

Their isolation must end. He could help, could he not?

The men had brought what he wanted. It lay in a box on their table in the low-lit café, close to their hands. Inside the box lay a gift for the woman to whom he had sent a blue feather, days earlier. An impossible choice. There was a proverb down in the valley where he had once made his home. *Neither dry in the sun nor wet in the rain*. How was he to get himself out of this difficulty?

One man had palms like soft leather cups, wrinkled and worn. The right thumb and little finger were missing, but on the left hand, only the middle finger was gone. This man was asking why the hands had reacted asymmetrically. Had he curled each differently each time they hosed him? Had he left one finger more exposed? He wanted to know also if it would have been easier to adjust if both hands had suffered the same fate. Because, now, he found he could do absolutely nothing with the left hand, even though it still retained a thumb. "The left hand uses the right as an image of itself, but it has lost this mirror. It cannot learn."

"It could have been worse," said the other man, who had only lost his toes. And he did a trick, making all but one of his fingers disappear. He held it up. The two men chuckled. They kept their shoes on.

Ghafoor kept appraising them, trying to place them from four summers ago, on one of his trips to Central Asia.

He had stopped in Kashgar for a few days, where he traded, among other things, leather for jade. The Chinese military were parked in the province for the month, to parade military hardware through the heart of the city. In the sky droned circles of fighter jets. On the ground trooped 100,000 boots, several dozen tanks, armored personnel vehicles, and camouflaged trucks. He had never seen so many uniforms before. He had never seen so many weapons. He had never seen so many planes. The chief of general staff of the People's Liberation Army was also present, along with more generals than he had seen even at one of Pakistan's military parades. It took longer than it ought to have to find the trader he was to meet, and when he did, he learned the reason for the display.

It would show the Uyghurs of Xinjiang that ethnic separatism under the banner of East Turkestan and religious freedom and the Turkic tongue would never be tolerated. This was not East Turkestan. It was China.

Ghafoor spent the week listening to the army's threats with one ear, and the bustle of the city's main bazaar with the other. There were many Pakistani merchants here, all buying joggers, socks, track suits with English writing, and the Pakistani housewife's favorite convenience: plastic buckets. He met a Uyghur who, after striking a deal for 4,000 pairs of socks, had closed shop for two months while feeding a family of twelve. He ate kebabs skewered on bicycle spokes. He bantered with peddlers who told him a joke that, in subsequent years, would grow slightly stale. ("What was the first thing Neil Armstrong saw when he landed on the moon…?") He watched more currency exchange more hands in more tongues than even down in Gilgit. For, though Uyghurs were proud of their Turkic heritage, for commerce, accommodations must be made. When currency was converted, so was language. The best clients were "Soviets" from Central Asia and Russia. If treated right, a Soviet could help a man close shop for *three* months. Ghafoor learned a little Russian himself, a skill that proved especially useful with the many Kazakh traders living in Xinjiang, men with whom he would travel to Ghulja on the border, forging direct links with artisans high in the Kazakh steppe.

But that was to happen later. Four summers ago, despite the windows he sensed were opening for him, Ghafoor was unsettled by the tanks and trucks occupying the city, and by the Han migrants being brought in from outside the province. They would pave the cobbled roads that cut through Old Kashgar, and force native Kashgaris to leave. He knew what it was to be forced out, to roam from field to field as though you were an upal in a buffalo's ass. It was partly for this reason that he had chosen to leave the valley of his birth. Better to choose, than to be forced. But the native Kashgaris were not choosing to leave, even when the cobbles beneath their feet were smashed, even when, for every donkey cart that sold polu and kebabs, there were two that sold liquor and pork. So he watched a history evanesce, alleys that once chimed with horsebells now clattering with cranes, mazes of mud-brick courtyards being flattened like naan, while, nearby, a colossal statue of Mao remained unshaken. "This is our al-Quds," an old man whose family had fled the previous year told him. "I will never leave." And when he added, "Will you help us?" Ghafoor had replied, "Of course." But his eye, saturated with the grief of those he knew he could not help—he had not even been able to help his own people, though God knows he had tried—this saturated eye began to wander.

By the end of the week, Ghafoor had a mound of Kazakh, Chinese, and American currency in his purse, and the news at his back. He was vaguely aware of what it said. An East Turkestan separatist had been arrested in Pakistan. He had confessed to being the ring leader of a group planning attacks on China's twelve new highway projects, each of which would cut through Xinjiang to connect China with Russia, Kazakhstan, Tajikistan, Pakistan, and ultimately, Uzbekistan, Iran, and Turkey. Upon his arrest, he publicly spat on the generous compensation Kashgaris would receive for resettlement. He spat also on the compensation for the herders whose nearby grazing grounds would be paved.

By the end of that same year, Ghafoor was far from Kashgar and Chinese tanks and Han donkey carts and the man to whom he had promised aid. The news was still at his back, and it could still be heard. The East Turkestan separatist had been executed.

His brother was now sitting opposite Ghafoor, without toes, and with a box. Ah—Ghafoor had not been able to place him, but the man now came out with his name! He need not have shown Ghafoor the photographs of those lovely mosques that would soon be razed. Of course Ghafoor had seen them, with his own eyes, before moving on from Kashgar into Kazakhstan. He had seen the military parade double in might, the fighter jets that spewed ribbons of white smoke into a sky that would not wear its natural color again for weeks. But by then, Ghafoor did not really care. Somewhere between the kebabs on bicycle spokes and the Chinese yuan in his pockets—or perhaps between the military tanks and an old man's defiance—he had fallen in love with a girl so white she could be a ribbon herself. She certainly weaved around him like one, her face a smooth oval, her lips small and pink, and with just the tiniest smile lurking at one corner. In one of those labyrinthine alleys in a photograph in a soft leather palm, he had followed her, over the remaining cobblestones and into a doorway and up a staircase and behind a madressah where her father was preaching, and on, into another doorway, up another staircase, through a window patterned with green tiles that took his breath away, on, past the blue and white vase standing on a pillar that was surely a work of angels. And there she pulled him into a room high above the minarets that seemed to point at the fighter jets, cursing them to hell. And she weaved around him again.

They met there each day, in a room in a sky in which birds had not flown for longer than anyone could say. They simply sat, the nightingales and the doves, the eagles and even the grayleg geese, on the eaves of houses and the domes of mosques, waiting for the planes to stop their din, waiting to be swept by the breezes that had also stopped, waiting, waiting, for the People's Liberation Army to look somewhere else, because it was getting late, soon, many of them would have to migrate south, including to Kaghan Valley, where he, the tall man with the sideburns and the belt on the floor, had once made his home. But in the meantime, while they waited, at least they had the advantage of a bird's eye view of the lovers who met each day in that room.

She wanted him to stay but he could not stay. He told her he had goods to trade in the steppe. He promised he would be back. He said her thigh was like the inside of a dove's wing, silken smooth and silken white, and outside, the doves shifted and almost cooed.

He was getting good at getting naked faster than her old man could climb one-third of the way up the stairs. Another third, and he had already had his fill. The final third, they had both dressed, and parted. By the time the midday prayer sounded from all the mosques—even the heavenly call from a hundred majestic minarets could not rival the din of the fighter jets, though not for want of trying; many muezzins lost their voices permanently that summer—the man with the sideburns and the girl with the feather-smooth thighs were nowhere to be seen.

And now, four summers later, the two Uyghurs had brought him what he asked. He opened the box. Two flowers, still fresh. The choice he faced was not easy, but it was worth trying to avoid. He paid them generously and stood up to leave. They laughed, reminding him that though he might prefer otherwise, their business was not over.

He sat back down.

After leaving the girl in Kashgar, his world had kept opening. He traded in the cities of Tashkent, Samarkand, Bukhara, and Almaty, traveling up the Oxus River and deep into the steppe, developing a special kinship with those who built the goods he sold in the markets. It was here the land spoke to him most, in a region that lay high in the north of what was now Kazakhstan, though to the nomads with whom he was to spend the next three summers, all of Central Asia was one land, divided not into states but into mountain and steppe, desert and oasis. The steppe nomads made him feel he was looking back in time—*his* time. It was the strangest sensation, the first day he was invited to break bread with them. It was as though a mountain inside him were melting, leaving him naked and cleansed, entirely in his own skin, the skin he used to inhabit in the valley of his youth, before he had to leave (he had not *entirely* chosen to leave; he had been sent away, banished, almost, even if he did prefer to think otherwise), before he had to don a thousand different skins. In the steppe he was undisguised, unwary, unwanting.

He found that the Turkic nomads shared an uncanny likeness to his own community: love of horses, hospitality to guests, and, most of all, a worshipful knowledge of the primacy of movement. The men had lush beards and liked their trees to look the same; they did not fell that which gave them life. Even some of their festivals were the same. They observed Nauroz, the first day of spring, by cleansing their homes with burning juniper branches, smoking out the vices of the previous year, a ritual now done in secret down in Kaghan, by a woman who, when she was a child, had licked honey from his fingers and danced to his flute. (The memory always made him smile.) The steppe nomads loved music too, bowed string things that made them kick. He was glad he had his flute. They sang as much as they prayed, and talked twice as much. They had their own shamans, those who could escort a soul back to a body, and those who could escort due justice back to a crime. They were born with a long ear and a memory as old as the Oxus. So was he. There was nothing said in his presence that he did not carry deep in his chest to the next yurt, the next town, the next valley. But he held it there. He did not talk. He merely listened, loyal to everyone who showed him only kindness. Their stories were his stories. Their enemies were his enemies. And their women, well.

Only a few weeks after leaving the girl with the feather-white thighs, Ghafoor found himself drinking milk from the arms of another. They had a peculiar diet, up here. It was the hardest thing for him to grow accustomed to. The worst thing he ever ate was a bowl of thick string made of something vaguely the consistency of rice, though the duck, also new to him, did make it easier to swallow, and the mare's milk made it easier still. He had never milked even a buffalo before—a sign that he was never a very good herder, even when he was one—but one day he saw her doing it, stroking the udder of a visibly pregnant mare, a girl who was not slight and not oval-faced, but who had the most perfect round arms, and who showed him how. *Press like this.*

Over the course of the summer he followed her through highland pastures the way he had, not too long ago, followed another through cobblestone labyrinths. An audience of eagles and hawks dipped and twirled in a sky free of fighter jets. Looking up from beneath him in the grass, she spoke a name of God that was older than Allah. *Tengri*. Tengri, he repeated, drinking her smell. He was getting better at getting naked faster than the milk still warm on her flesh could ferment. *Tengri*, she whispered again and again in his ear. *It means the endless hemisphere of the sky.*

There was some movement that even a free woman did not consider free. This time, before he could leave for the market towns, he was told to bid for her hand, which he did. He won the hand but before he could marry her, he had to win at two additional tasks. The first was assembling their home. A yurt was more luxurious than any Gujjar tent, and entirely sacred. It was a replica of *the endless hemisphere of the sky* and putting it together was an act of creation. His bride-to-be needed to know that he could create. After many tries, he eventually succeeded. Their yurt was a bright, plush home, with each aspect, she told him, representing a part of the human body. The walls were thighs, the smoke hole the eye, and the interior lattice frame with the ribbed plates that he gazed upon each night from beneath her, the womb. The second task was not divine, though, much to her amusement, he did not realize this till much later, when it ceased being a prerequisite to their marriage. It was a game in which he waited on a sandy outcrop on a horse till she rode up to him, at which point, he could chase after her. If he caught up with her, he could kiss her. If he failed, she could whip him. The game even had a name, kyz kuu, the kissing game. He never did win, even before she took pity and married him.

To their yurt and their games he returned, wherever he went, and for however long. She could weave the finest rugs ever seen, a skill that flowed in her blood for more generations than he could name, for which he fetched a handsome price, keeping her family well fed. He did not need to return to Pakistan very often for leather or other goods. He no longer found much use for jade.

Yet, lately, something was pulling him back, something that had not pulled him for a while. The comforts of the yurt had begun to ache. The duck no longer tasted sweet. Mare milk was rather sour when compared with buffalo milk. And the truth was, though it delighted her, kyz kuu exhausted him. Perhaps it was time for a visit. So he had sent the blue feather to the girl of the valley of his youth, smiling to himself as he recalled her amazement the first time he left her a sign in the cave. Their cave. And he sent word to all those he had met in his many years as a suitcase trader, a long, long network of associates who were Uzbek and Tajik, Afghan and Uyghur, men with a long, long ear and a memory as wide as the Lli River that flowed from Kazakhstan all the way into Xinjiang. He told them he needed something rare, very rare. Something he could give to someone from his past, something no one had ever thought to give before, the best surprise they could think of, and the most beautiful, and the most short-lived. For he was not staying long in Pakistan. It should last only as long as his trip. But it must be exceptionally radiant, silken, and sweet. In short, it must be *rare*.

And then he left.

From the open grassland of the steppe he eventually descended into the town of Almaty, and from there to Bishkek, swinging west into Tashkent—he had once told her their cave led all the way to Tashkent, he recalled, his step buoyant—repeating what he had already asked, and the answer was always the same. No, they had not found anything that rare but they would keep searching. It was July, the time of year when nomads all over Asia have moved from their winter homes into summer pastures, and he knew it would be the same for Maryam and her family. *Maryam*. He had not spoken her name for some time. She had always loved this time of year, away from the plains, high in the grazing grounds around Lake Saiful Maluk. Perhaps she was thinking of him, at just this moment.

Perhaps she was missing his version of the song about the prince, the princess, and the jealous jinn.

From Tashkent he descended into the Fergana Valley, and now he was getting close. He was approaching the passes through the Pamir and Karakoram ranges he knew so well he could have made the trek in his sleep, and he might have, but for one event that required him to remain fully awake.

It was this event that had tipped off these men.

It happened in Andijan, where he had stopped for just the day. The city Genghis Khan had burned seven hundred years ago, and that his grandson later rebuilt. The city where the Khan's most famous descendent, Emperor Babar, founder of the Mughal Dynasty, was born. The city where his most profitable clients now lived.

Ghafoor had arranged to meet his client in Babar Square. As he approached the square, he recognized the man, but the man was not alone. Beside him was a Uyghur from Xinjiang. Ever since leaving Kashgar, four summers ago, in haste, Ghafoor had been avoiding the Uyghur community as much as he could, which, given his business, was not always possible. His strategy was to always approach a Kashgari, in particular, from the side. He did not want to be recognized as the foreign merchant who broke his promise to a local girl. Repercussions could be—well, how would they be down in Kaghan? But this day, perhaps it was his excitement at nearing the mountain passes so familiar to him, or perhaps it was the way the sunlight fell on the statue of Babar's horse, whatever the reason, when both men greeted Ghafoor, they seemed amiable enough, and he relaxed. The Uzbek examined the rugs Ghafoor had brought, nodding appreciatively while promising, "God willing, we will find the just rate." When both men invited him to lunch at a crowded teahouse, he agreed.

He regretted it almost immediately.

How were the women up there, in the steppe, the Uyghur—who, it turned out, was from Kashgar—wanted to know.

"Well," answered Ghafoor, scooping handfuls of palov with his fingers. "The women are well." At the table next to him, he heard a

European refer to the rice dish as pilaff, the Kashgari at his table refer to it as polu, and of course, were he in Pakistan, he would hear it called pilau. It was piled high with mutton seasoned with herbs rather than spices and though he was now used to the difference, he ate with two tongues, one that did all the work while the other dreamed of flavors it did not touch.

"So you are married, then?" continued the Uyghur, who preferred to sip black tea without milk or sugar rather than eat. "To a Muslim?"

"Yes," he shifted in his seat. The Muslim of the steppe, he knew, was too animist for the Muslim of the town, and the Muslim of the town, for the Soviets and the Chinese, was just too Muslim.

"How many wives?" said the man, now lighting a pipe.

"One." Ghafoor licked a spoon of yogurt, thinking, *They like their yogurt sour here.*

A silence ensued, as deliberate as the slow burn of his pipe. The other man ordered a bottle of vodka, and, when it arrived, he began to talk. He spoke of the Andijan Massacre, two months earlier. Police had shot into a crowd of men, women, and children pressed together in Babar Square to protest the arrest of several businessmen. This was the same square in which their forefathers had fought Russian forces. They were not about to acquiesce to a president who behaved like a twenty-first-century tsar. More than 10,000 people came out in support of the prisoners. The Uzbek army blocked all routes to Babar Square with armored personnel vehicles and tanks. "Then every one began to panic," said the Uzbek. "We heard the *whit whit whit* of steel blades over our heads. At the exact moment when I looked up, the shooting began. It was like 1898 all over again, only now, they shot at us from the sky. We found the graves later. Fresh ones. Thousands of them. Even children."

The Uyghur listened. When the Uzbek was finished, he began to talk. More native Kashgaris had been forced out of their city as China's plan to develop Kashgar fortified. China had put more Uyghur organizations on the terrorist list, convincing the international community to do the same. There were even Uyghurs in Guantanamo Bay, handed over to America by Pakistan. The two men traded tales of injustice till long after the sunlight had slid off the statue of Babar's horse.

At last the Uzbek concluded, "We thought we were free, but now our own president works against us. Jailing those who are strong, shooting those who are weak!"

At which point, the Uyghur turned to Ghafoor (causing him to wonder later if every detail of this afternoon had been rehearsed), "*Your* country does the same. Why does it make friends with China? Why does it let China build highways and ports through the lands of its own people? Do you think it will make men like you rich?"

Ghafoor had stopped eating some time ago; the vodka he guzzled. He did not know how to explain that it had been a while, a very long while indeed, since he felt he had a country. Perhaps the last time was even before he had a single hair on his cheek. He had tried to fight for it, once, this country that had never been his, as though by fighting for it, he might earn it, but this had only resulted in his own people telling him to leave. He now belonged to the steppe. Even if he still carried his past in his shins.

"We herders have a very different fate," said the Uyghur, ordering a fresh pot of tea. "We may wear better clothes than those who still spend their lives looking for a field that welcomes them, but we will never stop wandering. Will we? *Even when we have an obligation to stay.*" The last words were spoken with the pipe clenched between his teeth.

Outside the teahouse, in the distance, Ghafoor could now barely see the statue of Babar on his horse. What he would give to call the horse to himself at that moment. Or call his wife. He could ride away with her. They could play kyz kuu.

"You say nothing, my friend? You must know that wherever men like us go, we are treated the same. Uyghur businessmen, Kazakh cattle-breeders, Gujjar buffalo herders. The same. Your in-laws do not speak of it? All the men who have passed through their land, as though they had the right? Taking anything they please. Giving nothing in return. Taking, even, their women."

The Uzbek was laughing. "Enough! The day is closing and the stars begin to call!" He picked up the rugs and tossed too few bills on the table. Then he left.

"You will help us," the Uyghur patted Ghafoor on the back. It was not a question.

The next day, Ghafoor was sent a message. That something he was looking for, which must be rare, very rare, that surprise that no one had ever thought to give—how had he put it? Yes, the most beautiful and the most short-lived—it would be waiting for him next week, in Gilgit, in northern Pakistan.

Before leaving Andijan, he caught sight of something twinkling just behind the ghostly statue of Babar's horse. It was even brighter than moonlight, and so he must follow it, a silvery cape of gauze draped around the shoulders of a woman in a gaily colored skirt. She had wide hips that pulled him to that portion of Babar Theater that still lay charred from the riots two months ago. Someone had started the fire before the army began firing on the protesters, but no one knew who, or why. The theater was black and crumbling and doves did not walk, nestle, or wait here, nor did hawks draw somersaults in the endless hemisphere of the sky. Here, there was no sky. Only broken walls and tattered curtains and cigarette stubs. She was older than he had thought and missing teeth. Why had he followed her at all? Perhaps to find himself getting better at getting naked faster than the ashes beneath them could turn to dust.

He held the box in his hands. Two flowers, still fresh. As fresh as the memory of those who had brought them. "They are what you wanted. Rare, radiant, sweet. And they will last only as long as you do." This was said by the man without toes but with all his fingers. He was the brother of the man who had been executed four years ago because Pakistan had given him away. The man without toes and without a few fingers was the brother of the girl Ghafoor had dishonored.

The box fit exactly in Ghafoor's hand, from wrist to middle finger. It was two-tiered, divided by a wooden plank. The flowers lay on top, on a white satin cushion. From beneath the plank escaped streams of packing material, but he was told not to look further. He was only to carry it. There would be other deliveries—the two men exchanged looks—after which, he must come back here, with news for them.

Ghafoor paused. They were not alone in the café. The Pakistanis milling around were mostly Shia, but even the Sunnis made him cringe. All of them spoke the word *Gujjar* with disdain. There were Kashmiris here, too, some with wretched stories of Indian prisons. The Kashmiris seldom insulted him. Outside, military convoys patrolled the muddy roads. He thought briefly that if the men with the box gave him trouble, perhaps in another country, the men in uniform might help. Then he remembered the military parade in Kashgar and the Uzbek army's massacre of civilians in Andijan, and he decided he had nowhere to run.

He could hear a Turkic tongue being spoken several tables away. He caught the word *cehennem*. Hell. *Jahannum* in Urdu. And in Gujri? What did it matter, since it was barely his language anymore? No Soviet worth his salt would do business in Ghafoor's native tongue. But then, who would?

The men had ordered food and the food now arrived, plates of mutton korma spiced the way he had been craving just a week ago, pilau piled high with peas—smaller peas than in the steppe but so much more flavorful—and kebabs skewered not on bicycle spokes but on *skewers*. The newspaper wrapped around the naan was in a script that was strangely familiar. Cyrillic. His wife could read it and had tried to teach him how, but he had failed as surely as at kyz kuu. He had not expected to see Cyrillic in Pakistan. But nothing surprised him now. What was it the Uyghur in Andijan had said?

Herders have a very different fate. We may wear better clothes than those who still spend their lives looking for a field that welcomes them, but we will never stop wandering.

Why was every mountain town the loneliest place in the world? Everyone here was scarred. Everyone here was in flight. Everyone was a passing flower in a dangerous box.

The men complimented the food, while insisting their kebabs tasted better. They attempted a joke. "What was the first thing Neil Armstrong saw when he landed on the moon?"

Not this again, thought Ghafoor.

"Two Uyghurs trying to sell him grilled kebabs!"

It was not even funny, this joke they repeated as often as their prayers.

In a moment of defiance he pushed the box toward them. "I must know what it is before I agree to carry it."

The men refused.

"Then my answer is no."

"We know you have done much worse. And that you have unfinished business."

Was he about to trade his life for two flowers?

"And you must know we can also do worse," they added.

What? Without hands and feet? Ghafoor was about to blurt, but then he paused.

The man without right finger or thumb was scooping food perfectly into his lips, without even trickling grease over those palms of soft brown leather. Watching those hands, Ghafoor was suddenly visited by a memory that had never visited him before. How could it have lived inside him all this time?

It was a memory of Maryam's brother, Adil, whose true friend he had once been. The two boys were at the edge of Lake Saiful Maluk, talking about Maryam without really talking about her. Ghafoor was frightened of losing his friend by admitting he had been pursuing her with music and honey. So they talked about music without talking about honey. Her brother played his drum,

Ghafoor played his flute, and while they paid attention only to each other, Maryam had arrived, cautiously, standing shyly behind a tree. A butterfly flit between all three of them, a yellow swallowtail with a shimmer of purple spots at the edge of two serrated wings. Maryam followed it with her eyes the entire time the boys played music. When it landed on her shoulder, she laughed, stroking it gently with her thumb. Her brother stopped playing and told her to leave. She did. The butterfly flew away. Ghafoor put away his flute and began to walk down the hill toward his cluster of tents. He did not want it to show, but he had not liked the way Adil had told her to leave. He was descending the hill when her brother caught up with him at a run, cupping something in his hands. The two boys faced each other. Adil opened his hands very slightly and Ghafoor leaned forward to find the butterfly pulsing inside. He reflexively extended his own hands. Then he began to feel the wings beat against his own flesh. For the longest time the two boys stood there, the hands of the brother in the hands of the friend, the hands of the friend in the hands of the brother, and there had been a silent agreement between them: her brother was passing her to him.

And what had he done instead?

The flowers in the box were the exact yellow shade of the butterfly, with the exact wingspan, and exact sheen. The man with the leather palms shut the lid of the box, and closed a half-fist around it. He extended both palms toward Ghafoor and Ghafoor cupped them in his.

FOUR

Hospitable Truths

I was feeling a little better.

As we prepared to leave, I found myself glancing frequently toward the tents. I noticed how shabby they were, each covered in a thin black sheet secured with sticks. The sheet flapped in the breeze and would surely leak in the rain.

Though I wanted another glimpse of the girl's mother, I feared it. She was young, younger than me, probably younger than Farhana. She must have borne her first child—the curly-haired boy who brought us the honey—in her early teens. *Her face.* So fierce, so proud. I wanted to talk to her. What I'd say I didn't know. But I'd developed an incapacity to do anything besides replay the angry glare she'd cast me twice, first when we headed to the lake with her daughter, then when I found the body first. It was absolutely the way I wanted to be looked at. *Damn you.* I wanted to hear it said in her voice.

Then I wanted her to like me.

Earlier today, after returning from the body to my tent, I looked for Irfan. I found him sleeping at the foothill where we'd lounged together while eating honey-dipped pears. He probably hadn't been sleeping much, and it was still early, but I shook him awake. I told him he had to go to the family, tell them I was sorry. He shoved me; it was very close to a punch. "Forgiving you is the last thing on anyone's mind, you fool."

A fool is absolutely what I wanted to be called.

I couldn't bear to look at Farhana. She couldn't bear to look at me. We were settling into the more bearable rhythm of avoiding each other. We were packing our things. At last, after days of listless shock, we had something to do. We threw ourselves into folding away Irfan's tent ("Let me do it," she snatched, eyes averted), zipping up his two sleeping bags ("Then let me do this," I pulled), ensuring the campsite was clean (both of us pacing, gathering imaginary peels and crumbs). Busywork, the mask of the socially impotent. Keep moving, away, except… where to?

We knew we had to head down the glacier back to our cabin to pack up from there and proceed—north or south? The question was growing fat. Many questions were growing even fatter. We waited for someone to make a decision, any decision, casting surreptitious glances at one another when we believed the other wasn't looking.

One thing was clear: the shores of the lake had grown very small. Our delay had drawn the mountains closer. They loomed over us, warning that no matter where we went, they could follow. And the tribes were also scorning us, though less surreptitiously. Of course they wanted us to leave. But they wouldn't say it, not to us, though I found out later that they'd said it to Irfan, and he'd had to ask them, much to his disgust, for time for me to heal. "As if you and Farhana hadn't exploited their hospitality enough."

Throughout our last day, as we packed—there was hardly anything *to* pack, but we kept the pace, the pace was key—Irfan met with Kiran's father, and they talked in low, rapid tones. I couldn't imagine what words Irfan could find. Green eyes, I thought. Eyes like enormous grapes. The mother's billowing shirt, ferocious glare, meticulously braided hair. *So young.* The baby's brown hand on the cold blue neck. She knew I hadn't wanted her there, in the boat. *Kola*, she said, daring me to take an interest, to know that I was making *her* feel like the intruder.

Somehow I found the courage to join Irfan.

Kiran's father tilted his head, now in a white turban, and folded his hands behind his back when he saw me. He had small brown eyes, a limp, and a gentle demeanor. He didn't appear angry or fierce but entirely depleted.

They were also leaving. To bury Kiran down in the plains. They'd migrated to the upper Kaghan Valley with their cattle in April, intending to stay through the summer before returning to the lowlands, where those who'd chosen a more settled way of life cultivated maize, potatoes, and beans. This had been the way for centuries. Their cattle needed to graze in these hills before returning to the plains for the long, merciless winter. But they were cutting the season short to return Kiran to her less transient home, near Balakot, where she'd been born, perhaps like her father Suleiman, and mother Maryam, and both her siblings. It would mean the cattle would starve over winter, or, equally troubling, that they'd spend the remaining summer crossing into fenced-off fields, costing the family hefty fines and possibly even confiscation. But Kiran had to rest.

The rapid murmurs between Irfan and Suleiman involved money. Suleiman's murmurs were lost to me, but there were more familiar sounds flowing from Irfan's tongue than I'd bothered to hear till now. I caught Urdu mixed with the Hindko-Gujri hybrid he'd so effectively been using since our arrival, and even a little English, for instance, "crop" and "full enough." My stomach clenched. Had Kiran understood Farhana and myself on the boat? She'd spent six summers here, around English-speaking visitors to the lake, like us. What had she heard? No, we'd spoken in code. She couldn't have comprehended us, even if we'd been speaking her very own tongue.

Irfan was saying that there could never be full enough. He was a Muslim, and understood very well that money could never make up for what had been lost. God was watching, and knew that he would sooner go hungry than presume to suggest otherwise. But the fact was, the family was going to suffer even worse in the coming years if their cattle died, or were confiscated. They had two remaining children to feed.

I understood enough of Suleiman's reply to know he was insisting God would guide them. He added that if needed, neighboring tribes were there to help. To which Irfan replied that the community was a wonderful source of strength, by the grace of Allah, but there was no harm in accepting help from him, Irfan, who was no stranger to this land. As Suleiman knew, from his many years here, Irfan honored and loved the valley and its people. (Irfan's voice cracked.) To which Suleiman replied by spitting. To which Irfan turned to me, his face red with rage, "Have you no shame? Leave us."

I wondered briefly why no one had crept into our tent the very first night, and killed either or both Farhana and me.

Her brother played the flute. Her sister dug in the dust with a stick, swaying her head from side to side. A boy from another tent joined them, lightly keeping beat on a tabla. He had only the left-hand drum. This was the boy drum, the bass. The right-hand drum—the girl, the one that dictates the melody—was missing. The heel of his left hand dug softly into the goatskin, cajoling, and the answer was deep and hollow, a swallowing, a sinking. A return to the water's depths. The brother blew through the bamboo bansuri as if in a prayer, or a kiss. The sister swayed. It was such a plaintive song, of such astonishing sweetness and hope and lasting farewell, that I bowed my head and wept.

There were tourists up here again, white-skinned and brown-skinned, filming.

On the glacier heading back down to our cabin, Irfan snarled, "If this had happened in America, you'd be in jail. If this had happened to the child of a landlord, you'd be in danger, and in debt." So that's why our lives had been spared: herders were disliked in this valley. They were considered outcasts. And now, so were we.

I scarcely noticed Wes and Farhana trudging ahead, or the jeeps skating by, or whether the bus that had fallen into the ravine the day before we made our way up had been removed. I noticed broken Coca-Cola bottles, biscuit wrappers, plastic bottle caps.

I didn't ask how the conversation between Suleiman and Irfan had ended. I didn't ask if money had been accepted. Or if, when Suleiman spat, he'd spat at me, or about me. I also didn't ask how damaging this entire sordid episode had been to Irfan's relationship with the valley and the communities he'd spent so much time with, bringing clean water to their towns. The question he'd spent most of his working life asking himself—*do they need it?*—had now been answered more brutally than even he might have foreseen. Knowing Irfan, he'd be blaming himself. I dared not speak to him.

Delicate negotiations, I thought. Years and years of delicate negotiations, to build a bedrock of trust. How easily it was spoiled.

An anger began to constrict my lungs.

There was a nagging thought, yes, I could only admit it now, walking back through the gray slush, our footprints ugly in the morning ice. I had no humor for snail-turd imagery, as on my way up. This fury inside me, it was far blacker and thicker than a snail or its turd. It nagged and nagged, though I tried to rub it off like a line of dirt, to tell myself it was only the movement of ice beneath my feet. And then it became a yellow-eyed fish, and I sat on that fish, I said to go down to the bottom of the lake and never again look up at the sun, or rise to the surface, for a sliver of air. But again it appeared, now a mean little fox, racing through the thickest sands of the shiftiest dunes, and I said to never disturb that sand, never kick up soft murky clouds, or shed a hair of that thick, furry tail.

Still my instructions went unheeded! This time it was a seagull, bobbing on a crest of a great, wide ocean, friendly and gay. Follow me! It said, with a flap of its wings. And it happened again, and again, till I had nowhere to hide.

The thought was this: *Did Farhana jump in?*

She was already in the boat when Irfan pulled me up. Did he pull *her* up? I hadn't had the chance to ask; I hadn't had the nerve. He might say no, she was already in the boat. That proved nothing. She could have hauled herself up. She had the strength. She was also cold and shivering that day… but how cold? How shivering? Was she as drenched as I? I couldn't remember. Knowing Irfan, that is hardly what he'd have noticed either. Wes? No. He wouldn't have seen. I remembered him pacing the beach, muttering something in agitation; no one was thinking clearly.

Irfan might also say that she was a woman: she didn't need to jump in. Just as she didn't need to be included in the decision to come to Kaghan—it had been for her sake, that's what mattered—she didn't need to risk her life. Had she tried, she could never have made a difference.

But she was a stronger swimmer than me. And it was her idea. Her damn return! She'd been warned to leave the girl alone. Instead, her meddling had drowned us all.

But so what if she was a stronger swimmer? Perhaps she didn't feel strong enough that day. Perhaps it was foolish of me to dive. I could have died. No one wants to die.

I'd fallen behind Irfan on the glacier; I now caught up with him. I asked, my voice shaking, "You have some idea how deep the lake is, don't you?"

He looked at me as though I'd walked into a mosque with slippers on.

"As deep as Lake Baikal," he eventually growled, adding, "that's in Russia."

"How deep is that?"

"Over a mile."

I waited, hoping he might add, *There's no way you could have found her*. Instead, he checked his damn phone. His way of shooing me away.

Why hadn't I seen Kiran when I dived? Had I waited too long? That horrible gurgling sound I heard in the water—how could I have heard it in the water? Where had I been? Where had Farhana been?

"In the weeks before coming here," I said to Irfan, catching up with him again, "Farhana started to change her mind. It had been her idea, yet she grew afraid. You know, because of all the bombings and the kidnappings. I started telling you that, you know, before it happened." I took a deep breath. "But by then, I was the one ready. She wanted me to call it off but I didn't want to. She'd already made the proposal so she wouldn't call it off herself. It was the same way she had doubts just before getting in the boat. Do you remember? It was her idea but then she grew afraid. Did you notice?"

The furrow between his brow sank like a chasm as he opened his mouth to speak. Then, changing his mind, he clamped his mouth shut. When the chasm lifted, he asked, "Did you notice the lake this morning?"

"Yes."

"What did you see?"

"Calm surface. Clear sky. Malika Parbat's twin peaks could have been etched in the water. As on that day."

He nodded. "A lake so clear and bright, but hideous underneath. For months after Zulekha's death—her murder" (I flinched at the word) "—this lake became a mirror of my own world. Then a voice started to tell me to look for a more hospitable truth. Not everything is as hideous as it doesn't seem. If I believed in God, I'd say the voice was His. I think it was the lake's."

Back at the cabin, we took solitary walks. We cloaked ourselves in shades of green, drinking forest smells. Even at night, I sought my camera. My landscapes of the River Kunhar were cool-headed, as if I'd been the third person in our tent.

Green eyes, green as the leaves of walnut trees, newly shed in the river, before turning black. Green as her bangles, and their incessant chiming.

I never did call my mother from Irfan's cell.

But I tried to take his advice. I devoted myself to reclothing us, Farhana and myself. I noticed she seemed to be doing the same. At night, we pecked each other quickly on the lips before lights out. When we met in daylight, she'd touch me on the thigh or on my back and the gesture was too deliberate, as if she were trying to recreate a lover she could touch. I'd do the same. I was glad when she followed Wes. She was glad when I followed Irfan. We created phantom foes—the lake, the jinn, the tourists—and phantom friends—each other, Wes, Irfan—but most of all, we created our own doubles. To these we assigned behavior, even roles.

I had dived repeatedly to look for Kiran. So had Farhana.

I had not given up. Neither had Farhana.

I had risked my own life. So had Farhana.

And the entire time, Irfan filled me in on the news. It was the only time he willingly talked to me. Apparently, there were real double agents in our midst, hunting real enemies. I couldn't have cared less.

I came to think of "him"—this mysterious killer and his double, the accomplice (accomplice to what exactly—a killing in Karachi? So long ago, so far away!)—as some kind of lynx and his shadow. He'd crept down the slopes of Kashmir, kicking up flecks of powdery snow, his footfall a hushed load of velvet, leaping across the crevices of glaciers that might have been growing or receding, this was Pakistan after all, and to a lynx it was all the same. Or he might be a snow leopard from Uzbekistan, lurking low into the new millennium, no longer Soviet or Russian but Central Asian, looking for a skin for his spots. Or a yeti from Tajikistan, slipping into Pakistan from the west, sweeping down to Chitral on a very long tail, before twisting east through Swat and into Kaghan. Or perhaps I was looking in the wrong direction entirely. Perhaps he'd come up from the south, through desert sands that hid airfields for days, a snake mangled by a cluster bomb, a pheasant dropped by a falcon.

What was it Irfan had said, that day he first told me about him? *That day*. Yes. The killer's link to this remote, peaceful valley was an accident of geography. *And accidents can happen anywhere.* I'd been watching Kiran in a magenta kameez walk up the hill to find her goat, Kola. Farhana had held her hand.

I took my camera to the closest town, the town of Naran. I learned that here he, the killer, was called Fareebi: the fraud, the shapeshifter. He was said to be hiding here to avoid suspicion, since all eyes were on the eastern border with Afghanistan. But Intelligence had tracked him—or was he tracking them?

At the store where I'd bought the Kashmiri shawl for Farhana, only five days ago, the shopkeeper unfolded a heap of shawls while a customer recited a local proverb. *Nature instructs every creature to shapeshift in case of danger*. Each shawl came in a dual pattern, with no clear front or back. The one I'd picked for Farhana had also been reversible. The customer rejected cloth after cloth, but he volunteered an opinion on the Karachi bombing. The death of seven Pakistanis and one Chinese man was revenge for the missile strikes in the killer's village.

I listened closely. Though the shapeshifter had sympathizers in Peshawar and Karachi, no one wanted him here, not even those angered by the missile attacks. What did the people of this valley have to do with it? No, he wasn't only tracking Intelligence but tracking them—the locals and their very way of life—this snow leopard, this snow leopard's jinn. And this false trail he was leaving, it was a deliberate distraction from some gargantuan avalanche about to hit those who weren't looking. The army rangers, Intelligence, and everyone else crawling along the valley's spine were fools for walking straight into the trap. Or else they were working together, to trap everyone else.

There was a cluster of men in the store now, all debating who was trapping whom, and none answered my greeting. I moved on. *A-salaam-o-aleikum*, I said, everywhere I went. No one answered. Geography may be an accident but no one in Pakistan ignores a greeting accidentally. I wasn't deaf, neither to the silence nor the whispers. "It's *him*." Of course they'd heard of Kiran's death. Of course their eyes were accusing, even if their words were delivered into each other's collars. But I never got used to it. It's *him*. Two words that sent my face igniting in shame. Two words that made me look over my shoulder, again and again, for *him*: the fraud, the shapeshifter. Two words that made me glad the herders had few friends. For otherwise, I would be dead.

I sought relief by immersing myself in the many murky legends of the valley. The one that preoccupied me most was the legend of Kagan, whose ancestry remained shrouded in secrecy.

Even if Kagan had been related to the pagan Kafir-Kalash tribe of Chitral Valley to the west, fact is, Kaghan Valley existed long before she was born. Before her arrival, the valley had been part of Hazara, whose history was a history of raids. Along the way, the story went, Hazara picked up more names than a pretty girl picks up suitors on her walk home from a well. Under Persian rule, Hazara doubled as Aroosa. Alexander of Macedonia pitched a plundered Aroosa to Raja Ambhi, who renamed her Abhisara. Abhisara next fell to Chandra Gupta, and then to his grandson Asoka. Upon converting to Buddhism, Asoka named the valley "Takht-e-Hazara," the throne of Hazara, and this must have been its name when Kagan arrived—from Chitral or the Caspian steppe or a fairy world—to wow the people with her beauty and black robes. Perhaps it was Asoka who graced the valley with her name. The details are lost. What remain are a cluster of sacred rocks from Asoka's day, though this may not be all.

According to Irfan, next to the Asokan rock edicts lay another holy site, a secret one. It was the site of a small cult of worshippers for whom Kagan belonged to another world, a world of animals and spirits. The only way to reach her was through the ancient practice of shamanism. They offered her lavish gifts and asked for her aid in keeping jealous jinns away from their homes, and their romances.

Though it was not possible to ask openly about the existence of the site, I could look for it. I took a bus down to Mansehra, near the site of the rocks, unsure how to begin. What did a secret pagan shrine look like? The bus had to pass Balakot, near where Kiran would now be buried, and her family would still be grieving. When we stopped in Balakot, I sloped into my seat. Thankfully, people got off but no one got on.

The Asokan edicts were engraved on three large boulders. I spent the afternoon photographing them, and the grove of blue pine and deodar trees on the stony slopes not far away. At the grove, I dug around discreetly, looking for evidence of goddess worship: burned incense; a small idol; flower petals. I found none. I walked back to the boulders for a last view of the edicts before heading back to Naran. That's when I noticed the children racing up the hill toward me. I hesitated. I continued photographing the rocks. The younger ones giggled, standing next to the rocks so they could also be in the frame. The older boys were more reserved. One of them, his head shaved and covered in a pristine white skull cap, whispered to another, in Urdu, so I could understand, though by now I'd know it in any tongue, "It's *him*."

I was surprised they'd heard about it even as far south as here, in Mansehra, which fell outside the valley.

The younger boy whispered back, "You mean Fareebi?"

And the older one replied, "No. I mean the killer."

I was considered even worse than the hotel bomber!

I turned around and headed back toward the bus stop. They followed me, a long line of boys, the older ones with hands behind their backs, the younger ones skipping ahead, brandishing sticks, their giggles turning malicious in the blood-red evening.

The bus was getting ready to leave. I raced toward it, only adding to my shame. The boys raced after me. With a chewed end of a pencil, the bus driver was twirling the tape back into a cassette; he didn't look up at the sound of the jeering crowd. As I stepped on the bus, a shadow slid just beyond the corner of my left eye. I paused, right foot on one step, left foot in the air. The specter slid between the boys: a green satin shalwar, a head of light tawny-blonde hair. As the head turned to face me, I ducked into the bus.

The next day, I stayed in the valley. I told no one what I'd seen the previous day, while hurrying onto the bus. *Her*, or someone like her. Someone who wore the same green pants. There was nothing special about the pants, and many girls had her hair color. It could also be that I was only imagining it. If I'd thought to photograph her—or it—specters do *not* have sex—the screen would have come up blank. Just as it had the night before we trekked to the lake. But *that* vision had been real… I had no idea where my thoughts were leading me and didn't particularly care to chase after them.

Does a man know when he begins to unravel?

I walked south to the next town, the town of Kaghan, where Kagan was believed to have died. Why did I care? I did not know. It was a long walk. It was the graves dotting the roadside between Naran and Kaghan that I had to see. I had to go there. I did not know why. If I had to find an explanation, I'd say it was a call. It was how I'd felt the night before heading to the lake, when I'd run beside the River Kunhar, and that wretched owl with the girl's face had cried *shreet!* I did not want to answer, yet I kept walking.

The graves were said to date from soon after the arrival of Islam, when the people converted willingly or by force, depending on whom you asked. There was a time when some might have said it was by force; not now. Nor would they risk acknowledging a pagan site. I felt their fear as I approached the graves. When I reached them, I saw immediately that the headstones were unlike any Islamic graves I'd seen. The first I came across had two birds joined by a floral wreath. The pattern resembled a peace sign, except the "doves" were more like ducks, with flat, wide beaks. There was a date, too faint to read. I passed a dozen others that were similar, with drawings better preserved than a date or a name. There were also headstones with horses—some arching beautifully toward the sky—pulling chariots of clearly defined wheels. Then came a whole series of headstones engraved with owls. Dozens of owls, some with wings in astonishing detail, others with heart-shaped faces intricately carved, the eyes large and fierce.

I took multiple shots of the graves. If the owls vanished from my screen, I'd know I was going insane. Irfan would help, if not with warm stones, then some other magic. Shouting, perhaps. Or a good punch.

Children found me here too. It was almost exactly a replay of yesterday. The younger ones giggled, following me around the headstones, pointing out others with owls. They caught on quickly that these interested me most. But the older boys, once again, stayed aloof. This time it was a boy without a cap and with hair about two days old who did the honors. "It's *him*."

I found myself feeling a little like a girl, and when I asked myself what this meant, I decided it meant hysterical. A growing panic bubbled up my gut and made me want to protest by flapping my hands and thrashing my head. I would have liked to be the size of these vicious children. I would have liked to be small and gay. I would have liked to lie on my back on one of the graves and kick my legs and scream. However, I did none of these things. The children followed me all the way down to the turn-off beyond which my cabin lay securely hidden in the thick palms of a walnut grove.

Their parents were no help. In the bazaar, the restaurant, the bus, even the damn road, eyes followed me long after I met them with my own. I was learning the full impact of the weight of those eyes. One moment they were heavy as clouds, the next, they moved through me like smoke. They could crush me and blow me away. They were a jury unto themselves, and would gladly have strung me from a telephone pole, if revenge on behalf of a herder had been worth it.

It was only me. Wes, Farhana, and Irfan were treated differently.

When children followed Wes, it was not to call him a killer. Nor to will him away. A white man, no matter how pale, is never see-through. Granted, he hadn't been in the boat. But he'd been with us: he was one of us. Yet, not to them. He casually distributed milk toffees and soggy chips and made them skip and squeal. Clearly, he'd come here to build schools.

If Wes was a guest-savior, Irfan was still a friend. I was glad for him—but, why *only* me? What about Farhana? She mostly stayed in the cabin, or walked around with Wes, beside whom she'd also be seen as a guest, perhaps even a guest's wife. Twice a guest! If not, she'd have said. She'd let it be known if people whispered, "It's *her*."

I, on the other hand, was neither guest nor savior nor friend nor wife. I was a murderer, prowling free across their turf.

One day I entered a glass and gem shop for ornaments to take back with me to Karachi for my sister, when I heard a customer ask the jeweler how "Maryam" was coping. Mysteriously, everyone around me now spoke in a tongue laced generously in Urdu. It didn't take me long to understand that the Maryam he meant was *the* Maryam: Kiran's mother. The jeweler answered that she was ill.

"Do not worry," replied the customer. "She will find how to live up to her name."

I decided on a different strategy. Instead of sloping away, I'd participate. In a manner I hoped was both casual and confident, I asked, "What do you mean, live up to her name?"

The man behind the counter began dusting a glass vase with

an old felt cloth. I waited. He turned his back to me, placing the vase gingerly on a shelf. The shelf was cramped; two glasses grazed each other. The sound gave me goosebumps. The customer and the jeweler began speaking in a language I could no longer understand.

I lifted a clump of pink topaz and cleared my throat. They continued not to acknowledge my presence in any way other than ignoring it. I asked for the price. I was quoted four times the number scratched on the tag. The quote was delivered to the felt cloth. Somehow I knew it would not do to bargain. I left the sum on the counter.

Back at the cabin, Irfan was waiting for me, with food. I assumed Farhana was with Wes, at the restaurant. Irfan was thawing toward me somewhat, possibly because his own treatment here hadn't soured too much.

"Eat." He watched me stare at the cubes of chicken tikka on my plate.

That did not stop me from staring at the cubes of chicken tikka on my plate.

He asked, for the millionth time, "Are you ready to leave?"

I shook my head.

"Where will we go," he persisted, "when you're ready? Back to Karachi?"

"Not now, Irfan."

"We have to decide. We have a booking up north that should be canc—"

"—I'm always running. Away. But not this time. I'm not avoiding it, the subject."

"What *is* the subject?"

"This time, I'm not running."

He sighed. "This time, maybe you should."

The next day, over another plate of cold food, he spoke in a tone more agitated than I'd heard from him yet. Much of what he said sounded like a distant call from somewhere silty and cold. There was heightened security in the valley, worse than before we'd left for the lake, hadn't I noticed? I couldn't think what to say. So he continued. Shia–Sunni riots had erupted in Gilgit district to the north, where we were heading, and Mansehra district to the south, close to where I was "merrily" taking the bus each day and night like a mad man. Again he waited for a response. Again I could think of none. It was especially bad near the town of Balakot—

Now I interrupted him. "Isn't that where Kiran's family's from?"

"They're not *from* anywhere. They're nomads. But, yes, they make a winter home near Balakot, near Syed Ahmad Barelvi's shrine, where his devotees are setting up training camps. Men from the camps harass the villagers, trying to recruit their sons." He paused. "It isn't safe." He threw up his hands. For Irfan, this was akin to smashing a chair. "The Karachi bomber and his accomplice are just a pretext for both sides, the militants and the government." He paused again. "Don't you understand? We carry a heavy responsibility, traveling with them." He nudged his chin in the direction of the wall between our cabin and theirs.

"She wants to return," I stated flatly, while he stared at me in disbelief.

"We'll need an armed escort," he said at last.

I shrugged.

"This isn't what we'd planned."

"I know."

"Something happens to them, international fiasco."

"I know."

"Something happens to us, so what."

"I know."

Never was a wind between teeth more exasperated.

I walked alone in the valley, aware of being shadowed, hearing whispers before they were spoken, ducking stares before they were launched. Twice I tripped over myself when a green shalwar slid along a wall. Once I saw her chubby toes, a brown stalk caught in a toe ring. I heard her bangles. I heard the goat bells too. I clicked my camera. Nothing. At least the owls on the headstones were there, in my viewfinder, as proof. Proof of what? Perhaps only this: they existed. Ergo, I couldn't be losing my mind. Or: they existed. Ergo, so did the green shalwar and the toe ring. Ergo, I *was* losing my mind.

At night I put a pillow over my head, and mostly lay awake. I assumed Farhana did too.

Irfan continued insisting a verdict had to be reached, and now Wes joined in too: were we to go on with our journey to the Northern Areas, or call it off? It was a decision Farhana and I had to make together. The problem was, we couldn't *be* together. Even looking at her caused me pain. Once or twice, we snapped at each other—*I said I'm not hungry! I said I don't know if I want to stay or leave!*—before withdrawing swiftly into our separate gloom. This was the only way to scrape off the pain. Snarling and retreating. It left us momentarily relieved, until we discovered ourselves erupting in a rash of rawness, followed by more pain, and the desire to scratch with increasing malice.

Many times, I asked myself, What *is* the pain? The pain of losing the girl, losing face, or—losing Farhana?

And then one night we did not retreat.

I'd come back to the cabin after taking the bus to Balakot to see Maryam. I learned through Irfan that the herders took their cattle to the forest nearby, to graze. I had no other plan besides walking into the forest to find her. I rode all the way there and all the way back without getting off the bus. Terrified of seeing her, I did it a second time. I rode all the way and back, my legs again refusing to move. It was cold and I was hungry. When I finally staggered back to the cabin, I tried to recall the poetry the darkness had evoked for me the night before we set out for the lake. I returned to the river, looking for the moon, and even a damn bird. Instead, I was almost attacked by dogs. I threw pebbles at canines all the way to the cabin. I knocked my toe against something. A carcass, a gun. I opened the door. Farhana was sprawled on the bed, naked from the hip down. Her face was turned away from the door. She wasn't breathing. She'd taken her own life! I rushed forward. She raised her left foot to scratch a mosquito bite on her right calf. The gesture enraged me. I'd thought her *dead* while all she did was *rest*! And what if someone else had walked into the cabin instead? It wasn't even locked!

And so it started, a himalaya of rage, our bodies exhausted with the effort of holding it back, stone by excruciating stone. I don't know exactly how it began. I don't know who said what, or in what sequence. But I do remember watching her lie there—I remember her legs and how, in the midst of my outrage, they triggered a memory, a happy memory, an extraordinarily happy memory—since when did fury come layered in honey?—and the next thing I know, I was saying:

"And do you really want me to say this. *Do you really want me to say it?* You were the one who started coming on to me!"

"Oh, so I'm not supposed to speak, while you can slobber over me any time you want!"

"When have I ever slobbered over you?"

"Ha!" She leaped off the bed. "At least I was *nice* to her. You didn't even talk to her. You acted like she wasn't even there!"

"Nice to her? *Nice?* Forcing her into the boat was nice?"

"She *wanted* to."

"Are you blind? Didn't you notice the way she sat in the boat? She hated it! She even said so! And didn't you notice her poor mother? Do you even know her name?"

"What has that got to do with it?"

"Everything! It has *everything* to do with it! You forced her mother. Maryam. That's her name. You forced her."

"Maryam. Thank you."

"And you forced her daughter—"

"Kiran."

"*I* was the one who said we should go back and drop her off."

"*Drop her off* is exactly right. She was a burden. You make everyone feel they're a burden."

"Oh, don't start."

"Oh, why not?"

"Because this isn't about you, Farhana. It's about someone else. *Someone dead*."

"It wasn't even my idea to come here! It was yours. And that friend of yours!"

"You *didn't* want to come to this valley but the girl *did* want to get in the boat?"

"That's right!"

"Well, it was your idea to come to your country. Are you having a nice *return*?"

She threw all the pillows off the bed.

I left.

"It isn't about you either," she'd say, in the middle of the night. And I'd pretend not to hear.

The sun had still not risen when we were both out of bed and I was saying:

"It's a question of finesse. *Finesse*! You do *not* barge into a place thinking you can fix it. Who are you? Who *are* you? What makes you think you can do that?"

She was sobbing. She was in the same shirt. I could still see her bush. "I didn't barge in. And for the hundredth time, it was Irfan's decision to come here. Neither of you deigned to even ask me."

"Irfan made the decision for you, but you made the decision for the girl. Who were you to make that decision?"

"At least I asked! I asked her family!"

"They couldn't refuse. You call that asking?"

"The girl wanted to come. She was just too shy to show it."

"You'll say anything to cover your guilt."

"*My* guilt?"

"Everyone's blaming me. In the market. Even outside the valley, in Mansehra. They call me the killer."

"They probably do the same with me."

"Probably? *Probably?*"

She blew her nose. "Everything would have been fine if you hadn't turned the boat around so fast."

"That's right! You're blameless!"

"We need to stop this."

But now I could not stop, not with the crown of the avalanche about to drop.

"Did you even jump in the water?"

"Oh God! You look *insane*."

"I need to know. You're the better swimmer. I learned to swim in a pool in Karachi, for heaven's sake. You learned in the sea. Did you jump in?"

"*Yes*."

"When? How long did you wait after I'd jumped?"

She slumped heavily onto the edge of the bed, her back to me. She started sobbing again. "I had her in my arms."

Six words that made the edge of the table where we'd had breakfast, all four of us, the morning of the accident, it was an accident, reel.

When I looked up, I was saying, "What do you mean, you had her in your arms?"

"Just that. I jumped, she clung to me. It was so fucking cold, Nadir. And she was *heavy*. She looked tiny. She wasn't. Her will to live wasn't tiny. It was huge. And it weighed a ton. She was pulling me down with her. Would you rather I hadn't let go?"

I couldn't understand what she was saying. Even if she had jumped, it would have been after me, and if I hadn't even seen Kiran, how could Farhana have caught her? "How could you have had her in your arms?"

"You said yourself. I'm a better swimmer than you."

"I jumped before you. If I didn't find her, how did you?"

"Because, Nadir, you were swimming away from us."

"I remember seeing fish. I remember how murky it was. But I don't remember seeing her."

"Did you not hear what I said? *You were swimming away from us.*"

The memory triggered by first seeing her sprawled across the bed, her thick muscular legs bare before me, was an extraordinarily happy one.

It was a memory from the honeymoon period after I was stabbed. It was a memory of her legs. Those steep legs, built by steepness. The slender ankles slanting up to her tennis ball calves. It had made my heart stop, that first time, when the slant was the braid across her back; it did the same the afternoon I shot those black and white photographs. How bright her muscles bulged, against our dark sheets, as we created our own *Male and Female Figures in Motion*.

Months later she lay across a bed in a cabin in Kaghan, and it was the sheets that bulged, her legs flat in shadow.

I'd seen the medals lining her shelves in her purple house in the Mission. She could ski, swim, dive, and even run better than me.

It was there—in the way her legs now receded in the dark, listless, asexual—that I felt the rawness of our every verbal assault, as if we were trying to scrub each other away with an increasingly astringent soap that broke in furious fists, leaving us more bloody, more exposed. I'd stepped into her shadow; she'd stepped into mine. Somewhere along the way, this war with a spook had become forever.

That day, and the next, Wes and Irfan didn't disturb us. Wes and Farhana were meant to check in with their boss about their work's progress, either by phone or fax, if possible. I found out later that when Wes called his boss from Naran, it was to tell him that there'd been a delay. His explanation? *There's been a bomb blast.*

"What do you mean by accusing me of swimming away?"

"I've had enough. I'm going next door to stay with Wes. Irfan can come here."

Oh, she was clever. "As usual, you haven't answered the question."

"As usual, you're avoiding the right one. Should I tell you what to ask? Why don't you ask what made *you* get in the boat?"

"You wanted me to."

"No, it was what Irfan said. Don't you remember? *If Wes says it's safe.*"

"I suggested taking a long walk instead."

"So why didn't we?"

"Because you said you wanted to go in the boat! Wes has nothing to do with it."

"Don't deny that you were trying to prove something to him—"

"I was trying to prove something to *you*—"

"—that you've been jealous of him ever since we got here. From even before we got here. Since the day he practically saved your life!"

"*What*?"

"Will you deny that too?"

"The wound was shallow, Farhana. It barely pierced my—whatever it's called!"

"Peritoneal cavity," she swiveled around on the bed to face me and the light streaming through the window—the sun was clearly up now—legs crossed, arms crossed. She swung those legs, suddenly amused.

"I've said it before. You want me to say it again, I will. You could have easily called an ambulance instead. They'd have *saved* me."

She started laughing.

"It's Irfan who saved me, you know. Twice. First by sending money. A second time by pulling me out of the lake. A third if you count how he warmed me, with stones."

She fell backward on the bed, laughing loudly. Her shirt was yanked up to her waist. Sunlight played across her crotch. "Well, he can come and stay with you here and warm you some more!"

She was so damn pleased with herself. "But before you fuck him, maybe you should fuck me!"

I aimed my words below the belt. "Who would *want* to fuck you?"

Farhana rose from the bed, pulling her shirt down. She packed in silence. She got dressed away from my eyes, in the bathroom, the door shut. (We seldom shut the door, even when pissing.) I followed her out to the adjoining cabin, though I didn't know why. Irfan was out. Wes, in. He was shirtless and reading *Flashman in the Great Game*. If he saw me standing behind her, he didn't show it. He wrapped a comforting arm around her shoulders, murmuring, "You all right?" as he shut the door.

I returned to our cabin. It was still ours. It echoed with the cruelest two accusations made.

Who would *want* to fuck you?

Nadir, you were swimming away from us.

Or,

Nadir, you were swimming away from us.

Who would *want* to fuck you?

I sat still for a long time. Really, which was worse?

Two months before we left—it was a sullen day in May, even in the Mission—I overheard her on the phone. I seemed to have come in at the end.

"… it boils down to. One person in the mood when the other isn't?"

There was a pause while, I assumed, the listener spoke. Farhana shook her head. "I'm not only talking about sex. Sex is just a metaphor."

I expected her to elaborate. A long silence instead.

Finally, she exhaled, "Yep, that's what I mean, uh-huh."

What did she mean?

"I mean, that day on the beach."

Now I feared I could guess.

It hadn't happened often but, often enough. Okay, increasingly often. Her wanting it while I didn't. It had happened the other way more. It had happened the other way most of my life. Like a forgiving puppy, I bounced back at the merest hint of encouragement. Until recently.

She was saying, "I know, nothing worse than letting go just to fall on your face. Though letting him decide, you know, what's hot, maybe that's worse." Silence. "Sure, I have, many times." Silence. "Uh-uh." Silence. "No. He doesn't."

I don't what? And then panic: it *was* me she meant?

"Wes? Oh sure, yeah. It bothers him a lot."

What?

I slammed the door. The door to the house with the five-sided bay window where she now spent more time with her laptop, searching for frightening headlines to text back to me. The door in the alcove where the gold rings of the columns now looked prosthetic, like gold teeth on a poor man from Tajikistan.

Why wasn't I aroused by her lately?

Our departure was just weeks away. Ours. We had our tickets. Our maps. Our separate allies, Wes and Irfan. If she wanted me to cancel, there was no chance of it. I was increasingly excited about what I'd do in northern Pakistan, with or without her, and this had renewed interest in my work. Nor would she agree to watch me leave without her. There was not going to be a *without*, no matter how many bombs were dropped or bombers martyred, not after working all year to claim a *with*. We were going. We both knew it. We saw it clearly in the shadow in our bed.

I bought a brand new Nikon digital, a 300mm lens, and a 20mm extension tube. I photographed small fry. The rainbow in a dragonfly wing. A single California poppy. Farhana's nipple.

I suppose the image of the magnified nipple and the blurred contours of the breast preoccupied me more than she did, but then, she was already preoccupied. Always on the phone, always talking about him, her work, her return, her anxiety about her return. Her breasts.

She liked me photographing them. Breasts that had begun to stir me only in the frame. At least I didn't get off on images of other women.

That day on the beach? It excited her, seeing herself magnified. And color-filtered. Image pre-processing, not to be confused with post-processing, to enhance maximum photorealism. To make the infeasible feasible. She lay on her stomach; I drizzled sand on the mound of her buttocks. It cascaded down her curves, featherlike, matching her skin tone. When we viewed the images together, the texture of the sandspill on her flesh made her wet. We were nestled between the same cluster of rocks where I'd found her the first time, on the far side of the cypress grove. There were others around, though none in our nest, or so we thought. She rolled back onto her stomach, raised her hips high into my groin. The sand scrubbed my erection. I heard the figure behind me, his breathing. I could feel it on my neck. I assumed she mistook it for mine or would have stopped. There was no way she could have seen his shadow on her spine.

Later, we both lay on our stomachs a long time. When we eventually got dressed, we didn't speak. *He came when I did.* She couldn't have noticed.

Now I looked in the viewfinder of my camera. I'd kept the photos of the weeks before we'd left, including that morning on Baker Beach. There were several shots of her—muted backgrounds, magnified nipples. I hadn't needed them since coming to this country, where secrecy seems to play the same role.

At lunchtime, I heard Wes and Farhana leave the adjoining cabin, presumably for the restaurant. I stayed inside. I hadn't slept in a long time. We'd been arguing for two days, almost without cease. I shut my eyes.

Nadir, you were swimming away from us.

I hadn't stopped seeing her, since that time at the bus stop. Sometimes she shrank into a distant, stamp-size image, as though I were looking through the gap in the front row of her teeth. A tiny girl in magenta and green, stick in hand, climbing a hill, chasing a black goat. But always, when she descended, the playback was at the wrong speed. Her movements grew rapid and jerky, trapped in a silent movie. Whoever shot that film had grossly undercranked it. The goat bounced like an epileptic, and Kiran shuddered backward and forward on the hill in the frame made by the gap between her teeth.

In this way, Kiran was my past.

Other times, I was looking at her from above, through a camera in an unmanned plane, and Kiran appeared in a burst of grainy images. Getting in the boat, hunkering in her seat, folding her hands nervously in her lap while heavy bracelets rolled down her wrists. Her movements slower now, her shape elongated.

In this way, Kiran was my present.

Or I was looking at her through a series of gaps, all cut into a cylinder, and she had not shrunk, rather, I was a mouse peering into a giant zoetrope. Her mother twirled nearby, black sleeves rimmed in pink thread, bangles sliding as her arm rose in objection. Ob-jection, OB-JECTION! When the cylinder spun, Kiran's bangles as she fidgeted in the boat and Maryam's bangles as she gesticulated in fury were in absolute synchronicity.

In this way, Kiran was my future.

I hadn't forgotten how her mother's shadow crossed mine in the sand, next to Kiran's corpse. Sometimes, as I slept, Maryam appeared in my room, throwing her image against mine. Sometimes it would become Kiran, her discolored face breathing on my pillow, wet hair tickling my cheek. And she'd touch my cold neck the way her baby sister had done, brown on blue.

I saw them, constantly, yet what I still could never see was my dive. I couldn't see myself make the jump. One minute I was in the boat, the next, in the lake. And the next, the boat was very far away. How to find the gap? I tried to recreate the scene at different speeds:

Kiran skidding with her left foot and falling backward. Kiran hitting the side of the tipping boat. Farhana screaming "Sit down!"

Farhana not reaching for the girl. Farhana trying to balance the boat instead. While I had done—what? Where was I?

Kiran skidding rolling backward hitting boat Farhana screaming Farhana leaning into boat and me—*and me?*

I was a slit in my memory through which I could see absolutely nothing.

KiranhittinghipcrackFarhanapullingboatbackKiransplash-Nadirnil.

And what about that rattle? Where was I when I heard it? Whose was it—Farhana's? Did she, in fact, dive first, as I waited safely on board? Had she been too kind to tell me this? Was the rattle the sound of her swallowing silt, risking being buried alive as the girl pulled her down?

Next I am shooting like a projectile down to the bottom of the lake. Terrible pain in my legs, the water so cold, and that sensation, the one of an eel locking itself around my spine. Kicking my way back up. Keep kicking. But by then, the boat is barely visible. Dive again, into a rain of sand. No Farhana. No Kiran. Just a fish. Large, too large. What is that fish? Floating away from me, a broad shadow, murky, oddly shaped, a misshape in the midst of an underwater avalanche.

And then I am touching the bottom of the boat. Circling it as the fish circle me. These *are* fish. Not misshapes. Their yellow eyes examine me. Eyes with weight. A swarm of eyes, surrounding me the way eyes now surround me on land. The feeling that if I linger too long, the watching will grow mean. The fear of not knowing when. And which. The large white one with the gray brow or the smaller one, with the gray teeth?

I am still circling the boat, listening to a keening above, watching those eyes enclose me, when a wave of fresh ice water hits me. I press the boat's hull with my palm. And listen. That misshape, floating near me in the water for barely a second. That was not a fish. What was it? Kiran? In arm's reach—*my arm's reach?*

A second wave of water hit me.

It was Irfan, in my cabin, throwing cold water in my face.

He was saying something, but I couldn't hear it. I wasn't ready to get back into the boat. I squeezed my eyes. I kept rubbing the skin of the hull into my flesh.

He threw a third cup of water in my face.

The boat began to recede. Instead of swimming toward it, I was swimming away, toward Irfan in the bathroom. He was filling the cup and running back to hit me again.

I shot out of reach just in time. "I *need* to go back there. I *need* to know. What if the too-large fish was Kiran?"

He blinked, meanly. Then he slapped my cheek.

If I hadn't swum away, if I'd helped Farhana as she held her, *if* she held her ...

"Are we continuing north or heading back?" Irfan was shouting. "I'm sick of waiting. If you won't decide, I will."

He pulled me out the door and pushed us both into the adjoining cabin without knocking on their door and repeated whatever it was he was trying to say.

More importantly: Farhana and Wes were seated neatly at a table, playing Scrabble. She didn't look up. She joined *amply* to *messy*. I was keenly aware of having to resist upending the board.

Wes made *search* and scored triple.

Irfan began to talk. He wanted to cancel the trip. "It isn't classy to go on."

"Why not?" asked Farhana, still not looking up. She had shitty tiles.

"It would be diminishing the weight of what has happened." He addressed her back, daring it to say what else could go wrong, for which he'd have to apologize.

Farhana joined *limb* to *amply*. *B* on double letter. "Sounds like you've decided."

Irfan looked at Wes. Wes said, "We've come this far. We go on." I couldn't help recalling that in Karachi he'd wanted to return to San Francisco.

Irfan looked at me. "I agree with Wes," I said, suddenly sure of what I was about to say. "I want to continue." I moved away from the table. I'd go on by myself if I had to.

Shaking his head, Irfan pushed me out the cabin with even more force than he'd pulled me in, slamming the door behind him.

"Careful, the cabins are old."

He didn't slap me again. "Did you not hear me the other day? It isn't safe."

"I heard you."

We stared at each other, daring the other to speak. In the past, I would have given in first. Now I didn't care.

He finally announced, "I need to return to Karachi and not go on to Gilgit and Hunza because it's the right thing to do, the safe thing to do, and—" he couldn't meet my eye now "—for other, personal reasons."

Perhaps I should have looked more closely then. Instead, I shrugged. "Okay."

He seemed surprised. "Okay? So, you will back me when I tell them the plan?"

"Yes." I kicked the dirt.

He opened the door.

"You could try knocking," Farhana said, still not turning around to look at us.

"Nadir has something to tell you," said Irfan.

"We're going," I said.

Irfan swung his neck like a dagger. *This isn't what we'd agreed.*

I didn't swing my neck in return. I was breaking my promise to him. I didn't care.

Irfan cleared his throat. I could feel him reaching for the right words, the right tone. "I may not be able to keep taking responsibility for you," he said to the room in general.

"Who's asking you to take responsibility?" asked Farhana, rearranging her tiles.

Irfan stood angrily at her back.

I explained to Wes and Farhana all that Irfan had taken responsibility for: Kiran's death; forging a truce with her family (I still didn't know how); our safety.

Farhana kept playing with her tiles.

"Nevertheless, I feel it would be a mistake to retreat," I continued. "But we should all agree to no longer expect Irfan to step up for any of us."

Farhana's fingers fluttered over her tiles as she cried "Oh!" All seven letters. *Traffic.* "I knew I took the blank for a reason!"

"Farrah," said Wes. "Maybe we should think more about this."

"It's your turn," she replied, not even looking up for him.

"There's worse trouble in the valley." Irfan saw an opening. "It's made people here—jumpy. And the death of the girl hasn't helped our popularity. Even if she is only a Gujjar girl. Was. We shouldn't stay or go on. We should head back."

Wes pushed his tiles away as he repeated, "What kind of worse trouble?"

Irfan told him about the training camps near Balakot. Was it me, or did I sense a little victory there, as though Irfan was pleased to deliver this final piece of rotten news? When he was finished, Wes asked glumly, "Who was Syed Ahmad Barelvi?"

"A martyr. He once called for jihad against the British. Now his supporters use his memory to cry for another jihad."

The air thickened. Was this fear I sensed in Wes? Well!

"There's an 8:00 a.m. bus to Abbottabad," Irfan continued rapidly. "From there we can take the connection to Islamabad. There's a flight to Karachi the next night. The same way we came."

"Once again," said Farhana, "you decide."

"Didn't you already say that?" Irfan snapped.

"Of course we leave!" Wes pushed his tiles away. "It's a no-brainer."

Farhana answered me, at last. "We go on."

"You're all nuts!" Wes overturned the Scrabble board for me. "How about you and I go back," he looked at Irfan, "and let these two go on?"

"We had an agreement." Farhana looked at Wes.

What agreement?

So did we. Irfan looked at me.

"Then it's decided," I said, bolting toward the door before Farhana changed her mind, and more agreements could be made.

In our cabin, Farhana's and mine, Irfan was sullen while unbuttoning his shirt. He said, "You and Farhana could fight your battle back in America."

"You don't have to come with us." It sounded like I was trying to get rid of him, when in fact I knew we needed him.

He knew too. He didn't bother answering me. Though no one said so, some of us at least seemed to hold to the belief that we all went forward or all went back. We had long ago ceased being mere friends. We were accomplices.

I watched him arrange his shirt on a hanger, then drape his jeans over a chair. Next, a fresh pair of socks, fresh underpants, and a pair of leather shoes. Joggers were only for trekking. He was always the most dapper man I'd known, second only to my father, who polished his shoes every night in slow, deliberate movements that were almost relaxed. The last time I was here, with Irfan's wife, there was no electricity in any hotel in Naran. To impress Zulekha, he'd taken all our clothes to the one laundry place in town, where the Khan had a coal iron. While the Khan put burning coals in the iron and waited for it to heat before painstakingly smoothening every wrinkle from our shirts and Zulekha's shalwars, kameezes, and especially her dupattas, Irfan and I stood by patiently, till one of us offered to get the other a boiled egg sprinkled with salt and pepper.

He had his own travel iron now. He was the only one of the three men in the group who shaved daily, keeping his beard clipped just so. There must have been shoe polish somewhere in his bag. Yet, apparently, even his fastidiousness had its limits. Irfan climbed into bed in his underpants without brushing his teeth.

But I smelled soap on him. I couldn't remember the last time I'd showered.

He checked his cell phone then switched off the lamp on his side of the bed. "We should avoid Kohistan and head northeast, with an armed escort. Everyone is being checked, and I'm not even sure who they're checking for. You've been so busy with your private battle I don't know if you've even noticed the nervousness of people here."

He was repeating himself. I let him.

"They don't know who's who, spies or militants," he jabbered on. "And who's working for who—America, Pakistan, or India. Or someone else we don't even suspect."

"You seem more nervous than anyone else," I said. Spies or militants, murderers or lovers, what difference did it make?

"You know Wes called his boss to say his work was delayed because there'd been a bomb blast? He was right. You and Farhana were generating that much smoke."

I had to laugh at that.

After a while, I said, "I need to ask you something."

"I'm listening."

"When you and the girl's brother came to get us, was Farhana in our boat?"

"Of course."

"Was she—wet. You know, as if she'd been in the lake?"

I could hear him turn in the dark. "She was shivering, yes. I didn't look at her that closely. She had to be wrapped in blankets too, but I don't think she fell in the lake. Her temperature didn't drop like yours. Why?"

"Do you think she dived?"

"To look for the girl? What would have been the point? She could never have saved her. Now, if I'd been on your boat."

I decided not to argue with him.

He reached over in the dark and scratched my head. "Sleep."

He was taking my betrayal of him remarkably well.

"Tell me more about her," I ventured.

"Who?"

"The girl. Her family."

I heard him shift again. "No one knows where they came from. Even they can only agree with each other on three things. They were always wanderers. They were once horsemen. They are still considered outsiders."

I listened to Irfan in the dark, grateful for the distraction. He spoke for a long time, uninterrupted, and after he fell asleep, I pulled on my jeans, laced up my shoes.

"Stay away from owls," he mumbled into his pillow, as I shut the door behind me.

I walked repeating his words in my head.

Eventually, a few tribes had lost their horses and, to some extent, their wandering lifestyle, while others retained both. On four legs or two, Gujjars had always been pushed out of grazing grounds by those who came before or after. Yet they'd managed to keep grazing in this valley, and in parts of Kashmir. And somehow, through time and distance, they kept in intimate contact with each other.

I knew where my legs were carrying me. It would be my last night in Kaghan, perhaps ever. I believed myself prepared for the ghosts I'd find. My head was clear. I felt calm, the way I normally felt on my nightly walks, the way I hadn't felt since the accident—no, I'd stop calling it that. I would call it a murder.

I reached the graves. There they were again, the ones engraved with owls, ducks, and horses. I shone my flashlight on the headstone that had caught my attention earlier, the one of three horses pulling a chariot, necks curved upward, toward the sky. Now I noticed others with chariot wheels, the wheels perhaps symbols of permanence, representing those tribes that had partially settled. And perhaps the ducks joined with floral wreaths represented the harmony between the different tribes, those who remained nomadic and those who became sedentary. No one had told me this; I was only guessing. But I did know that the two needed each other, those who moved and those who stayed. They formed a political system of co-tribes, together deciding on the limits of their pastures and forming ways of guarding against encroaching tribes, such as the Sawati Afghans, with whom the Gujjars of this valley had tense relations. The more stable group was the protector. The more nomadic group was the producer. And the two formed alliances through marriage.

Such as Maryam's.

Irfan believed that Maryam's family was from the protector group. They'd become laborers, merchants, and soldiers, with some migrating south to the cities, others to the town of Naran, perhaps like the jeweler at whose shop I'd been overcharged for topaz. In contrast, the family of Maryam's husband, Suleiman, were the producers. They continued to roam the Kaghan Valley as grazers, with little engagement in the world of commerce or defense. And so, while his family kept hers fed, her family kept his alive.

"They have a private system of justice," Irfan had said. "Nothing to do with the state. The state couldn't care less about them." After a few moments, he'd added, "They have no land, no nation. If you'd killed a child of the nation, well, you already know."

I'd listened in the dark, the air in the cabin slowly diminishing.

"It's her family, who are less low to the ground, that demanded compensation for Kiran's death," he'd continued. "His family are lowly herders. They asked for nothing."

I hadn't asked what the compensation was. It would doubtless involve money, putting me twice in Irfan's debt. I still hadn't returned my rent money.

Now I turned my attention back to the headstone with the three horses. I was not unaware of the presence at my back. I had heard footsteps. I had also heard whispers. I was not imagining it. I did not shine my flashlight behind me, but straight ahead, at the grave with the horses.

The arc of those necks arrested me. Three crescents on a rock, perfectly aligned. Together, they exposed to the world the most vulnerable part of themselves, inviting judgment. No, seeking it. It seemed to me, as I crouched in the dark, my hand shaking, the light-beam fading (why hadn't I changed the battery?), that the owls on the headstones were the jury. In contrast, the ducks, carved in profile (unlike the owls, who stared full in your face) with wings beating impatiently, played the role of neutral spectators. Their indifference was not unkind; they might represent absolutely nothing other than the random strokes of a playful mind and a long-forgotten hand. Or else, if one had been placed there on purpose, in all his flapping, noiseless glory as he looked down the barrel of those arcing necks, sleek and defenseless, surely it was to serve as a gentle reminder of a need for mercy.

Queen of the Mountains: The Whisper Chain

Maryam kept her back to him.

He was here, at last, the one who had left her a blue feather in her mountain shrine. The garlic breather and honey carrier. The one who once told her there was a land outside land, outside mountains, even. Now he was back, in her home in the plains, laden with stories, as when she was a child.

His voice was low and it was sweet. "You remember you used to ask from where the snow came? From where the river first flowed? You wanted to see the farthest away river, above the glaciers. And I would say this was asking to see heaven."

He was waiting for a response but she kept her back to him. Sometimes it was desirable to put a mountain between yourself and someone else.

"Well," he continued. "I have seen it. Heaven is in the steppe, where there live nomads like us, with names like ours, but with sounds added on, and, unlike us, they live free."

"What sounds?"

"The ones you used to think were funny."

She still did not turn to face him but she could never forget these oddities about him, from the signs to the jade—white jade did *not* bring calm, she would have to tell him now—to the flute, and his many attempts at changing his own name. Russifying, he called it. For instance, Rahman became Rakhmon or Rahminov or Rakhmanov.

"But you are not Rahman," she would say.

"But I *could* be. And now I'm Rakhmanov."

Another time he was Yousuf and his name was changed to Yusupov.

"Yusupov!" she giggled.

"Yusupov," he repeated. "Of Yousuf." He said they followed Islam, up in the steppe, where the Gujjars once came down from. But their alphabet had no "h." So they did not say Mohammad.

"What do they say?"

"Mamedov. Or even, *Mama.*"

She was horrified and grew angry with him for taking the Prophet's name in jest.

"But it's the truth!"

So now he was spending more time up there, amongst a people without the letter h. From there he had come to her, with stories to chase away her fever dream and return her to this earth.

He said he had also been to a place called Leninabad and a place called Chinistan, where he made friends who gave him jade in return for leather. Better quality jade than he had traded for in the past—except that once. He cleared his throat, and she could feel his eyes at her back, searching for a way to find the stone around her neck. She said nothing. He started talking again. They drank mare's milk and ate horse flesh, these new friends. He could drink the milk but not even taste the flesh of the animals so beloved to their tribe. He stuck to mutton and duck.

Maryam's only idea of a duck was from the graves lining the road between Balakot and Naran. She did not want to think about graves.

He told her about flowers. She listened more closely.

"They have rare cloth, embroidered with flowers. This part of a flower. Look."

He leaned over her reclining body, and dropped in her half-open fist a yellow flower. It was larger than her hand and he was pointing to its center, with his own hand, the hand from which she had once licked a honey tinged with garlic from his sweat. A hand darker than she remembered. The heart of the flower was the color of fire. From within the fire grew a cluster of silken threads, each tipped with a pale green bud. When she brushed the buds, she brushed his palm. A hundred pollen grains fell onto their flesh. Into the flower's heart would dive a bee, she knew, for she had watched this happen many times, though never to a flower such as this. The bee would carry pollen on its fur, and from the pollen would come honey, and from the honey would come bliss.

The Uyghur, he was telling her, as though their hands had not touched, had at one time sewn those glistening threads in the heart of the flower into their cotton garments.

She wanted to taste the pollen on her skin. She could not bring herself to do this while he watched. He had stopped talking, but she could hear him breathe. Then, in a whisper as weightless as the gold spores: "The Kazakh nomads have a saying. Everything alive is in movement and everything that moves is alive. Wind and water, flowers and bees." He paused again. "You must learn to move again, Maryam. Kiran has already found a way."

When he left, she pressed the tip of her tongue to the tip of her index finger.

In the morning, she offered rice to the idol in her hidden lowland shrine, the shrine which did not cup her like the one in the mountains, nor hold any of the drawings that so captured her imagination, but which, in better times, her mother would decorate with ram horns and a yak tail.

She crouched in this shrine, which offered barely enough room to dream in, remembering how she had covered it in haste this April, in her hurry to leave for the mountains. She had not uncovered it till now. She was not *meant* to uncover it till September, when her people were *meant* to return. And now it was too late to properly cleanse her home, the way she was *meant* to have cleansed it in the spring. No one waved smoking juniper branches through sacred corners in July. So she stooped, thinking.

Down here in the plains, she needed strength. She needed armor against the sedentary people of this valley, among them those who had attended Kiran's funeral rites merely to see if they were Islamic. If only they were still on the move, up in the highland pastures, where frictions between the settled and the free became as small as chicken feed. But they had been forced to cut the summer short; tensions rose like mountain walls. Maryam could hear their insults. Nomads were untethered. She could also hear the spirit of her mother answer, *Well, better untethered than sedentary*. To which the sedentary folk would retort, untethered women always went too far. They did not use the veil. They worked alongside men, herding cattle, gathering wood. They sweated like horses. And smelled even worse. *Well, sedentary women were fatter than cows. It was good they kept all that droopy flesh covered. It had the texture of wet dough, upon which no man could rise.* From behind double chins, they kept retorting, not a single nomad will rise to heaven. *And where will you go, if you keep sitting?* Still they kept on, nomads were riders. The men might know how to play polo and the women might know how to play men, but did either know how to play landlords? Or forest inspectors? No. They only knew how to kick their heels and run. *At least we can run.*

Maryam fingered the jade around her neck. It would not do to keep playing out abuses in her head. This only gave them life, made them fatter. She needed strength, and this meant starving the words that brought her pain. In truth, the valley was envious of nomads. They could tame the wildest steed, while sedentary folk, without even two legs to stand on, could not even saddle a chick.

When Kiran was a chick, Maryam carried her on her back in a cradle made of jute. She was quiet there, with toes against Maryam's rib, fist in mouth, slurping a cube of rock candy. Hair loose; even then she never accepted braids. Maryam talked. She told Kiran about the fat Australian sheep the government was selling them, to replace the thin desi kind. They were happy with the sheep at first, despite the cost. Indigenous sheep yielded twenty kilograms of meat and two kilograms of wool. Foreign sheep yielded forty kilograms of meat and eight kilograms of wool. But they were finding out, too late, that fat foreign sheep were not as strong as thin desi sheep. They could not survive the icy winds and sudden snowdrifts of Kaghan Valley. They were fussy eaters. And they were slow-moving, adjusting poorly to nomadic living and complaining too much.

"Unlike you," Maryam said, and Kiran kicked her spine.

"If they don't live even half as long as our sheep, where is the gain from all that wool and meat?"

Kiran waved her arm and her bangles chimed. They were tiny bangles, given to Kiran by her grandmother, and as her arm grew pudgy, they rolled along its length less and less. Maryam would have to remove them soon, to replace them with larger ones.

"Another thing," she kept on, "their wool. So long it gets all tangled up in thorns as we look for better feed, just for them. No. These foreign sheep are better off staying in one flat dry place." And she launched her final reprimand, "They are sedentary sheep."

After a while, she added, "If you don't let me braid your hair you will grow wool like theirs. All tangled up, and bald before you know it!"

In later years, she would tell her daughter more, how the Australian sheep, because of their silly diet, forced the herders into pastures that were closed to them. They were forced to pay fines. Huge fines. One year a fat sheep nibbled two stems of a ginger plant with twelve stems. The plant could afford to lose two stems. But no, they were made to pay a hundred rupees per stem. The government was closing off their freedom to roam the land the way Maryam had done when she was Kiran's age, and this too was killing the sheep they had been forced to buy. Even their goats were meddled with. The government replaced the sturdy Kaghani goats and the fierce Kilan goats with those that yielded more mutton but ate all the feed and left the indigenous goats bleating in hunger.

Kiran understood these things. This April, when they set off for Lake Saiful Maluk—the hills around which they were still free to graze in—Kiran had climbed onto the mare Namasha with an Australian lamb tied to her back. It mewed pitifully the entire way, ignoring Kiran's repeated warnings. Once they were at the lake, she abandoned it. "Go to your mother!" she snapped, and set about chasing her own goats instead. Kola, Bhuri, Makheri. Her own names for the only Kaghani goats left in their flock. Maryam had laughed. Her daughter, like her, would make a restless mother, preferring the child that could play on its own.

She had watched Kiran recede up the hill and gone back to arranging the hearth, piling up stones to light a fire to cook the maize bread for the guests.

Ghafoor was watching her at the shrine. His only reason for coming here, to the land that had banished him, was to see Maryam. Now that he had seen her, he could not leave. Kiran, at whose birth he had played the flute, had been killed. He would not leave yet.

He held to his lips a tall aluminum glass of lassi. What he had been suspecting for some time now was true. The milk of a mare could not compare to that of a buffalo.

She could feel him at her back, just as she had felt him inside the hut yesterday, when she lay on her side. She thought of silken tendrils and pale green buds and how easily each could snap. They did not speak. She willed him not to come close. She would let the weight of grief pull her to the ground. He would have to watch his one desire for her—*never grow old*—smack him defiantly in the face.

How could she keep the pieces of her heart warm? She had asked herself this repeatedly since Kiran's death. What was the point of a reprise without reprisal? She wanted justice. She wanted justice more than she wanted warmth.

"Maryam." He took two steps toward her.

She shook her head. In the years since her marriage she had tried to think of her husband as the pasture inside their barrier of mountains. She had tried to stop thinking of Ghafoor as her window to the world. The shimmering blue feather he left in the cave had both excited and worried her. And the pain of losing Kiran—it was all too much.

"Leave me."

He waited for her to change her mind but she knew he knew her better than that.

He left her, for now, but he would be back in a few hours. What was he doing traveling the globe and carrying everyone else's woes, when he could not even help his own people?

Before moving away he opened the box and took out the second flower. Still fresh. *They will only last as long as you do*, the men had said. How long was that?

He did as he was told and did not look underneath.

She had taken the bangles off before Kiran was buried. The heavy necklaces, too. The toe rings had to be cut; even after oiling the toes, they were too swollen. She had braided her hair, in both styles. First, a thick knot starting at the top of her forehead and woven all the way around her face. Kiran's face was so lovely in its oval form and the braid had cupped it as her own hands had done. But then

Maryam's fingers had untied the knot and moved swiftly into weaving a series of thin braids starting from the top of her dead daughter's forehead and converging down the back of her head as one. For a long time, she had stared at that one braid. The color of maize, the thickness of rope, it scraped the nape of her daughter's neck, the color of which was turning devilish. And the texture—she could not dwell on it, the cold clamminess against her fingers. In slow, deliberate movements, she eventually untied the braid. Kiran would want her hair as loose in death as in life.

She had hidden the bangles and the other jewelry in a box in a corner of the shrine. The box also held Kiran's two front teeth, the first of which had nearly cost Kiran her life. After it fell off, Kiran rolled the tooth on the floor, on her arm, between her palms, and in every corner and crevice she could find. Then she skipped to Maryam with a smile. "Guess where it is." Mayram could not guess. Kiran tapped her nose. "What does that mean?" Maryam asked. "Guess!" The child eventually revealed that she had stuck it up her nose. She wanted to see how far it would go. She was amazed to find the area "open." *The tooth kept going up! Up!* She would have pushed it all the way to her brain had her finger been long enough. "Don't breathe," commanded Maryam. "Sneeze!" When this did not work she slapped the back of Kiran's head, demanding, "Which nostril?" Kiran, now frightened, would not say. In due course, pure instinct told Kiran to squeeze shut the right nostril while, from the left, she blew and blew till a slick white stone shot forward, so large both mother and daughter stared in horror.

Now, caressing the tooth with her fingers (it was slightly larger than the second tooth, smoother too), Maryam remembered the legend of Maryam Zamani, who could will a stone to cease obstructing her way. And she fingered the bangles, the ones she still heard chime, every day and every night, including in her sleep. They had been a sign—don't let me go in the boat!—but she had not listened.

When Maryam eventually crawled outside her shrine, she found a second yellow flower waiting for her in the dirt, near the hole that served as entrance. The flower reminded her of a butterfly that had landed on her shoulder once, when she was a child. She had never seen the exact shade of yellow again, not till now. She did not know how to read this sign either. She twirled the stem till the heart of fire grew to the ends of the petals and the ends of her world. The day was too bright. She wanted to retreat into a mountain cave, into darkness lit by ancient markings. She wanted to carry this spiraling flame into the cool cover of her highland shrine, deep in the Karakoram's womb.

Mixed in with the weight of grief was the weight of caution. In the months between their departure to the lake and their return to the lowlands, the world had tipped unsteadily. It was not a reliable unsteadiness, the kind that leads from pasture to plain, according to the season's change. This motion had no rhythm. What it had was men in tanks and spies in plainclothes, all showing up at your door and demanding to be placated with the sugar you were saving for your children, or your guests, or a man who would leave you a sign in a cave.

And these men were different. They were not the kind who would shoot the guard dogs that warned the herders when a goat or lamb was being stolen. They were not the kind who would leave the dogs poisoned meat. They were not from the forest department either, those men who leashed the forest and then leased it. Men with a list of fines the length of a horse's mane, and a list of felled trees the length of three times three. Nor were they the policemen who lived in the forest department's pockets, nestling deeper into its silk linings each time the felled logs were tucked in the water wells of the Kunhar River's banks. Nor even from the revenue department, demanding taxes for every new buffalo that came bleating into the world. No. These men were, at least at first, as alien to her as Australian sheep, and, from the looks of them, as stupid. They said a man was hiding in their valley. He was a killer, and he needed to be caught. If they sheltered him, they would be caught instead. They accused anyone of sheltering him.

But, she wanted to know, if these men knew who sheltered the killer, how come they did not know who he was?

They ripped through their homes, kicking pots and dishes and goats and children. Then they demanded food. Over the course of the past few days, while watching them eat, she came to question whether they were that different, these men. Perhaps they were all in each other's pockets. The ones who tore down the old, old trees and poisoned the Gujjar dogs and fenced off the land and charged the moon for two stems of ginger and claimed a killer was hiding in their midst. Perhaps they were all exactly the same. *Everything alive is in movement and everything that moves is alive.* These men were unchanging. They were not alive.

While they ate, they kept on with their questions. Where was her son? He wasn't with the cattle—where was he? It was no use telling them he was running an errand at the market or studying at the mosque because they would look for him there. And find him. And take him away. No. She kept her son far from these men and offered them more sugar, more yogurt, and more bread.

In the days since her return from the lake, it seemed she did not even have enough time to retreat into darkness to grieve. Her sorrow was swiftly turning to fear for her remaining children, her remaining land, and also, for that palpitation in her chest, warning her of her remaining love for Ghafoor.

The flower in her hand had no smell. The jade around her neck had heat.

Soon after securing that stone, Ghafoor had gotten into trouble. His tumultuous relationship with the forest officials was the stuff of legend, though it was not the kind of legend she only heard about. In fact, she never heard of it at all. It was a legend she had watched take shape for most of her youth, with her own eyes, yet it did not bear repeating, neither in a shop nor at the mouth of a cave nor on horseback on the way to a pasture. Nor was it the kind of legend you could pray to, in a secret shrine, nor the kind to name a child after. This legend was never celebrated or exchanged or put to music with a flute. It was never invited to a wedding or a birth or a funeral. It was left entirely alone, to grow as bitter as truth.

Though Maryam had watched it take shape, this legend, she sometimes lost its exact thread, whether it began with the time they were charged two hundred rupees for two stems of ginger, or the time the thirtieth water well was destroyed by a stash of felled logs, or the time the rain tore another secret stash from out of a nullah and into a bridge, smashing the bridge into pieces that were also lost in the swell. Or it might have been the time the stallion was skewered by a barbed wire fence so slyly concealed in the forest even an owl could not have seen it. Or the time a friend of his was murdered after filing a case against the timber mafia. (Those who killed him were never called killers, thought Maryam, still fingering the stone around her neck.) There were many other possible beginnings to the making of Ghafoor the Legend, though the nub of it was not open to debate: he had been told to leave the valley. His presence was a threat to the entire community. Worse than a threat; it had already resulted in several deaths.

So he left.

Before fleeing, he left her a crow feather, and then a red cloth. These signs she had learned to read.

How did he do it? She asked him once, on one of his rare returns, taken at high risk to himself, and to all of them. How did he find a way to leave his mark with her, no matter where he went? Often, when she needed him most. Often, before she even knew she needed him.

He had answered with stories. The Silk Road had for centuries transported not only goods, but also, voices. Had she heard the name of Genghis Khan, King of the Universe? Founder of the greatest nomadic empire ever known? She shook her head. He had said *Silk Road* in English, her first words in a tongue she would hear more of in later years with indifference, but at the time, indifference was not known to her. The words had conjured images of a road made of silvery mist, left behind by the trail of a fairy. The silver of her trail fell all the way to the snow-capped mountains and down to the forested plains, and, like a dream, it was never something you could—or should—actually touch.

But Ghafoor described the road differently. While she saw a shimmering in the clouds, he saw the march of Genghis Khan in the dirt. And he tried to make her see it his way. Genghis Khan marched into Bukhara in what is today Tajikistan, he said—*names, Maryam, they always change, if you listen carefully*, though she did not care about the names, she cared about their color, and whether they tasted as sweet as honey. Again he snapped his fingers. "Are you listening?" She would try to look as though she was. So he continued. After the Great Khan marched into Bukhara and burned 10,000 villages and slaughtered 30,000 villagers, he set about building like a mad man. He constructed thousands of caravanserais and tidied up the *Silk Road*—she saw fat hands plumping up a glistening haze—and made it into a safe highway, without bandits like him, and also, he built something else. She was asked to guess but she could not guess.

The world's first postal service, Ghafoor answered with swank. No matter where Rahman or Rakhmanov, Yousuf or Yusupov, Karim or Karimov, Umar or Umarov would go, if she needed him, a message would be sent. When he told her this she smiled, despite his boastful manner (or because of it), remembering her mother's names for each mountain that enclosed them. *Look for windows. Don't walk into walls.* Apparently, Genghis Khan had thought the same. He had torn through them all, the Hindu Kush and the Pamirs, the Himalayas and the Karakorams, as if through mist, leaving behind a chain of whisperers and runners.

A red cloth meant he was going far away, and this was the last sign she received from him before Kiran's birth. The second last was a crow feather, and this meant he was in trouble. She had not needed to ask what kind of trouble; by then he was a legend of the unsung kind. The shimmering blue feather he left before Kiran's death had been the first sign in more years than she cared to count. And now there was no sugar to greet him with, thanks to the men who wanted to know if any enemies of the state were being sheltered in her home.

Maryam had kept the red cloth. The box with Kiran's belongings was tied in it, because Kiran had gone far away. Before burying the box and the cloth in the shrine, she had prayed. *May your skies be filled with skins that do not tear, stallions that do not bleed. May you live forever without hurt.* Now she walked the distance between her shrine and the hut, shielding her eyes from the brightness of the day. She frowned. Was it a premonition of Kiran's death that had brought him back, or something else?

What if the killer were really here? What if he did exist? What had he done that was worse than what the men tearing down their homes and forests still did?

In the valley, they were calling him Fareebi, the shapeshifter, and she did not consider this wise, for once you give a shape a name, you give it life. They said he came down the slopes of the Pamirs as softly as a cat and snuck into their huts while they slept. By the time his footsteps were tracked to a hut, he had become something else. A wisp of smoke, a jinn of the lowlands. Only after he left could the plains return to normalcy, even if this meant more dog killings and stupid sheep and sedentary wives.

He was inside her hut, she could feel him there. Her husband was in the forest, with the cattle. Her son would also not be home. It was the second time since Ghafoor's return that they would be alone, and she feared that this time, she could not turn her back to him. She had no sugar to offer, but she could still offer him tea. She almost smiled, imagining how his mouth would grimace at the taste. This man who drank mare's milk and wore a different name each day.

She pulled away from the hut, toward her husband in the forest. Sometimes, it was desirable to put a mountain between yourself and someone else.

Shapeshift

It was our last morning in the valley. I can't say I was as relieved as I should have been. Perhaps it was the beady eyes on the graves last night, or the knowledge that I'd become someone who could be unsettled by stone engravings, or the feeling that, even as I prepared to leave, I was still walking back from the graves.

My pessimism wasn't entirely without reason. While checking out of our hotel, we heard the news. The army had launched a missile strike in Waziristan yesterday, and, not even an hour ago, at a police station in Mansehra, a policeman had been handed a box of holy dates from a date tree near the Kaaba in Mecca. The firing pin was attached to the cover of the box and when he pulled the lid off, he tore himself and three others to pieces. It was a crude, Soviet-era device, and, within minutes, a second one had detonated at a police station in Balakot, south of the graves. No one asked if it was to protest the missile strike. The gloom thickening around us was born of more sinister knowledge: the bombers had succeeded even as the valley crawled with military convoys. Intelligence would have more reason to increase its presence here, the militants would have more power, and the people of this valley, even less. There never had been a killer hiding here before but now there would be. He need not even hide. Fareebi, the shapeshifter, had been set loose.

As we piled our bags into the jeep, Irfan and I discussed the other rumor adding to the despair. The missile had not been launched by Pakistan but by an American drone armed with missiles that were MALE, with Pakistan's consent, from one of its airfields, where, not too long ago, wealthy Arabs had been invited to launch their falcons on endangered Houbara Bustards. The thirty civilians dead included three children.

Despite this, astonishingly, some people didn't delight in seeing us go, or at least, seeing *them* go. They blessed Farhana and embraced "Mr. Whistly," who, genuinely caught up in the moment, executed the three-swing hug with such adeptness everyone lined up for more. Eventually, he settled in the front seat, Farhana angled herself next to Irfan at the back, and, reluctantly, Irfan shifted closer to me.

We took the road up to Babusar Pass, at the border between the North-West Frontier Province and the Northern Areas. No one spoke. I wished we could have flown over this part of the journey, avoided it entirely. Of course, avoiding the past week would also have been optimum. Seven years ago, Irfan and I had trekked up from here, to see the mating of glaciers. Zulekha had been with us. Her brother, who'd die with her, had been back at the hotel, playing escort poorly. Their absence filled the canyon.

Next to me, Irfan hunkered, pulling himself close, eyes wet. Though he still hadn't admitted it, I knew it was for a glimpse of the glacier that he'd suggested this route in Karachi. We were not going to avoid it now, no matter how tense the air grew inside the jeep, no matter how hard life was going to be for those we were leaving.

I could see Farhana lean back in the seat, on Irfan's other side. We seemed acutely aware of each other, or perhaps that was only me. I was sure she'd know which glacier we'd soon be stopping at.

My most beautiful moment, the one I'd shared with her in the bay window of her purple house. How changed she was from the woman beside whom I'd reclined, as we played opposites! How different the world had become! For instance, back then, I'd never been called a murderer.

I turned my head slightly in her direction, trying to catch more of her profile. Did she remember details of the ceremony, the way I'd describe it for her as we lay together at her window?

When we reached a place from which to look across the valley, Irfan asked the driver to stop. We walked to the edge of the road.

Beyond the chasm, I could see the glacier, the one that had crept down the cliff for the past seven years. I remembered the mat of husks and walnut shells so vividly I could smell it, and I saw the backs of those porters as they trudged, in a ritual of silent awe, all the way to the marital bed. With equal proximity, I could hear Zulekha kiss Irfan's cheek. And I could hear his sorrow, as he stood beside me now, alone, more alone than even I could feel, a sorrow that was louder than our combined memories. Two friends, one with a wife cold in the ground, the other with a lover cold on the road.

On the slopes beneath the glacier were scattered a few sheep and goats, and, closer, juniper trees, whose leaves were still burned by shamans on special occasions. The late afternoon sun fell just at the lip of the glacier.

"That's the one, isn't it?" It was Farhana, standing beside me. Her first words directly to me since leaving our cabin back in Kaghan, to move in with Wes.

"Yes," I replied.

"Tell me again."

I was surprised. Did she want evidence of just how terribly we'd changed? I did not question the request. I told her again, knowing, after uttering each word, that the story had lost its shine, that each word itself helped to erase the shine by exposing our loss.

First, I repeated, the village elders decided which glaciers to mate. The female ice was picked from a village where women were especially beautiful, the male, from one where men were especially strong. We were only allowed to watch after swearing an oath of silence, because words disturb the balance between lovers in transit. We were told it was bad luck for other eyes to watch…

"You never told me that part."

No, I had not.

A long pause.

Then, Wes was there. "What are you looking at?"

I said nothing. Neither did she.

"Is it one they seeded?" he asked.

"Yes," said Farhana.

"It looks young," he said. "It has to be at least sixty feet thick to be called a glacier."

"It's seven years old," I said.

"Seven?" he repeated. "You sure?"

"They've always made do without science," said Irfan, at my side again.

I took out my camera. As I photographed the glacier, I thought of one of the first things I'd learned about seeing through the lens: normalize the view. Which meant the right exposure on the area the human eye is most inclined to drift toward, which, at this moment, was that sliver of bright light at the edge of the white smudge.

Farhana began explaining to Wes what I'd once explained to her. The old tradition of marrying glaciers was coming back, as a way to offset a dwindling supply of meltwater. "Winter temperatures on the rise, summer temperatures dropping. More snowfall, but less melt. So," she concluded, pointing across the abyss, "after seven years, that could be sixty feet."

"Thanks for the lesson." He ruffled her hair. "How many glaciers have I studied?"

"Sorry."

"How far are we from Gilgit?" He asked Irfan.

"Not far," said Irfan, pulling him away.

Farhana and I were left alone. I lowered my camera.

Behind us, a row of military trucks raced up the highway, slowing to examine our group. I heard them call out to Irfan and watched as they waved their guns in the air as casually as cigarettes. I let Irfan tackle them.

Across the valley, a farmer was nurturing his field with water he'd probably helped create. The sun was creeping off the glacier's lip and onto the dark gravel. He stopped to enjoy the light, just as we did. A goat grazed at his feet, bells chiming. I pushed thoughts of Kiran's goat and bells far into the chasm ahead. In its place surfaced an image of us from last year. We were standing on guard, gazing out at the Pacific Ocean, where gunships once pointed to the minefields outside Golden Gate. *Take me back*, she'd said. *Take me back to the places you love.*

Gradually, the black earth immediately before us ignited, as if the sun had chosen that precise point upon which to rest its fiery fingers, swallowing the man and the goat. We kept at our lookouts, squinting into the glare, waiting for the sun to release the captives. From the corner of my eye, I noticed a rolling, as of a raincloud. As the glacier slid into shadow, we could still hear the bells of Kiran's goats.

Queen of the Mountains: On Justice

There was always someone looking to make a delivery, but he had not been looking. He was in the pocket of men whose city was being destroyed. Or so they said. He had not recognized them, that day in the café in Gilgit, when the man with the soft leather palms had passed him the box. He was sure he had not seen them four summers ago in Kashgar. They had each spoken a name and claimed an identity. It could be about as real as Ghafoor's. Rahman or Rahmanov. Umar or Umarov. What was he now? Names, he had once told Maryam, they always change.

So those men in Gilgit, he had no way of knowing who they really were. Nor the truth about the man who must have tipped them off in Andijan. It was what excited and exhausted him most about his trade. You were always passing through. You were always donning skins. And yet, to those Uyghur men from Kashgar—or so they said—he was entirely naked. They had known more about him than his relationship with the girl in the room at the top of the stairs, the one with the feather-smooth thighs. *We know you have done worse,* they had said. *We know you have unfinished business.* How did they know? And if they did, how did they not also know that he never had any intention of finishing the business, none at all? Because he did not have a country to finish it in. He did not have a city. He did not have a field. Nor even a buffalo. Or a friend.

All he had were handsome clothes and a wife who could beat him at everything.

He stood outside the forest inspector's new villa. The old villa had burned down some years ago, when Ghafoor had been told to leave. He did not stand there openly, but behind a tree. The forest inspector did not allow the timber mafia to fell the trees near his home, only those further away.

All the way down his long, swooping driveway were parked a convoy of military trucks. The soldiers smoked cigarettes and drank tea and scratched their balls.

Every day since his arrival, Ghafoor had watched them surround his valley. *His.* Why were they here? To catch militants? If that were so, why did the training camps keep getting stronger as these men moved in? The answer was simple. Each and every one of them slept in two beds: the mafia with the government, the militants with the mafia, the government with the militants.

So what were they going to do next, choke his skies with their planes? *His.* What was this, Kashgar or Kashmir? Andijan or Afghanistan? It was bad enough that they had been tearing down the forests for as long as he had walked on two feet. Now they were even tearing into people's homes, including Maryam's.

If there was one thing he had learned in his years away, it was that nomads everywhere were treated much the same. What the Uyghurs were to the Chinese, the Kazakh cattle-breeders were to Kazakhstan and, in the past, to the USSR. And the Uzbek herders of Afghanistan—how badly they fared, both under Russia and the Taliban. No less pitiful was the condition of shepherds all over Pakistan. Look what was happening in the south, in Baluchistan, with Pakistan selling its coast to China, throwing people off their own land. Or giving it to America. And look at the north, where China built a road straight through the heart of the Karakoram Range, just to reach the coast it had already robbed!

But he was grown tired of everyone else's wrongs. It was time to right his own. No one needed him more than those he had been told to leave. And yet, no one besides Maryam even wanted him here. He pulled away from the forest inspector's villa, toward her hut. If he had not been able to avenge the suffering wrought on his people, he could at least avenge the suffering wrought on his woman. Even if she was not his woman.

Maryam spoke tenderly to the two horses tethered outside their hut. Ghafoor was again here this morning, still waiting to talk to her. He could keep waiting.

These were the only horses left, a mare and her filly, both Kaliani. In her father's time, there had been the Nukra, Bharssi, even the Yarkandi breed, said to have come down from the Fergana Valley long ago, perhaps with her people. The way Ghafoor did now, by himself. Now all of those breeds were lost, forever. By the time Kiran was her age, the Kaliani breed too might be extinct.

She buried her head in the belly of the mare, inhaling deeply. *Kiran will never be my age.* The thought made her sick. She pushed down the sick, inhaling deeper, pulling her stomach high, all the way to her chest. The belly of the mare shivered. Then it moved two steps away, forcing Maryam to stand up straight.

The mare, Namasha, Kiran had named. After dusk: for the coat she threw around herself, dark and glossy. The coat was losing its sheen ever since their return from the highlands. When Maryam led her to water, Namasha did not drink. Her filly sucked at the waterhole; she merely watched. Maryam wondered if she should tether her again, or take her into the forest to feed. Everything was wrong this year. The animals were meant to graze high in the summer pastures, not down here in the plains. The lowland forests would be overgrazed, with no time to regenerate through the rainy season. And the rain was coming. They could sense it.

Sick of lowland grub, Namasha whinnied. She wanted the air of the mountains, the way it sweetened the grass. She wanted the crunch of snowmelt on her tongue. Why else did she wait for summer each year? Why else did she keep herself handsome, even at her age? Not for this pre-monsoon heat! Not for the flies around her eyes!

The filly, Loi Tara, taking a cue from her mother, tossed her mane haughtily. Then she nuzzled Maryam's neck. "What do you want me to do?" Maryam asked, stroking first the filly, then the mother. A shudder ran down Namasha's side again, loud as a thunderbolt this time. "We had to come back down early. To bury Kiran."

Namasha stared at her, accusingly.

Loi Tara inspected Maryam's palm. Kiran had named her too. Loi Tara. Morning star. The night and her morning star. Finding Maryam's palm empty, Loi Tara allowed herself to explore Maryam's fingers instead. Maryam teased the forelock; she smoothed the silken line of a perfect nose. It occurred to Maryam that her youngest child, Jumanah, had not yet found the words to name the creatures of her world, but when she did, would Maryam know? She was now with her father in the forest. She had been with him every day since their return because Maryam found it impossible to tend to her. Her husband folded Jumanah in his arms each morning as the sun began to stretch its own, at the hour when loi tara was still above their dera, and the girgiti too, pulsing together like a tribe.

The girgiti. The constellation of six stars she had looked for every morning since she could remember, till now, when it became so hard to get herself out of bed. Now she carried a rock around her neck, a rock even the legendary Maryam Zamani would not have known how to remove. So her husband did not wake her up; it would mean waking the rock. He took Jumanah with him without a sound, as he led the animals into the forest and returned them later in the morning, at which point he said that if she felt able, she could take them back to the forest at noon, for the second feed.

The rock lodged in her throat. It did not matter how frequently she swallowed it down. It kept growing, prickly and green, like guilt.

"He let her go in the boat," she said, returning Namasha's stare. She was suddenly livid with this animal for stirring the fury she had been holding inside. Now it threatened to spread through her veins faster than a snake bite, just as she struggled to find a routine again, by taking the horses into the forest for the second feed! "Do you think I could have stopped him?" She heard her voice give. "I tried. Do you hear me? *I tried*!" She stamped her foot, and the filly backed away. The mare stood her ground. "Who would listen to a wife over a flock of stupid foreigners? He said we could not refuse them. He said they were guests! They were *not* guests. They were thieves!"

Still the evil Namasha kept staring.

"What would *you* have done?"

The mare turned and walked herself indignantly into the forest.

"You better stay where you should stay!" Maryam shouted. "We are *not* going to pay any fines for a conceited old hag like you!"

The filly followed her mother, waving her thick brown tail like a taunt.

For a long time, Maryam watched them go.

She finally glanced again at the hut. It was good Ghafoor was inside, even if she was not ready to see him.

Early that morning, two policemen had torn through their hut.

She had been lying in bed listening to her husband move on one leg while Jumanah raced after him on two. He would take her to the forest that day, he said. She grunted in gratitude, though it was strange to feel gratitude toward a man who had given her older daughter away. It required all the effort in the world to sit up in bed. She sat up for her son, not her husband. Younis would need breakfast before he left for the shop. He was standing before an open curtain, the way Kiran had done each morning, gazing up at the sky. The light that poured through was a violet bleeding slowly to gold. Loi Tara would be there, high above his wide shoulders, and perhaps the six stars of girgiti too, in which case, the second from the bottom would be flickering the brightest. It was always the last to leave for the day.

Then came the boots and the police shoving Younis inside and the curtain pulling shut.

A bomber had blown himself up in the Balakot police station, they said, killing four policemen, putting four others in hospital, and leaving the rest in a rage. That last detail she found redundant. They kicked the stove and the bed where she still sat, her hair a mess, she had not braided it yet, and made Jumanah cry. They broke the teacups. "We will find him!" they declared. They took Younis by the ear and pulled him and shook him. "He is your friend, isn't he? Where is he?"

She watched as her son cried for the second time this year, first when Kiran was buried, and now, as he trembled in their grip. Only when a trickle of urine stained his shalwar did they release him, laughing. Then they sat down for tea. Then they demanded teacups. Then they demanded eggs.

She would not let Younis out of the house alone so Suleiman went to get the eggs and borrow teacups while the men stared at her. She could not fix her hair while they watched so she kept her hands at her side, folding her fingers. Her shawl was very far away. They asked questions that had nothing to do with the bomber. What was a woman from a family like hers, even if it was only a Gujjar family, doing with a man like him? He could not even walk. What else could he not do? How had he managed to have three children? Where was the third? Oh yes, they had heard. And they were very sorry, but not as sorry as they were to find her with a man like him. It was only a girl, after all, and she still had her son. A very fine boy indeed. He clearly took after her. But why only one son? She was still young or—had her husband not noticed? Did he need them to show him? They delivered their threats to her chest and neck and back again to her chest, grinning, while Younis seethed and Jumanah howled. She had slept in a kameez too thin because it was so, so hot and the rain was coming yet it did not come.

Suleiman returned and she made breakfast.

While they ate the buffaloes lowed in pain, their udders swelling like her shame, but she did not dare step outside to relieve them. The family of four sat in a straight line on the dirt floor—Younis, Jumanah, Maryam, and Suleiman—watching the policemen sit crosslegged on their rope bed with their boots on. They dug those boots deep into the bedding and into the weave of the rope. When the meal was finally finished, the men stood up, plunged their hands in the drinking water in the clay pot, and, still standing inside the hut, pissed against the curtain. "Remember, we will find him." Then they smashed the borrowed teacups. Then they left.

She scrubbed clean each thread of the curtain and each string of the bed till her knuckles bled and when she put them to her lips the salt was soothing, she wanted no one to disturb her, no one at all.

Now, as she watched her horses disappear deep into the forest, she was glad Ghafoor was waiting for her inside. He would not stand by passively while policemen destroyed her home.

The time he went away, when he left her the red cloth, was a few days after the villa of the head inspector of the forest department had been set ablaze. It was quite possible that this was when the legend of Ghafoor had first begun to take shape, though it was equally possible that it had always been taking shape, from the very first time she saw him, but she never noticed, because she had been too busy watching his fingers play the flute and her taste buds.

The inspector had fined them for grazing on prohibited land, and this time, it was not about a sheep nibbling two stalks of a ginger plant, but an entire flock ripping apart an entire field. It was a lie. The field had been rotten to begin with, and they had been nowhere near it. (The field had been rotten because the land was easily destroyed in the floods the previous year. The land was easily destroyed because it had no trees. It had no trees because the same inspector grew fat each time the forest was torn down. There was always a beginning, hard as it was to keep track of sometimes.) As punishment, the herders were told to pay four thousand rupees, as well as a weekly supply of milk, curd, butter, and ghee for an indefinite period of time. Sugar upon demand.

There were ways of registering resentment.

The night the villa burned, the inspector had been in the kitchen in the front of the house, drinking whiskey. The fire had started at the back, in his bedroom. The wall was made of wood; a walnut tree knocked against the wall. His wife was in the bedroom, his children in the room next to theirs. By the time the fire reached the kitchen, the inspector was intoxicated, though not enough to forget about himself. He tumbled out the kitchen window, drunken head first, and only later, remembered his family. He yelled at his servants—who were not in their quarters; *those* questions would come later—to go back inside the house to save them. The servants were able to retrieve the children but his wife was lost in a fire hotter than hell, and they would endure the hell on earth the inspector would put them through rather than risk the one in the bedroom.

A crow feather. And then the cloth.

Not one of the servants made to endure the beatings, kicks to the head, or severed pay, dared give Ghafoor away. He was as dependable as a stone come loose from a glacier. What he might do would be worse than anything they suffered now.

She was not proud of him for doing it. The inspector's children were sent to a city hospital and their burns were crippling. The girl especially, who would marry her now? And without even a mother.

The poor woman had played no part in the fine, neither the one imposed on the herders, nor the one imposed on herself, each time she opened her legs for that man whose whiskey tasted of their sweat.

Perhaps it had not been Ghafoor, she told herself, ignoring the rumors spreading through the valley faster than the fire had burned the wife. Faster, even, than Genghis Khan had burned 10,000 villages. From the ashes of the dead, she reminded herself, the King of the Universe had gifted the world its first postal service. Without that gift, she might not have survived her marriage.

He was happy for her when she got married.

He sang for her on her wedding day, the same song about Prince Saiful Maluk and Princess Badar Jamal he had sung before, outside her highland shrine. He suspected she was trying not to listen. She was angry he had not bid for her hand. Many men had come forward to offer their best cattle. Not he. Though his success as a merchant continued to grow, she had been given to Suleiman instead. Suleiman's family gifted hers almost their entire herd, and when the gift was accepted, members of the tribe had gifted his family some of their cattle. In this way, Maryam was made up for, in part.

He had brought her a wedding gift, that, he could see now, as he waited inside her hut, was nowhere. The two carpets made by women in Tashkent: they had hung on a wall, or so he thought. Would that space there not make a good place? He looked closely above the rope bed, which was unusually disheveled, he thought, but saw no carpets.

The hut was not too clean and not too comfortable. A yurt was lavish and beautifully lit. Kazakh herders were far better off than the Gujjars of Kaghan Valley, and a small part of him regretted coming down here at all. A yurt was sacred, and, after three summers living in one, he decided this was as it should be. It ought to be a replica of the endless hemisphere of the sky. No boots should be allowed to stamp their will inside. No broken teacups should litter the floor. No clay pot should lie empty. Why was there no drinking water here? These walls were not thighs, the smoke hole was an evil eye, and there was no lattice frame, no womb.

The similarities he had found to exist between the Turkic nomads of the steppe and his own tribe suddenly began to fade. It was true they both lived according to the cycles of nature, carrying goods on their backs, sharing their assets, welcoming guests, and driving their herds from one pasture to the next so a field was never overgrazed. But if what he saw in the steppe was abundance in spite of hardship, what he saw here was ruin because of it. Did Maryam still cleanse her home with juniper branches, or had even she given up keeping this ritual alive? He could not imagine a festival taking place here anymore. He was suddenly glad for the woman beneath whom he could lie each night, the woman with the round white arms, who was waiting for him high up the Oxus River and deep in the steppe.

He had to remind himself that he had been happier for Maryam when she got married than when he did. He had to remind himself that he was here now, in the midst of this wretchedness, for a reason. He needed a plan. He believed himself close to finding it.

She was happy for him when he got rich.

He had not bid for her hand, though he could have afforded to. Instead, Suleiman's family had placed the highest bid, and the marriage suited both their families.

In recent years, her family had increasingly succumbed to the pressure to settle more, and move less. Though the eye of the state could watch them more closely now, they had been left with little choice. They could not afford to keep ducking the eye. Living solely on cattle rearing was becoming a curse, given all the dying indigenous breeds and the restrictions on grazing in a diminishing forest. So they bought small plots of land and tried to be cultivators.

During her lifetime, her mother had vehemently opposed the change. *You can harness a horse, but not a Gujjar!* She watched in fury as Maryam's brother first planted instead of herded, then kicked his ice-encrusted plot, abandoning it for work at a mine. While the contractor pocketed his pay, he took to drink. Others in her family, however, proved more successful. They became traders and merchants, or joined the army. A few, like her brother's friend Ghafoor, even traveled the world and came home rich. They were welcomed in big shops in big towns. They wore good clothes; they owned good guns. And every now and then, though very rarely, if one went too far, he was asked to leave, and if he returned, the others looked away for as long as they could, without mentioning the crime, without mentioning the legend.

Her husband's family, on the other hand, had refused to change, a fact which won them immediate favor with her mother. They were herders and always would be. Only with tradition came pride and dignity. Only with seasons and stars, sturdy animals, and fresh spring grass, came peace. They did not own good clothes and avoided even bad guns. But this did not mean they could not benefit from the protection of those who, like Maryam's more cunning relatives, could knock on the *front* door of the forest inspector's new house in a crisp white shirt, carrying silver spoons for his very new wife.

She remembered the horse she rode to her husband's hut the night of her wedding and all the ghee and sugar her family distributed in celebration. The horse died soon afterward, and she did not know why, but she had cried for it. She remembered too the row of donkey carts that arrived at her wedding with guests who had been made to sit on a pile of felled trees. This was one of two favorite ways for the smugglers to transport their goods. They either sent them down the Kunhar to the big lakes of Mangla and Tarbela, where forest officials lay in wait, or they intercepted public festivities, layering the floors of carts and trucks with logs and forcing family members to pile up on them. It was all a façade anyway, since any policeman stopping them would be an accomplice. And since those who sat on the logs were also made complicit, no one dared complain. By the time Maryam's guests arrived, their clothes were torn and mud-stained. Some had bought them by saving for months. Others had sewn them on a shared Singer sewing machine that was older than all their children and some of their wives. But when Ghafoor started to sing about Saiful Maluk and his love for Badar Jamal, everybody started to dance and a few even dance-rolled, illustrating their journey on the logs.

She did not dance. She could tell that despite his merriment, Ghafoor's war with the officials was far from over. She did not care. He had not bid for her hand.

On their wedding night, her husband dislodged his wooden leg. She thought of felled trees hidden in water wells. She was his water well. On subsequent nights, she learned to take it all in, the gray and yellow swirls encased in a walnut cylinder, the smoothness, even the scent; it did not frighten her the way he feared it might. How did it happen? She asked. Two bullets, from a rival Sawati Afghan tribe to the west. If not a forest inspector or landlord or policeman or smuggler, it was other herders. They said his cattle grazed on their land, though they did not own the land either. The land owned them. He bandaged the wound himself, as he had done numerous times for his horses. But he was kinder with horses. When the lesion began to ooze, after attempting to ignore it, he cleaned it so roughly he pushed both the bacteria and the bullet—the second bullet was never found—deeper inside. And then one morning, he saw the color creep beyond the blood-encrusted edge of the bandage, the shade of a terrible bruise, like buffalo hide. He lowered his head and inhaled. The stench made him weep.

"This leg is much prettier," he said, curling his fingers around her own on the wood. She would stroke the grain of his torn skin too, the rubbery knob without bone. My husband is made of cartilage, she would think. Flexible, yet tough.

He would say he was a good husband. "You are lucky I am not like the others." He was right. He did not interfere with her rituals at the shrine, even in recent years, as the pressure to tether her more securely to the Islam spreading toward them increased. He left her to keep the old calendar in place of the Islamic one. They called it Moharram, she could still say Chaitar; they called it Ramzan, she could still say Mangeru; they, Safar, she, Baisakh. And she could continue to mark the date of their departure to the highlands by Nauroz and their return to the lowlands by Het. "Pagan seasons, for a pagan wife," the others said, but he ignored them, in his calm, dignified way. A dignity as stiff as his leg. The only time he interceded was last year, when she wanted to celebrate Diwali with her children, the way her mother had done with her. He warned, softly, that it would be leaving a sign. A sign too bright, brighter than all the constellations she was free to call by her own names. And so, last year, without his having to say more, she also ceased celebrating Lohdi and Baishakhi. She rejoiced at the passing of the bitter cold only in the privacy of her heart and welcomed the spring only in there too.

When, after Kiran's birth, Ghafoor started to leave her signs again, she drew inspiration from her husband's mild, uncomplaining nature. She would temper her pleasure at sight of a cloth or stone, and temper her longing for more. She would draw strength from restraint. Even if she faltered now and then. When one day, seeing the flash of anger in her eyes—*why didn't* you *try for my hand*—he offered, lamely, more lamely than her husband walked, "I would make a false husband, but I make a true friend," she laughed in his face. But she did nothing more. She continued to enjoy his stories. She also continued to ignore the rumors floating in the valley ever since the fire had burned down the inspector's villa: Ghafoor was grown as hard as the company he kept, the company of men from the north who were tough, but not flexible.

Now he was still inside her hut, this man who would not stand idly by while policemen tore through her home, bullied her son, and mocked her honor. And as calmly as that, Maryam threw open the curtain, ready to talk.

"At last." He was smiling.

"Why are you here?" she snapped.

"How is Suleiman? Suleiman*ov*?"

She did not giggle.

"Where is he?"

"Why are you here?" she repeated.

"Don't you want to know whose feather that was?"

She was none too pleased when her fury began to scatter.

"Do you want a story?" he pressed.

The way he spoke to her, it was not unlike the way she would speak to Kiran, when she was tied to her back. And Kiran would listen to Maryam the way Maryam always listened to Ghafoor, wide-eyed and willing.

He was talking. As he talked, her eye—unwide, unwilling—moved to the general space where his wedding gift had hung each autumn, on their return to the plains.

She remembered the day he brought them: two carpets from the north, made by gypsy women who used them to insulate their walls. They were different from the Kashmiri carpets sold in Kaghan. How? he had asked, rolling them out on the floor. She was no expert, and preferred to look, and touch, rather than speak. Kashmiri wool was soft and shiny; these threads were coarse as beards. And the colors! A red so rich it seemed to bleed on her fingertips, reminding her that she had touched herself, there, the night of her wedding, after her husband fell asleep. The red glowed in the center, and she loved how her eye moved from the edging to the bright heart, and back to the edging again. The second carpet did not bleed. It held a resolute zigzag pattern, each line sure and quick—red, orange, yellow, green—each shade sharp and distinct.

He had looked healthy, even happy, his light brown hair parted to the side, beard gone, sideburns thick enough to braid. Still stroking the carpets with pride (as if *he* had made them, she thought), he said the women dressed like men, in trousers made of animal skins and belts with clasps that pulled in their waists.

Maryam's shirt was loose but her stomach tight. She rubbed it discreetly as he spoke, wondering how the women could weave with their stomachs cinched.

When he left, she hung the carpets behind the bed she shared with her husband. When her son was born, she hung the red carpet over his cot. When Kiran was born, the cot became hers, and she moved the second carpet too. Her husband did not question the extravagance of the gift. Being a friend of her brother's, Ghafoor was considered part of her family. But over time, he said the gift attracted too much attention, not only because of who had presented it, but because it made them look wealthy. Too wealthy for nomads. So she had taken them down, hoping that when Kiran slept, she would fill the bare wall with her own colors.

She kept staring at the wall, her mind reeling. She hoped her husband had found Namasha in the forest. She ought to prepare lunch. Jumanah would be playing with the goats, as Kiran had done. Younis was at the market, searching for a better life. He wanted to be like Ghafoor, not his father. The convoys were everywhere. A week since Kiran's death but she only knew it by the number of meals she had coaxed down her family's throat.

"You did not like the story," he said.

She moved her eye away from the wall and centered them on his. They were light brown, like his hair, and devious, always. She was glad the sideburns were gone. Each time she saw him, he had changed his look in some way; no doubt he had again changed his name. He wore trousers, not a shalwar, and a belt around his waist with a large silver clasp in a pattern she would have liked to see up close. She moved her eye upward from the belt.

"You did not tell it well," she replied.

"Then let me try another." He smiled slyly. "I have been to the Fergana Valley. I have mounted its famous horses. They are beautiful, but none have Namasha's temper." He paused, still smiling. So he had been watching her quarrel with the hag.

"I should look for her in the forest."

"She is fine."

Maryam did not move.

"You know where Fergana is?"

"You know I do not."

"The Chinese took it before the Russians could, calling the horses by many names. Horses from heaven. Horses that sweat gold, even blood. But they could never tame even one."

Maryam took a deep breath, pleased that the fury she held in a knot did not scatter again. For today, Ghafoor's words lacked some honey.

"… Then came the Arabs, who fought the Chinese and won, and Islam spread through all of Central Asia. So did the horses that sweat gold and blood. The Arabs sold them to the Chinese they had defeated."

"Why are you telling me this?"

He made a face, looking at her without any trace of a smile. She remembered the rumor. He was keeping the company of hard men now. And even harder women. She wanted to know about them. Not horses. She already knew about horses.

"I have come to see you at great risk to myself," he said, still with that sour face.

Was she supposed to be grateful?

She thought of Suleiman again, and the gratitude she felt toward him when he took care of Jumanah. Why could he not have looked after Jumanah *and* Kiran? Why did men always expect gratitude for the smallest gesture, when their largest, most catastrophic mistakes were irreversible? Why did women always bestow it?

"Bukhara, Tashkent, Samarkand, Fergana," he continued, impetuously. "The people there are proud, Maryam. They are nomads like us, with centuries of power. They defeated the Chinese. They built the Mughal Empire that conquered India. They defeated the Russians. They did not let themselves become enslaved by fines, or by troops."

By loss? She wanted to ask. Did they let themselves become enslaved by loss?

"Why are the convoys here?" he kept on. "To find a killer? There is no killer! They want *us*. Our way of life. Our horses. Our children. Our freedom. They want to *own* us. It is happening to the east, in Kashmir and in Turkestan. To the south, in Waziristan. To the west, in Afghanistan. If not the Russians, it is the Chinese. If not the Chinese, Indians. If not Indians, Americans. And Pakistanis? Traitors who send people to *their* prisons! If they do not send us there, look what they do to us here, killing our sheep, fencing the land, looting our forests, insulting our women. They know nothing of us, the way *we* work the land. The way *you* do, Maryam. They cannot see your hands. Look at your hands!" He took a sudden step forward and before she knew to stop him, he had grabbed her hand. "Look how cut and bruised they are! They will not leave us alone!"

Maryam quickly pulled her hand away and took two steps back, into the wall. She had never seen him like this. He always liked to toss words at her, it was true, long, foreign words, flaunting his travels, his worldliness. But it was done to impress. Now she was unsure what the purpose was. Before, even when he swaggered, he retained a certain poise, one that was different from her husband's. Suleiman's poise stemmed from years of enduring pain and humility; Ghafoor's, from rejecting pain and humility. But now she did not know what he was rejecting, or enduring.

He was glaring at her, as if to gauge whether or not to continue.

If she had to guess, she might say his swagger was filled with fear.

Still glaring.

Yes, he was afraid. Like her.

Something he had said made the upper lid of her right eye flicker. It made her want to say, with a scorn wrapped in the play their previous encounters had always known, *You care more for jewels and money. You do not work the land anymore, so what do you care?* But she held her peace, burying the thought in her chest, where so many others were locked, including this one she might also have shared in the past: she preferred his stories of gypsy women with pinched waists, and of rare cloth made of the hearts of flowers, to tales of conquests and prisons.

Perhaps she could steer him back there again. First, she ought to calm him.

She cleared her throat. "Will you stay for lunch?"

He frowned. "I am leaving soon."

"You just arrived."

"I have been waiting nearly a week to speak with you."

She nodded, a little embarrassed.

"There is something I need to know before I go."

She looked up.

"Which one killed her?"

The question startled her. She took another step back but there was nowhere left to go.

"Which one, Maryam?"

"They all did." The sickness rose in her again. He was like Namasha, pulling her down into the whirlpool of her grief, when she had hoped he would save her from it.

"Are you going to do something or are you going to be just like the rest—throw your hands up to God and say it was His will?"

"What would you have me do?"

"When you see them, what do you *want* to do?"

"I do not see them," she whispered. It was a lie. She had seen him, not too long ago, at the graves. That friend of Irfan's, the one who was always looking sideways. She had noticed him on the road, when she went to the market to look for her son. And she had wanted to do something, anything, to rid herself of the anger he planted in her breast.

Ghafoor waited. Now he was more composed than she. Inadvertently, she had calmed him with her sorrow.

"It was not all of them," she said at last. "One of them, the smallest one, he speaks to us. He is kind. And one is American."

"We cannot touch him."

"And one is a woman."

"We cannot touch her."

There it was again, she could feel it rise, a taste so foul she had to spit, there on the floor of her hut. "It was *her* idea!" There were tears in her eyes, hot, furious tears.

"What about the fourth?"

"Did you not hear what I said? It was *her* idea."

He shook his head. "We cannot touch her. She is with the American."

"Then why ask me, if you already know about them? I thought you came for *me*!"

"I did. What about the fourth?"

The one who followed me, she was about to say, but hesitated. The one who gazed upon Kiran when the lake gave her back. The one who killed *and* blasphemed. What was he doing at the graves? She had heard that he was rummaging around for a secret shrine. *Her* shrine. Did he *want* to sink deeper and deeper into hell? Well, it could never be a hell as deep as hers, and anyway, he would never find it! She had ended up following him to the graves; it was the only thing she could think to do. And as she stood there, watching him, something about the way he crouched, gazing at the stones with the horses and the ducks, something about it was too familiar. She had seen him before. *Before* he had come to the lake. How could it be? The back of that head, the width of those shoulders, the length of the spine, even the shirt—she had seen it! She could not say when. But as she stood watching him, it seemed to her that he was trapped. And she had always known he would be. And he was very afraid. Everyone around her was afraid.

Ghafoor snapped his fingers, the way he would do when she was younger, trying to pull her back to himself. "What about the fourth?" he said a third time.

"I do not know," she formulated her thoughts slowly into words. "He is—strange."

"Strange—how?"

"*She* is the one who feels no remorse."

"The small one, he has been in touch with your husband."

She nodded. "He wants to pay. My husband does not want payment."

"But your brother feels differently."

"So he does."

He nodded. "They have struck a bargain. God is all merciful, and with His help, we will find the just rate." He looked away from her then.

"What are you going to do?"

"They are heading north."

"I do not care where they go, if they fall off the edge of all worlds."

As soon as the words were spoken, before Maryam unfolded a picture so clear it was as though a window had opened, a lake had stilled. Though Maryam could not see him, she could see the peak on which he lay trapped. The one who had followed her. The one she had followed. The one she had seen before. She could not see him, but she knew it was him, surrounded not by small headstones in a graveyard but by vast knife-edged stones on a precipice she had never seen before. The precipice was shaped like a glistening fang, in a place where snow was born and ice never melted. He was trapped. He was very afraid.

Ghafoor was smiling, honey in his eyes, finally. "At last I see her, the Maryam I used to know."

She looked down. The picture of the man on the mountain vanished.

And now Ghafoor's voice was low and sweet, as on the morning he had brought her the yellow flower. "Live up to your name, Maryam Zamani. Do not try to walk around this stone, or walk across it. You will only hurt more. It is an obstacle. It has to be removed." She looked up. "You will not worry."

As he continued, she thought, his words are a silken thread. A thread the color of fire. And fire will warm the pieces of me. But remember: more than warmth, I want justice.

"There are those who are walking toward a wall," he kept on.

"All we have to do is drive them forward. All we have to do is escort them. And you, Maryam, all you have to do is will it. Your mother would have done no less. And you are your mother's child. As Kiran is yours. I am the legs, but you are the will."

Aside from his finger, she had never touched him. Nor had she pulled the flesh around his knuckles with her tongue and teeth for the garlic tint of honey even once since her marriage. Nor would she.

She walked him to the curtain.

While stepping outside, he turned back to face her, and she saw that both the fear and the honey were gone. "They ride under the open skies, Maryam, these men and women of the steppe. Just as we do. And, like us, they are not foolish enough to point at the sun or the moon or the stars. They do not point at what gives them life. They only point at what takes it away."

She held his gaze. If he took her hand now she might not pull away.

"This morning I looked at loi tara with your eyes, Maryam. I also looked up at girgiti. You are not waking up early, your husband tells me. You are in too much pain. So I looked at those six stars in your place, and in Kiran's place. Six stars, for her six years. What did they want with her, those people who know nothing of our stars?"

When he left, Maryam nailed the curtain shut. Then she fell to her knees.

She let it come, the animal sounds that lunged from her throat with more anguish than a horse impaled on a fence. There was a puncture wound to her chest, and no amount of pressure with her palm—or smacking, or beating—could stop the bleeding. It seemed only one thought might begin to offer some relief, to fill the hole widening inside her breath. The thought was this. The part of her she had lost—and kept on losing, every hour of every day, it never stopped, the hole was growing so *big*, despite how fast she filled it with this thought—this part of her wanted him, Ghafoor, to do the worst thing his hard friends from the north had taught him. The *absolute* worst. She smacked the heel of her palm against the dirt floor—oh, *this* was relief! The way the wrist began to *give*! Again! Again!—she would go to the shrine this evening—May the goddess be with her! May the horns of her bulls clap their consent!—she would sacrifice a lamb *and* her wrist—Again! Again!—she would pray for the worst, the worst, the worst.

Blessed Are the Outsiders

I was beginning to wonder if this was a mistake. Perhaps Irfan had been right. From Kaghan we ought to have headed south, not north. My doubt stemmed from a series of events encountered after our stop at the glacier, each causing further delays.

First, soon after crossing Babusar Pass, our Jeep broke down and we ended up staying at a hotel. Once again Irfan and I shared a room. I slept poorly and each time I awoke, instead of Irfan, I saw Farhana lying beside me. In the morning, Wes informed us that Farhana was unwell. It was commonly known that the gas pressure at these heights was too low for boiling lentils, yet she'd ordered them the previous night and of course had spent it running to the toilet. According to Irfan the delay was necessary for a third reason, something to do with the "indemnity" agreed to with Maryam's family. When I asked to know more, he said "we're waiting for someone," and returned to his phone.

So we waited. The town we were stuck in afforded a glimpse of the real Naked Mountain, whose phantom lookalike we'd seen from the lake. There he loomed, shimmering at 8,126 meters, a bold and cocky devil also known as Killer Mountain. He'd killed thirty-one climbers before finally conceding to one man at his summit; he'd killed another thirty-one since. I wondered about the Queen's melt, down below. I wondered how the lake appeared today.

We finally left the next morning, in another jeep, with a different driver. Beside me, Irfan remained edgy, while beside him, Farhana reclined in the seat, sweating and pale. Despite her weakness, I thought I saw a smile lurking around her mouth. She seemed to be the only one who felt us advancing forward. *Leave it behind* was to be the essence of any truce between us, and we all seemed to understand this, even if we didn't all agree. As we ascended higher into the mountains, wheeling the Frontier firmly to our backs, it was as if we were the ones standing still while the edge of the world flew by. We were on the Karakoram Highway, a stretch of road that cut through the tallest peaks, creating passes within passes, rolling in conjunction with the Indus River that carved the gorges dropping inches from our jeep. I attempted a smile. Yes, we can rise above our mistakes! I doubt the smile or the sentiment would have convinced even a goat.

For starters, she and I could be sharing a room.

But I wasn't going to dwell on that now.

The mountain was following us. If at one bend he disappeared, at the next, he rose again. Naked Mountain, swaggering flame of Queen of the Mountains. The mountain that had cursed us at the lake. The mountain that moved. To bid him farewell, as though we needed his blessings to go on, after a few kilometers we left the jeep again, though we had only just piled in. Below us raged the dark, silty Indus; above, a thin necklace of purple-gray clouds. There was a rumbling in the distance as we followed Irfan and Nur Shah, the new driver, toward a cluster of rocks.

The rocks were scratched with inscriptions of horses, as on the graves in Kaghan, and with a nimbus of winged figures—fairies, perhaps, or, according to Nur Shah, shamans. His fingerprints mixing with those who came before him, he also decoded battle scenes left by warriors from the steppe, incense bowls scratched by

Buddhist monks, and, a few feet away, an ancient script. Thousands of codes were said to remain hidden in the rocks, perhaps meant for those who'd yet to cross the mountains or ford the Indus, in which the people of Chilas had at one time ridden dinghies, panning for gold.

"There is no gold left," concluded Nur Shah, turning away from the glyphs to view the west face of Nanga Parbat, as he pierced and shredded his crown of clouds. Perhaps it was only the altitude, but I was suddenly incapable of gauging where I stood in relation to him—forward or backward, west or east? I shook my head to clear it.

"What happened here?" said Wes, turning back to the glyphs.

In my vertiginous state, the glyphs were a welcome anchor. The floating in the sky—or in my head—began to still. I realized that the figure scratched on the rock before me had been defaced.

Nur Shah's face drooped as he shook his head. "You know the times. People think if you draw a new line across an old one, you can remake the past."

"We'll lose even more glyphs to China's development projects than to mad men crying jihad," said Irfan. And the three of them talked about the plan to expand this road and connect it all the way to the deep-sea port of Gwadar on Pakistan's southern coast, the construction of which was largely funded by China. The Chinese premier had even inaugurated the opening of the port this spring. The extended road would secure China's trade route from Central Asia down to Gwadar and on to the rest of the world.

"Some believe it will give us work. But when the work is done?" lamented Nur Shah. "What will become of us, without our homes? Without our past?"

The clouds were now at Naked Mountain's waist, like a belt. Farhana looked up as the belt began to peel away. "Let's go," she said.

"Not yet," Irfan replied.

"What are we waiting for?"

"Him."

A motorcycle halted beside our jeep, and a figure rolled off the seat with a bag swung over his shoulder.

"Who's that?" we asked.

"Our armed escort."

I laughed. "*That*?"

"I wouldn't laugh if I were you. He's a relative of Maryam's, he's from Kaghan, and he's coming with us. Now we're ready."

I'm sure I climbed into the jeep with an open mouth.

We were packed inside again, six of us now. The escort sat in the boot. When I looked back at his friend riding away on the motorcycle, I saw Naked Mountain, his jagged torso hovering just beyond my shoulder, following the bend of the road.

We were entering disputed territory. Wes and Farhana had to register at every checkpoint. It was a repeat of the inspections on the road to Kaghan, except here there were even more. At least we were in a private vehicle and wouldn't trouble an entire bus with the stops. But if before Farhana had been testy and Wes congenial, now it was the opposite. Perhaps she was making him sleep on the floor.

After the first stop, on returning to our jeep, Wes faced us from the passenger seat. "We *are* in Kashmir?"

"Yes," answered Irfan.

"We've left Pakistan?"

"In a sense."

"And yet you don't need a visa? It's us who are checked, by Pakistani soldiers."

"It's for your own safety," said Irfan.

"Yeah, you said that already."

After a while, he added, "So, will this ever be part of Pakistan?"

"We can hope. But not till India holds a plebiscite in Kashmir."

"It won't happen. Your country's wasting itself on a war you lost long ago."

"That is not how we see it."

"India has a lot of friends."

"It has the most important one." After a heavy beat, Irfan added, "Though it's us who fight its wars."

It was the first time Irfan had let himself be provoked, at least in my presence. They continued arguing, Wes saying, "It's a democracy," and Irfan insisting, "Third-world military dictators are especially popular with free-world *democracies*."

Nur Shah, who till our stop at the petroglyphs had been quiet, now turned his attention to me. "First time?"

"No, I've been here before."

"It's my first time," said Farhana.

He said, in English, "Welcome."

It was not something we'd heard in Kaghan Valley.

"Where are you going, after Gilgit?" he asked, in Urdu again.

In a mix of Urdu and English Farhana told him she'd come to study glaciers. He seemed unsurprised. "People come here for all reasons," he declared. He then asked if she knew that 25 percent of the Karakorams were under ice.

She laughed. "Of course I know."

"There are *thousands* of glaciers," he said.

"Well, hundreds."

"I can take you."

"Thank you."

"But not to Siachen."

She kept laughing. I couldn't remember the last time I'd seen her so gay.

Nur Shah knew not only glaciers. He knew stories and, at least at first, how to share them to dissipate the tension in the jeep. Originally from Hunza, he'd moved to Gilgit soon after the Karakoram Highway was built and claimed that, as a child, he was "best of friends" with the grandson of the Mir of Hunza. This Mir had famously joined the struggle for the creation of Pakistan, and, according to Nur Shah, it was the Mir's unique way of training his men that won us independence from Hindustan.

The Mir's way was indeed unique. The officers of the Eskimo Force had to plunge their hands in the icy Hunza River for hours at a time and wade through ice sheets without shoes. "They had skin as thick as a glacier," he looked at Farhana. Perhaps each time he made her laugh, he counted additional rupees. "It was an old technique," he continued. "Before the freedom fight, it toughened men for raiding caravans passing from Kashmir to Yarkand. You know Yarkand? In Chinese Turkestan? On the Silk Road?"

Farhana smiled.

"The Hunzakuts would walk on ice to reach the highest mountaintops, then pounce down on the enemy on the Silk Road and take his food and weapons. Later, they used the same skill to pounce down on soldiers in Kargil."

Farhana stifled a yawn.

Still the driver continued. "In Kargil, the Eskimo Force joined up with the Ibex Force. You know the Ibex Force?"

"No," said Farhana.

"The Tiger Force?"

"No."

"You do not know the Tiger Force—sahib?" He looked at me.

"No."

"They would advance while growling like tigers, keeping the Indian Force away."

Farhana started laughing.

"Millions of men growling is nothing to laugh about, baji," Nur Shah said softly.

"And what did the Ibex Force do?" she cleared her throat.

"It hopped."

Before she could laugh again Irfan motioned to her to stop. He whispered that it would be very rude to insult what was a well-documented strategy, and a source of pride.

She whispered back, "Do we need your permission to laugh now?"

Nur Shah whispered, "Many Pakistanis do not know their own history."

From the boot of the jeep, we heard a cough. Our man from Kaghan, Maryam's relative. He'd been so silent since joining us I'd almost forgotten him. Next to me Irfan whispered in English that this was the "concession" he'd made Maryam's family, in addition to the payment, in order for us to proceed peacefully on our journey after Kiran's death. He added, "You've no idea how lengthy the monetary negotiations were. Agreeing on the escort was the easy part." I would have to ask him for details later.

As Nur Shah continued to recount stories in praise of Hunzakuts, the escort muttered what sounded a lot like, *Tell this son-of-an-owl to shut up*. He sat hunched over an automatic weapon, knocking his head into the roof each time we hit a pothole, which was often. Irfan patted his shoulder and the man made a sound a tiger might make as he stifled a growl. If a million men were to growl like him, it might well encourage an army's retreat.

It was raining when we arrived in Gilgit, the largest town we'd seen since leaving Islamabad over a week ago. It was crowded, and the army was everywhere, in part to contain the not infrequent Shia–Sunni squabbles that erupted here.

In our hotel room, Irfan told me that our escort's black mood had in part to do with his distaste for the Shias of Gilgit, though differences transcended lines of sect. No matter how settled they might be today, the Gujjars who likely came down from the Central Asian steppe thousands of years ago would always be considered *grazers*.

"So why did he come?"

"He has work."

"What work?"

"Trade. What else have people ever done here?"

We took turns in the shower (hot, thankfully) before joining Wes at the restaurant. Farhana had gone for a walk, with the driver, in the rain.

Wes had already ordered food. Wet hair lay flat across his forehead and a line of moisture trickled down his temple. Irfan and I had dried our hair vigorously with towels before stepping into the chilly evening. It was a difference I'd noted to Farhana once, soon after we'd met. Pakistanis avoided combining wet hair with cold air, believing it a recipe for sickness. Americans didn't. Farhana didn't.

Whether he was courting a cold or not, with the arrival of the meal of spinach, mutton korma, and pilau, Wes's spirits revived. "Simple and great," he announced to the three waiters who topped his glass of water after every sip, proffered fresh naan before the one on his plate could grow cold, and apologized when his napkin fell off his lap.

The naan came wrapped in newspaper written in a script that was neither English nor Urdu. I asked one of our waiters where it was from.

"That is Kazakh," he said.

"You can read it?"

He shook his head and laughed, adding, "But I can sometimes hear it."

Irfan was looking over his shoulder at the table next to us.

I'd also noticed them: our escort, talking to two men who kept looking at us, one with dark eyes, the other blue. Our waiters seemed disconcerted by the trio.

Irfan asked the waiters if the men were speaking their language, Shina.

All three shook their heads.

"Kazakh?"

"It is possible," said the first waiter, before listening more intently. "The men are speaking a Turkic language. It could be any. Kazakh, Uzbek. No, I do not think Uzbek. They could also be Uyghurs. From China. They all come here for business and speak each other's tongues." After a longer pause, he added, with some disdain, "We have seen that man before. The one who came with you."

"He is not liked?" asked Irfan.

"He does not like us." He looked away.

Our escort snapped his fingers and the youngest waiter was told to answer. It seemed to me that they were all keeping their distance to avoid serving the table.

After a while, the eldest waiter continued, "Nomads have a way of finding each other. It is strange. Their bonds."

I waited. "And?"

The old man scratched his beard. "The two men over at that end," he lifted his chin, "I am sure now. One is a Uyghur merchant." I tried to look back discreetly but the man had shifted; my view was blocked by our escort. "The other is a cattle breeder."

"A free man," nodded Irfan.

"How so?"

"Kazakh means free man." He chewed vigorously. "They are the wandering cattle breeders that fired Dostoyevsky's imagination. Remember how he exiled Raskolnikov in *Crime and Punishment*?"

"I don't remember." This was better than admitting I never finished it.

"He sent him to Kazakhstan."

"Didn't he spend time there himself, after prison camp?"

"Yes, after his mock execution. Imagine thinking you're going to be killed, and then, at the last minute, being spared."

"I can't imagine it."

We were still recovering a sense of freedom and resurrection à la Dostoyevsky, when Irfan noticed her. Farhana, entering the restaurant. Before she could reach our table, he'd caught the old waiter's eye and ordered fresh food. Her hair was dripping; her skin glowed. She eyed our plates hungrily.

"It won't be long," said Irfan.

"Thank you." She sat down.

We were all getting along so well.

"How're you feeling, Farrah?" asked Wes. "Think you can eat?"

"Just watch."

So when the food arrived, we watched Farhana dip her fingers into the plates and suck steaming spinach off her thumb. It was probably the wrong thing for her to eat but I wasn't going to be the messenger. She spoke of her walk with Nur Shah along the Gilgit River, adding, "Nadir"—this was delivered casually, without looking up—"I'm beginning to understand your love of night walks along rivers."

"I go alone," I said.

She laughed, carefree, cold.

There was silence at the table as we continued watching her eat.

"So," offered Wes. "Ultar Glacier tomorrow? Batura the next day?"

"If the weather permits," replied Irfan. "We'll leave for Hunza early. Batura is north of Passu, where the road isn't good, especially in the rain. And it's supposed to keep raining. Even if we do get there, the trek will be slippery."

"Ultar is closer," said Farhana.

"But steeper," said Irfan.

She insisted we had to try. Wes supported her. After all, he'd climbed up glaciers in the Gulf of Alaska, Canada, and God-knows-where. Throw in the Andes and Mount Kilimanjaro. Patagonia while you're at it. Did I mention that he'd fallen down a crevasse in Antartica? There he wrestled with polar bears—the only ones in the Southern Hemisphere—before inching his way back to the top, on bloodied fingernails. Only to confront more polar bears as the nails grew back.

Farhana tossed her head about some episode or other they'd encountered together while taking ice samples on Mount Shasta.

I reminded myself: *Leave it behind.* We were here to go on. Even if we could not get along. I excused myself and headed out into the night. Before leaving the restaurant, I thought I saw one of the men at our escort's table scoop food into his mouth with a hand without fingers. It was not an image to look at twice.

Kashmiris have names for Indian prisons: Papa-2; Kot Balwal; Gogoland. The way the Indian government disappeared the men of Kashmir, I heard said, was not unlike how Pakistan's government disappeared the men of Pakistan. Only, no one was sharing names for Pakistani prisons, at least not those I heard around me now, as I walked down the muddy lanes of the main bazaar. The disappearances usually happened in more or less the same way: a boy leaves the house to get paan from the stall across the street, or to play cricket in the field around the block. Never returns.

I did not want paan. I did not know what I wanted, but I found myself staring at a wall, specifically, at a poster on the wall. Sylvester Stallone. Beside him, someone had scrawled, *Inshallah*. I thought of polar bears and kept walking.

It was after nine o'clock but the market was still crammed and I heard more languages spoken here than at an international airport. I learned that some of the people milling around had come from as far away as Andijan and Kashgar, either with bales of cloth, or with no clothes except the ones on their backs. The textile business had been thriving since the end of the Soviet Union; so had the business of war.

At one door, a sign read, *Hitt Fabricks of Sentral Asia*. The greatest hits included fabrics named after heroes and villains: Putin, Osama bin Laden, Tears of Shahrukh, Eyes of Ashwarya. My sister would drool, anticipating how women would whisper enviously at the next wedding, *Did you see her in Osama?*

I moved on. Here, as in Kaghan, a tale of occupation was a tale of names. So Gilgit was also Little Tibet and the Xinjiang Province was Turkestan, and almost everyone around me who wasn't from here was fleeing occupation of some kind.

Outside a different shop, I noticed a cluster of men speaking a language I couldn't identify, one of whom was definitely missing the fingers of his right hand. After the group left, two of them hobbling, I said to the shopkeeper, "They didn't look like lepers."

"Because they're not," he replied. "You should see their toes." He said they were Uyghur refugees, fleeing a quite unique persecution by China: their hands and feet were hosed with ice water. I was reminded of our driver's tales of the Eskimo Force, soldiers who were made to plunge their hands in the freezing Hunza River for hours, then wade through ice sheets without shoes. If for one it was torture, for the other, glory.

The men at the restaurant were a foreshadowing of the Gilgit I'd stepped into tonight. Where one group of men shared tales of Kashmiris tortured by Indian troops, another shared tales of Uzbeks fired upon by Uzbek troops. These mountains acted as walls, enclosing us in a lonely pocket where poverty was synonymous with diversity and conflict with hospitality. There was more than one dark-eyed Uyghur from China sipping tea with a blue-eyed Kazakh from Russia, whether at a restaurant, or in among a clutter of cheap chinaware, a mound of jade, or posters of Stallone.

Meanwhile, rumors of the man-and-his-double, Fareebi the shapeshifter, had traveled to these heights long before us. He was fleeing Pakistani torture cells, it was said, the cells with no names, where he would end up, eventually, in the hands of the Americans. But, the rumors continued, vehemently and unanimously, he wasn't here, in this epicenter of refugees and informers, traders and merchants.

On the walls of yet another shop, I read a telltale scrawl, *Pipelineistan 4 Hu?* Osama silk, dowdy dishware, and persecution weren't all that brought men to this corridor. There was also oil. Between sweet green tea and salty pink tea, there was much opining about the Kazakh–Chinese deal, in which a 3,000-kilometer pipeline running through the Xinjiang Province would start pumping oil as early as next year. It was a throwback to the ties forged on the ancient Silk Road, but with a twist. Despite the billions of dollars invested, ethnic Kazakhs and Uyghurs still lived below the poverty line, deprived of their ancestral homes. These men were refugees; they were also fugitives. Not all hobbled, and many carried guns.

How many were twenty-first-century Raskolnikovs, seeking banishment most of all from themselves? Perhaps only Dostoyevsky would know.

It was getting late, and I didn't wish to linger any longer through the night, not in a town I was only beginning to see. I left the muddy alleys and wound my way back toward the Gilgit River, a thick, brick-red arm of the Indus that chugged down Gilgit Valley like an impetuous train. As my footsteps grew more urgent, the rain started again, softly, yet even this caress seemed to aggravate the river's march. It kicked; it heaved.

Before I'd left the store with the crippled Uyghur refugees, the shopkeeper, polishing the inside of a chipped teacup with his spit, had said something that now thundered in my head. "Our valley is tight, but not impassable, if you know the way. How we all arrrived at the same corridor from different corners of the world, now that may seem like a mystery, but it is not. We found a way. Why? Trade, yes, but most importantly, freedom. And we know you need three things to be free. Mountains, for security and glaciers; rivers, for drinking and irrigation; farmland, for food and money. Here we have all three. Which is why the government won't leave us alone." He put the cup away. "And why we help each other." He then quoted a saying of the Prophet Mohammad: "In the beginning Islam was something strange and it will one day return as something strange." I said I wasn't familiar with the Hadith, but was glad to learn of it. The shopkeeper added, "It is why the Prophet gave glad tidings to the ghuraba. The strangers. 'Blessed are the outsiders,' he said, peace be upon him!"

I couldn't confirm it, but I had a feeling, as I hurried along the rash river, that I was being watched. I would have liked to find the courage to turn left at the mosque, and even left again at the end of the road, where, I was sure of it, soon after leaving the shop, I'd seen our escort slip into the shadows. I would have liked to stare down whatever it was I would meet. But I kept on, till, eventually, I stepped to my right, into the hotel.

The next morning, I was not altogether surprised to find us hit with more delays.

First, there was the raid. Among the seized items were two cars; 35,000 kilograms of explosives; fifty computers; hundreds of guns; electronic goods (VCRs, toasters, blenders); furniture stolen from schools and banks. And rickshaws. Rickshaws were to be banned for fifteen days. The "found" goods were displayed at a press briefing. There were also two arrests, a blind man and a cripple who had to be propped semi-upright from the hips. These were the cream of the bad crop. They weren't from Gilgit but from "outside the mountains." Given how many people here were seeking sanctuary from somewhere else—including, I realized with a start, Farhana and I—it was hard to know who hadn't come from outside the mountains.

Next, there were no buses leaving for Hunza that morning, and Nur Shah refused to take us in his jeep. We'd have to wait. Our journey's motif.

By afternoon, the rumor had spread. The real reason for the arrests was to deliver a clear message to those at war with the country. The state could do what it wanted with the grazing grounds and water of the land. It could, if it wanted, give it all to China. Pakistan and China had a history of friendship, and those who tried to undermine the friendship would be arrested under Pakistan's Prevention of Terrorism Act, and convicted on evidence. The evidence was before our eyes: the seized items, the blind man, the cripple. Those at war with any other government friendly to Pakistan—whether in North America or in Central Asia—would also be arrested.

Gilgit wore a gray cloud that day, thicker than any that cloaked the mountains around us. Everyone wants our land, people said. Everyone wants our rivers, our sea.

Others argued that this too would pass. The land had known many conflicts and many differences, but people had always found common interests on the Silk Road, and always would. Governments, on the other hand, would come and go. As would music. By nightfall, radios blared again from every shop, some with news, others, Bollywood hits.

Our foursome was suddenly a tiny part of the world congregating in this narrow corridor, whether for trade or freedom. I embraced our diminished status with relief. The spotlight here wasn't on me but on a bigger game being played around me. I stayed in my hotel room that night. Irfan was away till very late; where he went, he wouldn't say. He hadn't been in our room the previous night either, when I returned from walking along the Gilgit River in the rain. I'd thought nothing of it. Though it may sound strange, I'd even hazard to say that when I finally heard Irfan climb into bed, after a quick flicking on and off of the lamp by his side, I felt much like the mountains enclosing us. Impenetrable.

Even when he said, in the dark, "In times of unrest, everyone is implicated."

Always the optimist.

We go on. Leave it behind. Everyone is implicated. Our three mantras, blending into one.

I had this ridiculous image of Farhana and I running toward each other while people blew themselves up around us, and a bird swung circles in the sky, watching our grainy shadows crisscross in jerks. We couldn't tell if the blood that draped every tree and every rock was caused by the stupid eye in the sky or the stupid bomber on the ground. And in the background, there was jaunty music, and people dancing. And in the extreme background, there was a green shalwar and a magenta shirt.

But it was only an image. We were safe.

Queen of the Mountains: Everyone Is Welcome

They had grown lean. The buffalo, especially; each hip had too many angles. Suleiman had been forced to buy supplementary feed, but once these stocks were gone, he could buy no more. The way the animals moved told Maryam that, like her, they wondered how many would not make it through the winter.

Her wrist still hurt.

On the day she smashed it, Suleiman had returned home with the horses she had left to wander into the field unsupervised.

"You know how valuable they are," he began. "If we lost them, how would we climb the slopes to the pasture next summer?"

"On our feet," Maryam muttered.

"Your feet cannot even carry you as far as your daughter." Jumanah whimpered in his arms. "Though they carry you very well to your shrine."

She waited, but without offering to take Jumanah from him, for the additional reason that she could not have held her with a broken wrist. She kept the arm hidden behind her back. She did not tell him that the animals did not need her to look after them. They were better off on their own, and perhaps he would be too.

His silence conveyed a thicket of disappointment she wished her body could hack through. Who was he to judge her, after all he had done? He was like the mare Namasha, righteous and mean. Well, she could stare them both down. Suleiman eventually limped away, still holding the baby.

It was hours later, after returning with the animals and herding them into the enclosure for the night, that he noticed. He came into their hut to find her weeping. This time, she only wept because of the physical ache. A current was tearing up her right arm, and, though her left hand tried to squeeze out the pain, the current was strong. It fought her like a snake, his teeth to her blood, while her eye noted, with a precision separate from the rest of her, the way the wrist kept swelling and changing color.

Suleiman kneeled. It was not an easy position for him. "What good would it be?" he whispered, "me with a broken leg and you with a broken arm?"

She thought this funny. As the colors on her skin deepened, she stifled a laugh and the spasm caused the current to shoot through her arm with heightened intensity, causing her to clench her teeth in pain, a gesture she was certain made her look like the mare Namasha, which only made her chuckle and choke and grimace again.

"It is all my fault!" he said, taking her fingers gently in his, tears licking his long lashes. Though he did not say exactly what *all*, he did not need to. At that moment, she was glad for both the men she loved, the one who wept, and the one who fought.

The next day, her wrist sticky with Suleiman's balm for broken bones and cradled in a cloth like a child, the other one showed up again. This time, he waited for her outside the hut, near the water-hole. If he had heard about her injury, it was not why he was here. His reason was to tell her that he would either send one of his men to accompany the foreigners north, or do it himself. He would let her know the result. The result of what? she wondered, but instead asked the question to which she already knew the answer.

"How will I know?"

"Through whisperers and runners, Maryam. The way we always survive."

From inside his good clothes he took out a bottle of clear liquid, unscrewed the top, and drank. He eyed her over the bottle. "Your son, Younis, does he talk to them?"

"Who?"

"The police. They show no sign of leaving."

"What would he talk to them about?"

"Whatever they want him to say."

"He has nothing to do with them."

He drank. The bottle had a red label and was half empty.

"He can come with me, Maryam. After my work here is done. I can find him a job. As a runner—for jade, or a different kind of silk."

"He stays with me."

"There is money to be made. And he will be safe. Safer than here."

"He stays with me," she repeated, steel in her voice.

"It was just an offer." He tilted the bottle in her direction, his eyes equally glassy. "Vodka will ease your pain, Maryam."

So, he was now offering her liquor, in place of honey. Did it taste different from juniper brandy? Many men liked brandy in their cups, in place of tea. Many women liked it too. Once, as a child, she had spied a cup left behind by her mother. When Maryam lifted it to her nose, without warning, her tongue had licked the bottom clean. It had made her blood surge with a warm, acid sweetness. Afterward, knowing that her mother's nose was even keener than her own, she had rubbed her gums with milk.

But something in the way Ghafoor now tilted the bottle toward her made it a worse trespass than her own secret experiment. He had never looked at her this way, not in all the times he had come to her when she was a child. She pushed his hand away.

He began telling her more stories, about the people of the steppe, their drink, their food. After boiling the head of a sheep, they divided it between the family. Ears went to the children, eyes to those who would not see, tongue to those who would not speak. "Guess which part would go to you?" he asked.

She watched his eyes shine with a silver glint that made her think of boiling heads. On he went, spewing big words in her face about the world from which he had descended. And she was back to saying nothing more to him.

"They are strong. Stronger than us. What do you think they do, Maryam, when free grazing lands are turned to state farms? Do they become slaves?" His eye was turning from silver to red. "Never! Once we were free to graze in the hills around Saiful Maluk. But even there we are no longer safe. Anyone can rob our cattle, even our children. We have no fight in us! We have no leadership! We have no pride!"

The bottle was dry. His eyes were wet. He was teetering close to the waterhole.

She was suddenly enraged. *Get on with the plan*, she wanted to say. *Get on with it. Whatever it is. Your talk is meaningless.*

"People here do not listen to me, Maryam. I came back at great risk to myself."

Again he waited for gratitude; again she withheld it. He plunged his fist inside the waterhole, wasting the good drink. He looked like he needed cradling more than the wrist tied to her chest, the one he had not even noticed.

"They drove me away. But I am back! I will prove what I can do!"

"Prove it then," she hissed, spinning on her heels and walking away. Without looking back she added, "Your war with every man in uniform should leave us strong, not weak."

After a long pause she heard his reply. "The ones in plainclothes are worse."

She did not look back at him, and two days later, she saw that the flowers he had left her lay wilting in her shrine.

If she had looked back, and kept on looking, she would have seen Ghafoor slip away, far away, to walk the winding valley of his youth.

First, a few miles north, past Kawai, where the road ascended steeply, and it felt good, the way his thighs tightened to brace for what he knew would soon be a much steeper ascent. If he looked to his left he could see Musa ka Musalla, the prayer mat of Moses. He did not know a single person who could explain why the mountain was called this, for it did not look much like a prayer mat at all. What he did know was that he was unlikely to see it again. So he bowed before it, from one prayer mat to another.

He contemplated taking the road to his right, toward Shogran, the forest in the sky, but he did not like the idea of meeting the city folk who spent their summers there. He turned around and went back down, toward Balakot, intending to head all the way south to Mansehra.

He met several people along the way and some of them met his eye and some of them did not. The River Kunhar moved beside him almost the entire way, sometimes thin as a smile, sometimes wide as laughter. It was laughter that could turn seditious in the rainy season, and he could not forget the floods of 1991, when he was just a buffalo boy hoping to one day see the world. Even though the riverbed was steeply inclined, that year she had climbed to the edge of it, to unleash the worst of her mischief on the town of Balakot.

It was a fragile town; another flood or earthquake and it might not survive at all. It was already barely keeping afloat. Two years after the 1991 floods, Maulana Sufi first began imposing Islamic laws in the region. Now, many summers later, his followers were moving deeper into the forest, their camps creeping like mold. Maryam could turn her back to him all she pleased, but every herder knew that no agency really wanted to dismantle the camps. Why would they? It was thanks to them that they could keep up the fight in Kashmir and Afghanistan and, most importantly, in the forest that had once looked down from two hundred feet but that now stooped in shame. Everyone here knew it, but no one had a plan.

The sun began to dip when Ghafoor neared Balakot, still deep in thought. The refugees from Central Asia were finding brothers in those camps. And what was he—a brother to his friends or to his enemies? Were they even friends, those men, the ones who had given him rare yellow flowers in Gilgit, the ones with missing toes and soft leather palms? They had told him not to look beneath the flowers. He had not looked. He had delivered it, as promised, to a man waiting above a bend of the Kunhar that was well-known to him. It was a part of the river used for storing smuggled tree trunks. There was a knob in the rock face opposite the bend, about twenty feet high, and Ghafoor had seen the man standing there, waiting. He was from a rival tribe, and Ghafoor had not liked the exchange, not one bit. The man had given him a second, very different kind of box—slightly larger than the other and with a lid he must not even crack—and a second delivery date, after which Ghafoor must return to the men in Gilgit, with news.

He had not cracked the lid. But he was unsure whether to deliver the box. He had buried it, in the most secret place he could think of—Maryam's shrine, a foxhole, really—and would leave it there while deciding what to do. Before the delivery date, he could be gone. He could reach those men in Gilgit, to whom he was committed to return, before they found out what he had done. He liked this plan, but he had to think.

He kept walking, his footsteps growing surer as he approached another bend in the Kunhar. Here the river laughed gaily as she smacked the rocks on her way to meet the Jhelum. This was where she would cease being his traveling companion. His road twisted west, hers east. At the waterfall made by the river's pleasure at leaving this valley to meet the next, a Queen had once washed her tired eyes. The bend was still called Nain Sukh.

Ghafoor skipped off the road and down the embankment. He balanced on a rock close to the waterfall. His shirt was wet, his shoes slippery. He was alone with the roar of the cascade and the sunlight flickering between the branches of the pine trees that were suddenly their own true height. He gazed up at those branches that had for centuries trusted the law that said the people of this valley must wait fifty years for each pine, deodar, and fir to reach maturity. Only after maturity could each be cut. Hardly anyone waited anymore, though here, right here in this island where time moved only as it should, the trees had been left alone.

Ghafoor held his breath; he cocked his ear toward the tallest branches. He listened for a very long time. Yes, at last, he could hear them, the reason why the forest to the south was called Chor Mor, the peacock thief. This bend of the river was like a bowl, gathering echoes and swirling them around like tea leaves. The more you waited, the richer grew the cries of those peacocks. He was tempted to hop off the rock and dash into the forest to chase after their feathers, the way he had done many times as a boy.

He stayed on the rock. He leaned forward, and, instead of feathers, he gathered the pure filtered water of the cascading river in his hands. He brushed it over his eyes. His eyes were soothed as lovingly as Queen Nur Jehan's long ago. He gargled. The water was unpolluted here. He blew his nose. He wet his ears. He rolled the cuffs of his sleeves and let the water roll down the sleekness of his skin, to his elbows. He filled his palms again and poured water back from his widow's peak, down to the back of his neck, and further, opening his palms, spreading his fingers out like a fan, reaching past his shoulder blades. He took off his shoes, and then his socks. He extended each foot, right one first, beneath the falls. The water was deliciously icy; only now did he realize how much his feet ached. He wriggled his toes. He stretched his ankles. He thought briefly of his wife in the steppe, who did not perform the ritual ablution after sexual intercourse, or after her monthly flow. He decided that when he returned to her, he would make sure she did.

There, his ghusl was complete. He had never felt purer of mind, or intent.

His mind was made up. He had no need to keep walking south. What was in Mansehra anyway? Nothing of relevance to him. He was no mere delivery boy. He did not work for them. He was not *their* whisperer. He was not *their* runner. He did not care about their troubles, ultimately. And he told himself again that he was sick of everyone else's sense of wrong. It was time to right his own. They could find another pair of hands to lock with another pair of hands to cross the canal, or scratch the precipices of the most treacherous land route, or ride the air for all he cared, to wherever a message or parcel needed to reach. He was a free man, like the free men he now lived among. He would do as he wished. He wished to unlock his fingers altogether.

And so he retraced his steps north again, reaching Maryam's homestead as the moon began to rise. The buffaloes slinked into the night's shadows, horns blazing white against the darkening sky. He waited. In the middle of the night, when no one was looking, he unearthed the box he had hidden in her shrine. It was the color of earth. He had wrapped it in red cloth to make it easier to find, less for color than texture, in case it needed unearthing in a hurry and he had no means to find it except by the ends of his fingers. He was glad he had done this, for it did help locate it, and rather quickly too—though the cloth felt thinner to his touch, silkier even, and, when he lifted it up, it was lighter than he remembered, much lighter—but he had no time to dwell on this, for he was now in a great hurry. In the dark, it looked about right, and it had to be. He had only left this one. He flattened the earth to ensure that Maryam would not notice the mound he had dug up.

It was while he was leveling the ground that his fingers brushed something else, a bump that felt rough to the touch, closer to the texture he remembered leaving here, and he paused, confused. He began to dig. It was a second box. How could this be? Something was not right. Which one should he take? He had no time to decide. He must leave tonight. Which one was the right size, the right weight. *He had no time*. He piled both into his bag and again began leveling the earth, this time less thoroughly, so terrified was he of brushing against something else. There was nothing else.

Except, before leaving, he noticed that the ends of the two flowers he had brought Maryam were curling inward, shrinking and drying like mice on their backs, in the slight incline of the shrine just above where the first box had been buried.

Except for the flowers, Maryam did not see any of this, and now Ghafoor was gone and her wrist still hurt. She followed the animals into the forest. They walked themselves, barely glancing back at her, as she cringed at their gauntness. The air filled with their bells and with those of the neighbors' cattle and she could just about tell the sounds apart.

At one time, each homestead had been spaced far enough apart to allow the herds of each family territory in which to graze, but this was no longer the case. It was another reason to look forward to the summer migration; in the highland pastures, there was space. Kiran's death had disrupted the rhythm of the entire tol. While some families had stayed in the mountains, others descended the slopes with hers, to help rebuild their lowland dera, leasing timber and thatching grass from the forest department on the aggrieved family's behalf. Maryam knew that if one of them were in her place, she and Suleiman would do the same. If you ignored their cries, they would ignore yours.

In the days when Maryam was carried on her mother's back, the way she would later carry Kiran, her mother would explain that timber and thatching grass had once been free. The forest department would take away the materials each spring, when the families dismantled their huts and headed for the mountains, and give back the same timber each autumn, when they returned. She told Maryam it was the Angrez who invented the whole business, the whole revenue-generating forest policy that bound the herders, forcing them to pay a grazing fee and tree-cutting fee. Before the

Angrez, they had been free to graze and chop. And the sedentary folk had been friendly. They let the nomads camp in their fields during the migration, knowing that when the cattle moved on, they left piles of fresh, steaming dung. Free manure; what else did anyone want? The change had begun in Maryam's mother's day, and over the years, herders had become no better than the upal that lived in buffalo dung. "Everyone is welcome but us," her mother would grieve.

Which was why many members of her family had been tricked into buying. Giving up free grazing rights. Purchasing small plots of land from a state that told them what to plant, and when. The same cash crops, year after year, and for whom? The same people who took away their grazing rights. The ones who never smelled the seasons.

It was all very well for Ghafoor to boast that the nomads among whom he now lived were stronger than those among whom he was born, but what were they supposed to do? *We have no fight in us.* She hoped that whatever fight was left in him, he would apply to the only fight left worth waging.

Such were her thoughts when she noticed Laila, daughter of a nearby dera, trailing her goats a little too close to Maryam's. But the two knew each other well. They greeted each other by exchanging insults for the sedentary villagers. "Their bottoms stick to cushions like snails to a leaf," said Maryam, to which Laila added sounds with her tongue that were downright lewd.

Eventually, Laila asked, in a whisper, if Maryam had visited her shrine that day. Keenly aware that the others did not approve of her devotions—even though they had dwindled this year—Maryam began to move away. Laila followed her. "They are here," she warned, both their herds now feeding on the same shrub. "The men from Balakot."

Maryam felt the panic rise in her. "What do they want?"

Laila shrugged. "What do they ever want? The glory of Islam!" She giggled. "And no idols! And no shrines!"

Not now, Maryam thought. She mopped the sweat at her lip with her bandage, and winced. It was only a matter of time before they would find it, her little den in the center of a hill, large enough for a fox but not for men with a grudge. Or so she hoped.

They left their goats and tiptoed to a screen of kakwa ferns, from behind which they could see their row of huts. The forked fronds tickled her nose. *Pagan seasons for a pagan wife*. She was familiar with the taunt, but familiarity never thickened anyone's skin. Among those who said it were men who called themselves hajis, dangling the boast not only in her face, but in the face of every Gujjar in the area. Not many herders had performed the pilgrimage to Mecca. Of course they wanted to—who did not want forgiveness for her sins?—but how would they get the money? The hajis in the valley wore their skullcaps as though they were horns.

And she could see those fake horns now, from behind the ferns. They were the ones from Balakot. They were the worst. And the most recent. It was not till last year that they started showing up here, which was why her husband forbade her from celebrating Diwali. These men from Balakot knew how the nomads suffered because of the grazing fees and cutting fees and annual permits and taxes and fines and the pressure to be still. Like her mother, they knew the history. Though she was too far away to hear them, she could see them circling two young boys of another tol. The boys were no more than thirteen or fourteen years old. She could guess that the hajis, who did not look much older themselves, would begin their sermon by recalling the policies of the British. That is what the younger hajis with the little horns called them. Not Angrez like everyone else. So smart in their black vests.

The two women were now behind a row of tall bhekkar shrubs, the trunks barely wider than them. "The British colonized your lands and instituted a forest policy for their greedy pockets!" She could hear them clearly now, speaking Hindko in a strange accent. They knew it had never been their land, and never would be. "And before them, that Sikh dog Ranjit Singh and his followers, they also crushed the glory of Islam!" She could now see two older men, with turbans wound differently from Gujjar men. "Until the birth of the great martyr Syed Ahmad Barelvi, who devoted his life to jihad!"

Then issued a long account of the Battle of Balakot, where Barelvi was martyred. She had heard it before. She knew what was next. The martyr was buried in Balakot, making it sacred ground (yet they condemned idolatory!) and an inspiration for their cause. The British had gone, but there was another infidel stalking their land, for whom the government of Pakistan fought repeatedly, first against the infidel Russians in Afghanistan and now against our own Afghan brothers. Would they not join the cause, these brave Gujjar men, whom neither the British nor the Sikhs nor the forest nor the mountains nor the rivers had ever been able to tame?

She could see one boy nodding, while the other scratched the dirt with his broken rubber slippers. His feet were caked in dirt. The two young hajis wore Peshawari chappals, gold embroidered on beige and brown leather. On the center strap of each slipper was a large red pom-pom. The older men wore chappals of scuffed black leather. One of them now began cajoling the boy scratching the dirt. He ruffled his hair. He pinched his cheek. "What do you say?" He made kissing sounds. The boy, still looking down, mumbled something that made the men laugh. The other boy played with a gold chain around his neck. It looked expensive, that chain. He was still playing with it with one hand when he grabbed the bashful boy's hand with the other and welcomed everyone into a hut. Within seconds, the red pom-poms were leading the way.

Like the forest inspector and tax collector who had always plagued them, and like the policemen, soldiers, and spies who plagued them now, these wrongly turbaned men could also be placated with ghee and sugar, mutton and bread. The more they preached, the hungrier they grew. She did not know what would happen once their supplies ran out.

From what she could hear the men say tonight, outside in the baithak, whose walls did not reach high enough to touch the roof, allowing her to listen freely—for though she must work with men in the forest she must not gossip with them in the hut—this year the patience of the men from Balakot was also running out.

Unlike the preachers of last year, the men said, this lot was not going to stop at words. They were younger and had training camps. They were armed. They had already used their guns against villagers to the south and west. They wanted to recruit; their sons were not safe. They were waging a Sunni jihad against non-Muslims and all allies of the infidel, including anyone linked to the government. This meant the men in convoys, as well as the tax inspector and forest inspector. They were not interested in the forest, unless it was to use it as a camp, should they need to move from Balakot. They had told the Gujjar men that they understood nomadic living.

Maryam pulled away in indignation. Herders did not pray regularly at the mosque, since their migration took them too far. The men from Balakot had at one time chided them for this. Now they called themselves nomadic? She stilled her breast, then glued her ear to the wall again.

One man—it was the voice of a man who had bid for her hand before Suleiman's family had won—said it was a shame how these men, like their inspiration Syed Ahmad Barelvi two hundred years ago, targeted Muslims. "They say Americans are killing Muslims in Afghanistan and Pakistan, Palestine, and Iraq. Then why kill us?"

"They have not killed us. Yet." Maryam felt this to be the voice of Laila's father. It was like distinguishing between bells again.

There was a long pause.

"Who do we cooperate with? The government or the militants?"

"Both."

"Then they will both be watching us. And they will both strike at us."

There was another long pause.

"It is true," a voice broke the silence at last. "We will neither get dry in the sun, nor wet in the rain."

There were murmurs of agreement, followed by a different proverb offering the same disturbing truth: they were caught between two sides that rejected them equally.

"Do the convoys even care about Fareebi any more?" This voice was high-pitched and clearly peeved. "That shapeshifter?"

"Did they ever? Who was he anyway?"

"Is," said a young boy, his voice just beginning to crack. "I saw him just today."

She heard his head being smacked. "Do not lie." It must have been his father.

The boy muttered an apology.

"In what shape did you see him?" another man asked, his voice distended in a grin. This man too she could recognize. On her wedding day, he had ogled her, then too with a grin. He had bid for her with one sick buffalo, nursing juniper brandy in his cup.

"The boy is too active in his head," said the father, and there were mutters of support, the transgression swiftly forgiven.

She could hear teacups secured to the floor, hookahs inhaled. With one breath came eight words that spoke for them all. "Who even knows who is doing what anymore?" Followed by deep grunts of approval. "Dust rises when the cliff falls." More approval, more gurgles of smoke.

After a while, a voice she did not recognize asked, "What about that man from your wife's side? The one who has come back?"

On the other side of the wall, Maryam tried to keep very still.

"That crow on a stone."

She flinched. It was a saying reserved only for the most mistrusted. Ghafoor was being accused of preferring to be by himself instead of with his family. This was not entirely fair, given that they had told him to leave, all those years ago.

"What about him?" The voice was Suleiman's.

"Is he with the militants?"

This time the pause was so excruciating she wanted to knock on the wall, tell them to hurry up and answer.

"I saw him talking to them." It was the voice she had not recognized.

There were murmurs of surprise. "What do you mean?"

"First he tried to talk to me. Something about the police and how we must stand up to them. How we could not be enslaved. How we could learn from the Uzbeks and the Uyghurs and the nomads of the steppe," the man spit, "whose women are like men. He thinks he can come back after all this time and lead us? If you want to lead, stand in line."

There were shouts of "Well said" and "That one never brought us anything but trouble" and "Now he is back, he will bring worse."

"No." Suleiman's voice was surprisingly firm. "He is not with them."

"No? His mouth is well-slit."

A few men laughed.

"Indeed." Sulemian cleared his throat. "It is because he is full of contradictory speech that my wife's family turned to him. As you know, I have wanted no compensation for our loss."

There were murmurs of support, and the air was filled with blessings for Kiran.

"It is the will of God."

"It is the will of the skies."

"It is the will of the mountains."

"It is the will of the goddess."

At this last there was much shifting and throat-clearing. Maryam knew it was the father of the child who had spoken out of turn. Clearly, the child had taken after his father, for people did not call out to the goddess in public anymore.

It seemed the only way to end the awkward silence was by steering the conversation back to the crow on the stone.

"Are you sure he is not with the militants?"

"I am sure," said Suleiman, his voice still unyielding.

"If he is, he can tell us what to do," countered another voice, also a stranger's.

"If he is, he will *not* tell us what to do," said Suleiman. "But I have said he is not. He is with other men. Men who might have contacts with these men, but who have different interests. I do not know what. But I know it is not Sunni jihad."

"What is it then?"

Perhaps Suleiman knew she was there. She had listened to their chatter on many nights, after her family had eaten and the children were in bed. Perhaps each time he returned to her from the baithak, her eyes revealed all that her ears had received.

"Well?" repeated the peeved voice. "If he is not with them, what is it he wants?"

"Justice."

"Justice?"

Then Maryam heard a sound, unnatural, like winter rain, or summer snow. It fell everywhere around her, from high above the wall. No, it was neither snow nor rain. What fell was far worse. It was the sound of men bonded together in derisive laughter.

She moved away from the wall, out into the open air, into her true home.

The night was moonless and thick with moisture. She searched for stars but not one revealed itself. She searched for Ghafoor but he was gone. Perhaps trailing the foreigners further north. She had heard nothing from him since their last meeting. Remembering the meeting left her aching for the way she used to think of him. Wherever he was now, she hoped he might see some stars. And when he did, she knew he would not point, no matter how inebriated, or enraged. *They only point at what takes away life.*

It pained her, too, the way the people of the valley regarded him. In the past, they had shown him both respect and fear. To the young, especially, he had been a hero, even if, to the old who carried the burden of honor, he was an embarrassment. But now, while some did not even know of him, others dismissed him outright. Had they not heard of his courage, the way he showed the forest inspector what happened to those falsely accused of a crime? Did they not pass the inspector's burned house, and cringe? Did they not see his dead wife's ghost, hear her children scream? No, apparently not. And, apparently, she had been proud of him for doing it, though she had not been able to admit it till now.

Though change was a part of their way, not this change, not this Ghafoor, the one who had become a stray.

She understood now that the way he had looked at her the last time said he was searching for his own worth. If others had rejected him, was she going to do the same? If he could not be a leader of his men, could he not even own a piece of her? Though their alliance depended on restraining desire, he still expected to be desirable to her. This was to be depended on. Though everything else must change, these were the two fixed variables of their love—*never consummate our love, never overcome it*. He had looked at her expecting this assurance, and was angry when he could not find it.

She walked back into the hut. Her free hand pulled a cup from off a plank behind which she hid their remaining supplies, including the brandy. Her children were asleep. On the other side, the men still talked. She poured a little brandy, her mind still churning.

She feared this change the most: could it be that her trader and merchant, the one with the vodka stench in place of the garlic tang, the desperate leer in place of the honey, did not have the fight in *him* anymore? Could it be that he was following the foreigners to the north to no purpose? He clearly needed cradling, but she was in no condition to offer this, even if she wanted to, which she did not. Not after all the effort it took to keep her broken heart from growing cold.

She carried the cup into the forest. No matter how bad things got in the valley, no matter how badly the herders were caught between the government and the militants, what happened to Kiran could not be forgotten. The fight had not left *her*. If only she could take Ghafoor's place, as he trailed the foreigners.

The trees before Maryam rose higher in the dark than during the day. She could name each shadow. Diar, bhentri, chalai. There were also shadows closer to earth, plants whose rhizomes and leaves cured ailments from insomnia to gonorrhea, and even cancer. She recited these names too—asmani booti, birmi, and of course, muther. She rubbed the soil between her fingers, her eye keen, searching for the ginger beloved to the animals.

The year the sheep ate the two ginger stems and they were forced to pay the fine, her mother had said something that now, as the warm, acid sweetness of juniper seeped through her pores, Maryam at last understood. Caressing the ginger root, her mother had said the ewe was wise to eat it. She said the best things in life were like the ginger plant, pungent, plentiful, and most of all, horizontal, with no clear beginning or end. Always on the move, in the middle, between things, between being. Leave the vertical world to trees and mountains. Everything else with any sense at all—including gods and jinns—moved like the ginger plant: parallel to the horizon, to reach whatever space was available.

Well, so would Maryam. Even if it could only be in her head. She drank. The warmth spread through her veins as when she had been a child licking the dregs of her mother's mana with guilt. Now she was guilt-free.

Fragments of the men's talk returned to her. As much as the words, it was the way in which they were spoken—distant, elevated—that played in her head. Her mother had taught her that women spoke to each other in a language that was direct and intimate, while men spoke in idioms, to raise them in height. But this did not mean women talked directly *to* men, only to each other, nor that women could not possess the power of public speech. She herself was proof of this. Who had not praised her skills? She would tell Maryam to grasp the nuances of speech before she married. She would ask, "Have you filled your mouth with flour?" It was a way of urging Maryam not only to speak, but to speak correctly. If Maryam could not fill her mouth with flour, how then could she see that a chasm could be a window, or a mountain a door?

Maryam settled at the foot of a chalai tree, though it could well be the torso of a jinn. She shut her eyes, feeling herself grow flatter and flatter. Trans-limbed, like a worm, buffeted by feathers and leaves. She slithered and she flew. She followed the foreigners north.

Almost immediately, he was there.

In the jaws of a glistening fang—the place where snow was born and ice never melted—a man lay hunkered, his shoulder braced against a fall. He was not going to fall, but he was in pain. How he got there, she could not say. Perhaps he had slipped.

The image was so dazzling in clarity, so fluid in motion, it was as though her hand orchestrated it. She could feel the pain in the right shoulder of the man who had followed her to the graves. It was not only a physical pain. And she could make it worse. If she willed him to moan, he did. If she willed him to look up, he did.

Her first vision, at last.

She heard the heavy wingbeat, just as she had heard it earlier this summer, the first time she saw the image of the man, before she realized what she was seeing. The wingbeat came closer; her vision was going to be interrupted, though she longed to see what would happen next inside the glistening fang, to the man with the pain that was not only a physical pain, the one who, like her, could not stop seeing a girl step inside a boat. It angered her that they had something in common, but they did.

The wings settled. Her vision disappeared. It was gone, the way a star is suddenly gone no matter how hard you stare at the space in the sky where it shone.

In place of the vision of the man in the mountains, there, staring down at her from a bhentri tree, was an owl.

"Hoot!" called the wings to the next world, leaning very slightly forward. Her face was ringed with braided feathers the shade of her own human hair. Her cheek was pale, her eyes, dark as a cave. Of course she would pick her beloved juniper tree to rest on, the one whose leaves she smoked, whose bark she burned, whose berries she roasted.

Maryam called back. “Have you filled your mouth with flour, Mother?”

The owl adjusted her wings, a hint of a smile at the corner of her beak.

FIVE

A Sudden Peace

I dreamed Farhana slept beside me again, talking in her sleep. I couldn't decipher her words. Perhaps they were again of her mother, who blew prayers over her flesh. "And I dream of my mother when I am scared..." She slept beside me while I sat up on my elbow, watching as the moon kissed her cheek. It left a perfect circle there, a circle that shuddered very slightly, before dipping to her mouth. Her best feature, even without the moon. How many times had I gazed upon its fleshiness, admired the pale beige tinted with the softest pink, run my fingers along that subtle arch? The moon kissed and it kissed. Farhana continued talking, though I knew she was asleep, and I knew it was left to me to do as her mother had done. I lifted myself into the air like a ball of feathers, and from there, I blew cool air upon her lips, just as the moon planted a second circle, before moving to her throat. "Breath for breath. That is how you love someone." I loved her. I loved her more than a mother, or a moon. She slept beside me in the cabin in Kaghan, and we had only just arrived, and everything was sweet. Our door was open to the night, inviting it inside. Around us rose scoops of velvet green, and beneath us, a brick red earth. It was for this we'd come, not to fall into ourselves, apart. But we hadn't fallen apart yet, we'd just arrived, and the valley undulated like an embrace, cupping in its curves Farhana, me, and nine blue lakes, motionless and pure.

Throughout the night, in my sleep, I blew blessings over her neck, her nails and knees—wherever the moon left circles.

In the morning, I was overcome with a peculiar lethargy. I reached for her hair, a blanket to shelter in, but the space beside me was bare. I registered her absence with dull panic, the fingers of one hand switching off an alarm while the other reached for a dream. And then I recognized it as a dream. We hadn't just arrived, so much had happened, we couldn't undo it, any of it. And we weren't in Kaghan; we were in Gilgit. Farhana's space beside me had been bare for more days than I cared to count. Now, even Irfan was gone.

I glanced at the clock. Seven in the morning. I left my bed and drew back the curtain, in search of the moss-layered hills of my dream. I couldn't see beyond the parking lot. The rain pounded Gilgit, leaving the lot slick with red dirt. It hadn't stopped raining since our jeep pulled into this town two days ago. A mudflow of riverbed sediment had gushed a kilometer up the highway. Our way was blocked. And yesterday, I now remembered, the dream abandoning me so completely it was breathtaking, we were told we'd have to wait at least another day. Yesterday the Gilgit River had thrust into a mosque, sweeping away twelve worshippers, including three children. Two children were still missing, the third was dead. If not floods, raids. The two arrested three days ago, the blind man and the cripple, were never heard from again.

In Pakistan, it was hard to know which tragedy to dwell on most.

I lay in bed, picking at blood-crust. Two days ago, as I'd walked back to my hotel room, I'd knocked into something—a scrap of metal, a skull. My foot, in the damp, was slow to heal. I felt neither pain, nor even, at this added delay, frustration. Once I'd registered Farhana's absence, and registered especially that it was a continuous thing, much like rain and roadblocks, I felt very little at all, except, quite unexpectedly, a sudden peace. *We still had time.* The longer our stay in the north, the more opportunities would present themselves to me, to us. In the meantime, I was sapped of energy. It was a peculiar feeling, and I'd never felt a fatigue like this before. It was as though I was being swept in a mudslide, swallowed and crushed. But this was okay, it didn't hurt. Someone was blowing something over *me*, as I'd blown love and blessings over Farhana in my dream, except, this was neither to love, nor to bless. And it was okay.

Ironically, it was Wes who knocked on my door that day. He came into my room to ask if we should have breakfast together. I agreed. Afterward, we played Scrabble. I noticed he'd stopped shaving. Plenty of clean-shaven men around, so I didn't think it was to fit in. He arranged his tiles on the board, unable to come up with anything better than *road*, and I laughed and said we were all thinking the same thing. It was very congenial, and even this was easy, because I didn't really feel I was there with him, and it was peculiar but not unpleasant.

I said, "The beard literally suits you."

He laughed. "Makes me look skinny, huh?"

"I wouldn't go that far."

He stood up, stuck his thumbs into the waist of his jeans. "What do you call this?"

"Skinny thumbs."

He sat back down again. "You're all right."

"I wouldn't go that far."

Afterward—the game was so low scoring I didn't even remember who won—our driver Nur Shah joined us, and we drank salty tea, listening to his many tales of Mirs and forts, listening to the rain and the men who had gone missing.

That night, I felt another absence. It took me longer than it should have to understand that the rain had ceased. I turned to

Irfan's side of the bed to wake him to ask whether this meant we would leave tomorrow. He wasn't there.

In the morning, Nur Shah drove us as far up the highway as the road would go. Where the mudslide rendered it impassable, we got out of the jeep, and, carrying our bags on our backs, walked tentatively across a stone pathway slippery with black clay. Our escort, whom I hadn't seen again after the first night in Gilgit till we set out this morning, leaped across like a gazelle.

Once across, we were met by a second jeep. I'd grown attached to Nur Shah and was sad to lose his company. He made us promise to visit Baltit Fort and, once there, imagine the throne from which the Mirs would command the Eskimo Force to walk on glaciers with bare soles. We promised.

Hunza lay nestled in the Karakoram Range as sweetly as a cat in a closet. I knew that the mountains took their Turkic name of Karakoram, meaning black gravel, from the rubble that covered the glaciers everywhere around us, for we were now in the most densely glaciated part of the globe outside the poles. To pick one to study or photograph was like plucking an apricot to roll along your thumb when granted a basket of thousands.

It was the contrast that took my breath away, the layers and layers of contrast. At the furthest end soared the snow-topped seven-thousanders, including the spear of Rakaposhi, dominating this valley as surely as Nanga Parbat dominated my dreams. A little closer loomed a row of brown and barren peaks, smeared in gray glaciers that, from our perspective below, held none of the dazzling white beauty of the glacier Irfan and I once witnessed in marriage, nor even the one all of us had walked across on our way to Lake Saiful Maluk. Along the valley's waist rose an erect forest of poplar trees, somber witnesses to the misdemeanors of earth, sky, and ice. Across the valley floor sprawled terraced fields, all the way down to the Hunza River.

Without the mountains, the valley might be too pretty. Without the valley, the mountains too stark. A rose has thorns, a cat has claws, an owl the ferocity of her gaze, and Hunza, location. If geography is an accident, then for thousands of years this one had worked out well.

Hunzakut settlements could reach several thousand feet up the valley; we passed many shepherds and their flocks grazing in these high summer pastures as we stretched our legs that first day. They met us openly and warmly. They hadn't heard of us here. We were welcome!

Smitten with the way Hunzakut women and men greeted each other—by blowing kisses when apart, and, when near, planting kisses on each other's fingers—Wes kissed the air and Farhana's fingers repeatedly. Her attention lay elsewhere. Laughing at Wes's flamboyant overtures, she pulled away, to walk with the women, who were as visible as expressive, and far more so than in the valleys to the south. She also photographed them. And grew friendly with their daughters. I told myself, *Leave it behind.* Not all girls were about to be annexed, not all women about to be aggrieved.

I tried to hope instead for the freedom we'd have here, Farhana and I, if we allowed ourselves. In my mind, I fed her air kisses. I brushed the tips of her fingers with my tongue.

Though the valley offered up glaciers as easily as fruit, first thing tomorrow, it was still to be Ultar Glacier. The hike was notoriously steep, as we all knew, but, also as we all knew, we were traveling with the incredible hulk, the one with skinny thumbs. And, though I was of course a pale (or dark) shadow by comparison, I'd done a fair bit of daredevilry myself, what with all the places I'd walked in the night without even a flashlight. It was the Hunza River I'd fallen into once, under a moonless sky, on my last visit here. I'd pulled myself out somehow. I could manage Ultar.

The glacier sat near the crest of the incredibly sheer Ultar peak, or Ultar Sar, which rose behind Baltit Fort. Before retiring to our hotel, we decided to see both. In this way, we'd keep our promise to our driver Nur Shah, who'd been "best of friends" with the grandson of a Mir.

We stopped first at the fort. At a windowless bay window, criss-crossed with spider webs, I recalled another—one that was five-sided—in a world of purple houses and art-glass windowpanes. But Nur Shah had wanted us to imagine the Mir on his throne in this room of the fort, and so I did, happy to inhabit a memory that wasn't mine. The floor was now thick with debris, and chalk marks in the design of a hopscotch grid. I stepped into the grid, while, through the spider webs across the window frame, I searched the valley for Ultar Sar. The peak lay to my back; for some reason, I hesitated to leave these ruins to look at the mountain directly.

So we lingered at the spider webs and the hopscotch grid, while our new driver, Danyal, deciding he was not to be outstoried, told us that the first people to settle here had walked south from the foot of K2. Like the Eskimo Force that succeeded them, they'd crossed the ice on bare feet. All but two had died in a landslide that, he assured us, originated from Ultar. The survivors were a girl and her grandmother. Those now living here, and in the twin valley of Nagar across the river, were descendants of the girl. She'd been beautiful and had worn on the soles of her feet a skin that could walk across any glacier (and, clearly, any avalanche), gifting her people with both.

The legend wasn't tough to believe. Everywhere around us, Hunzakuts trudged up mountain slopes carrying hefty loads of fodder on their backs, many without shoes, with stunning features, and most of all, with poverty and age. I saw countless men and especially women, including the very elderly, engaged in all manner of physical work. While the men had been able to move into commerce, owning shops in big cities, or becoming drivers, the women stayed back to manage the small farms and orchards. And children.

Now I could see Farhana walking away from the fort and down a trail, toward a woman carrying a basket of apricots on her head. A girl skipped beside her. Before I saw it, I knew it. She had a black goat.

"What is she doing now?" asked Irfan, standing beside me at the window.

I shook my head.

"It's been a long day."

"One of many."

"I'll ask Wes to get her."

"I hear you," Wes said, behind us.

Nobody moved.

Farhana, the woman, the girl, and the goat were turning into a side lane, presumably to one of the many thatched-roof shacks we'd passed on our way to the fort.

"Not now, Farrah," Wes mumbled, not without irritation. Despite all the finger-kissing, maybe he was still sleeping on the floor.

Farhana disappeared from our crumbling lookout.

Danyal parted a spider web. "The hike is not so good in the rain. Tomorrow, it may rain."

We gazed at the sky. Perhaps five minutes passed. Perhaps twenty. Irfan scratched his head. "Have you seen our escort?"

I hadn't. And I didn't care. I began walking toward Farhana. Of course the rain didn't wait till tomorrow. It began as soon as I left the fort, marching with me on the trail.

She was coming out of a shack, with the girl.

"The woman knows a bitan who tells the future."

"What's a bitan?"

She was pleased to inform me a bitan was a "religious authority" who inhaled the smoke of burning juniper branches. "She also dances, to her own music."

"What?"

"And drinks blood, from a goat's head. Then she goes into a trance. Then she talks, with spirits. And fairies."

I couldn't tell if she was making fun of me. "You mean, like the fairy Badar Jamal?"

"I didn't ask which."

I wondered briefly what Farhana had smoked.

Behind me, Irfan and Wes were still on the trail, allowing us some privacy, though I could feel them wondering if the strategy was working. All of us were getting slammed hard by the rain, and it was ridiculous, the way we eagerly gave up pieces of our flesh to its teeth.

"Are you cold?" I said with absolute futility.

Wes jogged up to us. "Let's check out the trail for tomorrow, then go back to the hotel."

I nodded; Farhana wouldn't move.

"Are we climbing in the morning or what?" said Wes.

"Not in the morning," said Farhana.

"Jesus." Wes wiped his wet beard. "Does anyone even remember why we came here?"

"Why don't you remind us?" said Farhana.

Oh, *this* was pleasant.

"Hey, I was ready to head back, in Kaghan. After you guys," Wes pointed, not at me but at her, "fucked up."

It was possible I could begin to like him.

"People live here," she said, all shaman-like. "We can't ignore them. We're not just here to take a few readings and photographs and be on our way."

I had to turn my back to her to prevent myself from screaming.

Wes and Irfan decided to move away, giving us privacy again.

Leave it behind.

"You want to see the shaman?" I said, facing her again.

"Oh, I already did. And they're called *bitan*."

"Actually, in this valley, they're called danyal."

"Like our driver?"

"That's right."

We stared dumbly at each other. If we didn't leave, *we'd* turn into a sacrifice—for the bloody rain.

"When?" I asked.

"When what?"

"When did you see the shaman?"

"You mean danyal."

"When, Farhana?"

"She'd smoked already. Before I went to see her."

"And what did she say?"

"She said we would… You know what? I don't feel like saying. But I want to spend the day here."

"We should scope out the trail for the morning."

She shook her head.

"What?"

"We climb at night. When there are fewer landslides and icefalls. That's partly what she said." Her voice was quiet. "She also said you're not to come."

The rain and the wind were making me shiver.

"You know how many have lost their lives on this peak," she added, soothingly.

"Did she say I was going to die?"

"No. Of course not."

And then Farhana turned around and walked back into the shack.

Ahead of her, the girl and the goat skipped into the field.

Ahead of me rose Ultar Sar, a serrated finger of solid granite, the Hunza River snaking around its knuckle. This much I was already mapping in my head.

I spent my last day in Hunza wondering if it was my last day. I walked in the nearest town, Karimabad, from where Ultar was invisible. The sky had closed around us, a mountain range of rain inside a mountain range of gravel. At these heights, the battle between earth and sky was always won by sky; my visibility was limited to the images playing in my head.

Ultar had never captured my imagination the way Nanga Parbat always did. It wasn't frequently photographed. Nor written up as deadly. Nor did it draw mountaineers from every corner of the world. It wasn't one of the Tallest Ten. Standing at roughly 5,300 meters, it was almost 3,000 meters shorter than Nanga Parbat. It wasn't a smooth ribald white from top to toe. Sexless, it had no lover.

Even so, that day I learned it did have a jinn. For whatever reason, this jinn stoked the appetite of the Japanese in particular, many of whom had attempted to summit Ultar, and many of whom had died. Years after his death, the valley still remembered Akihiko Ito, for he'd spoken to the people in their tongue, before setting out, in alpine style—as we would—without ropes, porters, or supplemental oxygen. And at night.

Of course, our plan wasn't to summit. Ultar Glacier was not as high up as, say, Ghulkin Glacier, so we had no need for fancy expedition gear. And though I didn't want to hear more, I couldn't help myself. It was like staring at a drop while teetering at its edge. I had to look.

Ito had set out at midnight, expecting to summit before sunrise, before the rocks and ice could heat and shift. He'd succeeded in this. The problem occurred, as it so often does, on the descent. A storm engulfed him, he lost his way, he spent two days on a ledge without food. Even then he survived. It wasn't till his return to basecamp that the jinn had entered Ito's liver and, slowly, extinguished all his lights.

I had to pull myself away from the edge. I stopped asking for stories.

I ended up spending the day in a most unexpected way. I spent it with Wes.

I was walking up a dirt road through an orchard. Around me, baskets of apricots had been left to dry in the sun. As I walked, two women greeted me, each with two long braids and a cap. The older woman, her body spry, her face lined by a thousand landslides, offered me a soup made of dried apricots and qurut, a kind of cheese. When I politely refused, she laughed, pointing to the shade of a tree where Wes sat spooning the remains of his gift. "He is not shy," she said. "You should be like him."

But I was unable to accept any more generosity. "You are very kind," I mumbled, increasing my pace.

He caught up with me. "These are your resources," he said, "good, kind country folk."

I thought, built any schools lately?

I said, "You have a strong stomach. Normally, one sip of the water here and even a brown man from the city is shitting liquid."

"Nice."

"No. It isn't."

"So that's why you refused?"

"No. That's not why I refused."

To my left rose the silver fin of Rakaposhi, bright as a mirror, graciously illustrating the truth of her name: luminous wall. Some called her by an older name, Dumani, mother of mist. But she was free of clothing today. The rain had passed completely, the air was cool and clean, Rakaposhi dazzled after her bath, and I was at liberty with my camera. The longer I stayed in these valleys and the more photographs I took, the more I came to understand how each peak had to be seen apart from all others. Rakaposhi, despite her height, did not inspire dread in me the way the shorter Ultar peak had, earlier today. Nor did she turn her spire against the hearts of men, like Naked Mountain, or open her arms temptingly to us, like Queen of the Mountains, when Farhana and I had gazed upon her in the lake. Rakaposhi's summit was elegant in its lines—razor-sharp, yes, but with a gentler grade—and it was no surprise that many insisted she was Pakistan's most beautiful mountain. But this did not mean she hadn't committed murder; the wild wolves who sheltered in her breast famously claimed her prey.

Wes leaned into my viewfinder. "Farrah's right. Climbing's better at night." A thumbnail of yellow hair was sprouting beneath the green stripe that lay across his head. The green was fading to a pale copper hue, blending almost entirely with the rest.

"That's how we climbed Mount Shasta. At night. With lights on our heads and drills to pull out the ice. She carried her own gear. Strong woman."

"You're going to drill Ultar?"

"No. Not this time. You could call this a reconnaisance mission." He laughed; I didn't. "For whenever we come back. Depending."

The road sloped up toward the Hunza River. As we followed it, Rakaposhi began to slip away.

"American Indians believe Mount Shasta's seven glaciers are the footsteps of the creator, as he descended from the clouds. I've wished sometimes, on this trip, that I understood the stories from here."

Something tweaked in my breast just then; I felt bad for him. In place of the silver fin of Rakaposhi dipping into a tree-lined horizon, I saw a black and white image of Bridalveil Fall plunging down a frame on a wall, and remembered how I'd stared at it, after an encounter with a man who rejected me completely. I remembered the loneliness, the absolute absence of anywhere or anyone to turn to. I didn't think Wes's loneliness was that complete—or even if it was loneliness. He had Farhana, after all, and any number of folks who'd happily give him their last bowl of soup. But something in the way he said it made me regret my coldness toward him. It was a regret I told myself I had to overcome. *He had Farhana.*

"It's beautiful here." He slipped his hands in his pockets, breathing deeply.

I was being rude. I needed something to say. The sky was the benign blue of a child's drawing of a sky. Too benign to photograph.

"Course, you don't always need a drill to read the ice," said Wes.

I laughed.

"Why don't you just propose to her?" he said.

"What?"

"What better place do you need?"

"Has she told you she wants me to?"

"Does she need to?"

"What do you talk about? At night?"

"You mean when we're alone?"

"What else would I mean?"

"Why not give her the pleasure of saying no?"

"Why?"

"You humiliated her."

What had she told him? Every drop of sympathy I'd felt for him moments ago vanished.

"Humble yourself," he kept on, "or she'll find a way to make you."

"Hasn't she already?"

"How's that?"

"You want me to spell it out?"

"Be my guest."

But I wasn't going to give *him* the pleasure of humiliating me. I started walking back.

He called after me. "You know that friend of Matthew's, who hooked you guys up?"

I stopped.

"Guess that was me."

I turned to face him again. The *former boyfriend* who knew a *nice little Pakistani girl*? It couldn't be!

"What do we talk about at night, alone? Among other things, if you're ever going to open your eyes."

"But you and Matthew…"

"What?"

"You don't look…"

"What?"

A dryness in my throat prevented me not only from articulating my thoughts, but even admitting them.

"This doesn't look like Pakistan," he said. He was very, very amused.

Slowly, the wheels started turning, and as they accelerated, the wheels began to sing. They weren't fucking. Pure and simple. Wes did not desire women. And Farhana was a woman. Relief! Relief!

Within seconds, the singing came to an abrupt halt, much as the sympathy I'd felt for Wes had done earlier. They'd been mocking me, toying with me, *for days*. Even longer. Why would Farhana accuse me of being jealous, that day in the shop, when she'd discarded the shawl? That was before Kiran, before moving in with him. They were enjoying my misery, even bonding over it. They were enjoying how malicious my misery was making me. The worst part of me cemented their alliance. You could argue that was worse than fucking.

I walked up to him, barely reaching his chin. "Why didn't you tell me before?"

"Why didn't you tell me?"

"What would I have said?"

"That you're an insecure bastard who can't trust a soul. I could've helped."

"I trust Irfan!"

He laughed. "And where is he?"

"What does that have to do with anything? You knew how I'd feel, when she left. You could have told me. You could have said she came to you only as a friend."

"Yeah. And as her friend, I let her say it. Or not."

"So why tell me now?"

He paused. "You'll know soon enough." He started walking away.

Soon enough? My thought-wheels began to creak.

"One last thing." He was back, towering over me, copper stripe a tongue sticking out in the sun. "She jumped before you. I saw her braid hit water. You were in the boat. When you did finally jump, you stayed in longer. Too long. But you already know that."

I buckled then, on the road. My knees in the gravel, scraped raw through the holes in my pants. *It feels good to cry.*

Irfan wasn't in the hotel room that evening. We needed to eat before setting out later; perhaps he was already at the restaurant.

My body was at ease. I felt as though I'd been washed, as though a thick mud had been scraped off my bones by a torrential rain from within. It was a comfortable fatigue, more comfortable even than my fatigue in Gilgit. I was without rage, without blame, even directed at myself. What I felt when I took off my shoes and socks and crawled under the blanket and stretched my arms over my head before folding them neatly just at the bulge of skull above the bend of my neck was an almost pleasant mist of melancholy. I thought of my family.

First, my sister Sonia and her vivacious chatter, her refusal to ever sit idle and mope. Once, when she was perhaps thirteen or fourteen, Irfan was over at our house. He was already in love with Zulekha then, the two of them bound to each other by hands more powerful than their own, like two budding glaciers tied to the strongest of backs, to be carried, in sacred silence, several thousand kilometers up a mountain slope, to be married in the most perfect bed on earth. But that day he'd looked at her, my sister, for just a flicker, and I believe it was the first time I registered her as a woman. She was lovely and she'd known she was lovely long before I cared to see it. Now the whole world saw it, and I was glad. I came as close to saying a prayer for her as I'd ever come: God keep the madmen stalking the streets of this land far, far away…

As I went up the chain of command, my prayers caught in my throat. I still hadn't called my mother since leaving Karachi. Sonia I didn't need to call. She knew I was always with her. But my mother needed guarantees, and I didn't know what guarantee to give when, aside from comforting others, she spent every part of every day since I'd known her being comforted in prayer. She'd secured her place in heaven; it was her husband and her children who must secure her place on earth. *Are you earning well? Are you coming home? Is Farhana the one?* All this she'd ask the son, and the son, it was clear, failed to answer. So she offered her own solution—how did she manage it, demanding assurance while supplying her own?—*God will provide.*

Next, my father. Throughout our stay in Karachi, he hadn't been told about Farhana. She was introduced as Wes's sister. Did he believe it? With him, it was hard to say. But if she *had* been the one, he would not have thought well of a daughter-in-law who traveled alone—without family, that is—before being married. (My mother refused to think ill of her. That was my mother.) As Wes's sister, she was adored. With Wes, my father was loquacious, and with her, chivalrous. Too loquacious. Too chivalrous. The way only a brown man sees a brown man become in the presence of a white man and his white "sister." And it embarrassed me, the way he asked Wes's opinion on everything, while, with me, it was the same taut silence, sliding around the parameters of our encounters like a striker around a carrom board. At times the striker would fall into the net of Pakistan's grief, and we might have a conversation. Other times, it rammed into every disc on the board in a spitfire of rage. There was more fury than sound, however. *What are your plans for the future?* would become *I'll be back in a while*, and the board was deserted as he sank into a deep gloom. He was a man whose conviviality was intimately wed to God, work, and family. When even one of these indicators was amiss—and clearly, thanks to me, all were amiss—his world tilted. Simply put, I upset his conscience. Perhaps he upset mine.

I remembered one particularly painful afternoon with him. Farhana was on a mission to somehow fix things. (It's a fine line, the one between helping and hurting. She never saw the line.) In this spirit, she showed my father a few prints of my desert shots from outside Tucson. I'd never shown him even one and didn't know she'd packed them. It was a grotesque tableau that inversely mirrored my meeting with her father in some way I couldn't quite pinpoint, but if with hers she'd wanted to stay away from the subject of my work, with mine she went too far.

His expression didn't change as he looked, without interest, at a flaming orange cactus. I'd been especially pleased with the close-up, the way each "petal" of the fiery ball was dotted with feathered white spines that looked almost like flowers. I hadn't seen the spines as flowers when I took the shot. I saw this only later, which was why the image mattered. It had come together as a kind of miracle.

Setting it aside, my father asked Farhana her opinion of the photograph.

It was as if I wasn't in the room. "Well," she hesitated. "I've never seen a cactus that color. He didn't use a filter. It's—natural."

"Natural." He nodded. Still without looking at me, he told me to get Wes, who was watching the BBC in the next room. "What do you think?" he asked him.

Wes looked at the photograph. "Neat."

My father waited expectantly. When it was clear Wes had said all he was going to say, my father asked, "Do you see talent here?"

Wes scratched his head. "Sure. I see talent." He went back to watching the BBC.

In the hotel room now, I held my camera. My melancholy was growing sharp around the edges, like the cactus itself. It seemed to change in color too, as though radiating the sun's glare. Before long, I began to burn. I got out of bed.

Farhana had been on a mission to fix things ever since we'd come to this country, or even before we'd come, but what about her niyat—her intent? Who was I to say?

Should I do as Wes recommended and propose to her, so she could have the pleasure of saying no? I didn't think Farhana needed to get her pleasure in this way. If she wanted, she could have humiliated me worse, by telling me herself that she'd jumped first. She'd spared me that. It occured to me that Wes might have been lying and no braid had ever hit the surface of the lake. But I dismissed the thought. I knew as surely as I knew the pain in my chest that I was right to believe him.

There were pictures of her, from so long ago. Her somber profile that day at the baths, as we watched the pelicans dive like missiles. Then Farhana stripping, taunting me with her back, hours before my attack in the park. And those shots of us at play, our bodies in motion together. Her mountain legs and lean torso; her slender hips and luscious lips. And me? She'd photographed my scrawny legs, and my penis, resting on my thigh like a petal on a floor. She photographed her finger caressing that petal to life. And more, from that day on the beach, the shots increasingly raunchy, but without play, only appropriation, her ass raised high in the frame.

I skipped forward. I came to my landscapes. I'd taken several in Kaghan—of the lake, the graves, the River Kunhar—but they all left me cold, as did this afternoon's series of Rakaposhi after the rain. Even the ones of the glacier—that luminous white above a dark gravel, the progression of shepherd into shadow, and then into light, as the glacier descended into darkness—they were missing something. If I could have put into words exactly what, I might not have wanted to be a photographer. But I saw no miracles there.

Her father once said, even the act of seeing can be a theft, even a murder. He might also have said the opposite. The act of *not* seeing can be a theft, even a murder. It was my refusal to see Kiran—first in the boat, then in the lake—that had killed her. And if Farhana hadn't seen her, ever, Kiran would still be alive.

So where did this leave us? I wanted her, pure and simple. Tonight, I really would leave it all behind. She was not with Wes. She was still with me. All I had to do was get her back and get her back I would, in the dark, on a climb I was told I shouldn't make. She said I wouldn't die, so what reason was there to stay away? It would be even better than courting her with calla lilies. I would court her on ice.

Queen of the Mountains: Blue Is the Flight

They stood inside the hut.

"What about that man Ghafoor? The one who burned down the forest inspector's house years ago? We know how dangerous he is. Do you? Do you know the company he keeps? There are bad ones in every flock. They always find each other. And make trouble for others. Especially true believers. Like you. You are a believer?" The larger man poked Suleiman's chest with his rifle.

"Oh yes," answered Suleiman.

"Because there are rumors that your wife here prays to another god. Even—" he spit "—a goddess."

"Oh no, sahibji. You must not believe these things."

"Because I have heard that she is a kafir."

"Please! Don't say such things."

"Because men have sworn she prays to *buth*, and is herself quite dangerous."

"No! I beg you—"

"She practices witchcraft."

"Kind sir, what you say—"

"But I do not believe it." He moved the rifle to Suleiman's

wooden leg, and began tapping it through Suleiman's shalwar. "Because you are God-fearing Muslims who are unfortunate victims of some evil gossip. It is the way of your kind. No unity, no nation. No sense of loyalty at all. Yet I fully believe even you would never go against those who are here in this valley, far from our families and homes, just to protect you."

"Yes!"

"You will work with us?"

"Yes!"

"For the sake of your family and your home."

"Yes!"

"Say the first kalma."

Suleiman began to recite. The policeman kept the butt of his rifle on Suleiman's leg, but his eyes were on Maryam. Tap tap tap. She moved her lips. She was only halfway through the very short prayer when the tapping was replaced by a shout, "If you are believers, why don't you treat your guests according to the recommendations of the Prophet, peace be upon him?" She withdrew in mid-recitation to make them breakfast.

When they left, she noticed that the dogs had not barked. She realized that all summer long, the dogs had not barked. They had not barked the day the two policemen—different men, they were always different, yet they were exactly the same—had come looking for the bomber and eaten breakfast and soiled her bed and pissed inside their hut. They had not even barked at the lake, the morning Kiran's body had washed up on shore. They were gaddi dogs, at one time so fierce no one could come near them. But some time this year, she could not say when exactly, they had grown as listless as the dry grass they slouched on all day.

It was the same the next morning. A messenger came to deliver the news: two boys had gone missing in the valley. The dogs did not stir when the man arrived and, with the exception of the left ear of one, the dogs did not stir when the man left.

Maryam waited for the ear to droop. A tail rose slightly, as if to register her anticipation. She found this more arresting than the news. She could not think about the news. The news could not be allowed even a corner in her home. The news about the two missing boys, especially. It could find a space and it could build a web and then you fell into it and never got out and then the news became you and you turned into the missing boys, or else your children did.

Her hands were still wet from milking Kola's mother, who had given birth again. She could milk a goat with one hand; it was the buffaloes that needed milking with two. She could just about hold the teats with the fingers of her right hand but squeezing them caused her pain. She needed her son for the buffaloes and he had helped her this morning, as he had helped every morning since her injury, before leaving for the store.

He was good with teats. He stroked them in a way that made her wonder what else he was stroking. He never had to be taught. The first time, she was amazed at how easily the buffalo, Noor, accepted him. His fingers moved up and down her udder, petting, cajoling, alternating between the four teats as though he were ringing bells. He played each in a rhythm all his own, back and forth, at times barely brushing one to make it swell, other times, lingering with his knuckle. Within moments, all four had distended till they threatened to burst. Then he took one in each hand, pressed hard, and tugged. Two teats at a time. It took him twenty minutes to relieve Noor; it used to take her thirty.

She was still studying the dog's ear. Of the two boys who had gone missing, neither was her son. Her relief was warmer than milk. The news began to creep away. The dog's ear stayed upright as she returned to the goat. And that was when her relief faded. The news raced back on a hundred little legs. *The dogs had not barked.* If the men who took the boys were to enter her dera, the dogs would let them. She would wake up in the morning to the lowing of buffaloes, wondering why they had not been milked before

Younis left for the store, and, rushing to his bed, find him gone. Outside, the dogs would be lying idle in the dirt, one ear cocked.

The messenger had not been able to say who had taken the boys. The men in uniform or the men in skullcaps? "They all begin to look the same." He had said, voicing the fear of everyone in the valley. He was a year or two older than her son. Like her son, he would be wondering which side to join.

Kola's mother, Makheri, had small teats, even after a second kidding. She carried them the way she carried her head, high and erect. Maryam had hoped that by now her udders would loosen, but no, they were still tight, still difficult to milk. She could brew a tea of cardamom and mint, as in the past, but it had not helped then, it would not help now. Kiran had named her, because troublesome is what she was, yet Kiran had always defended Makheri when Maryam complained about her teats. Like her brother, Kiran took naturally to milking the animals. Maryam brushed the thought away. She could not let the spirit of her beloved girl shame her into slowing down with this goat! She hastily finished—perhaps with excessive force—and left with the bucket, failing to return a few minutes later to check that the job was truly done. So what if a few prized drops remained in the teats? So what if she was grown as listless as the dogs!

All her children had their father's patience. Perhaps, when she was old, the two who remained would be patient with her.

Inside the hut, she poured the milk into an earthenware pot that sat on ice in a tray. Twice a day, her son delivered the ice, to keep the milk cool. In the mountains, they did not have to worry about these things. But they were not in the mountains. She ought to accept it. She ought to slosh the milk, make the butter. This too was difficult with one hand but she was not going to ask her son to stoop so low. Nor would she bother her husband.

It was not the season to make butter, but they were running out of supplies, in part because so much had been given away to placate the men who now occupied her valley. The milk too. They wanted tea brewed in raw milk on every "visit." They called it God's blessing, milk straight from the source, while leering at her breasts, while telling her to pray. They wanted it stirred with all the sugar the cup could hold. She would have to see about getting smaller cups.

Maryam sat at the edge of the bed, staring at the pot with the milk.

So now they were after Ghafoor. They had a name and a face for their own mess. And those two boys who had gone missing—what did they have to do with it?

The news had taken up residence in her home.

Years ago, before Ghafoor burned the forest inspector's home—*if* it was him—before the inspector was even hired, his boss had singled out her dera to harass. This man claimed that their grazing permit was fake. He said they had made it themselves. When her husband showed him the state stamp, the man laughed. "This? No, your stamp must look like *this*." And he took from his pocket a piece of paper, the likes of which they had never seen before. They could not read. They could only say sorry. The man fined them a month's worth of milk and tried to force them to accept a settlement program. "Learn to farm," he said, tearing up their permit.

She had watched members of her dera give in, allowing meager plots of land to be allotted to them. She saw the fight seep from their pores like moisture from a milkpot. She saw her brother, still living in the Punjab as a laborer, bound to contractors who pocketed his sweat. She even had a cousin who would likely be a forest inspector one day, smuggling trees downstream or in wedding caravans, while fining the herders for over-grazing. When her husband, who vowed never to become sedentary, berated the betrayal over dinner one day, her son, who was then no more than six, said he would rather be a forest inspector than a herder. She had slapped him. Kiran, then barely four, had not spoken to her brother for days.

And now, with all the other kinds of men moving into her valley without a permit—for them, movement was free—now what betrayal was going through her son's head? He had the fingers of a god when he stroked the teats of a buffalo. But the rest of him was a man. No longer a child. A man.

Ghafoor's offer, before he left, reverberated in her head. *He can come with me, Maryam. He will be safer.*

Maryam shuffled her way to the milkpot. Shuffling was new to her. She poured half the milk into a wooden container which she dragged back to the bed, then sat down again, propping the container between her knees. With a long wooden paddle that reminded her of an oar used to row a boat on a lake at the banks of which, not too long ago, her family had camped, she began to churn. It was not easy, agitating the milk with one hand. The day was growing hot; she had to do this now.

Perhaps it was the sound of the butter thickening that pulled her into a strange, sweat-induced dream. She sat upright, her body swaying with the rhythm of the paddle, but her mind drifted so far away she might have called the dream holy. Only, the visions playing in her head could not be called holy, not even by the most devious gods.

She was watching, through someone else's eyes—the eyes of a man she did not know—a group of Gujjar boys leave their homes early one morning. As she watched, through these strange pair of eyes, a second man began to follow the boys. A cigarette dangled from between his lips, not the bidi cigarettes the herders smoked, but the filtered kind she saw nestled behind her son's ear one day, *Dunhill*, he had called it, when she went to the store to give him the lunch he forgot to take that morning. He stalked his prey, this man with the *Dunhill* dangling from his lips, taking his time before singling out the weakest of the pack, the one with the curly brown hair and trusting eyes and godly fingers, drawing him aside with the promise of a ride into the city in his car, a car the boy could drive. And this man who was watching it all: he was in the car.

The image changed. Now she was herself, Maryam, and she knew that what she saw was not a prophecy but a memory, one from earlier this year, weeks before they packed their belongings to leave for the mountain pastures. She had seen her son bathing in the stream with a group of other boys his age or older. The water was still cold and it was their yearly ritual, before they left for the summer, they had to jump in the stream. This year, as she watched, she told herself that he had only just turned nine. Yet, there was a change, a change she recognized because she had been his age when she licked the honey from the fingers of her brother's best friend. The boys splashed each other's smooth, sleek skin and laughed and splashed the hair beginning to stream from between their legs. She knew this laughter was no more innocent than her own had been. She knew too the ritual within the ritual, what exactly they were displaying, those older boys. As a nine-year-old to a nine-year-old was not a boy, so to a twelve-year-old, he was not an adult. The older boys relished the power they pulled from their younger audience, a power that caused the very currents in the river to flow. Hoping that, while they waited impatiently for the same miracle to happen between their own thighs, some boys would never do more than look at the miracles of others, she had steered herself away from the stream.

At the edge of the bed, Maryam opened her eyes. There was a scraping on an outside wall. The dogs did not bark. If this was a knock, the men never knocked.

She waited. She could not identify the sound. She expected the curtain to part. It did not. Whoever was there began to walk away, his footsteps heavy. Or he was still there, and only pretending to leave, to draw her out. More likely, it was all in her mind, a place where too many pictures had lately played. Perhaps it was all a symptom of being trapped inside, like this, instead of moving under open skies, the way she always felt the most at peace.

Still she stayed inside, with the pictures.

She saw a figure walking in the night. Ghafoor was behind him. A cluster of village folk surrounded them. They were all there, the four who had been at the lake that day. It was late at night and the wind was relentless and the rain was worse. Ahead, a serrated spur of rock. The one she had seen three times already. The figure was walking toward the rock, because she knew it had to be just so, she had made it this way. So had the Queen and her lover. So had her mother. So had Kola and Namasha and Noor. So had Maryam Zamani and Kiran and the unnamed thousands who had passed through this valley, or stayed, without committing murder. She could feel the peace slipping away as surely as the long wooden paddle through her fingers. Nothing stuck to her skin anymore, not a paddle or a teat, not sweat, not butter. It was all slipping away.

It began to rain, the same vicious rain that ripped through the man's jacket as she watched him set his first foot high on the rock. He had a red dot on his forehead, this man. Like a bindi, or a ruby. What kind of man decorated himself like a woman? The rain did not wash it off, no matter how emphatically it lashed his skin. No matter how near it came to her hut. The first torrent of the season, drowning out the sound of boots stomping outside.

Quietly, she began to scoop the butter onto a board, before adding the salt. Quietly, she watched it melt.

With the rain came more mosquitoes and flies and the mare Namasha turned her indignation inward. She continued to cast judgment at Maryam with the ferocity of her gaze, but she now refused to walk herself into the forest. Nor would she allow herself to be walked, even with one wrist. Nor would she accept the maize Maryam cooked for her every morning with extra salt to help with her digestion, though salt was growing scarce. She was on a hunger strike, and hunger made her gnash her teeth. Her daughter, Loi Tara, was learning the price of loyalty to the womb. Did it have to mean starvation?

For the first two days after the rain began to flog them, each time Maryam clicked her tongue and pulled the rope, Loi Tara galloped forward eagerly, before curtsying back to Namasha. "Don't be a donkey!" Maryam shouted over the rain. "You are a growing child!" Loi Tara would nuzzle her mother and shake her head at Maryam and shiver in wretchedness under a shelter of graveyard cypress. Namasha would wind her neck around her daughter once before standing upright again, daring Maryam to intercept.

The third day, Maryam took the dare. She went into the forest and brought back something even more tempting than an egg from a sedentary farmer. A peach, covered in golden down with a blush of crimson. There was no hesitation. Loi Tara burrowed her sweet lips in Maryam's palm. Namasha bucked her once. Loi Tara did not stop eating.

The fourth day, the filly scampered toward Maryam as soon as their eyes met, and once untethered, bounded into the forest. "Will you not follow us?" pleaded Maryam. Namasha gnashed her teeth.

Maryam caught up with the filly, who had found the buffalo Noor at a papra plant, wrapping soft lips around lacy leaves. Loi Tara looked momentarily perplexed: where were the peaches? In truth, Maryam had plucked the peach from a fruitseller, in exchange for butter, and planted it in the forest before bringing it forward to the filly's ready nose. Now she stroked her smooth, velvety neck, the color of egg yolk in the setting sun, murmuring, "Silly, peaches grow in orchards forbidden to you. And little horses don't eat papra leaves." She untangled the wet mane with her fingers. "How to bring your mother back?" Loi Tara nodded, nuzzled, and forgot. She began plucking the tall grass at Maryam's feet.

The forest dripped with rain. She looked at it: her forest. The slender stems of the kakwa fern glistened jet and violet, glossy emerald fronds tossed as proudly as the filly tossed her mangled mane. In the past, when Kiran complained of toothache, a malady she was prone to, Maryam had boiled those fronds and left the water to cool. Kiran would sip it later, her pain gradually subsiding. *In the past.*

Maryam pulled Loi Tara further into the forest. Around them towered blue pine and long-leaved pine, branches whorled, cones at her feet. Closer to the soil, the small, pink flowers of the khatambal. She could not remember the last time she had seen these. The herb flowered only during the monsoons, when they were in the mountains. She let the filly tear apart the bloom.

She could hear thunder. The buffalo bulls of the goddess clashing their horns. That was how thunder used to be known, in her grandmother's day, even her mother's. When the goddess's bulls were at war, so was the world. Maryam stepped inside a canopy of chir, a warm, dry canopy, where nothing could find her. Not even the rain.

Inside her canopy, she contemplated the life hers had become. Earlier this morning she had stayed in bed, as had become routine, with a listlessness coated in dread. Would policemen bother them? Or would it be plainclothesmen today? Neither had come; she still had to force herself out of bed. It seemed the only thing pulling her into the world was the battle with her horse. That was the power of the occupation: whether the men showed or not, they now resided in their home, just like the news, on a multitude of legs. They could appear at any time. They were already there—behind the curtain, beside the teacups, in the weave of her bed. No one could hide, though they kept on trying. She mostly stayed inside her hut, worse, she stayed inside herself, in a way of life she knew she could never grow used to, even as it became routine.

At night, when she listened through the wall, she heard the men and their radio. When they rolled the dial they could catch the voice of the mullah arrested three years ago, for fighting America in Afghanistan. Though still in jail, he had supporters in Swat, and even closer, in Mansehra. The same men setting up camp around Balakot, and pushing into their huts? She did not know. The voice on the radio always said radio was sin. TV, computers, cinema—all, sin. In Naran, there were stores with computers; her son knew all about them. But the radio? That was not so new, and Maryam could hear the men roll the dial, as her own father had done, to catch the news as far away as Peshawar. There was the mullah, cursing the radio he was inside, promising that soon this would be a Country of God, with no music, no dancing, and with madressahs in every valley. To fulfill the dream, they needed the local boys.

Through the wall she could hear her husband vow that it would take the hand of God to make the valley surrender to these men. A flood. Or an earthquake.

Inside the canopy inside her forest, Maryam continued stroking Loi Tara. The filly was back to nuzzling the buffalo. Maryam's eye fell on a drop of rain rolling to the lip of a leaf Noor had missed. The drop halted just at the lip. The leaf seemed to curl, holding it in.

If that drop of rain were her son, how long could she hold him?

This morning, after milking the buffalo, he had told her he wanted to be a trader, like his uncle Ghafoor. He did not want to be like his father, a mere herder. He wanted Ghafoor's clothes, the trousers with silver belts. He wanted to barter jade and leather, not milk and butter. He wanted to travel, outside the valley, outside the mountains, even. But he had a soft temperament, her son, more like his father than his uncle. And he was impressionable. If yesterday he would rather be a forest inspector, and today, a trader, what would it be tomorrow? A "local boy" in a camp—even if the locals themselves did not consider Gujjars local?

Anger began to well in Maryam's chest, as she continued staring at the raindrop at the tip of the leaf. If the government knew these men trained in the camps near Balakot, or down in Mansehra, or even as far as Swat, why not get rid of the camps? It was a question she heard the men ask too, as she listened through the wall, their anger almost as bitter as hers when their talk turned to the two missing boys. So much security and the boys had still not been found? Who had taken them, and why? Enemy suspects: buffalo herders? Keepers of stupid Australian sheep?

Maryam was not going to lose a second child. Was keeping Younis here a way of losing him? Was sending him away, with

Ghafoor, a way of keeping him? It seemed the only options that presented themselves brought her right back to the dilemma voiced by everyone around her now. No matter what they did, they would neither be dry in the sun, nor wet in the rain.

The buffalo pulled the leaf that held the raindrop. She caught the drop with her long, purple tongue, her focus still on chewing. "Drink well," said Maryam. "Eat well too."

Behind them grew a cluster of wild pistachio trees, one of the most beloved trees in the forest. In late winter would bloom a mass of flowers the color of red dirt. It was a blessing, the way the color lit the freezing air. To Kiran, it had been a sign of an order she trusted in completely. Upon finding them each February, she would smile, but not once did she ever point. (It would take a special kind of jihad to enforce pointing.) And every September, soon after they returned from the mountains, when the red nuts had matured to blue, all the children of all the returning deras would shake the trees, gather the nuts, and carry them home to salt.

This September, Kiran would shake the trees from a different place. Maryam sank her face in the filly's, and breathed. Over the years, she had cured the coughs of all her children with the tissues of pistachio bark. Now she inhaled the scent of the filly—a fresh manure scent, with hints of wood and incense—and wondered if she could cure the mother too. But of which malady? She smiled, still buried in horsehair. And which mother—the one on two legs or four?

Loi Tara had eaten enough. She raised her head, remembering her stubborn mother. "What should we bring her?" asked Maryam, still untangling that thicket of forelock with the fingers of her left hand. Loi Tara exhaled into Maryam's stomach. She could feel the warmth through her rain-soaked kameez. She wondered, vaguely, if they should go deeper into the forest, to meet her husband. He would be bringing the rest of their herd back to the homestead. Jumanah would be with him, and Maryam could untangle her hair for a while, instead of Loi Tara's.

She pulled Loi Tara gently back toward the hut. The rain fell as a series of ruthless barriers, pushing them back as they pulled ahead. They moved in stages, breaching one watery wall, pausing beneath a tree, and charging forward again, into a thicker, heavier wall. She could barely see where they were headed, yet there were others in the forest too, she could sense them, navigating their way through a world of fences, both solid and liquid, singing softly to their cattle, whose bells she had been hearing the entire time the filly fed. The sound was so known to her she could forget to notice it.

On she walked, keeping the rhythm that out-tricked the rain, a rhythm that was almost enjoyable, like a game. She hoped there would be no floods this year. They had endured enough. She hoped the glaciers would behave, and not gallop down the mountain slopes to block their roads and break their bridges. There was nothing more worrisome than a glacier that looked around and decided it no longer wanted to mate and melt gradually, but instead, to run like a horse. You could harness a horse but not a Gujjar—or a glacier.

On she went, in the rain, in the shelter of her game, her thoughts. Through the wall at night, no one had mentioned Ghafoor again, not since the time they had laughed at him. She had even been to the shrine clandestinely at night, risking being caught by the uniforms or skullcaps or both, in the hopes of finding him there. Or finding something—a feather, a cloth. But she found nothing, except the two flowers, crisp to the core. It was unlike him. If he said he would let her know what happened, he would let her know. Perhaps nothing had happened. Or perhaps… If the men were looking for him, had his plan changed? Where was he? Perhaps she ought to pray for him, if only in her heart, because during the day, she kept away from her shrine. Her husband insisted that under no circumstances was she to go anywhere near it. So she never again uncovered the box with Kiran's jewelry and two milk teeth, the one she had wrapped in red cloth. She said a quick prayer over the place where it lay buried, and let it rest.

In truth, she did not need signs from Ghafoor any more, at least not to tell her where *they* were. She knew. She continued to see them, there at the foot of the mountain, moving toward the serrated brown rock. But each time the man lifted his foot and began the climb, Maryam's vision would fade. One minute he was approaching the mountain, the next, he was trapped. In between, there was rain, goatbells, and that low chorus of singing and lowing.

Maryam halted abruptly. They were perhaps two hundred feet from the homestead when she realized she was also listening to something else. Loi Tara heard it too, she could tell by the way the filly pulled nervously back. A commotion, a rumble—of voices, or thunder? A landslide? An earthquake?

She could hear a scream, followed by a whole chorus of screams.

A ripple of fear pulsed down the filly's back. More screams, and wailing too. From two deras away. Not Laila's family, but the family next to hers. They were in distress, and what was Maryam doing? Listening from afar while stroking Loi Tara? Is this how she repaid the kindness of those who had sacrificed their summer in the highland to return to the plains with her family, in her time of grief?

Maryam pulled Loi Tara toward something heavy and familiar in her gut. If she had to name it, she would name it death, and a whole universe of pain that never existed before death, until, it simply did.

They had found one of the missing boys in his family's waterhole. The rain filled the hole and he rose to the top and his bloated limbs nearly spilled over the edge of the trough. But they did not. He bobbed in the slime-gilded pool with mango peels and goat entrails. Petals of eritrichum littered his hair. In the sky, a murder of crows. On the ground, too many men and women to let Maryam through. Yet, within moments, she held the history of the boy's young life in her flesh while her eyes reflected what others would see. His arms and legs were broken, hands burned, buttocks slashed, and a portion of his head crumpled like an aluminum can stamped on by a horse. From this wound a stream oozed into the waterhole; that was not the blood nor bile of a goat. He was recognized by the chain around his neck, a present from a rich relative that appeared to have helped choke him.

Maryam froze. She recalled the two boys seen several days ago while she hid in the forest with Laila. One boy had been scratching the dirt with a broken slipper. The other had been wearing a chain. She remembered the second one inviting a group of men into a hut. She remembered the red pom-poms.

The second boy was not found. It was his mother who cried the loudest. The one whose son was being dragged out of the waterhole did not cry. She was cursing God so loudly, eventually she had to be slapped into silence. It was a silence that would last the rest of her life.

Meanwhile, the valley talked. It was a talk that began as a murmur and grew and grew. The boys had been taken "for information." They were "enemy suspects." They had been taken by plainclothesmen. No, they had been taken by uniforms. Laila said they wore turbans and expensive slippers. Maryam said the slippers had pom-poms. Still others said they were taken by men last seen on the banks of the Kunhar, smuggling trees, in expensive slippers. They were from the camps. No, others insisted, they had come down to the plains from the mountains. No. They had come up to the plains from hell. No, it was the mountains. Which? The mountains to the east. No, the ones to the west. And it seemed to Maryam that those doing the talking kept growing in number, and included both plainclothesmen and men in uniform, and were from the government and from the camps, from the mountains and from hell.

But that day, after the woman whose son was fished out of the waterhole was slapped, Maryam did not really listen to them. Through the noise, she kept her poise, speaking the words she needed to speak, to whom she needed to speak them. She did not know from where the strength came. Perhaps from listening to the silence of the woman who had been slapped. She could feel the silence begin to consume her and thought it better that she scream her way to the other world, but when she whispered this into the woman's ear the woman swooned, and Maryam could do no more than hold her, so hold her she did, through the moment she fell silent forever. She blew gently over her face. She brewed her a tea of sweet herbs that made her sleep. Nobody called Maryam a pagan wife, not that day, because she was the only one who could do more than talk and curse and swoon after being slapped into a comatose dream. They watched her, and despair became their glue, and glue became a tangle of arms in which to carry the woman to her hut. It untangled to lay the woman down, over her bed, and then Maryam could not remember where it went. She spent the day moving between the homes of the two families—the one whose boy had been found and the one whose boy had not—her own home—she returned Loi Tara to Namasha, who received her daughter with moderate reproach—and the store where her son Younis worked. On her way she noticed a ginger plant pushing its way into their allowed part of the forest from some disallowed part. At the store she pulled Younis into her arms. He was alive. She held him till he pushed her away. Afterward, she stole into her shrine and, for the first time since the man who played a double flute and told tales like a prophet and danced like a jinn first let her pull the honey from his fingers, she did not wait for any more signs. She did not wait for any more songs either. She made up her own. She sang to the woman whose silence was forever, a melody in which her boy would be with Kiran soon, in a valley of fairies and princes and roasted pistachios and flying horses. She sang to the woman whose silence was forever about heaven. Heaven was not a warm place but a world of ice, a world of placid lakes and two single peaks made of windows and doors called the Queen and the Nude. The Queen more or less stayed in the valley but the Nude had been to places far away, farther than the mountains even, and he would find those who had taken her child from her and caused a silence as deep as the lake to enter her womb. He would find them and do as he must and the woman should rest peacefully through it all and listen to this song of a heaven made of ice and fairies and roasted pistachios and flying horses, a heaven nestled between two peaks that watched over Kiran and this boy who would soon be with her. They would have good clothes to wear, Kiran and the boy. He might even convince her to braid her hair. He might even braid it for her. He would pay attention to the chime of her bangles. He would feed the goats they had lost down in this temporary world to the greed of fat Australian sheep. They would all be there, and the filly's father too, the one who had leaped into a barbed wire fence and caused the filly's mother to grow mean in this other world. The children would ride him together sometimes, over the two peaks, finding the surest footholds, stepping across the flattest stones, through rivers and glaciers and sweet mountain grass. And if they felt sleepy they would rest their heads against his velvet smooth back and their dreams would fill with a velvety smoothness. Their dreams would hold the best colors of their young imagination, which for Kiran would include every breathing shade of blue. Blue as a fairy's wing, blue as a kingfisher's tail, blue as the flower of the Jan-i-Adam.

So sang Maryam to the woman whose silence was forever as the talk in the valley grew and grew, alongside the boots and the pom-poms and the tanks and the appetites of those who had taken over their lives.

Ultar Sar

It was one o'clock in the morning when our driver dropped us off near Baltit Fort, to begin our ascent of Ultar Sar. He would not come with us, though he waited till we walked up the trail that twisted past the house where Farhana had spent yesterday. News of our plan had reached the village and many stood outside their homes in the cold to see us off, including the woman who'd led Farhana to the shaman. The girl and the goat were there too. My flashlight accidentally fell on her face and the face was deeply serious. I mumbled an apology for shining the light in her eyes and she replied by lifting her right hand and waving goodbye.

I tilted the flashlight away, looking for a magenta shirt, a green shalwar. But I'd seen no phantoms since entering this valley and, thankfully, I saw none now.

Before me walked Wes and Farhana. How different they seemed! Beside me, as always, Irfan. Behind us, the escort from Kaghan. I didn't know why he, a merchant, would want to make this trek with us. But as it seemed to me that thus far I'd been asking all the wrong questions, I decided not to ask this one. If what he desired was to follow us all the way to the glacier, who was I to require an explanation?

I'd seen no armed convoys since entering this valley either. It was peaceful, quietly ceremonious, and freezing.

I was glad for the extra sweater beneath my windbreaker, the same windbreaker as on that night in San Francisco. *Jack-eet, jack-eet*, the man had said. I was glad he'd left me with my jack-eet. My shoes were sturdy, and Irfan had picked up a headlamp for me at the market in Karimabad. That's where he'd spent his day—being practical, being Irfan. I'd never worn a headlamp on any of my night walks, and this one didn't fit well. The straps were loose, despite all my adjustments. Nor could I get accustomed to the sensation of carrying a load at the center of my forehead, however illuminating the load might be. Besides, it was a red lens. It cast an oddly devious sheen on the pristine valley. Irfan wore his as easily as a bride wears a bindi. It even looked good on him.

As we reached the base of the mountain, I noticed a glow on each of Wes's shins. Then I noticed Farhana's, though hers were smaller. They'd come equipped, down to foothold lighting. "Did you think of that?" I asked Irfan. He shook his head. In silence, I recalled that on the shores of Lake Saiful Maluk, when we needed a tent, Irfan had provided his. Would Wes and Farhana now give up one light each, allowing all four of us more visibility? Perhaps we were both waiting to see if the offer was forthcoming.

When it was clear that it wasn't, Irfan said, "Let's keep each other in view. But maybe we should change partners. You stay with Wes."

He must have thought I'd prefer this, despite how uncomfortable she made him. He didn't know my plan was to pursue her on the mountain. For now, I agreed.

"You have water?" I asked, and he nodded.

"You have biscuits?" he asked, and I nodded.

"Five hours to the glacier, maximum. The sky's clear."

We both looked up at the serrated knives of Ultar rising before us. I couldn't see too much sky.

"Dark," he mumbled. Those were his last words to me before he stepped up onto a trail that was scratched through blocks of granite as large as a table for four. The rock edges were sharp. I put my head down and began the climb.

A few meters up I realized I was climbing on all fours. It was easier that way. I'd slipped my flashlight into my backpack and was relying solely on my headlamp, with peripheral aid from the two dots of yellowish light several feet ahead. The shins of Wes. I didn't call out to him to slow down. I was alone with my thoughts, the adrenaline in my veins, and the weight on my back. My pack was heavy; inside lay more than water, biscuits, and a flashlight. I had to keep adjusting it, and adjusting the headlamp too, the latter mutating into an odd kind of mental strain. If I had a third eye, it would always give me a headache. The lens washed the wall rising before me in the same devious red hue as it had the road, and the world was like a rusted photo print. For a long time I was distracted by the eeriness of it. Color is location, I thought. And dislocation.

My eye eventually did adjust, and I began to see variations in the tint. Brown from black, burnt sienna from gray. There were rain puddles and the occasional snow melt, but, amazingly, the rocks were not too slippery. We were lucky the rain had stopped. I was glad for the sensation beneath my rubber soles, the way my toes nudged into corners to assess the size and stability of the foothold, the way my fingers scraped the edges of a cliff to assess the height. I knew I was in a rhythm when I stopped checking my watch, when even knowing I'd stopped couldn't entice me to check. My chest opened wide and the cold rushed in with teeth, leaving me raw, invigorated. I didn't attempt to catch up with Wes, Irfan, or Farhana, whose mountain legs would no doubt take her higher than us all. I'd catch up with them, with her, eventually. I'd say all that I'd rehearsed. For now, there was plenty else to do without worrying about the nuances of human disclosure.

Over time, the sky moved closer. I could see stars, bright fragments of ice the width of my nail, at times so close I felt I could grasp them in my nail. Ultar's silhouette was not etched in stone. It moved when I moved, and with each step, the sky of ice chips slid higher or lower around its pointed shoulders. *Her* pointed shoulders? Why not. All beautiful things are feminine to me, and Ultar, at this height, was suddenly beautiful. She moved when I moved. Below me, the Hunza River curved around her rotating feet, like a jingling anklet.

I could also hear scratching and scraping. Someone lay down on her back then heaved herself up; someone else jumped, or tripped. We were only five but we made enough noise to better keep each other in view by ear than by third eye.

But Ultar did not carry sound to us the way we received it.

It must have been an hour after we'd left when I thought I heard Farhana fall. I was heading up a boulder that shook beneath my weight and I knew I had to leap across quickly or it would give. I let it give. It rolled away from me and I fell. When I stood up and wound around the path where I thought Farhana had lost her footing, I found no one. I'd left my pack where I tumbled. I retraced my steps—holding my headlamp in place with one hand—but couldn't find the pack. I crawled on my knees and cut my free hand; I felt it ooze. I waited, listening for the river, listening for footsteps. The river now flowed in angles rather than curves, like a child skipping down a flight of stairs. Apart from this, I heard only the occasional stone fall. "Farhana?" I called. But I'd already lost the direction from which I thought I heard her.

"Farhana?" I called again. In the distance I heard a faint, vanishing call, and now I moved faster. From where had it come? To my right. Yes, I was sure of it. I climbed recklessly now, the stones rolling under me and into the river that was perilously near. I knew I could slip if I did not slow down, but I did not slow down. I knew if I slipped no one would hear me, and I knew I did not know where I was heading. I knew it was no longer toward Farhana, for by now she must have moved on, but still I did not slow down. I could still hear something, though I could not say what. Perhaps a footfall. A leopard? I began to feel afraid. Something was breathing near me, I was sure of it, and from its step, I knew it did not wear shoes. I hurried on, till the river was above me—though, how could it be? How could I hear the sound of running water from high in the sky, a sky that had pulled away from me as surely as I was pulling away from those velvet paws, that ravenous panting? A waterfall? No, there were no waterfalls on this mountain. The soft padding began to fade; the wet wheezing began to slow. In its place was a sound I'd heard earlier, of a river flowing not in curves but in angles, and then I saw a figure skipping up a flight of stairs, a small child receding in a burnt sienna world, in a rusted photo print. Her back was to me but she was tilting her head to the side, as though she knew I was watching. I could hear hooves—*click click click*, the most delicate mincing steps—followed by the joyous ring of a bell.

At last I stopped. It was only when I stopped that I realized I'd been following her, she who did not exist. There was nothing there. I was imagining this. There were no shepherds on this mountain at night. No hungry leopards. And Farhana had probably not fallen at all.

Ultar muted the footsteps that were upon me before I had a chance to move away. It was the escort, and he was carrying my pack.

"You dropped this," he said.

"Thank you." I sat down, disappointed and yet strangely relieved. Disappointed it wasn't Farhana. Relieved it wasn't a ghost. Disappointed too to find myself missing human company, when I'd believed myself content to make the beauty of the night and the challenge of the climb, for now at least, my only companions.

I leaned against a cliff wall, wondering vaguely if I would have followed the phantom all the way into the chasm ahead.

"This is not a good place to stop," said the escort.

I couldn't hear Farhana. How would I carry out my plan to court her on this mountain?

I was about to ask if he knew where the others were when I heard the rumbling. My palms lay flat against the gravel and that is where it seemed to start, just beneath my skin. I pressed harder, listening with my hands, as though, by bearing down, I could balance myself *and* stop the tremor. Only now did I realize that the wall against which I rested was wet and crumbling and that I sat alarmingly near the edge. The rumbling grew louder.

"Turn around slowly," he said, "without standing up."

I did as I was told, keeping my hands on the gravel, leaning forward while turning toward him. At that moment, a bolt of lightning fell over Ultar's edge, illuminating the mountain across the gorge. It was Ultar's height, and it even spit into a series of needles and minarets in the same fierce angles. A second bolt: I saw a rock the size of a house charge down the mountain's side. A third: the rock smashed into three pieces as it bounced on the slope. When the largest piece disappeared into the chasm, the lightning in the sky and the rumbling under my palm ceased.

If I were on that side of the ravine instead of this one, I'd be dead.

I halted, unable to lift my hands off the gravel, unable to move at all. I knew if I leaned back again the wall could break, knocking me over the edge. On the other hand, my position right now was ludicrous. I was leaning forward at about a 40-degree angle and to my left lay emptiness and to my right a dark figure on a dark mountain was still waiting for me to turn. I grew increasingly dizzy. If I did not pull away, I could still fall, without even breaking that wall.

"I felt it clearly," I said, clinging to the gravel with my fingers. "The rumbling." I was breathing so loud whoever was climbing *that* mountain would surely feel it. Perhaps it was my own heavy panting I'd heard earlier, just before I saw the girl.

"We sometimes think we feel the other side. I would not worry. At night, Ultar seldom slides." He paused. "But I would not stop here."

He disappeared into the night.

It was three-thirty in the morning and it was silent. I was checking my watch compulsively now. I was beginning to feel the altitude. I stopped for water, often; I chewed on biscuits. My lungs no longer felt clean but swollen. So did my feet. They were heavy; my shoes were heavy. The pack on my back, even heavier. Worse, I was beginning to get the same feeling as in Kaghan, and even Gilgit. I was being watched. Perhaps by Ultar's jinn, or Ultar's double, rising menacingly behind us like a shadow. I was alone, but I was not. I told myself it was nothing, just the residual panic of nearly falling into the chasm. I had nearly died. That was all.

I pushed on, replaying my moment on the edge. I'd pulled away eventually, though I couldn't say how long I'd sat there after the escort left. Because I hadn't wanted to lift my hands, I hadn't been able to check the time. I'd kept sitting in that 40-degree angle, my body stiffening. It might have been the fear of never being able to move again that caused me to slowly inch away on my buttocks, one push at a time, looking at anything but my shoes. They were on solid ground. Push. They were *still* on solid ground. When I finally stood up, Ultar was silent. No rumbling. The river flowed in curves again. But I did not. A stitch of fear had fallen off onto me from that wavering wall, and now I carried it with me as I moved forward.

Of the route I was unsure, but there was evidently still a long way up. Irfan and Wes had said the glacier was not at the summit. They'd estimated four, maybe five hours. I might only be halfway there. I tried not to feel angry with Irfan. We were meant to keep each other vaguely in sight, even if we were to follow the shin-beams. Why wasn't he looking out for me?

A new worry seized me. Should I be looking out for him?

And what about the others? Was Farhana safe?

I would have heard a shout. No one was in danger. I did what I'd resisted doing ever since pulling away from the ravine. I shone my headlamp into it, as it plunged thousands of meters to the valley floor. Nothing—though what exactly I was looking for, I didn't know. Landslides? No, Ultar and her shadow were at peace.

I drank more water. I unloaded my pack from off my back. I'd packed my camera before setting out, and the 300 mm telephoto zoom, which added extra pounds. So much for being a photographer by day and a happy man by night! Before leaving, I'd told myself I wanted to change. If I were a photographer by night, would I be a happy man by day? If I were a happy man by day, would I make Farhana happier? So I'd packed the camera. My plan was to take images of the glacier before courting Farhana beside it, before descending to our hotel with her beside me.

Perhaps it was the camera that made me feel watched. I was aware of it, in my bag, in my company. I'd had it with me that night at the graves, before leaving Kaghan, when I could feel eyes behind me. And as on that night, my legs were not guiding me. It was my mind that guided my legs. Granted, climbing up a mountain that was not so much sloped as scissored was likely a good occasion to use one's head. But I'd trusted my instincts better in the past—even if they did ocassionally fail me—and I liked how I saw the world differently without my camera at night. Now I felt obliged to do something with it. I took it out. I put it back inside.

As I tucked the camera away, I noticed a box wrapped in a red cloth beneath the zoom. I hadn't put it there. It was likely that this had also been adding to the weight. Perhaps Irfan had slipped it in, with mithai or fruit to break into at the glacier.

I kept climbing.

I grew excited at the thought of a celebration waiting for us at our meeting point. I wouldn't open the box. I'd let Irfan say when. And with this thought, it was again all right to be by myself. I had the company of a surprise that I'd been designated to carry, I was the good messenger, and in the meantime, the stars were again sparkling almost at nail's reach, the night was clear.

My mind began to drift. This time, instead of muffled footsteps, or goatbells, I heard Farhana's voice, sweeter than a bell. We were at the Sutro Baths that day in May, her birthday. Before me on Ultar Sar I saw her orange scarf roll across the green peat as she asked,

"So, which is more beautiful. The desert, or the mountains?" I hadn't known how to compare them, a horizontal wilderness with the most impenetrable perpendicular wilderness in the world. Now here I was, in a dark upright world that moved when I moved, in jaws that grew teeth when I tried to slip by them, and with no one to call out to if I fell into that widest jaw of all, the one below. I'd told her the experience energized me by removing me from myself. *Like seeing the world from behind a camera.* Except now, I had my camera with me, and I'd put it away.

Okay, which makes you happiest, the desert, the mountains, or these scummy baths with me.

I'm happy anywhere with you.

Soon I'd be happy again. Soon.

Half an hour later I was walking in mud, and a soft rain began to fall. My hands were filthy from guiding my feet through the muck. I wiped them on my jeans. The rocks were caked in soil and my shoes found no traction. I would have to walk around the mountain side, instead of going up. But which side? I was completely disoriented. I headed to my right, keeping my hands out in front, feeling in the shadows for a dry surface to hold. What I felt instead, more acutely this time, was a pair of eyes.

When I tried to look around to my horror I realized that I'd wound my way to the edge of a turn, past a gap, and onto a ledge. Again! Only, this time I wasn't simply leaning against a crumbling wall but standing on it! Worse, I couldn't even see it! My headlamp hadn't illuminated the path; my feet were entirely in the dark. To go forward would mean falling into the chasm, witnessed only by Ultar and her echo. There was nothing for it but to slink to my left toward the mud again, raising my foot so it wouldn't catch in the gap I'd been lucky to avoid without even knowing it. It was far worse than the last time; now it was raining, the earth was increasingly slick, and there was that gap. Plus, my feet were anchored in a space so small I couldn't even think of sitting and inching my way to safety on my behind. I had to jump. I had to jump in the dark. I pushed the panic in my gut down a few inches but it rose by twice as many. Worse was to come. The headlamp was growing increasingly dim and I hadn't brought extra batteries. Once again I cursed Irfan. Then I cursed myself for depending on him.

Why did I keep doing it? Why had I twice stepped so near to my death? It was as though something was willing me to do it. It was not my will! These were not my legs! I wanted to shout, and then I think I did. I think I shouted, *These are not my legs!* before it dawned on me that this was a terrible time to shout. I had to get off the ledge. I could not afford to stand here indefinitely, the way I'd sat indefinitely on the gravel earlier. I could not afford any distractions. I had to think clearly what to do next. And then I had to stop thinking. I had to act. Stop thinking. Stop thinking. I took two deep breaths, scooped to the left, felt the gap with my toes, jumped. I fell face down in the mud. But it was mud, not air. I was safe. I pulled my bag off my shoulders and fished inside—I could *not* afford to think about what I had just escaped, I had to think about small things, such as, I could *not* afford to drop my camera here—I fished inside without upsetting the camera, or the box, for the flashlight. Instead, a flashlight was in my face.

"Not far now," he said. It was the escort, and he was bloody calm.

"Is there a way up from here?" My voice was shaking.

"Oh yes." He offered me his hand.

I was hauled up as easily as a twig, though I'd believed him to be scrawnier than myself. I followed him further into the belly of the mountain, away from the torn crook of her arm.

It was raining harder. My jacket had a hood. His didn't. He seemed unperturbed by this. This was a good thing to focus on. It was a very good thing.

"What's your name?"

"Askarov."

"Askar*ov*?" I laughed. "From Kaghan?"

He did not answer.

"What is it you trade?" I tried again.

"Jade."

"Jade? In return for what?"

"Many things."

"Such as?"

"Ghee."

"Ghee? Don't you make plenty of that already?"

He grinned. It was the first time I'd seen him grin. It wasn't pretty.

"Is there jade at the glacier, or ghee?"

He lost his grin. I think I preferred it.

"Have you climbed up here before?"

"It is not far now. You will hear it."

Again he disappeared.

"Hear what? And where are the others?" I called after him, expecting no reply, and getting none. Twice he'd helped me, both times when I was lost, and in danger.

He was watching me.

The sky was growing pale. It was turning on its side, leaving behind a softer shade of black. The perpendicular wilderness began to seem less impenetrable. Just as well, because my headlamp quietly extinguished with a flickering that was not unlike a silent fart. I tore the straps off. I had only my flashlight now. I heard more rocks fall, not the defeaning shatter of the landslide on Ultar's double, but a rumble nonetheless, followed by a roll of smaller rocks. A leopard or the escort? A ghost or Farhana? There was a creaking too; like the night, the stones were turning in their sleep.

I ate more biscuits. I drank a little water. I must save the rest. I had about half a bottle left. I took one last sip then screwed the top back on. When I looked up, I saw two shins, glowing about twenty feet above my head. Like the mountain, my inhibitions were growing less impenetrable too. "Wes!" I shouted loudly. "Where the hell is everyone?" I was so excited to see him I almost forgot to take my pack.

"Right here," he turned back. "We're almost there."

"Wait!"

But he did not.

I was alone again. Damn Irfan. Damn Wes. And damn Farhana. Wouldn't *she* have wanted a word alone with me, just once on our way up?

And "Askarov"—where was he now? Tired of watching me? Just as well! I would *not* let myself ask—not here, not now—*why* he was following me. Maybe Irfan had asked him to look out for me. Irfan, who knew I wouldn't follow Wes. Irfan, to whom I foolishly left all the practicalities of every trip. Maybe Farhana had been right. I did defer to him too much. Maybe I was going about this courtship in a very wrong way. Maybe she needed to see me at the front of the line, not stuck back here, bringing up the rear. Maybe she'd walk beside me if I were leading.

I pushed on. I couldn't lead now. All I could do was push on. I concentrated on the small circle thrown by the flashlight at my feet. That little glow was just what I needed to coax me into a rhythm again, and nudge all my idle thoughts away. I hoped the battery would last till the sky turned gray, even gold. I tried to focus only on this. Flashlight, don't die! Flash a little longer!

I began to see colors in my head. A wash of ash gray, charcoal at top, cream below, and a frayed edge that blossomed delicately from the faintest yellow to the most luminous salmon pink. It was so vivid before me I wondered if my sister had a dupatta of that pattern, or perhaps a sari. It might even belong to my mother, a stranger walking down a silver floor to a side street lit with white lamps, the cloth billowing behind her like a cloud. I didn't know how long the image sustained me but, finally raising my eye past the light at my feet, I noticed there were patches of snow all around me now, mounds that glittered in the night.

The sight was so beautiful I thought I'd stumbled onto the silver floor of my imagining. I was in the middle of an oasis! How thirsty I was! I scooped a snow heap with my fingers; the taste was bitter and familiar. It pulled me back to that moonlit night in Kaghan, a night heavy with the silence of seduction, like tonight, and I was kneeling at the banks of the River Kunhar, gathering silver filigree deep into the folds of my tongue, while a reflection broke in the water. Instantly, I looked up. No owl. No opal moon.

The sky grew even lighter, a gentle gray streaked with gold. I thanked my flashlight and switched it off. More snow crystals stretched awake while others fell asleep. Surely they were stars, fallen from the sky! The hand of a fairy had strewn them on these slopes! I wanted to stuff myself with them, foul taste and all.

With the burn of glacial melt still in my mouth, I started walking again. Yet more snow. The palest apricot sky. I could hear birds now, distant and small, but there was an unmistakable thrill in the air nonetheless, and it was rising. I'd never known a daybreak as joyous as this. I looked toward the sun; it was still invisible to me but I was not invisible to it. I was shivering and sweating and I was alone but I was not alone. Perhaps I was delirious but I did not care. I spun toward the sun, again and again. I laughed.

When I stopped spinning I pulled my feet apart to steady myself, still laughing. In return, I heard a groan. It was not a human voice. It was not a rockfall. This was a groan that came from somewhere else. The first thought that entered my mind, *a whale*. The second, *but I'm on a mountain*. The third, *a whale on a mountain*.

I'd never heard a whale sing but I imagined it might be like this. It was the sound of sheer bulk. A lunge through a dark void of unimaginable weight, as the lungs sought release. And I was carried along, higher, higher, till I heard the first suck of air in the form of a crack. The beast kept pulling me toward itself. As the snapping and heaving grew louder, I heard the distinctive tone of ice, and it was as if an ancient corpse were trying to break free of its colossal tomb.

I was at the glacier.

The portion that met me first was the classic deep blue of polar glaciers, a color I'd never seen in the Karakoram before. But then I'd never been this high up. I climbed higher still. Before me stretched the gray sea of rock and gravelly moraine of the glaciers of the lower valley, but also a dozen ethereal blues, a dozen delicate violets. My mind was clear. I couldn't remember when I'd taken the camera out, or snapped on the zoom, but apparently I had. I wasn't thinking of the photographs my fingers took, but I trusted my hand completely.

As the cracking of the glacier continued, it released a memory.

How does sunlight travel through ice? I am asking Irfan. What happens to this light? We are in class eight; I think I am twelve, he thirteen. I am teamed up with Irfan in the physics lab to watch the rainbow in a prism, while our teacher says the sun has different colors, each with different quantities of energy. Orange and red hold only a little; violet and blue, considerably more. Irfan says he is blue; I am red. I agree, happily. Beside me, in my plastic thermos cup, floats a single cube of ice. I ask him if light passes through ice in the same way, blue first, and he says yes.

There near the summit, the crystals of Ultar Glacier sucked me in. The reds and yellows were vanished, the blues limning the ice prevailed. When my camera rotated, I saw them. Irfan, his lips on Farhana's. I believe I photographed them before I knew what I'd let myself preserve.

A prince and a fairy in a crystal, one planting on the other the softest of kisses, his movements so tender they were devotional. Their eyes were shut as they felt each other through layers of clothing—he even kissed the sleeve of her red jacket—and both faces wore identical expressions: a look so sublime it was as though they were soaring on a carpet of feathers. And how united they were in their ascent! Free of haste, free of shame. If till then it had been a secret, they were through with secrets now. In the arms of discovery, they suffered no fear of being discovered. I knew I hadn't kissed her in this way in a long, long time. For the briefest flicker before my fury set in, I registered the truth of the moment. And captured all of it. My camera clicked; my mind could not stop the hand it trusted so well. It was what had been missing in my work so far and I was ill-prepared for the moment when I would find it: beauty, sweet and true. It was a miracle.

Then came ugliness. I saw the crevasse behind Irfan. I saw the indigo wash of light pouring off the drop, the fin-like gash of ultramarine swirling around the snowy edges now melting in the sun, and farther, the wide black mouth into which he might fall. It would be easy to slip. I couldn't see the depth; perhaps it would only cause minor injury. Still, it would likely be impossible to haul him out without the gear we hadn't brought.

My mind stepped in and slapped my hand away. How could I picture Irfan this way? What demons had possessed me? My hand lashed back. Good demons. Easy, just walk up and push. He was too wrapped up in her sleeve to resist. And he might be smarter, but he was smaller. Were he to fight back, you'd win. But first, pull yourself away from the kiss. How? Whose hand would help with *that*?

My skin burned with the warmth between them. Breathing didn't come easy. I could feel my resolve crumble. I couldn't pull away from watching. *What was so spectacular about her sleeve?* And what was he going to do next—kneel? Kiss her damn shoes? In reply, the glacier groaned. High-frequency lust; low-frequency torture. All that pressure pooling at its surface in the sun! Wasn't sunrise meant to be the hour of hope? *The season of creation* some poet or other had once called it. Fucking poet.

Next I was overcome with a desire to vanish myself. That cascade of light pouring down the side of the drop: I could pour with it. It was the only way to free myself of thought, now that I was thinking again. They looked so young, in their union of trust, my former lover, my former best friend. All the shame the two refused to carry was swiftly encumbering me. I needed to be rid of it. I needed to be someone else. Only then would I release all the cracking and heaving from somewhere deep inside.

Vanish me. I squeezed my eyes shut. My legs did the rest.

The day was searingly hot already. I'd left my pack behind. I felt no need to retrace my steps. There was that half bottle of water left inside. I was sure I wouldn't make it back down without it. Yet I stayed, on a ledge, letting the thirst pool on my tongue. Perhaps it was the same ledge as earlier this morning, when I'd nearly fallen to my death. That would have been better.

The questions I could not leave behind. Their first time? Or with her all those nights away from our hotel? His own desire prompting him to ask, on the shores of the lake, if she and Wes had ever been lovers? Or had it begun even earlier, as early as Karachi? No? At the cabin in Kaghan, then, the day before we left for Gilgit? He said he wanted to return to Karachi for—how did he put it?—*personal reasons*. Had he been trying to warn me? And what about that look of disapproval, the morning after the owl-sighting, the morning Farhana and I last made love—had it, in truth, been envy? Hadn't he been different with me ever since? And what of poor Zulekha? He'd come here to say goodbye to her, and in the process, stolen Farhana?

The questions would kill me before my thirst could. What difference did it make? Perhaps she'd found a better man to *return* to. Or simply, a better man.

I couldn't hear them anymore.

Which is worse, a crime committed because you don't look, or because you do? The one that is an accident, or the one that is calculated?

It was a chance calculation. More like an accident.

What exactly had happened when I'd approached them? *Had* I approached them? I couldn't remember. I remembered some things only, such as wondering if I'd have the strength to push him. And the glacier had heard. A ray of sun had tickled her rib; she began to sweat. Adjusting her spine, she shrank, expanded, then advanced. They were fools to stand on that rib, but even so, I would not have thought it possible, the way their position moved, sliding closer to the edge, as she oscillated so very slightly, to and fro, a micrometer shrug, and Irfan was slipping backward, while Farhana's eyes opened at last. He reached for her when he saw me. He reached for that red sleeve he'd been kissing just moments earlier, when the ice was firm, when the sun was still behind Ultar's spire. And I saw it: she pulled the sleeve away. She did not want to fall with him. She would not hold another drowning body. She had let him go, while crying for help.

Across the chasm, I could see it now. Ultar's shadow. The sun had peeled off his mask. Underneath lay a russet tongue of gravel between a file of punishing teeth. There was a legend about that mountain but I couldn't remember it. No doubt it involved a demon and a death. The wind was kicking up now and it probably wasn't a good idea to keep sitting here; I leaned back and let the gale tear at my flesh. They'd looked sublime. Eyes shut, cheeks flushed. Hands roaming. More sublime than she and I had looked in the water, on the edge of Saiful Maluk.

I'd tossed him my pack. "There's water left." He hadn't moved. I'd also noticed two mithai boxes, not just the one, pushed to the bottom. Both wrapped in red cloth. I decided to take one for myself at the last minute, then I threw the pack. He caught it. I waited for him to look up. When he finally did, I was glad the light obliterated his face.

Wes and Farhana watched me leave. "Are you going for help?" Wes called after me. "I think his leg is broken." He was asking me? The man who could wrestle polar bears by himself? He could surely haul a small brown man off a slippery shelf.

At least he was kind enough to announce himself this time. The escort cleared his throat, waited briefly, then hopped down to the ledge where I was hiding from the world. By now I could barely open my eyes.

"I need water," I whispered.

He said nothing.

"Do you have any?"

He shook his head.

"Why are you on this mountain? There isn't jade or ghee up here." I didn't really care how he answered; all my questions were tired now.

He answered with a hideous grin, reminding me of someone else.

"Do you want my jacket?" I asked.

"What for?"

"You're following me." It wasn't a question. It was closer to acquiescence.

He laughed.

"Why are you following me?"

He was nodding and grinning and laughing all at once. "To kill you."

"What would you be trading then?"

He kept laughing.

My eyes were drooping less. I saw that he was not bad looking. His teeth, the part of him I'd been speaking to, were his worst feature. But the expression in his wide brown eyes was surprisingly mild. It might have been my own desire to see him this way, but see him this way I now did. A silky head of hair, the color of wheat, fell almost to his shoulders. Slightly darker than Kiran's and better kept. In fact, all of him was better kept. His clothes were good. A thick gray jacket of rough weave, perhaps yak wool, with white embroidery around the buttons. The embroidery was not as smeared with mud as it ought to have been, given the conditions. A necklace of large black stones, jade perhaps, though not in a color I'd seen before; a belt of real leather; solid shoes. I'd thought he went without shoes, he'd been that silent. But this man did not walk on glaciers on the soles of his feet.

A gun lay at his feet. I only noticed it now, while taking in the shoes. If he'd carried it around his shoulder, as, after all, an armed escort should, I might have noticed—though it was dark, how would I? But it wasn't the kind to sling around the shoulder. It wasn't the automatic weapon I'd seen him with when we first picked him up, on our way to Gilgit. It was a pistol.

From the inside pocket of his jacket, he pulled out a bottle. Thirsty, I reached out. He gladly proffered it; the scent turned my mouth sour. I shook my head.

So this was breakfast.

"They hibernate, you know." He pointed behind him. "Like mammals and birds. When the sun shines, and the ice melts, they roll over. The thin ice rolls the loudest."

So we'd talk first.

It sounded like some kind of Chinese proverb. *The thin ice rolls the loudest.* Yes? And how did the man on the ledge roll? And which man, the one who'd landed here by choice, or the one on another ledge, higher up, who'd—slipped? I decided not to ask.

He drank. His lips were moist, his skin as tawny as his belt. "Shh," he whispered, lifting a finger to those wet lips, though he was the one talking. "Listen." From his throat poured a sound like a gurgle. "RrrrrRrrrr!" It sounded like an engine, though, apparently, it was meant to represent water. "Low sound is water gushing, finding a new opening. RrrrrRrrrr!" I heard no low sounds, no gushing water. Only him. "There are always openings in the mountains. Always. You can find them. If you learn to track with sound." He grinned. "It is a skill that will suit you, when you go."

Suit you, he said, in English. Suit me how? And go where? He spoke in an Urdu with no trace of a northern accent. He threw in many English words. And his talk was beginning to make less and less sense.

"It is hard to endure, you know?"

I nodded.

"What do you know?" His voice was growing brittle as the bottle in his hand.

I hesitated.

"Can you play the flute?"

I shook my head.

"Drums?"

I shook it again.

"What good are you?"

I nodded.

"Here, try this." From another pocket, he pulled out a double flute, embellished with multicolored tassels, many intricately braided.

I held it in my hands.

"Play," he commanded.

When I held it to my lips, I tasted paint. No sound came from me.

He laughed. He began to play.

I heard again the melody played the day Kiran's body was taken down to the plains. I remembered the way her brother's cheek had filled with air kisses, the way his farewell filled the shores of the lake, the way Queen of the Mountains and Naked Mountain sang back the notes. I did not recognize this man from that day. As his dirge grew more elaborate, it rolled into the valley like twin armies of dark clouds, each shadowing the other with thunder in its breast. The mountains answered back, with deeper thunder.

When he stopped, I did not weep. But I began to feel afraid.

He dried the lip of each pipe tenderly with a corner of his shirt. "I played at her birth," he said. "You know?" His eyes were not mild at all. He spat on the wood and began to shine it. He was humming. "Six years for six stars in girgiti. I promised. I keep my promises. Hmmhmmhmm."

I could feel myself slowly slink away from him, though I didn't have much room. It was either the chasm, or him.

Without looking up from the flute, he said, "I was coming down from the steppe when it happened. From Kazakhstan. You know Kazakhstan?"

I hesitated.

"She sits on two hundred billion barrels of oil. You know?"

I nodded.

"America says no, no, *no* pipeline, not through Iran!" He was laughing vigorously now, unbuttoning his jacket after resting the flute on his lap, the black stones at his throat glistening with sweat. "But others, they say yes, yes, yes!"

I had nowhere to go.

"China ships it, the crude. All the way to Iran, from Pakistan. Then back up to China. China, Kazakhstan, Pakistan, Iran. The new Silk Road. You know?"

I nodded.

"But still they are poor. So they want my help, my friends." He fingered the bottle. It had a red label and he drank it slow. "Are they my friends?"

I kept very still, hoping he wouldn't notice *me* searching for an opening. How did he put it? *There are always openings through the mountains*. Another Chinese proverb?

"The way it used to be," he kept on. "Except, now we run on land *and* water." He stared past my head, at the chasm beyond. "We have always run," he added, still gazing with some longing at the drop.

I could not speak.

He picked up my camera. "I have seen many others. Better than this." He shook it, roughly. He flipped it back and forth, searching for the on button.

"Uh." I cleared my throat, trying to indicate the button with my eyes and my chin.

He pushed it. I looked away. The photographs would begin with the most recent. The one of them, at the glacier. Reason for the broader grin, no doubt. He'd probably seen them first. He was always ahead of me on the trail. He could have killed me any time, on the way up. But he'd waited, wanting me to see. And he was pleased. He began to skip through the pictures backward. I began to see them all in my mind again. I ought to have been offended at his obvious interest in Farhana as a nude and I was, even as I told myself it didn't matter anymore, but, in fact, I was more offended than I had been on the beach—that *must* be the one he was gaping at, his wide eyes about to burst—when I'd hardly been upset at all, when the voyeur had been a voyeur not of film but of flesh.

He took his time. I didn't interrupt.

Eventually, he put the camera down in the gravel, outside its case, and without switching it off. I fought the urge to tuck it away securely.

Moments passed. The sun was high, higher than the man beside me.

After a while, I dared to ask, gently, "Should we leave?"

He scratched his chin, where thin wisps of golden brown fluttered in a wind that scraped my throat so dry, I was tempted to drink his drink.

"Maryam's mother. She was an escort."

It chilled me to hear her name spoken. "Yes?"

"Of the sick. When a soul would wander away, she would bring it back."

I kept looking at him with as much interest as possible.

"You are sick," he announced. "But I am not here to help."

It was curious how the will to live now burned bright in me, where earlier this morning, I'd lost it entirely.

"I thought I was going to kill you." He grinned.

I hadn't lost the will, not at all. It was a discarded friend I welcomed back. And as it raised its head to fill the space I cleared for it, I wondered about Irfan. Still conscious? An ever-expanding part of me hoped he was, even as I wanted to silence this part. They couldn't have reached help yet, Wes and Farhana, though they might be close. No, I couldn't count on that. It would be some time before they made it all the way back up.

By then, what would have happened to me?

He said I *thought* I was going to kill you.

He was peering into my face with eyes now small and red.

"You know?" he asked, seeming genuinely lost.

I took a chance. "Have you ever killed?"

Seeming to remember something, he frowned, as if to chase the thought away. "You are a sick man. A dying man. I have never killed a dying man."

Well, this was hopeful.

"A life of exile is worse than death. You will forever be alone."

Another proverb?

He smiled, suddenly pleased. It was different from his grin. He looked almost pretty. "I was going to give you a choice, but the dying have no choice. I do not think there is need for this." He pointed to his gun. He picked it up. He fired into the chasm.

I pressed my hands to my ears. If before the mountains had answered his flute with a series of thundering echoes, now it was the valleys and the bluffs of my skull through which the gunshot ricocheted first. There were hundreds of surfaces inside me to strike, no matter how hard I squeezed shut my ears.

A very long time passed before I found the courage to remove my hands. And when I did, I vomited. I had only biscuits and water to bring up and they did not surrender with ease. A string of froth fell on my chin, on my shirt, and at his heel.

He offered the bottle again.

I nearly vomited again.

"I would not have to do anything except make sure you were never found." Still with that smile around his lips. The bottle lay with his gun, the cap back on.

I returned the smile. I could taste the acid still rising in me.

"You know the choice?"

I shook my head.

"Go outside the mountains and never return. Or, die." He pointed again to his gun.

"No!" I squeezed my ears.

He shrugged, feigning surprise, as though I'd just declined a sweet.

I shut my eyes and thought quickly. It would be just fine with me if I left. Distance is a great protector! A quick stop at my mother's in Karachi, then back to San Francisco, or perhaps the desert. I'd forget all of it. I'd live unencumbered by shame or yearning, history or memory. The farther into the future I'd go, the less my past would shadow me.

"Should we leave?" I hazarded again.

"I said no. No choice." He fired the gun again.

This time I bowed my head like a coward. My eyes, however, stayed open. I was listening and watching, even if that meant the crack through the canyon made my ears hum and every sound fade as though I were plunging to the bottom of a lake. My ears were filling with water but I would have to keep listening.

I waited. He seemed almost to be in a trance. He'd look at me, then gaze dreamily at the abyss beyond. Look at the bottle, then look at his flute. Look at my camera, then look again at the chasm. Speaking in circles, as though delivering a chant.

"Not south and not across the seas, from wherever it is you came. No no no. I mean north."

"North?" My voice already sounded very far away. "This *is* north."

"China north." He was laughing again.

And then he began to outline, in the most labyrinthine detail, and still in that trance-like voice, the destiny he had mapped out for me.

Disguised as a trader, I would arrive at the frontier town of Tashkurgan, where I would pass into Kashgar. After that would come a checkpoint, the keeping of which was the bitterest of jobs, when the thermometer dropped to below zero. It made the men cranky, the ones who would tell me to take off all my clothes, there in the cold. And I would be given a new name. And different clothes, clothes worn by the last man to make the passage, and the one before him, crossing in the other direction, perhaps, with no fingers or toes. And the clothes would not have been washed and they would be live with creatures that had survived the cold, and I ought to learn from them. Only after that would I be ready for the Silk Route proper, which I would take from Kashgar to Yarkand, tracing the footsteps of those who had done the same for thousands of years. And this route was more often called the Ghost Route, for it was haunted, so I would need to prepare. I would track ghosts by listening, learning which to avoid and which to sit beside, at a fire, sipping tea mixed with millet seed, telling tales of flying horses whose names changed like the colors of the nimbus through which they soared. Pegasus, Tulpar, Jonon Khar. I would hear them go. And the fire would blow out. And the spirits would vanish. And if my skin were thick enough, I would eventually find my way to Karakol Lake, the blackest of lakes, surrounded by the Pamir Mountains. And the Pamirs would be reflected on the surface of the lake, her peaks and valleys swooping into Karakol's depths, blue wings in a dark deep, and I would again be visited by fairies and jinns, owls and full moons, and I would kneel by the banks of that lake and wash my tired feet and drink the glacial melt and see the two of us, myself and my love, though he did not say this, he said the two of *us*, the Queen and the Nude, reflected as on another lake, one in which an unspeakable crime had been committed, for which someone had to pay.

He was blinking like a lizard in the sun.

My lips were cracking. I could taste the warm comfort of salt and blood.

"No." He shook his head. "That is not how it will be."

I did not know if I preferred it when he looked at me or past me.

"You are already paying. You know?" The smile returned to his face. "But tell me, you would not choose this life, if I let you choose?"

A life of banishment in place of death? Without love, with only the company of barren rocks? At one time I believed myself desirous of anonymity and solitude, but I was trembling now. He was right. I was sick.

"The dying have no choice," I answered.

He laughed. "You hear me well."

"You speak well."

He grinned.

Again a long pause.

Then, "Can you hear it?"

Behind me, I thought I could still hear the glacier crawl. I said as much.

"No no no. Not the glacier. Your friend. He is moving."

I decided to stand up, very, very slowly.

"One last thing." His eyes flew open.

I slid back down.

"If I let you go, you must give me something in return."

In return for what—my new lease on a lonesome life?

"I want this."

He took my camera.

"One more last thing."

I waited. He was looking beside me, at the box wrapped in red cloth.

"Where is your bag?"

"I gave it to him," I pointed to the general area where Irfan lay trapped.

He seemed alarmed by this. "Did you take anything out?"

"Just that." I pointed to the camera in his hands. "And that." I pointed to the box.

He looked away, still troubled. I thought it atypical for him.

"Why?" I asked.

"I was never going to kill you with a gun." He began to laugh.

As I climbed down the mountain, he played the flute. *Goodbye!* The melody was at my back, and then *on* my back. It swung around, knotting a pair of tassles around my waist. It pranced before me in the dust as I walked. *Goodbye, goodbye!* It was leaping and kicking, skipping and taunting, this jealous jinn, this giddy guide. *Not even a fairy princess is worth falling for!* It was what Irfan had said, at the edge of a different glacier, on our way to the lake. We'd nearly slipped, both of us. I'd pulled his jacket for support. He'd let me.

Did he only have a broken leg? Was he even alive? A yearning began to rub me raw.

The descent did nothing to relieve me of it, not even when the melody finally faded and my thoughts grew heavy and dull through sheer bodily fatigue. Now my most steady companion was time, time in which to re-live my tale as I scraped my shins against Ultar's jagged fangs, forging a distance between me and all that I loved, a distance that was no protector at all. I made my way by listening to rocks fall, and to memories surround me: I ought to turn back. I ought to help Irfan. He was in danger. I'd swum away from Kiran and Farhana. Now I was running from Irfan. Farhana and Wes would also leave him. Where was the help? He was abandoned. He was in danger. I, on the other hand, was now out of danger.

I did not turn back.

Before I could reach the first village, I saw a convoy of trucks heading for the foot of the mountain. They stopped when they saw me.

"That's him!"

"No. That is not him."

"Then what is *that*?"

Two men got out of a truck and told me to put down the box. While one kept watching it, the other searched me roughly. He sneered at my ID card and pocketed the forty dollars I still had in my wallet. They asked what was inside the box and I said food and they asked where I'd been. I tried to explain that I was with a group of friends, but my tongue was stuck somewhere at the back of my throat. Irfan would have been better at this. Besides, they weren't my friends.

"We are wasting time," said another man from inside a second truck.

"This man is lying."

"Where are you going?"

"Hurry up!" They called from inside.

"I—I don't know."

"What did you say?"

"He isn't the one we want."

While they argued, a black Honda and white Hyundai drove up. "Check it," called a man from inside the Honda, before it had even screeched to a stop.

"Be careful, he might be carrying explosives," said a man from inside the Hyundai.

Did I hear them correctly? I began to laugh.

Immediately I was surrounded. There were six men around me now, each pointing a gun to my head, and one of them began to shout. "*What's this*?" He pushed my head so I was leaning forward, gaping at the box wrapped in red cloth. They would not touch it.

"That's mithai," I said, my voice shaking.

"It's him," a skinny man with a face like a screw said to the large man whose hand was still pushing my head. The large man kicked the backs of my knees so I fell to the ground. "Get up!" said the skinny man, and when I tried to get up, he slapped the back of my head and told me to kneel. And now the most extraordinary thing began to happen.

While the trucks and cars started driving away, the six men took long steps backward, still with their guns pointed at my head. They walked steadily and heavily away from me, as though in me they had stumbled upon an unexploded mine. I was entranced by their mistake. They were afraid of *me*. The weak one, the one to always bring up the rear, the one who ran away. The man moving the slowest was the skinny one, who had two diagonal lines extending from his cheekbone to his nose, and two more diagonal lines on the other side of his face extending from his nose to his jaw. I was looking at those lines as he began to bark his orders.

"When we are there, at that tree with the cloth tied to its branches," he pointed behind him and I raised my head to see the end of the road and what might have been a tree, "you will open the box. Understand?" I nodded. In truth, behind him I saw only shimmering brown earth. The day was scorching, and the dust on the horizon was growing thick. Where was everybody? I'd never been entirely alone even once on this trip, even when I'd wanted to be. Eyes had followed me everywhere. Where were they—my accusers? Didn't they want to see me now?

"*Do you understand?*" he kept repeating as he withdrew into the searing sky. I kept nodding, even when I knew he couldn't see me. "*Understand?*" Yes. Yes, I understand. My neck agreed. My spine too; all of me was bowing in consent. All of me was jerking up, and flopping down. Yes! I understand! It took me a while to see that I was not merely nodding, but sobbing.

"*Open it now.*" Perhaps they had a megaphone, for the voice appeared to reach me from very far away, yet it was clear.

I stared at the sky. I stared at the red cloth.

"*Open it NOW!*"

There was a bomb and they were making me open it. It was not mithai or fruit. Irfan had not put it there. How did it get there? I remembered dropping my pack, when I got lost on the mountain the first time. The escort had found me, and the pack, and returned it. And before we'd parted, he'd asked me where the second box was. It was with Irfan.

Then I remembered the holy dates. The ones gifted to the policemen in Mansehra and Balakot. The ones that came in a box inside which lay a small handmade bomb, with the firing pin attached to the lid. The blast was enough to kill those within range. I was definitely within range; the other men were not.

I stared at the red cloth. I did not touch it. There was no picture of a date anywhere I could see. Those other boxes, I imagined them wrapped in shiny gold paper that folded neatly around the edges. I imagined the paper crinkling at the slightest touch, though the touch of those men would not have been slight. I imagined the pictures of fat, juicy dates on a glossy cover, perhaps with nuts. But this was just a red cloth.

Farhana was with Irfan.

I heard a gunshot and then a shout. "*Son-of-a-swine, open it NOW!*"

Naturally, it wouldn't always come disguised as holy dates. It could be anything. Including mithai. Including fruit.

The skinny man was walking toward me, yelling that he would shoot me first, before I could open it. This confused me. I thought he wanted me to open it? Before I could understand, the butt of his rifle hit my cheek. I heard a crack. I fell sideways. Two more men had joined him and only now did it register that none of them were in uniform. This confused me too. *Thwack!* This time the blow was aimed at my gut. The fist that pulled away was as large as a melon. I drooled blood on his shoe. I could not see very much.

"We are telling you one last time. When we are at that tree," he lifted my chin and yanked it sideways, and I screamed, because under his fingers the side of my face rippled like oil, "when we are there, you will open it. Do you understand, you bastard? You son of a whore?"

They began to back away again.

"Now: OPEN IT."

I could hear my voice come out of my throat in a gargle. "No! Please! Please no!"

There was no answer.

Let me walk away. Like you. See how it is, in that innocent wrapping? Let it lie there. Let it rest. Bury it. No one will know. I will never tell. I promise. On my life.

I straightened myself as best I could to a kneeling position again. I kneeled before these men, who were now safely beside some tree I could not see. My mind was raging but my body was capitulating. I kept kneeling, even as I wanted to tear them apart with my teeth. I wanted to thank them too, for letting me live, if that is what they chose to do, out of the goodness of their hearts. I wanted to kick them to pulp. I kept kneeling. I wanted to silence the part of me that asked why we live subject to those we can't respect. Why? Why do we agree to live like this? How can we respect ourselves? How would I ever get up again?

I began to gargle again. "Listen, please listen! Let me live!"

Gargle gargle gargle.

It occurred to me that it might be better to die.

I could simply open the box. No more humiliation. I could end this right now. I reminded myself that I'd wanted to end this even earlier, on the glacier, before the escort reminded me that I wanted to live.

I picked up the box. It was light. Very light. Weren't bombs heavy? What else could be inside? Cherries? Small slippers?

Very slowly, I twisted loose the knot that tied the four ends of the cloth together. It was a style that would have perfectly suited the wrapping of a stack of hot chapaatis.

The box was uncovered now. The box was small and white. I smelled no chapaatis and that was okay because I wasn't hungry.

I touched the lid of the box.

I tried praying but it didn't really work. I was angry with God, at that particular moment.

Again I pleaded for life. "I beg you, I'll do anything!" Again I hated myself.

After what seemed like a very long time, I received an answer in the shape of a kick to my teeth. I lay curled on my side in the dirt and continued to receive the blows.

I did not know how much time passed before I noticed that the sun was drying the blood in my mouth and this was uncomfortable. It is curious how, even when every inch of the body is in pain, it is possible to isolate a hurt, make it a separate thing, cushion it with exclusive attention and care. I tried to wet the dried blood with my spit but moving my lips made me tear the scabs at their corners. I kept trying. I had to wet my lips without moving them. I could do this.

Ahead of me, a field was aflame. If this was delirium, it was not unpleasant. The fire in the distance had a warm orange glow. At its center sizzled a cluster of seeds with a purple sheen. The chaos was elsewhere, far from that orange glow, and no one would disturb me as I focused all my desire on tending this small corner of a troubled earth: the corner of my mouth.

A small white box lay inches from my nose.

I still concentrated on my lips. I made a very tiny bubble but the sun took it away. I made another. I was having trouble opening my eyes. I could, however, make a slit, a very narrow one, and from between this slit I could still look out at the world, I could face the box.

I pulled the box toward me. I was facing its side. Again I touched the lid. It was not secured with a latch or even a tongue of tape. It would be very easy to tear off. I squeezed my eyes shut. This hurt, so I loosened the muscles of my eyes and counted to ten. *Goodbye.* I counted to twenty. I counted to a hundred. *Goodbye.* Two hundred. I pulled off the lid.

My eyes were still shut. I counted to three hundred. I was not dead. My lips tore as I shouted, "Hurry up! Hurry up!"

Again time passed. Again, against my will, I began to think.

Why had the bomb not detonated? Was it a different kind of device? Which? Why did I know so little? Why was I at the mercy of those who tormented me for knowing so little, when there were those who knew even less?

"Hurry up! Hurry up! You fucking cowards, hurry up!"

I was not pleading for life but for a more predictable death. This seemed reasonable. A quick death had been the promise. I would open the lid and be torn to pieces and not feel a thing. It was reasonable. Instead, the kind of death waiting for me two inches from my nose was unknown. This was not reasonable at all. This was betrayal. "You promised! You sick bastards, keep your fucking promise!" Who would do a thing like this? Who would lie to a man resigned to death? *Who would do a thing like this?*

What if the explosion came while I was kicking and ranting? Is that how I wanted to go? Imagine the expression on my face! My eyes squeezed shut and my mouth wide open, bleeding. What a monstrosity! No, I preferred to go in dignity. I preferred to close my mouth, around a spoon of poise. I preferred to go with hands folded, eyes shut but not squeezed, lips loose. This could not be denied me. This was in my control. I could take my life by holding my breath. It would take longer than a bomb but it might work. I pulled my ribs up to my chin and they screamed but I did not. I held them in my mouth.

"Look inside!" I heard a shout. "Get up and look inside!"

Had I grown deaf or had they grown tired? The shout was wimpy. I lifted my head off the ground, still holding my breath, but I could not see into the box. I lifted it more.

Bangles. A necklace. And what might have been two milk teeth, their ends brown.

The air surged from my mouth and I choked. Then I passed out.

I do not recall clearly what happened after that. The men must have seen for themselves the mystery I'd unraveled. When I regained consciousness, the jewelry lay smashed everywhere around me. I was aware, despite my weakness, that water was to be found somewhere. I was thinking I might scoop snowmelt onto my lips. I was thinking I might follow the migration of buffaloes and goat herders who treated me with tolerance, even kindness, inviting me near their fire for tea. On a grassy hilltop, I know I caught a glimpse of a silhouette with horns longer than my legs. A yak? A demon? I glimpsed, too, a red blur, and, squinting, saw the ends of a dark braid scatter sunlight before my eyes. *She jumped before you. I saw her braid hit water.* And I began to see more, the way she frowned when she untangled her hair at night. It was a very different frown from the one she wore in the boat, as Kiran fell into the water, close to me, and I simply watched. Farhana was screaming. "Grab her!" Before she fell backward into the side of the teetering boat, her left foot had brushed my arm. I heard it—the anarchy of bangles, the crack of bone—while I only watched. I heard the splash as Farhana jumped, on her side of the boat, so she would have had to swim very fast to rescue Kiran sinking on my side. And I heard the rattle, as Farhana was pulled deeper into the dungeon of silt Kiran was pulling her to. Only now, on that grassy hilltop, long after the men had smashed the contents of the box and left me with a parting kick, only now did I attempt a run toward the vision—I jumped off the boat, finally, I could see myself make that jump—but I did not know what came of it.

Eventually, I must have fallen near someone's hut. It might not have been far from the mountain, or perhaps it was very far; I did not know where I was. I slept there for a long time, waking to bandages and a watered-down version of apricot soup. This time, I accepted the gift. I would have to consider myself worthy of the generosity of strangers again, somehow. But the gift did not sit well with me. I remembered vomiting, many times. Till one day, I did not.

I also remembered the voice of a radio. I had not been dreaming when I heard it. I had stumbled far from the fort by then, and I had been noticed, and offered water, and help, but I had not accepted the latter—not till I fell in front of that hut—in a part of the valley that was less like a village and more like dotted outcroppings of a shack or two. I remembered stopping in a corner of one such shack, surrounded by soap, flour, a cat, and a shopkeeper who turned the dial of a radio till the static stilled. I wondered if I'd just arrived in Karachi, and none of what happened had happened, because it was the same story, at least at first.

A bomb exploded in a hotel this morning, killing one foreigner and seven Pakistanis…

I left the shack, then hurried back inside when I heard this:

…Reports say the explosive was carried in a box, similar to other devices used this summer. Among the deceased was the bomber. Witnesses say he had arrived in Gilgit several days earlier, with a broken leg.

No group has claimed responsibility for the attack.

Several children were staying in the hotel at the time of the blast. Six persons were killed, including the American national. Three policemen, three women and two children were among the injured. One child succumbed to her wounds on her way to hospital. The family of the deceased American have been notified.

The woman who tendered the soup had green eyes and wound a braid around her oval face. She wanted to feed me qurut and lamb, almonds and cherries. She kept goats in the cattle pen, and spun a wool so fine it could pass through an earhole. Her children had clear skies in their eyes. Her husband healed without words. I had to ask what he was treating me for, and his daughter, giggling, said bleeding and broken bones. And worms. I must drink the flowers of arusha to expel the worms by stunning them, she added. And to stop the bleeding. And swelling. It was the bitterest remedy, with an aroma that made me see only flat things with too many legs.

Several times, a boy helped me to the hole by the cattle pen. I could not keep anything down, not even water. I told myself: Irfan had made it back down the mountain, with only a broken leg. He'd been alive. He might still be alive, if I hadn't tossed him my pack.

But then I might have opened the box instead.

The cattle pen had a wretched stench.

Who was the American national? If a woman, the gender would have been specified.

Surely, Farhana was already on her way home to her father. But this would mean it was Wes who was the—how could I say the word—*deceased*. How could I hope for that?

The blast was in Gilgit, which meant they were on their way back south—without looking for me first—I abandoned him; he abandoned me—but I'd never stolen his love, his Zulekha. If he had looked for me, would I have wanted to see him?

When he opened the box, had Farhana been with him? Had

they looked in my pack and noticed the box and, laughing, sat down together to share whatever they hoped to find inside?

The gender would have been specified.

Wouldn't it?

Wouldn't it? I asked the boy. He stood by and waited till I had finished before carrying me back inside the hut to the woman with green eyes and the man who healed without words.

It might have been days, even weeks—I did not ask to be shown the time—before I could feel the contours of my face again. I could take a shallow breath. I could sip a little soup.

I asked the girl who told me about the flowers of arusha for the way to the nearest bus stop, or even if she knew of a driver who might carry me south to the highway in his jeep, or if she knew anyone at all, a kind soul to take me home. She smiled with warmth, perhaps even pity. Then she called her brother, who had carried me to the cattle pen, possibly for weeks. The brother's expression was the same as hers, except, perhaps, he exuded a little dismay. He called his father. The father had long slender hands that were cool but my forehead was cooler. He shook his head; I supposed it meant I needed no more cures, at least none his fingers could provide. He called his wife. She entered the room smelling of woodsmoke and sweet oils. She offered me cheese. Good for the spirit, she said. I accepted a small piece, and reiterated the question I'd put to her children and to her husband, but which the whole family was clearly avoiding. At my insistence, and with a little more cheese, she answered me at last. Home? You want to be taken home? There is only one time to come home, and that is after death.

I turned my back to her then. I could still smell her scent of woodsmoke and oil, perhaps it was almond oil. She said I should stay till I felt strong enough to—she hesitated. To come home? I thought. No, she could not say that now, because then I would be dead.

She kept standing there, basked in a quiet like infinity. Instead of completing her sentence, she gave me another, sweeter proverb, one I will never forget, though I may never have use for it now. *Beware the guest one does not feed.* I'd heard Irfan say it once, on the shores of a lake, after we'd eaten a pear, after the honey. After Farhana had left with the girl. I hadn't thought to ask him what it meant. I asked my hostess now. She explained that it referred to people who did not do things from the heart, or, even worse, who ignored the heart entirely. The heart is a guest, she stated in a smooth, liquid voice. It must be nourished, made welcome.

So is that what Irfan had decided to do? Feed his guest?

I lay there hunched on the cot—vaguely aware that this was likely the only cot they owned—my back to the woman who smelled of almond oil. I faced a window through which I could see an apricot tree. Hopping between each fur-eared fruit was a warbler, its delicate yellow throat vibrating when the woman spoke, pausing when she paused. The heart is a guest, she kept on in a voice that was as still and rich as the surface of a lake. It deserves the best room in the house.

Postscript

It was time to lay the needles down. Fresh pine needles for a clean floor and a bed softer than most things, except feathers, or flesh. Her flesh was ruddy as a peach and the child would rest her head of thick brown curls against it when she tired of gathering the needles and the branches. The sheet had to be propped securely if the house was to stay dry, Maryam explained, though she need not have. The girl, at age four, gathered all the materials swiftly without being asked, and brought them to her mother.

Her son had candles. He would be leaving this year. The candles were not too sensible—it was windy here, at the edge of the lake, and it rained—but he said they were better than the little oil lamps and so they lit the long wax sticks with threads that sizzled at the slightest change in weather, while she laughed in private, for her son would cut the wicks and blow the flames back to life with some tenderness and a lot of pride.

Maryam watched them, her two remaining children, Younis and Jumanah. They carried the candles out into the night after the tents were secured.

They had taken longer to reach the mountains this year. After the earthquake, they all moved more slowly, and besides, they had been forced to change their route. Last year, they had camped at the foot of a glacier, in potato fields that ripened swiftly under the blanket of steaming dung the cattle bestowed. But during the monsoons, the fields had been washed away. It had happened plenty of times before, though never like this, and in her mind, she could hear it, the way the glacier groaned. Done with keeping all that pressure locked inside, it let the world feel its pulse, taking the fields, the homes, the cattle, and the grain. When the earthquake buckled the land, it left behind a small artificial lake. They had been forced to trek around this.

They had also taken longer to leave the plains. A part of her had feared they would never leave at all, and she still could not entirely believe that they were here, nor that her children were slipping out into the night, in secret, excluding her, two candles, two whispers, and one destination, which she believed she could guess. She watched them go. She had to let them go eventually.

Down in the lowlands, the convoys had also left. They left soon after Fareebi, the shapeshifter, was found. They left as silently as they came: every man in uniform and spy in plainclothes, or so the people said. They had been replaced by different convoys, carrying food and blankets for the shocked survivors who stared past the cameras and far into the heavy dust of their past lives. *Balakot is completely lost*, they said. Maryam had never heard so much terror, or breathed so much death. The goddess had finally unleashed upon their valley the full weight of her wrath, and more men, women, and children than Maryam had ever seen now lay buried beneath it.

Even now, months later, she could do no more than isolate a few details of their combined devastation, like the way she had been watching the buffalo Noor in the forest just before it happened. Noor's eyes had begun to roll high into her head. And her tail! It did not swat her back so much as stand upright, like a snake, jerking and twitching, as though about to drop! Maryam had been staring at the monstrous movements of her most placid beast when Makheri, the goat with the too-high teats, rammed her from behind, saving her life. In the space where Maryam had been standing crashed a pistachio tree. How could it be? She had been harvesting the nuts of that tree not two weeks earlier. Noor now lay beneath it. Her tail still twitching. A man from Laila's dera pulled her away from the sight. And as they ran, so did the world.

But up here in the mountains, even this year, time kept defiantly still. Lake Saiful Maluk lay slick and dark, like a cold, sleepy eye. It had kept the eye shut through the wretchedness of the winter, and now, in spring, it was coming awake, lapping the shores beneath the two lovers, the Queen and the Nude. Tonight, Maryam could feel the lovers at rest. They would be watching her children, and watching the tents, but they would have no reason to complain. Except, perhaps, when they noticed that three tents were missing. The first for the family of the boy found in the waterhole last year, the second for the boy who was never found, the third for the family that was crushed by a boulder when the earth moved. The first two families had left for the city, the husbands and remaining sons to work as thekedars, loading and unloading the gunny bags of grain from state farms, the wives and daughters to pull all their silences closer to their now-sedentary hearts. The space for all three tents lay bare.

There had been other deaths, even before the earthquake, and who knows if the goddess had played a hand in these too. A shopkeeper beaten to death by policemen for withholding information. The information he withheld was his identity. There were no papers to prove it, the police claimed. Who was he? To which state did he pledge allegiance? He had no papers to answer for him. And there was a round-up, all the people of the valley—the sedentary, the nomadic, and everything in-between—had to show their identity papers. Maryam had pulled out every scrap they ever owned. Deeds showing permission to graze; taxes paid; materials leased each autumn and one summer, for a temporary home. But there was no proof of her birth. Her husband's, yes, and he could not remember how and from where the proof had come, it was a gift from God, that little rectangle with his thumbprint and his name. But Maryam had none. The men had reached for the closest thing they could find. Younis. They pulled his ears and slapped his head, again and again, till his neck hung limp and she screamed and beat her wrists against the hard floor (including the wrist that never again healed). When he fell, and they began to beat his back with their boots and their rifles, she saw the boy in the waterhole, and said anything, *take anything you want but the children.* They took the filly. Loi Tara, with the coat the color of sunset in a yolk. Taken in her third year, still tethered to her shell, still only a mare in name. She had been nuzzling the buffaloes, the rain-kissed leaves, and those who let her go.

Maryam did not dare approach Namasha any more. Only her husband had that privilege now. Only he fed and watered her. Only he administered to her pain. Maryam did not inquire how. But even her husband did not ask the mare to carry a single item—not a lamb or even a copper bowl—on her back on their migration to the highlands. She would have thrown it off anyway, sent it spinning all the way past Naked Mountain to the callused hand of God, Who would have dropped it.

There was a limit to the extent of baggage any creature should hold.

It was soon after they took Loi Tara that she agreed to let Younis go. This time, it was she who left Ghafoor a sign. A red cloth, just as he had done. And he came, with a new look and a new name, still glowing from his success with the foreigners. About that, he had casually declared, "You will never see him again." She never asked to know more. There was a slight, very slight, unease lurking inside her, born of an image too fleeting to hold, one which she admitted only to herself. It was never clear to her *which* man she envisioned trapped in the serrated mountains, his back to her, because once, just once, he looked up, and she did not think it was the one she had thought. The man she saw had pointy features and a brooding brow, like the good man, the friend of her people, Irfan. Trapped. It had confused her. A mistake? Hers or his? And she thought of the night the forest inspector's house had burned, the way the man got away while his wife did not. It made her uneasy—how could there be any likeness? *That* had been a fire, *this* a fall, *this* was easy—and, shaking the image away, she thanked the gods that this particular mutation of it had never returned. So when Ghafoor had assured her, "You will never see him again, no matter how much juniper you smoke," she did not ask to know more. All she said was that she never smoked; she could see very well without it. He laughed and so did she. He added, "Even your mother, bless her spirit, will never see him again," and then too she could not help but smile, though it was not altogether respectful, the way he spoke of spirits.

When she asked him to take Younis with him he scratched his thick new beard—black; he had even dyed his hair—wiped her cheek—which had suddenly grown damp—and licked his finger free of her tears the way she had once licked the honey.

Hold on to nothing except your children and your herds, her mother would say. Sometimes, even these possessions were too many.

Maryam quietly crept to the far side of the shore, where the two candles had disappeared. The night was cool and still and she wrapped her shawl close to her chest, and felt the sand give beneath her feet. This was her first night back in the place that had taken Kiran. It was her first touch of the icy water that had pulled the child to itself. She had warned Younis and Jumanah to stay away from the lake, and though she trusted them, she followed nonetheless.

They were heading for her shrine, the one in the cave. The one that could still exist. The one in the lowlands she would have buried before leaving, had the goddess not done this first. She would have had little choice, even after the rumor began to spread that the killer had been found, and the uniforms and the plainclothesmen began to leave, and the relief workers began to arrive. Over them all one voice could still be heard, as Maryam prepared to leave for the mountains. It was the voice of the mullah, claiming victory was coming to every valley in every district, and every city, village, and town. So Maryam had abandoned the cleansing rituals entirely this spring, pleading in her heart that her family not be punished, it was not her fault the rituals could not be kept alive. She had one further evidence of the degree to which her own way was in danger. Just before the earthquake, she had dug a small patch of dirt in her shrine, for the box with Kiran's belongings. The box was gone. The shrine had been tainted, and apparently the goddess agreed.

The mullah had still been claiming victory when they began their ascent.

They had seen their mother do it and so they did it too, when they thought she was not looking. They climbed the hill farthest from the boats and the tents and kept on going, toward the mountain that could only be seen when imagined. The candles blew out twice and Younis patted his trousers, the way he saw men do. He pulled out the box of matches, lit two together, cupping the double flare in a tent made of his fist, and re-lit the sticks.

Finally, the two children arrived at the cave.

While Jumanah looked inside, Younis talked. He was telling her all he would do, when he left. He would become a trader and because all good traders had beards—"Ghafoor bai says you trade best when scratching your beard"—he scratched his naked chin, and she scratched hers. As a businessman, he would bring her things, he said, things that would make her blush the way their mother did, when Ghafoor bai brought her flowers. And Jumanah lowered her eyes, practicing how to look pleased. It was easy, because she was already on her knees, arranging on the uneven floor a bed of pine needles. She carried a big bundle in her hands—she had been careful not to let the candle burn them—and now she took her time softening the floor while Younis talked.

When the carpet was made, they sat together, holding the candles out toward the drawings on the cave wall. There was the horse, Loi Tara, in different poses. Sometimes alone, her mouth busy, her head turned to return their gaze. Sometimes prancing toward a peach. There were buffaloes too, and at times, Loi Tara went to meet them. She was a little yellow and the buffaloes a little blue, but mostly, their world was black and white. There was also a girl. Kiran. She only appeared once, and you had to come very close to see her, so close that the candle left a mark on the wall. Jumanah was standing now, her bare feet absently sweeping the pine needles to and fro, her toes digging into them while she concentrated, holding the candle just so, above the girl and to the left, for this way, the light fell on her face and the face was neither blue nor yellow but the color of the wall. Pinkish, like the real Kiran, though she was no longer sure.

Jumanah steps back—perhaps she will see better from a different angle—and notices a pine needle has caught in her toe ring. Bothered by this, she tries to pull it away. A thought comes to her, a thought-image, blurry yet insistent as an earache. It is of toe rings on a row of bloated toes. She remembers that it worried her. How would her mother get the rings off when the toes swelled like teats? Overcome with a terrible fear that her own toes will be squashed inside these circles of bells, she begins to pull them off.

Delighted, her brother pulls her toes, pulling so hard it hurts, and she wishes she could explain to him why she is afraid, but she cannot. He kisses her only when the tears fall, calling each drop a jumanah, a silver pearl. When she has shed several dozen pearls, she grows mesmerized by how quickly each disappears. Soon, she forgets the reason she cried in the first place and the tears stop falling. There is nothing to hold her attention. They go back to talking.

They decide to mimic their mother and dead grandmother. They make their own offerings, chant their own prayers, drink their own brandy, smoke their own leaves. Younis smacks his pockets, finds the matchbox again, and lights a pretend branch because this is better than going outside to get a real one. And they play pretend vision.

"Say, 'I see evil,'" says Younis.

"I see evil," says Jumanah.

"Do not despair, my child!" cries Younis.

Jumanah laughs.

"Do this and say 'I want more sugar!'" cries Younis.

Jumanah snaps her fingers. "I want more sugar!"

And with this signal the game has changed. They are mimicking the men who have bothered them all year.

Younis dons a belt that is in fact a drawstring, sticks bullet-stones inside, carries a pine cone beard at his chin, swishes as he walks. "Who am I?"

When Jumanah smiles at him with pearly teeth, he leaves the stage to whisper quickly in her ear.

He returns to his place, repeats, "Who am I?"

"Jihadi!"

And now he wears a mustache made of fat leaves, spits, scratches his balls. Narrows his eyes, convincingly lecherous. Before asking who-am-I, he whispers in Jumanah's ear.

"Who am I?"

"Inspector!"

He fingers his hair to bring it down to his shoulders—though it does not reach, the effect is clear—and wears a silver sheet—perhaps a biscuit wrapper, one of many items left behind from some traveler, who could not know this is a sacred shrine—as a clasp around his drawstring-belt. He holds two pine needles to his chin for a wisp of a beard. He even carries a bottle. "Who am I?"

This time, Jumanah does not need help. "Ghafoor bai!"

And next he is extremely serious. He walks with a limp, carries his chin low, and his brow is furrowed. "Who am I?"

"Baba!"

And now they are back to their first game, mimicking their mother and grandmother again, except, this time, they are very solemn indeed. Younis carries the pretend smoking branch—cleverly pretend re-lit—around the cave, crying, "Leave our house!"

Jumanah follows him, chanting the same. "Leave! Leave!"

"Not like that," says Younis. There is much concentration and commentary, as the rituals are tidied up, rehearsed, and re-performed.

"Carry it like this," insists Younis, and Jumanah sticks her arms up straight.

He then proceeds to tickle her.

While Jumanah squeals, Maryam sucks in her breath, reminding herself and the spirits that they are only children. It is not sacrilege if it is innocent, she says under her breath, where she stifles a laugh, and everything else building up inside. What she really wants, more than anything, is to join them. She would gladly give up fear and sorrow if it meant that for these months in the mountains, she could play. Instead, she watches from the crack in the side of the wall, a tiny space she has peered through many times over the years before entering her cave, for it would be unwise to enter with a traveler inside. She watches the two children, who are solemn once again, and pulls another breath, and holds it, waiting for the breakneck craving in her breast to pass. Of course, it does not pass. But she will not disturb them to satisfy the fierceness of her love. She will leave them enrapt in their game, one in which they do not await the end of the world so much as enjoy it.

Soon after she leaves, their work complete, the children fall asleep. Younis on his back, Jumanah pressed against his chest. In the middle of the night, a feather falls on them, white as the wings that flew through the night to secure it.

Acknowledgments

During my work on this novel, the following sources on north Pakistan and northwest China proved especially enlightening: *History of Northern Areas of Pakistan: up to 2000 A.D.* by Ahmad Hasan Dani (Lahore: Sang-e-Meel Publcations, 2001), "The Martyrs of Balakot" from *Partisans of Allah: Jihad in South Asia* by Ayesha Jalal (Cambridge: Harvard University Press, 2008), and *Eurasian Crossroads: a History of Xinjiang* by James A. Millward (New York: Columbia University Press, 2007). I would like to extend my appreciation to their authors, and would recommend their work to all those whose love of these areas cannot be sated.